the towering sky

*The Thousandth Floor*
*The Dazzling Heights*
*The Towering Sky*

# the towering sky

## KATHARINE McGEE

**HARPER**

*An Imprint of HarperCollinsPublishers*

The Towering Sky
Copyright © 2018 by Alloy Entertainment and Katharine McGee

alloyentertainment
Produced by Alloy Entertainment
1325 Avenue of the Americas
New York, NY 10019
www.alloyentertainment.com

Library of Congress Control Number: 2018942092

ISBN 978-0-06-241865-4 (trade bdg.) — ISBN 978-0-06-284248-0 (int. ed.)

Typography by Liz Dresner

18 19 20 21 22  PC/LSCH  10 9 8 7 6 5 4 3 2 1
❖
First Edition

*For Deedo, and in loving memory of Snake*

# PROLOGUE

*December 2119*

**THERE HAS ALWAYS** been something otherworldly about the first snow of the year in New York.

It gilds the city's flaws, its hard edges, transforming Manhattan into a proud, glittering northern place. Magic hangs heavy in the air. On the morning of the first snow, even the most jaded New Yorkers pause in the streets to look up at the sky, stilled by a quiet sense of awe. As if every hot summer they forgot that this was possible, and only when the first flakes of snow kiss their faces can they believe in it again.

It seems almost that the snowfall might wash the city clean, reveal all the monstrous secrets buried beneath its surface.

But then, some secrets are best kept buried.

It was on one of these mornings of cold, enchanted silence that a girl stood on the roof of Manhattan's enormous skyscraper.

She stepped closer to the edge, and the wind whipped at her hair. Snowflakes danced around her in splintered crystals. Her skin glowed like an overexposed hologram in the predawn light. If anyone had been up there to see her, they would have said that she looked troubled, and sharply beautiful. And afraid.

She hadn't been on the roof in over a year, yet it looked the same as ever. Photovoltaic panels huddled on its surface, waiting to drink in the sun and convert it to usable power. An enormous steel spire twisted up to collide with the sky. And below her hummed an entire city—a thousand-story tower, teeming with millions of people.

Some of them she had loved, some of them she had resented. Many she had never known at all. Yet in their own ways they had betrayed her, every last one of them. They had made her life unbearable by depriving her of the one person she had ever loved.

The girl knew she'd been up here too long. She was starting to feel the familiar slippery light-headedness as her body slowed down, struggling to adjust to the decreased oxygen, to pull resources in toward her core. She curled her toes. They were numb. The air downstairs was oxygenated and infused with vitamins, but here on the roof it felt whip-thin.

She hoped they would forgive her for what she was about to do. But she didn't have a choice. It was either this, or go on leading a shriveled, starved, half life: a life deprived of the only person who made it worth living. She felt a pang of guilt, but even stronger was her profound sense of relief, that at least—at last—it would soon be over.

The girl reached up to wipe at her eyes, as if the wind had stung them to tears.

"I'm sorry," she said, though there was no one around to hear. Who was she talking to, anyway? Maybe the city below her or the entire world or her own quiet conscience.

And what did it matter? New York would go on with or without her, the same as ever, just as loud and electric and raucous and bright. New York didn't care that those were the last words Avery Fuller ever spoke.

# AVERY

*Three months earlier*

**AVERY DRUMMED HER** fingers restlessly on the armrest of her family's chopper. She felt her boyfriend's gaze on her and glanced up. "Why are you looking at me like that?" she asked, teasing.

"Like what? Like I want to kiss you?" Max answered his own question by leaning over to drop a kiss on her lips. "You may not realize it, Avery, but I always want to kiss you."

"Please prepare yourselves for the final approach to New York," the chopper's autopilot cut in, projecting the words through unseen speakers. Not that Avery needed the update; she'd been tracking their progress this entire trip.

"You okay?" Max's eyes were warm on hers.

Avery shifted, struggling to explain. The last thing she wanted was for Max to think she was anxious about *him*. "It's just . . . so much happened while I was gone." It had been a long time. Seven months, the longest she'd ever spent away from New York in all her eighteen years.

"Including me." Max gave a conspiratorial grin.

"Especially you," Avery told him, mirroring his smile.

The Tower swam up rapidly to dominate the view through their flexiglass windows. Avery had seen it from this perspective plenty of times—all those years of traveling with her family, or with her friend Eris and her parents—but she'd never before noticed how much it looked like a massive chrome headstone. Like Eris's headstone.

Avery shoved that thought aside. She focused instead on the autumn sunlight dancing over the choppy surface of the river, burnishing the golden torch of the Statue of Liberty, which once seemed so tall but now was absurdly dwarfed by its great neighbor, the thousand-story megatower that sprouted from the concrete surface of Manhattan. The Tower that her father's company had helped build, in which the Fullers occupied the top floor, the highest penthouse in the entire world.

Avery let her gaze swoop to the boats and autocars buzzing below, the monorails suspended in the air as delicately as strands of spider's silk.

She'd left New York in February, soon after the launch of her father's new vertical living complex in Dubai. That was the night when she and Atlas had decided that they couldn't be together, no matter how much they loved each other. Because even though they weren't related by blood, Atlas was Avery's adopted brother.

Avery had thought then that her entire world was shattered. Or maybe she herself was shattered—into so many infinitesimally small pieces that she'd become the character from the nursery rhyme, the one who could never be put back together. She had been certain she would die from the pain of it.

How foolish she'd been, to think that a broken heart would kill her, but it was how she'd felt.

Yet hearts are funny, stubborn, elastic little organs. When she didn't die after all, Avery realized that she wanted to leave—to get away from New York, with its painful memories and familiar faces. Just as Atlas had.

She had already applied to Oxford's summer program; now she simply pinged the admissions office and asked if she could transfer early, in time for the spring semester. She met with the dean at Berkeley Academy to request high school credit for Oxford's college courses. Of course they all agreed. As if anyone would say no to Pierson Fuller's daughter.

The only source of resistance, surprisingly enough, was Pierson himself.

"What's this about, Avery?" he'd demanded, when she came to him with her transfer papers.

"I need to leave. To go somewhere far away, somewhere completely free of memories."

Her father's eyes darkened. "I know you miss her, but this feels extreme."

Of course. He assumed that this was about Eris's death. And it was, in part—but Avery was grieving Atlas too.

"I just need some time away from Berkeley. Everyone stares at me in the halls, whispering about me," she insisted, telling the truth. "I just want to get away. To somewhere no one knows me, and I don't know them."

"They know you all over the world, Avery. Or if they don't yet, they will soon enough," her father said softly. "I was going to tell you—I'm running for mayor of New York this year."

Avery stared at him for a moment in mute shock. Though she shouldn't really have been surprised. Her father was never satisfied with what he had. Now that he was the richest man in the city, of course he would want to be the most prominent too.

"You'll be back next fall, for the election," Pierson told her. It wasn't a question.

"So I can go?" Avery asked, her chest seizing with a violent, almost nauseous relief.

Her father sighed and began to sign her permission papers. "Someday, Avery, you'll learn that it's not much use running away from things if you have to eventually come back and face them."

The next week, Avery and a jostling band of mover-bots made their way down the narrow streets of Oxford. The dorms had been full midsemester, but Avery posted an anonymous ad to the school discussion boards, and found a room in an off-campus cottage with a delightfully overgrown square of garden out back. It even came with a roommate, a poetry student named Neha. And, it turned out, a house full of boys next door.

Avery slid easily into Oxford life. She loved how unmodern everything felt: the way her professors wrote on green boards with funny white stencils; the way people actually looked at her when they spoke, rather than letting their eyes slide constantly toward the edge of their vision to check the feeds. Most people here didn't even own the computerized contacts Avery had grown up using. The linkages in Oxford were so weak that Avery had ended up taking hers out too, living like a premodern human with nothing but a tablet to communicate. Her vision felt delightfully raw and unencumbered.

One evening as she worked on an essay for her East Asian art class, Avery was distracted by noises from next door. Her neighbors were having a party.

Back in New York, she would simply have turned on her

silencer: the device that blocked incoming sound waves, creating a little pocket of quiet even in the loudest places. Actually, this wouldn't have happened in New York, because in New York Avery didn't *have* next-door neighbors, just the sky stretching out from the Fuller apartment on all sides.

She cupped her hands into earmuffs over her ears, trying to focus, but the raucous shouts and laughter grew even louder. Finally she stood up and marched next door, not caring that she was wearing athletic shorts, her honey-colored hair piled atop her head and fastened with a turtle-shaped clip that Eris had given her years ago.

That was when she saw Max.

He stood at the center of a group in the backyard, telling a story with animated fervor. He had shaggy dark hair that stuck out in all directions and wore a blue sweater paired with blue jeans, something the girls back home would have teased him mercilessly for. But Avery saw it as a sign of his elemental impatience, as if he was too preoccupied to be bothered by something as mundane as clothes.

She felt suddenly ridiculous. What had she been planning to do, come over here and *scold* her neighbors for having fun? She retreated a step—just as the boy telling the story looked up, directly into her eyes. He smiled knowingly. Then his gaze slid past her, and he kept talking without a break in narrative thread.

Avery was startled by the flash of irritation she felt. She wasn't accustomed to being ignored.

"Of course I would vote for the referendum, if I could vote here," the boy was saying. He had a German accent, his voice sliding up and down along a wild range of emotion. "London *must* expand upward. A city is a living thing; if it doesn't grow, it withers and dies."

He was talking about her dad's bill, Avery realized. After

years of lobbying the British Parliament, Pierson Fuller had finally gotten his nationwide referendum, to determine whether Britain would tear down their capital city and rebuild it as a massive supertower. So many cities around the world had already done so—Rio, Hong Kong, Beijing, Dubai, and of course New York first of all, two decades ago—but some of the older European cities were more reluctant.

"I would vote no," Avery butted in. It wasn't the most popular opinion among young people, and her dad would have been appalled, but she felt a perverse desire to grab this boy's attention. And, anyway, it was the truth.

He gave an ironic, half-foreign bow in her direction, inviting her to continue.

"It's just that London wouldn't feel like London anymore," Avery went on. It would become another of her dad's sleek automated cities, another vertical sea of anonymity.

The boy's eyes crinkled pleasantly when he smiled. "Have you seen the proposal? There are battalions of architects and designers to make sure that the feeling of London is preserved, that it's *better* than before, even."

"But it never really turns out like that. When you're in a tower, there's less sense of connection, of spontaneity. Less of"— she held out her hands a little helplessly—"of this."

"Party crashing? For some reason, I think people do that in skyscrapers just fine."

Avery knew she should be flushing with embarrassment, but instead she burst out laughing.

"Maximilian von Strauss. Call me Max," the boy introduced himself. He had just finished his first year at Oxford, he explained, studying economics and philosophy. He wanted to get a PhD and become a professor, or an author of obscure books about the economy.

There was something decidedly old-fashioned about Max, Avery thought; it was as if he'd stepped through a portal from another century and ended up here. Perhaps it was his earnestness. In New York, everyone seemed to measure their superiority by how contemptuous and cynical they were. Max wasn't afraid to *care* about things, publicly and unironically.

Within a few days he and Avery were spending most of their free time together. They studied at the same table in the Bodleian Library, surrounded by the tattered spines of old novels. They sat outside at the local pub, listening to the amateur student bands, or the soft sound of locusts in the warm summer night. And not once did they cross the bounds of friendship.

Initially Avery treated it like an experiment. Max was like one of those bandages from before people invented mediwands; he was helping her forget how much she was still hurting after losing Atlas.

But at some point it stopped feeling like a Band-Aid, and started feeling real.

They were walking home one evening along the river, a pair of twilight shadows against a tapestry of trees. The wind picked up, sending ripples along the surface of the water. In the distance, the university's white limestone arches gleamed pale blue in the moonlight.

Avery reached tentatively for Max's hand. She felt him jolt a little in surprise.

"I assumed you had a boyfriend back home," he remarked, as if in answer to some question she'd asked, which perhaps she had.

"No," Avery said quietly. "I was just . . . getting over something that I lost."

His dark eyes held hers, catching the glow of moonlight. "Are you over it now?"

"I will be."

Now, in the enormous plush seats of her father's copter, she shifted toward Max. The cushions were upholstered in a scrolling navy-and-gold pattern that, upon closer inspection, revealed itself to be a series of interlocking cursive *F*s. Even the carpet below her feet was emblazoned with her family monogram.

She wondered, not for the first time, what Max thought of it all. How would he handle meeting her parents? She had already met his family, one weekend in Würzburg this summer. Max's mom was a professor of linguistics and his dad wrote novels, delightfully lurid mysteries where people were murdered at least three times per book. Neither of them spoke much English. They had both just hugged Avery profusely, using their contacts' funny auto-translate setting, which despite years of upgrades still made people sound like drunken toddlers. "It's because language has so many musics," Max's mom tried to explain, which Avery took to mean nuances of meaning.

Besides, they had all communicated just fine with gestures and laughter.

Avery knew that her parents would be nothing like that. She loved them, of course, but there had always been a carefully maintained distance between them and her. Sometimes, when she was younger, Avery used to see her friends with their mothers and feel a sharp stab of jealousy: at the way Eris and her mom romped arm in arm through Bergdorf's, bent over in conspiratorial giggles, looking more like friends than mother and daughter. Or even Leda and her mom, who had famously explosive fights but always cried and hugged and made up afterward.

The Fullers didn't show affection that way. Even when Avery was a toddler, they never cuddled with her or sat near her bedside when she was sick. In their minds, that was what the help was for. Just because they weren't the touchy-feely type didn't mean that they loved her any less, Avery reminded herself. And yet—she wondered sometimes what it would be like to have parents she could pal around with, parents she could be irreverent with.

Avery's parents knew that she was dating someone, and they had said that they couldn't wait to meet him. But she couldn't help worrying that they would take one look at Max, in all his disheveled German glory, and try to send him packing. Now that her dad was running for mayor of New York, he seemed more obsessed than ever with their family image. Whatever that meant.

"What are you thinking about? Worried your friends won't like me?" Max asked, cutting surprisingly close to the truth.

"Of course they will," she said resolutely. Though she didn't know what to expect of her friends right now, least of all her best friend, Leda Cole. When Avery left last spring, Leda hadn't exactly been in a great state of mind.

"I'm so glad you came with me," she added. Max would only stay in New York a few days before heading back for the start of his sophomore year at Oxford. It meant a lot that he'd crossed the ocean for her, to meet the people she cared about and see the city she came from.

"As if I would pass up the chance for more time with you." Max reached to brush his thumb lightly over Avery's knuckles. A thin woven bracelet, a memoriam to a childhood friend who had died young, slid down Max's wrist. Avery squeezed his hand.

They tipped a few degrees sideways, tilting into the airstream that shot around the edge of the Tower. Even their copter, which was weighted on all sides to prevent turbulence, couldn't avoid being buffeted in winds this strong. Avery braced herself, and then the gaping mouth of the helipad was before them: sliced from the wall of the Tower in perfect ninety-degree angles, everything stark and flat and gleaming, as if to scream at you that it was new. How different from Oxford, where curved uneven roofs rose into the wine-colored sky.

Their copter lurched into the helipad, whipping up the hair of the waiting crowds. Avery blinked in surprise. What were all these people doing here? They jostled together, clutching small image capturers, with lenses gleaming in the middle like cyclopean eyes. Probably vloggers or i-Net reporters.

"Looks like New York is glad you're back," Max remarked, sparking a rueful smile from Avery.

"I'm sorry. I had no idea." She was used to the occasional fashion bloggers taking snaps of her outfits, but nothing like this.

Then she caught sight of her parents, and Avery realized exactly whose fault this was. Her dad had decided to make her homecoming a PR moment.

The copter's door opened, its staircase unfolding like an accordion. Avery exchanged a final glance with Max before starting down.

Elizabeth Fuller swept forward, wearing a tailored luncheon dress and heels. "Welcome home, sweetie! We missed you."

Avery forgot her irritation that their reunion was happening like this, in the heat and noise of a crowded helipad. She forgot everything except the fact that she was seeing her mom again after so many months apart. "I missed you too!" she exclaimed, pulling her mom into a tight hug.

"Avery!" Her father turned away from Max, who had been shaking his hand. "I'm so glad you're back!"

He hugged Avery too, and she closed her eyes, returning the embrace—until her dad deftly swiveled her around to better angle her toward the cameras. He stepped back, looking sleek and self-satisfied in his crisp white shirt, beaming with pride. Avery tried to hide her disappointment—that her dad had turned her homecoming into a stunt, and that the media had obliged him.

"Thank you all!" he declared in his booming, charming voice, for the benefit of everyone recording. What he was thanking them for, Avery didn't exactly understand, but from the nodding faces of the reporters, it didn't seem to matter. "We are thrilled that our daughter, Avery, has returned from her semester abroad just in time for the election! Avery would be delighted to answer a few questions," her dad added, nudging her gently forward.

She wouldn't, actually, but Avery didn't have a choice.

"Avery! What are they wearing in England right now?" one of them cried out, a fashion blogger whom Avery recognized.

"Um . . ." No matter how many times she said she wasn't a fashionista, no one seemed to believe her. Avery turned a pleading glance toward Max—not that he would really be any help—and her attention fastened on the neckline of his flannel shirt. Most of the buttons that marched up the collar were dark brown, but one was much lighter, a soft fawn color. He must have lost that button and replaced it with another, not caring that it didn't go with the others.

"Clashing buttons," she heard herself say. "I mean, buttons that don't match. On purpose."

Max caught her eye, one eyebrow lifted in amusement. She forced herself to look away so she wouldn't burst out laughing.

"And who is this? Your new boyfriend?" another of the bloggers asked, causing the group's focus to swerve hungrily toward Max. He gave a genial shrug.

Avery couldn't help noticing that her parents' gazes had hardened as they focused on Max. "Yes. This is my boyfriend, Max," she declared.

There was a mild uproar at her words, and before Avery could say anything else, Pierson had put a protective arm around her. "Thank you for your support! We are so glad to have Avery back in New York," he said again. "And now, if you'll excuse us, we need some time alone as a family."

"Clashing buttons?" Max fell into step alongside her. "Wonder where that came from."

"You should be thanking me. I just made you the most stylish guy in New York," Avery joked, reaching for his hand.

"Exactly! How will I handle that kind of pressure?"

As they walked toward the waiting hover, Avery's mind drifted back to her father's final words. *Some time alone as a family.* Except they weren't a family right now, because they were missing one very important person.

Avery knew she shouldn't be thinking about him, yet she couldn't help wondering what Atlas was doing, half a world away.

# LEDA

**"ISN'T THIS NICE?"** Leda Cole's mom attempted, her tone remorselessly upbeat.

Leda cast a brief, disinterested glance around. She and Ilara were standing in waist-deep warm water, surrounded by the jagged boulders of the Blue Lagoon. The ceiling of the 834th floor soared overhead, colored a cheerful azure that clashed with Leda's mood.

"Sure," she mumbled, ignoring the hurt that darted over her mom's features. She hadn't wanted to come out today at all. She'd been perfectly fine in her room, alone with her slender, solitary sadness.

Leda knew that her mom was only trying to help. She wondered if this forced outing had been suggested by Dr. Vanderstein, the psychiatrist who treated both of them. *Why don't you try some "girl time"?* Leda could hear him saying, with invisible air quotes. Ilara would have seized gratefully on the idea. Anything to drag her daughter out of this unshakable dark mood.

A year ago it would have worked. Leda so rarely got a chunk of her mom's time; she would have been grateful just for the chance to hang out with her. And the old Leda had always loved going to a hot new spa or restaurant before anyone else.

The Blue Lagoon had opened just a few days ago. After last year's unexpected earthquake, which sent most of Iceland sliding back into the ocean, a development company had bought the now submerged lagoon from the bewildered Icelandic government at a bargain price. They'd spent months excavating every last sliver of volcanic rock, shipping the whole thing to New York, and re-creating it here, stone by stone.

Typical New Yorkers, forever determined to bring the world to them, as if they couldn't be bothered to leave their tiny island. *Whatever you have*, they seemed to be saying to the rest of the world, *we can build it here—and better.*

Leda used to possess that same kind of cool self-confidence. She had been the girl who knew everything about everyone, who dispensed gossip and favors, who tried to bend the universe to her will. But that was before.

She ran a hand dispassionately through the water, wondering if it was treated with light-bending particles to make it that impossible blue color. Unlike the original lagoon, this one wasn't filled from a real hot spring. It was just heated tap water, infused with multivitamins and a hint of aloe, supposedly much better than that old foul-smelling sulfuric stuff.

Leda had also heard a rumor that the lagoon managers pumped illegal relaxants into the air: nothing serious, just enough to make up 0.02 percent of the air composition. Well, she could use a little relaxing right now.

"I saw that Avery's back in town," Ilara ventured, and the name splintered through Leda's protective shell of numbness.

It had been easy not to think about Avery while she was in England. Avery had never been reliable at vid-chatting; as long as Leda replied to her occasional one-line message, Avery was distracted into thinking that everything was fine. But what if seeing Avery again dredged up all those memories—the ones Leda forced herself not to think about, the ones she had buried deep within her, in the pitch-darkness—

*No*, she told herself, Avery wouldn't want to think about the past any more than Leda did. She was with Max now.

"She has a new boyfriend, right?" Ilara fiddled with the strap of her black one-piece. "Do you know anything about him?"

"A little. His name is Max."

Her mom nodded. They both knew that the old Leda would have bubbled over at the question, offering various conjectures and speculation about Max, and whether or not he was good enough for her best friend. "What about you, Leda? I haven't heard you talk about any boys lately," her mom went on, even though she knew perfectly well that Leda had been alone all summer.

"That's because there's nothing to talk about." Leda's jaw tightened, and she sank a little lower in the water.

Ilara hesitated, then apparently decided to forge ahead. "I know you're still not over Watt, but maybe it's time to—"

"Seriously, Mom?" Leda snapped.

"You've had such a rough year, Leda; I just want you to be happy! And Watt . . ." She paused. "You never really told me what happened with him."

"I don't want to talk about it."

Before her mom could press her further, Leda held her breath and ducked all the way under the surface of the lagoon, not caring that the weird vitamins would make her hair crunchy. The water felt warm and pleasantly quiet, stifling all sound. She wished she could stay submerged forever, down here where there were no failures or pains, no mistakes and misunderstandings, no wrong decisions. *Wash me and I shall be clean*, she remembered from her days at Sunday school, except Leda would never be clean, not if she stayed under forever. Not after what she had done.

First there had been that whole mess with Avery and Atlas. Hard to believe now, but Leda used to like Atlas—even, foolishly, thought that she *loved* him. Until she learned that he and Avery were secretly together. Leda flinched, remembering how she'd confronted Avery about it on the roof, the night when everything went so terribly wrong.

Their friend Eris had tried to calm down Leda, despite Leda's shouts that she should back off. When Eris came close, Leda pushed her away—and inadvertently pushed her off the side of the Tower.

After that, it was no surprise that Avery wanted to leave New York. And Avery didn't even know the full story. Only Leda had learned the darkest and most shameful part of the truth.

Eris had been Leda's half sister.

Leda found out last winter, from Eris's ex-girlfriend, Mariel Valconsuelo. Mariel had told her about it at the launch party for the new Dubai tower—right before she drugged Leda and left her for dead, abandoning her at the water's edge during a rising tide.

The truth of Mariel's words had resonated in Leda with sickening finality. It made so much more sense than what she thought was going on: that Eris was secretly having an affair with Leda's dad. Instead, Eris and Leda *shared* a dad; and worse, Eris had known the truth before she died. Leda realized that now. It was what Eris had been trying to tell her, that night on the roof, which Leda so drastically misunderstood.

The knowledge that she'd killed her own *sister* burned Leda from within. She wanted to pound her fists and scream until the sky split open. She couldn't sleep, haunted by plaintive images of Eris up on the roof, staring balefully at her with those amber-flecked eyes.

There was only one way to find relief from this kind of pain, and Leda had sworn never to touch it again. But she couldn't help herself. With a shaking voice, Leda pinged her old drug dealer.

She took more and more pills, mixing and combining them with a shocking recklessness. She didn't care what the hell she took as long as it numbed her. And then, as she'd probably known deep down that she would, Leda took one too many pills.

She was missing for an entire day. When her mom found her the next morning, Leda was curled atop her bed, her jeans and her shoes still on. At some point Leda must have gotten a nose-bleed. The blood had trailed down her shirt to crust in sticky flakes all over her chest. Her forehead felt clammy and damp with sweat.

"Where were you?" her mom cried out, horrified.

"I don't know," Leda admitted. There was a flutter in the empty cavity of her chest where her heart should have been. The last thing she really remembered was getting high with her old dealer, Ross. She couldn't account for anything else in the last twenty-four hours; she didn't even know how she had managed to drag herself home.

Her parents sent her to rehab, terrified that Leda had meant to kill herself. Maybe, on some subconscious level, she *had*. She would only be finishing what Mariel started.

And then, to Leda's surprise, she learned that Mariel was dead too.

In the aftermath of that terrifying confrontation in Dubai, Leda had set an i-Net alert to flag any mentions of Mariel's name. She'd never expected it to catch an *obituary*. But one day in rehab, she found the obit waiting in her inbox: *Mariel Arellano Valconsuelo, age 17, has gone to the Lord. She is survived by her parents, Eduardo and Marina Valconsuelo, and her brother Marcos. . . .*

*Has gone to the Lord.* That was even more vague than the usual *passed away* or *died suddenly*. Leda had no idea what had happened to Mariel, whether she'd been in an accident or suffered a sudden illness. Perhaps she too had turned to drugs—out of grief at losing Eris, or regret for what she'd done to Leda in Dubai.

At the news of Mariel's death, a chilling new fear began to seep into Leda. It felt oddly like some kind of omen, like a terrible portent of things to come.

"I need to get better," she announced to her doctor that afternoon.

Dr. Reasoner smiled. "Of course, Leda. We all want that for you."

"No, you don't understand," Leda insisted, almost frantic. "I'm caught in this vicious cycle of hurt, and I want to break away from it, but I don't know how!"

"Life is hard, and drugs are easy. They insulate you from real life, protect you from feeling anything too deeply," Dr. Reasoner said softly. Leda caught her breath, wishing she could explain that her problem was more than just drugs. It was the gaping vortex of darkness within her that seemed to pull her, and everyone around her, inexorably downward.

"Leda," the doctor went on, "you need to break the emotional patterns that cause your addiction, and start over. Which is why I've recommended that your parents send you to boarding school when you've finished your treatment here. You need a fresh start."

"I can't go to boarding school!" Leda couldn't stand the

thought of being away from her friends—or her family, as broken and fragile as it was.

"Then the only way you can escape this cycle is with a complete and total overhaul."

Dr. Reasoner explained that Leda would have to amputate the poisoned parts of her life, like a surgeon with a scalpel, and move forward with whatever remained. She needed to cut out anything that might trigger her problematic behavior, and rebuild.

"What about my boyfriend?" Leda had whispered, and Dr. Reasoner sighed. She had actually met Watt earlier that year, when he came to Leda's rehab check-in.

"I think that Watt is the worst trigger of them all."

Even amid the blind haze of her pain, Leda realized that the doctor was right. Watt knew her—*really* knew her, beneath every last scrap of deceit, all her insecurities and fears, all the terrible things she had done. Watt was too tangled up in who she had been, and Leda needed to focus on who she was becoming.

So when she got back from rehab, she broke up with Watt for good.

Leda's thoughts were interrupted by a bright-red notification flashing in the corner of her vision. "Look! It's time for our massages!" Ilara exclaimed, glancing hopefully at her daughter.

Leda tried to muster up a smile, though she didn't really care about massages anymore. Massages were something that had belonged to the old Leda.

She waded through the water after her mom, past the mud mask station and carved ice bar to the cordoned-off area reserved for private spa treatments. They stepped through an invisible sound barrier, and the laughter and voices of the Blue Lagoon cut off sharply, replaced by harp music that was piped in through speakers.

Two flotation mats were arranged in the sheltered space, each anchored to the bottom of the pool with an ivory ribbon. Leda froze with her hands on her mat. Suddenly, all she could see was the cream-colored ribbon of Eris's scarf, fluttering against her red-gold hair as she tumbled into the darkness. The scarf that Leda had so drastically misinterpreted, because it was a gift from Leda's *dad*—

"Leda? Is everything okay?" her mom asked, her brow furrowed in concern.

"Of course," Leda said stiffly, and she hauled herself onto her massage mat. It began heating up, its sensors determining where she was sore and customizing her treatment.

Leda tried to force her eyes shut and relax. Everything would be fine, now that all the darkness of last year was behind her. She wouldn't let the mistakes of her past weigh her down.

She let her hands trail in the artificially blue waters of the lagoon, trying to empty her mind, but her fingers kept splaying and then closing anxiously into a fist.

*I'll be fine*, she repeated to herself. As long as she kept herself remote, cut away from anything that might trigger her old addictions, she would be safe from the world.

And the world would be safe from her.

# CALLIOPE

**CALLIOPE BROWN LEANED** her palms on the cast-iron railing, looking down at the street seventy stories below.

"Oh, Nadav!" her mom, Elise, exclaimed behind her. "You were right. This is absolutely perfect for the wedding reception."

They were standing on the outdoor terrace of the Museum of Natural History: a real exposed terrace, its doors thrown open to the syrupy golden air of September. The sky gleamed with the polished brilliance of enamel. This was one of the very last floors where you could actually step outside. Any higher and the terraces were no longer real terraces, just rooms with a nice view, enclosed in polyethylene glass.

Calliope's soon-to-be stepsister, Nadav's daughter, Livya, gave a little *ooh* of approval from where she stood near the doors. Calliope didn't bother turning around. She was getting pretty tired of Livya, though she did her utmost to hide the feeling.

She and Livya were never going to be friends. Livya was

an insufferable rule follower, the type of girl who still sent embossed thank-you notes and gave a shrill fake laugh whenever one of their teachers told a lame joke. Worse, there was something unavoidably sly and beady-eyed about her. Calliope had the sense that if you whispered secrets behind a closed door, Livya would be the one with her ear pressed hungrily to the keyhole.

She heard Nadav say something indistinguishable behind her, probably another quiet *I love you* to Elise. Poor Nadav. He really had no idea what he'd gotten into when he proposed to Calliope's mom at the Fullers' Dubai launch party. He couldn't know that Elise was a professional at getting engaged, that his was the fourteenth proposal she'd received in the past few years.

When Calliope was a child, living in London, her mother had worked as a personal assistant to a cold, wealthy woman named Mrs. Houghton, who claimed to be descended from the aristocracy. Whether or not that was even true—which Calliope doubted—it certainly didn't give Mrs. Houghton the right to abuse Calliope's mom the way she did. Eventually the situation reached a breaking point, and Calliope and Elise ran away from London. Calliope was only eleven.

They had embarked upon a life of glamorous nomadism: jetting around the world, using their wits and beauty to, as Elise liked to phrase it, *relieve wealthy people of their excess wealth.* One of their many strategies for doing so was a proposal. Elise would trap someone into loving her, get engaged, then take the ring and run before the wedding. But it wasn't just fake engagements; over the years, Elise and her daughter had fabricated all types of stories, from long-lost relatives to investment scams, tales of tears and passion—whatever it took to make people dip into their bitbanc accounts. The moment they had separated the mark from his or her money, Calliope and Elise would disappear.

It wasn't easy slipping off the grid like that, not in this day and age. But they were very, very good at it. Calliope had been caught only once, and she still didn't know how it had happened.

It was the night of the Dubai party, just after Nadav and Elise had gotten engaged—after Elise had turned to Calliope and offered to stay in New York for real. To actually go through with the wedding and live here, instead of taking the first train away. Calliope's blood pounded in excitement at the prospect. She had been feeling a strange urge lately to settle down, to live a real life, and New York seemed like the perfect place to do it.

Then Avery Fuller had confronted her.

"I know the truth about you and your mom. So now you're both going to get the hell out of New York," Avery had threatened, unbearably icy and distant. Calliope knew then that she had to back down. She didn't have a choice.

Until a few hours later, when she saw Avery and Atlas *kissing*, and realized she had something on Avery that was just as treacherous as what Avery had on her.

She'd confronted Avery about it back in New York. "I'm not going anywhere," she'd declared. "And if you tell anyone what you know about me, I'll tell what I know about you. You can take me down, but you'd better believe you're going down with me." Avery had just looked at Calliope with weary red-rimmed eyes, as if she weren't even seeing her: as if Calliope were as insubstantial as a ghost.

Calliope hadn't realized back then what she was signing on for, staying in New York and playing out this con. She should have paid more attention to her mom's narrative. Elise always tailored their backstory for whomever she was trying to target—and for intense, soft-spoken Nadav, the quiet cybernetics engineer, Elise had gone all out. She presented herself and Calliope as a pair of sweet, serious, bleeding-heart philanthropists who had traveled the world for years, volunteering for various causes.

Calliope got to stay in New York and live a stable, "normal" life for the first time in years. But it came with a tremendous price tag: She couldn't be herself.

Although, was anyone really themselves in New York? Wasn't this the city full of people from nowhere, people who remade themselves the moment they arrived? Calliope glanced down at the twin rivers, flowing around Manhattan like the cold River Lethe—as if the moment you crossed them, your entire past became irrelevant, and you were reborn as someone new.

That was what she loved about New York. That feeling of utter *aliveness*, a rush and flow of ruthless, furious energy. That New York belief that this was the center of the world, and god help you if you were anywhere else.

She glanced in resignation at her costume—she refused to think of it as her outfit, because it was nothing she would have chosen for herself—a tailored knee-length dress and low kitten heels. Her rich brown hair was pulled into a low ponytail, show-ing off a pair of modest aquamarine earrings. The whole thing was ladylike and elegant, and excruciatingly dull.

She had tried at first to push the limits of Nadav's tolerance. After all, he was engaged to her mom, not to Calliope. Why should he care if she wore tight dresses and stayed out late? He'd seen her at the Under the Sea ball and the Dubai party. Surely he knew that Elise's daughter wasn't as well-behaved as Elise was—or rather, as she was pretending to be.

Yet Nadav had quickly made it clear that he expected Calliope to follow the same rules as Livya. Everything about him was direct and uncompromising. He seemed to view the entire world like a computer problem, in stark black and white. Unlike Calliope and her mom, who operated in shades of gray.

For months, Calliope had thrown herself headfirst into this part. She'd kept her head down, actually studied at school, obeyed curfew. But it had been a long time, much longer than she'd ever kept up any con, and Calliope was starting to chafe beneath her constraints. She felt as if she were losing herself in this never-ending performance—drowning in it, even.

She leaned her elbows onto the railing. The wind teased at her hair, tugged at the fabric of her dress. A shard of doubt had wiggled into her mind, and she couldn't seem to dislodge it. Was staying in New York truly worth all this?

The sun had lowered in the distance, a furious golden blaze above the dragon-back skyline of Jersey. But the city showed no signs of slowing down. Autocars moved in coordinated strands along the West Side Highway. Motes of the setting sun danced over the Hudson, glazing it a fine warm bronze. Down in the river, an old ship had been repurposed into a bar, where New Yorkers stubbornly clutched their beers as the waves buffeted them. Calliope had a sudden, fervent urge to be down there among them, caught up in the laughter and the rocking of the boat—instead of standing up here like a quiet, breathing statue.

"I was thinking the guests could do cocktail hour out here, while we're finishing our photos," Nadav was saying. The corners of his mouth almost, but not quite, turned up in a smile.

Elise clapped her hands girlishly. "I love it!" she exclaimed. "Of course, it won't work if we end up with a rain day, but—"

"I've already filed our weather request with the Metropolitan Weather Bureau," Nadav cut in eagerly. "It should be a perfect evening, just like this one." He threw his arm out as if offering the sunset as a present, which Calliope supposed was exactly what he was doing.

She should have known that you could purchase good weather on your wedding day, she thought wryly. Everything in New York was for sale, in the end.

Elise held up a hand in protest. "You shouldn't have! I can't imagine how much that must have cost—you have to cancel it and donate that money instead. . . ."

"Absolutely not," Nadav countered, leaning in to kiss Calliope's mom. "For once, everything is going to be about you."

Calliope just barely refrained from rolling her eyes. As if everything wasn't *always* about Elise and what she wanted. Nadav had no idea that he was falling for one of the world's most basic manipulation tricks: reverse psychology. With certain people, the more you begged them not to spend money on you, the more determined they became to do exactly that.

The museum's event planner ducked out onto the terrace to inform them that the appetizer tasting was ready. As they began to file through the doors, Calliope cast a lingering look over her shoulder, at the great wide expanse of sky. Then she turned to walk with dutiful, mechanical steps back inside.

# WATT

**IT WAS FRIDAY** evening, and Watzahn Bakradi was doing the same thing he did every Friday. He was out at a bar.

Tonight's bar of choice was called Helipad. The midTower clientele probably thought that was some kind of hilarious hipster irony, but Watt had another theory: It was called Helipad because no one had bothered to name it anything more creative.

Though Watt had to admit that this place was pretty cool. During the day it was a real, functioning helipad—there were actual skid marks on the gray carbon-composite floor, mere hours old—until every night after the final copter departure, when it transformed into an illicit bar.

The ceiling soared above them like a cavernous steel rib cage. Behind a folding table, human bartenders mixed drinks out of coolers: No one dared bring a bot-tender up here, because a bot would report all the safety violations. Dozens of young people, dressed in midriff-baring tops or flickering instaprinted T-shirts, clustered in the center of the space. The air hummed with excitement and attraction and the low pulse of speakers. Most striking of all, though, were the helipad's main double doors—which had been thrown open jaggedly, as if an enormous shark had taken a bite out of the Tower's exterior wall. The cool night air whipped around the side of the building. Watt could hear it beneath the music, an odd disembodied hum.

The partygoers kept glancing that way, their gazes drawn to the velvety night sky, but no one ventured too close. There was an unspoken rule to stay on this side of the red-painted safety line, about twenty meters from the gaping edge of the hangar.

Any closer and people might think you were planning to jump.

Watt had heard that copters did sometimes, unpredictably, land here at night, for patients with medical emergencies. If that happened, the entire bar would pick up and evacuate with four minutes' notice. The type of people who came here didn't mind the uncertainty. That was part of the appeal: the thrill of flirting with danger.

He shifted his weight, holding a frosted beer bottle determinedly in one hand. It wasn't his first of the evening. When he began coming out like this, right after Leda broke up with him, he would skulk around the edges of whatever bar he'd come to, trying to conceal his hurt, which only made it hurt worse. Now at least the wound was scarred over enough for him to stand at the center of the crowd. It made Watt feel marginally less lonely.

*Your blood alcohol levels are higher than the legal limit*, reported Nadia, the quantum computer embedded in Watt's brain. She projected the words over his contacts like an incoming flicker, communicating the way she always did when Watt was in a public setting.

*Tell me something I don't know*, Watt thought somewhat immaturely.

*I just worry about you drinking alone.*

*I'm not drinking alone*, Watt pointed out mirthlessly. *All these people are here with me.*

Nadia didn't laugh at the joke.

Watt's gaze was drawn to a pretty, long-limbed girl with olive skin. He tossed his empty beer bottle into the recycle chute and started over.

"Want to dance?" he asked once he was standing next to her. Nadia had gone utterly silent. *Come on, Nadia. Please.*

The girl pulled her lower lip into her teeth and glanced around. "No one else is dancing. . . ."

"Which is why we should be the first," Watt countered, just as the music abruptly switched tracks to a grating pop song.

The girl's reluctance visibly melted away, and she laughed. "This is actually my favorite song!" she exclaimed, taking Watt's hand.

"Really?" Watt asked, as if he didn't already know. It was because of him—well, because of Nadia—that the song was playing. Nadia had hacked the girl's page on the feeds to determine her favorite music, then hijacked the bar's speakers to play it, all in less than a second.

*Thanks, Nadia.*

*Are you sure you want to thank me? This song is garbage*, Nadia shot back, so vehemently that Watt couldn't help cracking a smile.

Nadia was Watt's secret weapon. Everyone could search the i-Net on their computerized contacts, of course, but even the latest contacts operated by voice-command—which meant that if you wanted to look something up, you had to say it aloud, the way you sent a flicker. Only Watt could search the i-Net in surreptitious silence, because only Watt had a computer embedded in his brain.

Whenever Watt met someone, Nadia would instantly scan the girl's page on the feeds, then determine what he should say in order to win her over. Maybe the girl was a tattooed graphic artist, and Watt would pretend to love old 2-D sketches and small-batch whiskey. Maybe she was a foreign exchange student, and Watt would act urbane and sophisticated; or maybe she was a passionate political advocate, and Watt would claim to espouse her cause, whatever it was. The script always changed, but in each case, it was easy to follow.

These girls were all looking for someone like them. Someone who echoed their own opinions, who said what they wanted to hear, who didn't push them or contradict them. Leda was the only girl Watt had ever met who *didn't* want that, who actually preferred to be called out on her bullshit.

He forced away the thought of Leda, focusing on the bright-eyed girl before him.

"I'm Jaya," she said, stepping closer and draping her arms around Watt's shoulders.

"Watt."

Nadia provided him with a few conversation starters, questions about Jaya's interests or her family, but Watt wasn't in the mood to make small talk. "I have to leave soon," he heard himself say.

*Wow, really jumping the gun tonight, aren't you?* Nadia remarked drily. He didn't bother to reply.

Jaya startled a little, but Watt quickly forged ahead. "I'm fostering a rescue puppy from the shelter," he said, "and I need to go check on him. I have one of those pet-minder bots, but I still feel weird leaving it with him. He's so young, you know?"

Jaya's expression had instantly softened. Her dream was to be a veterinarian. "Of *course* I understand. What kind of puppy?"

"We think he's a border terrier, but we aren't totally sure. Apparently he was found alone in Central Park." For some reason the lie tasted rancid in Watt's mouth.

"No way! I have a border terrier rescue too! His name is Frederick," Jaya exclaimed. "They found him under the old Queensboro Bridge."

"What a coincidence," Watt said flatly.

Jaya didn't seem to notice his lack of surprise. She looked at him through her thick fluttering lashes. "Want me to come help? I'm really good with rescues," she offered.

It was exactly what Watt had been fishing for, yet now that Jaya had suggested it, he was shockingly uninterested. He felt as if nothing or no one would surprise him ever again.

"I think I'll be okay," he offered. "But thanks."

Jaya recoiled. "Okay, then," she said coolly, and stalked away.

Watt ran a hand wearily over his face. What was *wrong* with him? Derrick would never let him hear the end of it if he knew Watt was rejecting cute girls who invited themselves over. Except that he didn't actually want any of those girls, because none of them could erase the memory of the one he'd lost. The only one he had ever really cared about.

Instead of heading for the exit, Watt found himself walking the other direction. His toes edged against the painted safety line. The stars glittered far up in the sky. To think that their light was careening wildly toward him at three hundred million meters per second. But what about darkness? How fast did the darkness rush toward you after a star died and its light went out for good?

No matter how fast light traveled, Watt thought, the darkness always seemed to have gotten there first.

Inevitably, his thoughts turned back to Leda. This time he didn't even try to distract himself.

It was his fault. He should have watched Leda more closely, those first few weeks after Dubai. She had insisted that she needed some time alone, after everything that happened. Watt tried to respect her wishes—until he learned that she had overdosed and was going back to rehab.

When she got home several weeks later, Leda didn't seem all that eager to see him.

"Hey, Watt," she'd said woodenly, holding open the front door. She was wearing an oversized charcoal sweater and black plasticky shorts, her feet bare on the hardwood floor of her entryway. "I'm glad you came by. We need to talk."

Those four words filled Watt with a shiver of foreboding. "I—I was so worried about you," he'd stammered, taking a step forward. "They wouldn't let me talk to you at rehab. I thought that you were . . ."

Leda abruptly talked over him. "Watt, we need to stop seeing each other. I can't be with you, not after everything I've done."

Watt's heart thudded. "I don't care," he assured her. "I know what you've done and I don't care, because I—"

"You don't know what you're talking about!" Leda cried out. "Watt, Eris and I shared a father. I killed my half sister!"

Her words reverberated in the air. Watt felt his throat close up. Everything he wanted to tell her now seemed inadequate.

"I need to start over, okay?" Her voice was shaking, and she seemed determined not to meet his eyes. "I can't get better with you around. You're one of my triggers—the *worst* of my triggers—and as long as I'm with you, I'll keep turning back to my old behaviors. I can't afford to do that."

"That isn't true. You and I make each other better," he tried to protest.

Leda shook her head. "Please," she begged. "I just want to move on. If you care about me at all, you'll leave me alone, for my own good."

The door shut behind her with a definitive click.

"Hey, step back!" someone shouted. Watt realized in a daze that he had wandered past the painted safety line, toward the gaping maw of the helipad.

"Sorry," he muttered, and retreated a few steps. He didn't even attempt to explain. What would he tell those people, exactly? That there was something soothing about looking out over the edge? That it was a sharp reminder of how small and insignificant he was, surrounded by this vast city? Of how little his pain mattered in the scheme of things?

Finally Watt turned and walked away from the bar, just as he had forced himself to walk away from Leda all those months ago.

# RYLIN

**RYLIN MYERS SAT** cross-legged on the floor, old vid-storage devices scattered around her. Some of them were shaped like shiny circular discs, others boxy and square. Rylin's delicate half-Korean features pulled into a frown as she considered each piece of hardware in turn, pausing over it as if internally debating its merits, before shaking her head and moving on. She was so engrossed in her task that she missed the footsteps that sounded in the doorway.

"I didn't expect you to work so hard on your last day." It was Rylin's boss, Raquel.

"I wanted to organize this last collection for you before I go. We're almost up to 2030," Rylin said eagerly.

To Rylin's surprise, Raquel came and knelt on the floor next to her. The lightning bolt inktat on her forearm—which was timed to flash every sixty seconds—appeared, darkened, then vanished again like smoke. "What do you think this one is?"

Raquel mused aloud, reaching for a disc that was emblazoned with an animated snowflake and a pair of girls with braids.

"I like that one," Rylin quickly said, reaching for the disc before Raquel could dismiss it. She sorted it into the pile marked SAVE: POSSIBLE ADAPTATION.

A smile curled at the corner of Raquel's mouth. "I'm going to miss you, Rylin. I'm really glad you applied for this job."

"Me too."

Rylin had spent most of last year, her junior year, attending an upper-floor private high school on scholarship. She had assumed that when June arrived, she would do the same thing she did every summer and get a mindless job downTower to pay the bills. But just when she'd been about to swallow her pride and beg for her old job at a monorail snack station, Rylin had learned that her scholarship actually continued through the summer—as long as she got an academic internship.

She had applied to as many internships as she could find, especially ones that had to do with holography, the creation of three-dimensional holographic films. And she had found this internship: working for the Walt Disney archivist.

Rylin had been startled to learn that the job was located here, in the bowels of the main public library location, in midTower. She'd never been to this location, though Rylin and her best friend, Lux, used to spend hours at their nearest public library. They would trade their favorite e-texts back and forth, then make up plays about them and stage them for their bemused parents, complete with a loud, improvised sound track.

On her first day, Rylin had walked in to find Raquel sitting cross-legged on a swivel chair, spinning it back and forth like a distracted child, her ponytail whipping sideways to smack at her cheek. "You're the new intern?" Raquel had asked, somewhat impatiently, and Rylin nodded.

Raquel explained that Disney had hired her to sort through all the old films from the pre-holo age and flag any that were ripe for adaptation. "Holographs fully saturated the market fifty years ago," she told Rylin. "At that point, everyone stopped producing 2-D films, and the machinery to play them. A lot of content was adapted in those first few decades, but there are still so many that no one has ever bothered to redo."

Rylin knew that 2-D–to–3-D conversion was an expensive and painstaking process. It was like turning a stick figure into a sculpture, taking a flat sheet of pixels and making it inhabit space. The whole thing required hundreds of hours of computer design and human creativity.

"Why isn't this stuff on the cloud somewhere?" Rylin had wondered, gesturing at the walls of old tapes and discs.

"Some of it is: the big blockbusters and all the classics. But people lost interest trying to catalog and upload every last thing. That's where we come in."

To Rylin's surprise, the more time she spent watching these old 2-D films, the more she appreciated them. The directors had so little to work with, yet accomplished so much with what they had. There was an elegance beneath the films' celluloid flatness.

"By the way," Raquel said now, as they kept methodically sorting the boxes, "I really enjoyed *Starfall*."

Rylin glanced up in surprise. "You watched it?"

*Starfall* was a short holo that Rylin had written and directed this spring, in several weeks of angst-ridden shooting after her return from Dubai. It featured some dark interior shots of the Tower, juxtaposed with sweeping views from the terraces and zoomed-in shots of Lux's eyes: because of course Lux and Chrissa, Rylin's sister, were the only actors she'd been able to coerce into it.

"It's a lovely film," Raquel replied. "You made your friend feel almost . . . capricious. Is she like that in real life?"

"She is," Rylin managed to reply, gratefulness blooming in her chest. Raquel was acting as if it wasn't a big deal—and maybe it wasn't, for her to have watched a five-minute film—but it meant a lot to Rylin.

After she'd said good-bye, Rylin trotted out the library's main entrance, with its grandiose carved stone lions. She boarded the A express lift downTower, disembarking on thirty-two and walking the ten blocks to her local neighborhood recreation center. Then it was through the broad double doors, down a long hallway, and out into the direct afternoon sunlight.

Rylin lifted a hand to shade her eyes. She glanced around the deck, the narrow strip of the 32nd floor that extended out farther than the floor above. The sun felt like a searing kiss on her skin after the cool darkness of the library, even though the library was hundreds of floors above her. She quickly shrugged out of her soft green zip-up and started through the maze of basketball courts, searching for one person in particular.

Several courts later, she found him.

He didn't notice her at first. He was too focused on the team of fifth-grade boys that he coached. They were running drills now, jogging back and forth in trailing zigzag lines as they passed the ball back and forth. Rylin stifled a smile as she leaned on the railing to watch her boyfriend, silently cataloging all the things she loved about him. The strong tanned lines of his arms as he demonstrated something to the group. The way his hair curled around his ears. The quickness of his laughter.

He looked up and noticed her, and his entire face broke out into a grin. "Look, guys! We have an audience," he announced, flashing Rylin a geeky thumbs-up.

She laughed and shook her head, tucking a strand of dark hair behind one ear. After she and Hiral broke up the first time, Rylin had never guessed that they would get back together. Which was incontestable proof that you couldn't predict where life might take you.

---

Rylin had started dating Hiral Karadjan when they were both in eighth grade. He lived near her on the 32nd floor and went to her school. Rylin remembered being instantly drawn to him: He had an effervescent sort of energy, so palpable she imagined she could see it. She came to realize that it was joy—a hazy afterglow of laughter, like the light that still streaks across the sky after a shooting star has disappeared.

Hiral laughed a lot back then. And he made Rylin laugh—the sort of deep, helpless laughter that you can only spark when you truly know someone. Rylin had loved that about Hiral: the way he seemed to understand her in a way that no one else ever could.

Until Cord.

Last fall Rylin had started working her mom's old job, as maid for the Andertons on the 969th floor. In spite of her best intentions, she'd fallen headfirst for Cord Anderton. She tried to break up with Hiral, except by that point he was in *jail*, having been arrested for drug dealing. Things got messier and messier, until eventually Rylin ended up betraying Cord's trust—and ruining things between them for good.

Then, unexpectedly, Rylin won a scholarship to Cord's upper-floor private school, and she started to wonder if they might have another shot. She'd even gone to a party all the way in Dubai, hoping to win him back: only to stand there like a fool as he kissed Avery Fuller, the richest, most flawlessly beautiful girl on earth.

Rylin told herself that it was better this way. Cord belonged with someone like Avery, someone he'd known since childhood;

someone who could join him on his life of lavish ski trips and black-tie parties and whatever else they did up there in the stratosphere.

Several weeks later, Hiral had knocked on Rylin's front door. And for some reason—maybe because she felt so alone, or because she'd learned one too many times that people don't always get the second chances they deserve—she opened it.

"Rylin. Hi." Hiral had sounded shocked that she'd actually answered. Rylin felt the same way. "Can we talk?" he added, shifting his weight. He was wearing dark jeans and a crewneck sweater that Rylin didn't recognize. And there was something else different about him, more than just the clothes. He looked softer, younger; the shadows erased from the hollows beneath his eyes.

"Okay," she decided, and opened the door wider.

Hiral walked in tentatively, as if expecting some wild thing to jump out and attack him at any moment, which might have happened if Chrissa were home. As it was, Rylin followed him with slow steps to the kitchen table. The silence between them was so thick that she seemed to be wading through it.

She saw Hiral's eyes dart to the missing table leg—he'd been the one to break it, in a burst of anger, when he learned that Rylin had hooked up with Cord—and his expression darkened.

"I owe you an apology," he began clumsily. Rylin wanted to speak up, but some instinct bade her stay silent, let him say his piece. "The things I did and said to you, when I was in jail—"

Hiral broke off and looked down, tracing an irregular pattern carved into the surface of the table. It was a series of half-moon indentations, like bite marks, from where Chrissa used to bang her spoon as a baby. *If this were a holo*, Rylin thought bizarrely, *the markings would be important. They would* mean *something*. But this was real life, where so many things had no meaning at all.

"I'm sorry, Rylin. I was a complete asshole to you. The only thing I can say is that jail scared me shitless," Hiral said baldly. "The other guys in there . . ."

He didn't finish the sentence, but he didn't need to. Rylin remembered visiting Hiral in jail: an adult jail, not juvie, because Hiral was over eighteen. It had felt unbearably soulless, permeated by a cold sense of despair.

"I know," she said softly. "But that doesn't excuse the things you said, and did."

Hiral looked pained at the memory. "That was the drugs talking," he said quickly. "I know it's not an excuse, but, Rylin—I was so terrified that I kept on using, anything that I could get my hands on in jail. I'm not proud of it, and I wish I could take it back. I'm sorry."

Rylin bit her lip. She knew plenty about doing things you wished you could undo.

"I'm not sure if you heard, but the trial went well. I got my old job back." Hiral worked as a liftie, one of the technicians who repaired the Tower's massive elevator shafts from the inside, suspended by thin cables, miles above the earth. It was dangerous work.

"I'm glad," Rylin told him. She felt guilty that she hadn't even shown up at his trial—she should have been there, if only for moral support, for the sake of their former friendship.

"Anyway, I just wanted to come say that I'm sorry. I've changed, Ry. I'm not that guy anymore, who was so awful to you. I'm sorry that I was ever that guy at all." Hiral kept his eyes steady on hers, and Rylin could see the regret burning there. She felt oddly proud of him for apologizing. It couldn't have been easy.

She thought, suddenly, of what Leda had said the other day in Dubai—that Rylin wasn't the same girl who'd shown up at Berkeley, defensive and uncertain. Hiral might have changed, but she had changed too. They'd *all* changed. How could they not, after everything that had happened, after all they had lost?

Maybe this was what growing up felt like. It hurt more than Rylin had expected.

"I forgive you, Hiral."

She hadn't expected to say that, but once she did, she was glad that she had.

He looked up with an intake of breath. "Really?"

Rylin knew that she should say something else, but she felt overwhelmed by a sudden flurry of memories—of how it had been with Hiral before. The little notes Hiral used to leave for her in the silliest places, like on the peel of a banana. The anniversary when he'd served her a picnic dinner in the park, complete with flameless candles. That time she had to go on a long road trip to visit her grandparents, when Hiral had made a playlist for her that was sprinkled with little audio clips of himself telling jokes, saying again and again how much he loved her.

And when Rylin's mom died, Hiral was the one who'd been there, steadying and certain, helping her make all the awful decisions that no daughter should ever have to make.

He stood up. "Thanks for letting me come by. I know you're with Cord now, and I won't bother you again. I just wanted to tell you how sorry I am."

"I'm not," Rylin said. "With Cord, I mean."

Hiral's face broke into an incredulous smile. "You're not?"

She shook her head.

"Rylin." Hiral faltered, sounding hoarse. "Do you think that we could ever . . . try again?"

"I don't know." A week earlier Rylin would have said absolutely not. But she was starting to learn that things were always changing, that nothing was ever quite what you thought it was, and that perhaps that was a good thing.

"Maybe," she clarified, and Hiral grinned.

"Maybe sounds good to me."

Standing at the rec center now, watching Hiral run back and forth across the basketball court, Rylin was glad that she'd given him another chance.

They'd been together for months, and Hiral had remained true to his word. He *was* different. He was totally clean: He didn't smoke or drink anymore, not even around their old friends. When he wasn't at work or spending time with Rylin, he was here at the rec center, playing basketball with these kids.

"All right, team! Huddle up!" he cried out, and the boys all gathered in an eager cluster. They all put their arms toward the center and let out a yell.

When he'd high-fived the last few boys and sent them on their way, Hiral hopped to Rylin's side of the fence. He threw an arm around her and leaned in to plant a kiss on her forehead.

"Hey, you're all sweaty!" Rylin protested and pretended to duck from beneath his arm, though she didn't really mind.

"The price you pay for dating a star athlete," Hiral teased.

They turned along the path that edged the deck, lined with benches and sprays of foliage, a few burger and frozen fruit stands scattered along the way. Rylin saw a community yoga class clustered in one corner, tipping into salutations toward the sun. As always, the deck was crowded with people, all of them gossiping, arguing, bantering.

It was one of those glorious New York fall afternoons, with a rich clarity to the low light that cast a dreamlike significance over everything. Far below, particles of sun glittered on the traffic of 42nd Street, hovercars floating in and out of the Tower like swarms of jeweled flies.

"This is my favorite time of year," Rylin declared. Autumn had always felt to her like the season of beginning, far more than spring. Children laughed on their way to school. The air was crisp and full of promise. The hours of daylight grew shorter, and therefore more precious.

Hiral lifted an eyebrow. "You do know that we live in a temperature-controlled building, right?"

"I know, but just look at this!" Rylin threw out an arm to indicate the deck, the hazy sunshine, then spun impulsively on her toes and kissed him.

When they pulled apart, Hiral was looking at her intently. "I'm going to miss you."

Rylin knew what he meant. Even with her internship, they'd had a lot of time to spend together this summer. That was all about to change, now that Rylin would be commuting upTower for school again, focusing on homework. Applying for college scholarships.

"I know. I'm going to miss you too," she said.

Neither of them mentioned the fact that Cord—the boy who had come between them last time—attended Rylin's school too.

# AVERY

"ANOTHER YEAR, ANOTHER costume party," Avery joked, glancing to where Leda stood next to her. The other girl didn't even crack a smile.

They were at the top of Cord's staircase, the same place they always caught their breath at Cord's annual back-to-school party, except it all felt wrong. Or rather, *Leda* felt wrong. Normally Leda was in her element at events like this, her energy seeming to increase in proportion to the number of people around her. But tonight she was subdued, even sullen, as if she resented Avery for dragging her here.

Ever since she got home, Avery had been asking when they could meet up, yet Leda kept putting her off with vague excuses. Finally Avery had decided to stop by on her way to Cord's. She didn't even pause to ring the doorbell, just blinked up at the Coles' retina scanner; she'd been on the entry list for years. The door instantly swung open to admit her.

Leda's mom stood in the living room, pulling a sumptuous coat around her shoulders. "Avery!" she had cried out, with audible relief. "I'm so glad you're here. It'll be good for Leda to see you."

*Good for Leda?* Avery thought, marching up the stairs in confusion. Then she reached Leda's bedroom and understood.

It was entirely changed. Gone were the bright persimmon carpet, the vintage Moroccan pillows, the hand-painted side tables. The shelves, which used to hold an eclectic assortment of things—a chipped celadon vase, a mobile sunlamp, a funny stuffed giraffe that sang "Happy Birthday" when you pressed on its stomach—were bare. Everything felt dismal and utterly Spartan. And most starkly changed was Leda herself, who stood in a pool of shadow near her closet.

Leda had always been thin, yet now she was startlingly skinny, new shadows gathering at the base of her collarbone. Her hair was cropped close to the scalp, making her look more boyish than ever. But it was her twitchy nervousness that frightened Avery the most.

"I've missed you," Avery cried out, crossing the room and engulfing her friend in a hug. Leda stood there stiffly, barely returning it. When Avery stepped back, Leda crossed her arms over her chest in an instantaneous defensive motion.

"What's going on, Leda?" *How did I miss this?* Avery remembered what she'd said to Max the other day, that a lot had happened while she was gone. Clearly much more than she'd realized.

"I made a few changes when I got back from rehab," Leda said tersely. "My doctors wanted me to start over fresh, with no reminders of my old life. So I wouldn't slide back into my old habits."

Avery refrained from pointing out that when they told Leda to start over, the doctors probably hadn't been talking about furniture. "Should we do dinner before Cord's party? I'll wait while you change."

Leda hurried to shake her head. "That's okay. I wasn't planning on going."

"You *live* for this party!"

"I used to," Leda said quietly, her eyes hooded. "Not anymore."

This wasn't Leda at all. The person before her was a hollow pod-person version of Leda, a mannequin Leda, who looked and sounded like Leda but couldn't possibly be Avery's sharp and vibrant best friend.

Well, if anything could snap Leda back into herself, it was a good party.

"Too bad," Avery said briskly, pressing her palm against Leda's wall to open her closet. "You're coming, even if I have to drag you the entire way. I promise not to let you drink a single thing," she said loudly, over Leda's stammered protests. "I'll even vid-chat your rehab counselor in real time, if that's what it takes. But you're coming. I want you to meet Max."

Now, as they looked out over Cord's living room, Avery couldn't help thinking that she'd made a mistake. Leda stood there vacant and glassy-eyed, utterly disinterested in her surroundings.

A pair of freshman girls strutted up the stairs, both of them wearing cat ears and holographic tails that swished lazily behind them. "That's her. Avery Fuller," one of them whispered. "She's so gorgeous."

"You would be too, if you were genetically designed for it."

"Can you believe her dad is running for mayor?"

"I'm sure he's buying his way in, the same way he bought Avery. . . ."

Avery tried not to listen as the girls brushed past, but her grip on the railing tightened imperceptibly. She should be used to the gossip by now; it had been going on her entire life.

Everyone in New York knew the story of Avery's creation: that her parents had custom-built her from the pool of their combined DNA in a very expensive genetic mining procedure. The year of her birth, her baby photo had even been on the cover of *Time* digital magazine, under the headline "Engineering Perfection." Avery hated it.

"Want me to kick them out?"

Avery looked over in surprise. Anger was stormclouding over Leda's features, fracturing her formerly cool surface.

She felt the strangest urge to laugh in relief. The old Leda was still in there after all.

"We're at a party. No need to stir up unnecessary drama," Avery said quickly.

"Where else does unnecessary drama belong, if not at a party?" Leda asked and then smiled. It came out a little rigid, as if she hadn't smiled in a while and had half forgotten how to do it, but it was a smile all the same.

*Unnecessary drama.* Suddenly, Avery couldn't help thinking of this time last year, when she and Leda had been standing at the top of these very stairs, both hiding the same monumental secret—that they were in love with Atlas.

"Where is he, anyway?" Leda asked.

"Who?" Surely Leda hadn't been thinking about—

"This Klaus von Schnitzel of yours."

*Oh, right.* "It's Max von Strauss," Avery corrected, hoping Leda hadn't heard the beat of hesitation. "And I'm not sure. He disappeared earlier this afternoon, saying that he had to do something urgent. He promised to meet me here, though."

"How mysterious," Leda said, and it was almost teasing.

Avery swallowed and decided to ask the same question she'd posed earlier. "Leda. What's going on?"

Leda opened her mouth as if to reassure Avery with a lie, only to pause. "I didn't have the easiest year," she admitted. "I needed to work through some things."

Avery knew precisely what Leda was wrestling with: the fact that she had killed Eris. "She wouldn't want you to beat yourself up like this." She didn't bother clarifying who she meant. They both knew.

"It's complicated," Leda said evasively.

"I wish you'd told me." Avery felt her chest clench with sorrow. Had Leda been like this all year long, avoiding their friends, hiding from the world in that hollowed-out bedroom?

"You couldn't have helped," Leda assured her. "But I'm glad you're back. I missed you, Avery."

"I missed you too."

Avery glanced down at the living room, and her eyes lit up at the sight of Max, threading his way through the crowd below. He looked tall and imposing and woefully lost. The world felt instantly lighter.

"Max is here!" she exclaimed, and reached for Leda's hand to tug her down the stairs. "Come on, I'm so excited for you guys to finally meet!"

"In a minute," Leda said, gently untangling herself from Avery's grip. "I need a breath of fresh air. Then I promise I'll come find you both."

Avery started to argue, then paused at the sight of Leda's eyes, liquid and serious. "Okay," she said at last, and then headed down the stairs alone.

When Max saw her, his entire face—his entire body, really—broke into a grin.

"You made it," Avery breathed. Not that she had ever doubted he would. Max always showed up exactly where he'd promised to be, at the exact time he'd promised. Ruthless German efficiency, she supposed, even if he did usually look like a college professor who was running late to class. "You didn't have any trouble finding the apartment?"

"Not at all. I chose the one with the girl throwing up outside," Max replied. "Don't worry, I put her into a hovertaxi home," he hastened to add.

Avery shook her head in amusement. She watch Max glance around the room at all her classmates, dressed in wild assortments of sequins and neon spandex, their hair temporarily colored or lengthened thanks to the styler's many custom settings. Compared to college parties, she realized, it probably felt silly and a bit affected.

"I'm sorry. I forgot to warn you that it's a costume party."

Max looked down at his own outfit for a moment, as if to check that he had, in fact, remembered to put on clothes that morning. "You're right! What can we tell everyone I'm dressed as? A vagabond?"

Avery couldn't help laughing. She felt everyone watching her, burning with curiosity about Avery Fuller's new boyfriend. She knew they were all surprised that *this* was who she ended up with, after so many years of being pointedly single. Max was nothing like the boys she'd grown up with, with his floppy green shirt and clunky, unstylish boots. He was so lanky and European looking, that predatory hawk-like nose dominating his otherwise handsome face.

"You, of course, look stunning." Max's eyes skimmed over her outfit, a black sequined dress and feathered headpiece she'd thrown on at the last minute. "Who are you, Daisy Buchanan?"

"Absolutely not," Avery said automatically. She had never liked *The Great Gatsby*. Something about Daisy's isolation—cold and alone, surrounded by all her money—struck her with an odd sense of misgiving.

"You're right; Daisy is far too frivolous. You're more of a Zelda Fitzgerald, beautiful *and* brilliant."

Avery waved away the compliment. "I'm so glad you made it. I'm dying to introduce you to everyone."

"And I can't wait to meet them all," Max said heartily. "But I need to talk with you first, alone. Is that okay?"

His words sounded portentous. Avery wondered if it had to do with his mysterious errand from earlier. "This way," she offered. She knew just the place.

As always at these parties, Cord's greenhouse already contained a group of underclassmen trying to hotbox with their halluci-lighters. A heavy cloud of smoke hung around their heads. The moment they saw Avery, they scrambled to leave without being asked. She sighed and pushed the aerate button near the door, then leaned back as the greenhouse's internal system cycled in new air.

She'd always loved it in here. The Andertons' greenhouse was on the corner, so two of its walls were lined with triple-reinforced flexiglass, offering floor-to-ceiling views of the dusted purple sky. Unlike her parents' greenhouse, which was strictly ordered and labeled, this one was a riot of color. Roses, bamboo, and sunflowers grew together in a haphazard tangle, all of them genetically tweaked to bloom in the Tower's conditions. A few pea-sized pods were scattered in the soil—biosensors, monitoring the plants' levels of water, glucose, even their temperatures, so the greenhouse could make adjustments on a micro level. Avery knew that this was exactly how Cord's mom had left it.

The air seemed warm, as if Avery's blood were rushing out to her extremities. It felt as if they were no longer in the Tower at all, but in some remote and uncharted jungle. She pushed toward the window and Max followed, ducking beneath one of the oversized orchids.

"I didn't want to say anything before, in case it didn't work out, but I just had a meeting at Columbia," Max began and then paused, as if to gauge Avery's reaction. When she didn't answer, he forged ahead. "One of the professors here, Dr. Rhonda Wilde, is the world's leading expert in political economics and urban structures. She advised my professor at Oxford when *he* was at university! I've always dreamed of the chance to study directly with her, and now I have it."

Max took Avery's hands and looked into her eyes. "What I'm trying to say is, Columbia and Oxford have both agreed to let me take my classes here this year as an exchange student. So I would spend the year in New York."

Avery was momentarily bewildered. She and Max hadn't discussed what would happen when he went back to England in a few days. She had hoped that they would stay together, but didn't want to assume anything. Max was in college, after all.

"You're saying you won't go back to Oxford?" Avery repeated. "You'll stay?"

"Only if you want me to," Max said quickly. The lingering smoke seemed almost blue in the darkness; it gathered around his head like a halo.

Avery let out a breathless laugh and threw her arms around him in delight. "Of course I want you to!" she exclaimed, her words muffled into his chest. "But are you sure this is what you really want? You would be missing your sophomore year of college—all those traditions you love, house parties and that dawn banquet and your crew season—"

"It's worth it, for the chance to study with Dr. Wilde. And to spend time with you," Max assured her. "But are you sure that *you're* okay with it? We never really talked about what would happen after the summer ended. I know it's your senior year. I'll understand if you want to just spend time with your friends, without your summer boyfriend hanging around."

"Max. You know you're more to me than a summer boy-friend," Avery said quietly, and was warmed by the broad, eager smile that broke over his face.

"You're more to me than a summer girlfriend, Avery. So much more. You're part of my life now, and I want you to keep being part of it."

He paused before the final three words, words that balanced on the edge of the sentence like droplets of rain. "I love you."

Avery had known somehow that he would say it, and yet Max's declaration still sent a delicious shiver down her spine. She let the words echo for a moment, savoring them, knowing that with those words their relationship had shifted into some-thing new. "I love you too."

She snaked her arms around Max to pull him closer, feeling the muscles of his back through the fabric of his shirt. He leaned forward to drop a kiss on her forehead, but Avery tilted her face up, so that his lips met hers instead.

The kiss was soft and tender at first, almost languid. But then Max's hands were tracing over her body with increasing urgency, sending little tingling whorls up and down her nerves. It felt as if her entire body was sizzling beneath her skin, or maybe her skin had grown too small to contain her. Avery's breath came faster. She clung tighter to Max, feeling like the vines draping along the walls, as if she wouldn't be able to stand without his support—

"Oh my god, get a room," someone said, sliding open the door. Avery tore herself back in a sudden panic. She recognized the voice as Cord's.

"We have a room, thanks. It's this one," Max replied blithely.

Avery couldn't even bring herself to speak. She just watched the horrified amusement spread over Cord's face as he realized who he'd interrupted. "Sorry, Avery, I didn't realize. You two, um, carry on."

He gave a funny double tap on the wall and started to beat a hasty retreat, but Avery had found her voice at last. "Cord, I don't know if you've met my boyfriend, Max?"

Cord looked the same as ever, Avery thought, broad and imposing in his pirate costume, a crimson sash flung dramatically across his open-necked white shirt. He was holding a packet of potshots; a couple other guys, Ty Rodrick and Maxton Feld, were clustered behind him. They'd clearly all been about to smoke.

Cord's ice-blue eyes held hers for a meaningful moment. Avery wondered if he was thinking about that night too—the one and only time that they had kissed, back in Dubai. It had been reckless and foolish and Avery hadn't cared; she'd been tumbling down a dark and perilous spiral after losing Atlas, and nothing at all had mattered to her. Not even the implications of that kiss, and what it might do to her relationship with Cord.

She knew it was cowardly and immature, but she and Cord had never spoken of it. She'd barely even *seen* him afterward; she'd left the next week for England, and then met Max. Part of her felt that she owed Cord an apology. Because afterward, in the cruel light of day, Avery saw that kiss for what it was: a selfish attempt to wipe Atlas from her brain. Cord deserved better.

He smiled at Max and held out a hand. "Great to meet you, Max. I'm Avery's friend Cord." And Avery understood without being told that everything was folded into that word, *friend*. She and Cord would be just fine.

"Oh. This is *your* greenhouse!" Max edged past Cord, toward the door. "In that case, we should find another room. Maybe one less in demand. Or more geographically convenient." He said that last bit to Avery, though loud enough that the rest of them all heard. She pursed her lips against a smile and dragged him back out into the party.

The rest of the night passed in a joy-soaked blur. She introduced Max to everyone—Leda stayed just long enough to say hi, though Avery was glad to see that he coaxed a smile from her. Finally, as the party was winding down, they slid into a hovertaxi home.

"You and Cord used to date, didn't you?" Max asked abruptly.

Avery blinked, caught off guard, but Max didn't seem to notice.

"He's the guy, isn't he? The one who broke your heart before you came to England?" Max sounded almost proud of himself for having figured it out. "I just felt a strange vibe between you, and I wondered."

Avery's heart was pounding wildly, echoing in her ears. "You're right," she said quickly. "Cord and I had a thing. But it didn't work out."

"Of course it didn't," Max agreed, as if pointing out the obvious. He wrapped his arm around her shoulders and pulled her close. "Because you belong with me."

Avery loved that about Max: the way he seemed so self-assured, so certain of the world and his place in it. The way he noticed things no one else paid attention to. But right now she needed him to pay a little bit less attention, or he might realize that she hadn't really told him the truth.

She hadn't wanted to lie to Max, but what other choice did she have? He couldn't ever know who had *actually* broken her heart last year. If he knew the truth, Max wouldn't want her anymore.

It didn't matter that she and Atlas were long since over. If *anyone* found out the truth about them, Avery knew, her life would come crashing down around her.

# CALLIOPE

**CALLIOPE HATED HER** bedroom at Nadav's apartment.

It used to be the formal guest room and still contained the same set of heavy furniture, with clawed feet and angry-looking eagle heads carved into each drawer. The heavy velvet drapes seemed to crush the very air from the room. On the wall facing the bed hung an antique image of dogs killing a deer. Calliope thought it was morbid, but Nadav had won it in an auction and was terribly proud of it. She'd gotten in the habit of throwing a sweater over the painting before she went to bed, so the deer's mournful eyes wouldn't haunt her in her sleep.

When Calliope first moved in, she'd instantly begun planning how she would redo the room. She would buy light, airy furniture and colorful pillows and paint the wall with pigmaspectrum paint, in the bold primary palette. But when she mentioned her intention one night at dinner, Nadav had been so shocked that he let his fork clatter loudly to his plate.

"That paint is intended for *toddlers'* rooms," he pointed out, clearly affronted by her suggestion.

Calliope didn't care that the paint was made for children. She loved the way it subtly shifted colors throughout the day, from a deep angry red all the way to purple and back again. "If you hate it, I can pick something else," she'd offered as Elise met her gaze meaningfully across the table.

Nadav shook his head. "I'm sorry, Calliope, but you can't redecorate. We need that room as a guest room for when my mom comes to stay."

Why couldn't she change her room just because Nadav's mom would eventually be sleeping there? "When your mom is staying in my room, where will I—"

"You'll share Livya's room, of course."

The only person who'd seemed unhappier about that than Calliope was Livya, whose lips pursed into a thin, pale line.

Calliope had grown used to a long litany of no's from Nadav. When she signed up for the school play: *No, you should try student government instead.* When she wanted to go to a party: *No, you have to be home by curfew.* When she wanted to get a puppy: *No, puppies are a frivolous distraction—at your age, you need to be focused on your studies.* As the months went by, Nadav had eventually started to say no before she'd finished voicing her question.

She told herself that it was fine, that she didn't really care about that stuff anyway. Except maybe for the puppy. At least that would have made her feel less lonely.

Standing now in her bedroom, Calliope let out a petulant sigh. This room might as well have belonged to a stranger. Even after eight months, there was something decidedly temporary about it all, as if Calliope were only camping out here: boxes and suitcases stacked haphazardly in the closet like the belongings of a criminal who might have to run from the law at any moment.

She stepped toward the closet and pushed past the rows of hangers, covered in demure silk dresses and high-waisted slacks. Even the clothes didn't feel like hers; before they moved in, her mom had sorted through Calliope's wardrobe with ruthless abandon, tossing out anything tight or revealing or remotely sexy. Thank god that Calliope had secretly managed to salvage a few pieces before that bonfire of the vanities.

She stretched toward the edge of the wall, past an enormous wool coat, until her fingers brushed the bag she was looking for. Quickly she began sifting through it, pulling out an electric bracelet, a pair of gaudy clip-on earrings, her favorite red lip gloss: things she hadn't worn in months. When she was finally ready, Calliope lifted her eyes to the only thing in the room she *did* like—the mirror-screen that took up an entire wall.

She kept the room bulbs on their maximum setting and gave a self-satisfied smirk. Her beauty was as vivid, and almost as harsh, as the overbright lighting.

"Here goes nothing," she said to herself, and was down the hallway without a backward glance.

Calliope felt a little shiver of adventure as she slipped out of Nadav's apartment. Because she wasn't just sneaking out of the house. She was sneaking out of her *life*, shedding her skin, sliding neatly from the role of Calliope Brown into another role. One that she was making up as she went along.

She knew this was risky. But Calliope had hit breaking point. She couldn't take another night in that cold, gilded apartment, with its thick carpets and ticking clocks. It was the sort of apartment where she knew exactly what was happening at any given moment, because it all ran with such monotonous efficiency. Even now, for instance, Nadav would be sitting at his modular recycled-aluminum desk to review some contract or message before going to sleep. Livya would be tucked safely into her four-poster princess bed, her room comp whispering SAT questions to her throughout the night for some osmosal learning. It was all so terrifyingly predictable.

As she stepped onto the downTower lift, filled with clamor and conversation—all the messy chaos of real life—Calliope felt an overwhelming sense of relief. New York was still here. It hadn't gone anywhere.

She switched to the monorail at Grand Central, heading out of the Tower altogether, toward the lower Manhattan neighborhood known as the Sprawl. It was as unlike the sleek, ordered reality of the Tower as night from day; parts of it were still radically low-tech, with warped wooden floors and twisted railings. Church steeples rose into the sky alongside bright holograms.

Calliope glanced back at the Tower as she stepped off the monorail. From this angle it seemed to burn more brightly than ever. Next to it, the half-moon looked alone in its isolated glory.

She paused at the corner of Elizabeth and Prince Street, her eyes closed with deceptive nonchalance. It was almost nine on a weeknight and the streets were mostly quiet. But Calliope could feel the Sprawl's thrum of excitement—the seething, excited pulse of things young and thrilling and illegal.

She pushed open an unmarked brown door and stepped inside.

A wall of sound roared up to meet her: crowds erupting in screams, the slippery beat of electronic music. Another turn down the stairs and Calliope emerged in a bar, all done up in neons and pulsing LED lights, like some kind of video-game speakeasy. The ceiling was lined in prisms of glass that reflected the garish illumination, separating it into a million glowing strands and tossing it down again. The colors were so vibrant that it almost hurt to look at them.

Calliope didn't bother getting a drink, though she could have; she was over eighteen. She just lingered in the corner, her eyes flicking expertly around the room. It was crowded, with a mix of nerds, tourists, and others who were simply curious. The afternoon show was meant for children, she knew; but the night performance was supposedly much edgier—and more violent.

Someone sounded a gong. The crowd obediently shuffled through the bar to the stadium beyond, clutching their drinks to their chests. Calliope let herself be caught along in the surge, her hair falling loose around her bare shoulders. She was wearing a strapless silver dress and boots, and had even sprayed a temporary inktat patch on her tanned cheek, just for fun. It would leave a sticky film over her face for several days, but the effect was worth it.

The stadium smelled like popcorn and grease. Calliope sank eagerly into her seat and leaned forward, elbows on her knees, to study the ComBots—Combat Robots—waiting around the room. A team of handlers huddled near each of them, clutching tablets as they engaged in last-minute system checks. Calliope caught a surreptitious movement in the corner of her eye and smiled. Probably bookies, recording under-the-table bets. ComBattles might not be illegal, but gambling on them assuredly was.

ComBattles were an expensive and arguably illogical sport, like racing cars used to be—how wasteful to build these sleek, elaborate bots, only to let them tear one another apart. Calliope wondered what it was about humans that made them relish destruction. This was the modern version of gladiatorial fights, or bear baitings, or reality television. For whatever reason, people loved watching things explode.

She hadn't been to a ComBattle in years, not since the time Elise took her to one in Shinjuku. She wasn't really sure why she'd come here tonight. Perhaps the loud anonymity of it seemed reassuring. This was as far from the Mizrahis' world as she could get.

Calliope let her eyes drift to the boy sitting next to her. "Did you bet on one?" she asked. For some reason the words came out in an Australian accent.

He looked around, startled, as she might be talking to some other, better someone lurking behind him. "Oh. Um, the three-headed snake," he said after a moment.

"That thing? Mine will crush it," Calliope declared, knowing that her voice would forgive the insult. Calliope's voice—soft and purring, with that seductive accent—had always been her secret weapon. It allowed her to say anything she wanted and get away with it.

White teeth flashed against ebony skin as the young man smiled. "I wouldn't have taken you for a gambler."

"And why not? Where's the fun, without a little risk to spice things up?"

He nodded, conceding the point. "Which did you bet on?"

"My money is on that scaly thing," Calliope fabricated, pointing toward a robot that was half lion, half dragon. Little whirls of fire emerged from its gullet.

There was something whimsical about the battle bots, despite their ruthlessness. It was against international regulations to make robots that resembled people; and in America, it was also illegal for robots to resemble real animals. As a result, the ComBots became something almost otherworldly. Calliope saw a dinosaur, a fanged unicorn, and a winged tiger that sizzled with electricity.

"Care to up the stakes?" the guy asked and held out a hand. "I'm Endred, by the way."

"Amada." It was a name she'd used back in Australia. Easy to remember. "What did you have in mind, exactly?"

"Loser buys dinner?"

Calliope hadn't come here to run a con. God knows she didn't need anything off this guy; she could buy her own dinner, now that she had access to Nadav's money. And yet . . . for her, it had always been as much about the thrill as it was about money. That eager breathless sensation of living on the edge, of knowing she was pulling off the impossible. *That* was what she wanted from Endred—attention, adventure, a night of being someone else, rather than the excruciatingly boring character she'd been playing these past eight months.

"I never say yes to dinner without drinks first," she told him, with an inscrutable smile.

"Done."

The stadium went suddenly dark and erupted in wild screaming as the first two ComBots faced off.

It was the dinosaur against her lion-dragon. Calliope reached beneath her seat for her glowstick and waved it in the air, shouting like everyone else until her throat was ragged, watching wide-eyed as the dinosaur and the hybrid creature began slashing at each other. They breathed fire; they shot small ballistics; they lunged forward and then quickly fell back. A pair of commentators narrated the action in a guttural, excited mix of English, Mandarin, and Spanish. Strobe lights flickered overhead. She felt Endred's gaze heavy on her and couldn't resist giving her head a proud toss.

The dinosaur's barbed tail slashed at the hybrid. Calliope jumped to her feet, one hand still wrapped tightly around the lime-green glowstick. "Get him!" she cried out as the lion-dragon's jaws unhinged—grotesquely wide, wider than a real creature's jaws ever could—and a torrent of flames erupted from it. The dinosaur stumbled, a gash in its side exposing a bright red tangle of wires. Its arms flailed, as if its computer was short circuiting, and then it tottered to one side and fell still.

Amid the roar of the stadium, Endred looked over at her and

grinned. "It seems congratulations are in order."

"I always know how to pick a winner," Calliope said provocatively.

Endred waved over a pitcher of a sticky lemon drink and handed her a glass. Down in the arena, a team of human specialists had run forward to sweep away the debris of the broken ComBot. The team managing the winning bot were high-fiving one another, readying themselves for another round.

Calliope took a tentative sip of the lemon drink, wincing at its tanginess. "So, Endred, tell me about yourself. Where are you from?"

Endred preened, predictably, beneath the attention. "Miami. Have you ever been?"

Calliope shook her head, though she and Elise had run cons in Miami countless times.

He began describing the city's waterlogged streets; which had been flooded for half a century, ever since the sandbars surrounding Florida crumbled into the ocean. Calliope didn't listen. As if she hadn't taken a Jet Ski up and down those very streets. She loved Miami, loved the stubborn sexiness of the city, the way it refused to admit defeat even when it was flooded, and instead rose boldly from the waters like a modern super-Venice.

But Calliope could tell that Endred was the type of guy who could be easily won over by talking about himself. Like most boys.

As she peppered him with questions, slipping in the occasional lie about herself, Calliope felt herself reviving like a plant in water. She'd forgotten what a rush it was, playing this game. But now she was in her element again, and all her self-confidence came rushing back as she did what she did best: become someone else.

"If it isn't Calliope Brown," an unexpected voice said behind her.

Calliope turned around slowly, trying to mask her trepidation. It was Brice Anderton, Cord's older brother. He wore a dark jacket and oversized sunglasses, which he lifted now, his eyes roving unabashedly over Calliope's skintight dress. He was swarthy and tall and far too good-looking, and he knew it.

"I'm afraid you have the wrong girl," Endred interrupted, oblivious to the tension between them. "This is Amada."

"Yes. You must have me confused with someone else," Calliope heard herself say in the Australian accent.

"My mistake." Brice's mouth twisted in amusement.

Endred tried to pick up their conversation where it had left off, but Calliope's smile was beginning to slip from her frozen features. "Excuse me," she murmured, and ducked back up the narrow stairs to the neon-decked bar just as the lights began to dim for the next fight.

Brice was leaning negligently against the bar, as if he'd known that she would come. "Calliope. What an unexpected pleasure," he said in that unmistakable entitled drawl.

She refused to back down. "The unexpected pleasure is all mine. I had no idea you were into ComBattles."

"I could say the same thing. This doesn't exactly strike me as your scene."

*This is far closer to the real me than the Little Bo Peep version of me everyone has seen all year.* "I like to think of myself as a thing of mystery," she said flippantly.

"And I like to think of myself as a person who solves mysteries."

The smart thing to do would be to ignore him and head home. Brice was the only person aside from Avery with the power to blow Calliope's cover. She'd met him once before, in Singapore, when she'd conned his friend and then skipped town. Whether or not he recognized her—which she never could quite figure out—there was always a dangerous, and slightly magnetic, edge to their interactions.

But instead of leaving, Calliope leaned forward over the bar, kicking one boot behind the other. She held Brice's gaze. "I haven't seen you in a while. Since last year's Under the Sea ball, I think."

"I've been traveling a lot. To East Asia, Europe, all over the place."

"Is New York too boring for you?"

"Not anymore," Brice said meaningfully, his eyes on her. "But really, what were you doing in there, telling people your name is Amada, using that fake accent?"

For once, Calliope felt an urge to tell the truth. "I was bored. I guess I just wanted to be someone else for the night."

"Want to be someone else some*where* else?" Brice offered. "There's a great dumpling place around the corner, and I'm starving."

The prospect was oddly tempting. But Calliope knew better. She'd already risked too much simply by coming out tonight; she couldn't be seen with the infamous, notorious Brice Anderton. Not when she'd worked for so long to convince everyone on the upper floors that she was a soft-hearted philanthropist.

"I actually need to get home," she told him, hating how much she sounded like a teenager on curfew. Part of her hoped that he would try to convince her to stay.

Brice just shrugged and took a step back. "All right, then," he said easily. He disappeared downstairs, back into the roaring darkness of the ComBot arena, taking with him the only flicker of excitement that Calliope had felt in months.

# RYLIN

**THE FIRST DAY** of school, Rylin stepped out of Berkeley's main quadrangle, lifting a hand to her eyes to shade them even as her contacts switched to light-blocking mode: one of the few things they were able to do on school grounds. The UV-free solar beams prickled pleasantly on her arms.

Ahead of her rose the science building, surrounded by a turquoise reflecting pool that was filled with multicolored koi and a few croaking frogs. Rylin shuddered as she passed. She'd had to dissect a frog last year in biology class, and even though she knew it wasn't real—that it was actually a synthetic frog-like thing built specifically for high school students to avoid animal cruelty—she still didn't like the sound of the real ones.

She hadn't wanted to take a science class this year at all, but since it was mandatory, Rylin had settled on the most innocuous-sounding option: Introduction to Psychology. Actually, her summer boss, Raquel, had been the one to suggest it. "All good storytellers study psychology," she'd proclaimed, drumming her fingers idly over the film storage boxes. "Novelists, filmmakers, even actors. You have to know the rules of human behavior before you can make your characters break them."

That sounded reasonable to Rylin. Besides, psychology seemed so much friendlier than the other options—no test tubes or scalpels, just surveys and "social experiments," whatever that meant.

She started down the two-story science hallway past the robotics lab, where electrical sparks jumped from one wire to another like fiery spiders; past the meteoroculture lab, where students gathered around a massive holographic globe, studying the weather patterns that broke in soft gray waves over its surface; past the massive steel door marked SUBZERO LAB: THERMAL PROTECTION REQUIRED. The so-called "ice box," where the Advanced Physics class conducted below-freezing experiments in subatomic particles. Rylin didn't even want to know how much it cost to maintain that temperature.

When she turned into room 142 at the end of the hall, Rylin was relieved to see rows of two-person lab stations, each equipped with nothing but a pair of holo-goggles. She took a seat at one of the empty tables and pulled up the notepad function on her school tablet—just in time.

"Humans are illogical and irrational. That's the first rule of psychology." A glamorous Chinese woman strode into the classroom, instantly skewering them all with her stare. Her heels clicked lightly on the floor.

"Psychology as a science was born because humans have been trying for millennia to understand why we do the things we do. *Psyche*, meaning mind, and *logos*, study. We've been doing this since the ancient Greeks, and yet we still haven't come close to making sense of it all.

"I'm Professor Heather Wang. Welcome to Introduction to Psychology," she announced and narrowed her eyes. "If you're here because you think this is the 'easy' science class compared to physics or chemistry, think again. At least elements and chemicals behave in a predictable way. People, on the other hand, are shockingly unpredictable."

Rylin couldn't agree more. Sometimes she felt as if she couldn't even predict her own actions, let alone those of the people around her.

The door to the classroom pushed inward, and a familiar dark head appeared. Rylin barely bit back a sigh. Of all the classes he could have taken, Cord had to be in this one?

Professor Wang gazed coolly at him. "I know you're all seniors and have one foot out the door already, but I don't tolerate lateness from anyone."

"I'm sorry, Professor Wang," Cord said, with his usual charming forgive-me smile. Then he marched right over to Rylin's lab console—ignoring the several other empty spots—and slid into the seat next to her.

Rylin kept her gaze studiously forward, pretending not to see him.

"Despite being coerced and at best halfhearted," the professor went on, addressing the class, "what you just heard from Mr. Anderton was an *apology*, a prime example of the types of social interactions we will study this year. We will explore the different forces influencing human behavior, including established social norms. We'll discuss how these norms came to be, and what happens when someone chooses to violate them."

*Like violating the unspoken norm of sitting next to your ex-girlfriend in class when there are plenty of open seats?*

"Today we'll be performing the Stroop effect, a classic

demonstration of how easily the human brain can be tricked. Our brains are the computers with which we interpret the world, and yet their operations are compromised far too easily. We mis-remember information, we forget whole stretches of time. We convince ourselves of things we know to be untrue. Now let's get started." Professor Wang clapped, and their tablets all lit up with the text of the lab instructions.

Cord leaned forward onto the lab table. He'd rolled up his sleeves, in blatant defiance of the dress code, revealing the mus-cles of his forearms. "Long time no see, Myers."

Rylin kept her eyes on the lab instructions to keep from looking at him. She'd been avoiding Cord since she saw him kiss Avery at the Dubai party last year. And she had been mostly successful, until now.

"It says here that one of us needs to put on the VR headset," she pointed out. If Cord noticed that she was tapping at her tablet with unusual vehemence, he didn't comment on it. He just kept looking at her with that amused smile, his lips slightly parted.

"How was your summer?"

Why was he trying to make small talk? "It was good," Rylin said shortly. "You?"

"I traveled with Brice for a while, mostly around South America. Windsurfing, scuba, you know." *No*, Rylin thought, *I really don't know.*

Cord was close with his older brother, Brice, but then—like Rylin and Chrissa—they were all each other had. The Andertons had died years ago in a freak plane crash, making Cord an orphan, a celebrity, and a billionaire all at once. He had been ten years old.

When Rylin's mom died, Rylin had inherited nothing but a massive stack of unpaid medical bills.

"What about you, did you go anywhere fun?" Cord asked.

*Go anywhere fun?* "Not really. I had a job working for an archivist, going through film at the public library."

"Oh, right. I saw your snaps. That looked cool," Cord agreed. Rylin was startled to hear that he'd been following her on the feeds.

"I missed you at my party on Saturday," he added. "I was excited to see what you were going to be dressed as—I couldn't decide which was more likely, Catwoman or a punk rocker."

"I don't really do costumes." Did Cord seriously think that she would show up to the very party she'd worked for him last year, the party where he'd first kissed her?

"Don't do costumes? Where's the fun in that?"

"It doesn't always have to be about 'fun,' you know," Rylin snapped, more curtly than she'd meant to. She knew she wasn't really being fair. But Cord needed to stop and *think* sometimes before just saying whatever popped into his mind.

And there wasn't anyone else in Cord's life who was about to call him out like that.

She picked up the virtual reality headpiece and settled it clunkily over her brow, shutting out the whole world, including Cord. "I'll go first," she said into the silence. Illuminated before her on the goggles was a blank white background.

After a moment, Cord tapped at something to begin the lab. "Tell me what color you see."

The word *hello* appeared before her in vibrant green. Rylin blinked at it for a moment, disconcerted, before remembering that she was supposed to say the color. "Green."

The word disappeared, to be replaced by a dark red block letters that read *purple.*

"Purple," she said automatically and felt herself flush again. "No, wait, I mean, red—"

Cord laughed. She tried not to wonder what his expression looked like beyond her blocked-out field of vision.

"Don't you see how easily your brain can be tricked!" Professor Wang's voice crowed nearby.

Rylin flicked a switch on the side of the VR headset and its screen evaporated into transparency. She glanced through her now clear goggles to see the professor hovering near their lab station. "I just read the word automatically," she tried to explain.

"Exactly!" the professor cried out. "Your analytical and visual identification neurons were firing at cross-purposes, and chaos broke out! Your own brain betrayed you!" She tapped one finger to her head before swishing off to another lab station.

*It only betrays me when Cord is around*, Rylin thought with some resentment.

She reached up to flick the side of her headset, letting the view screen repopulate with the lab program. "Okay, I'm ready."

"Rylin . . ." Cord reached over as if to lift the VR headset from the crown of her head, but Rylin instinctively jerked back. He didn't get to touch her hair as if it meant nothing. He'd forfeited that right a long time ago.

Cord seemed to realize that he'd crossed a line. "Sorry," he mumbled, chastened. "But—I'm confused. What's going on? I thought we were becoming friends again last year, and now I feel like you're attacking me."

*We* were *becoming friends, until I wanted to be more, and then I saw you with Avery.* "Don't worry about it," she said stiffly. "It's fine."

"It's clearly not fine," Cord protested.

"Look, can we just get this lab done with, and—"

"Forget the lab, Rylin."

She was startled by the flash of anger that ran through Cord's words. Reluctantly she took off the VR headset and set it on the table.

"What is it?"

"Why are you acting like this?"

"I don't know what you mean," Rylin protested weakly—because she knew exactly what he meant, and felt suddenly ashamed of herself. She fiddled awkwardly with the strap on the headset.

"Did I do something to upset you?" Cord pressed.

Their eyes met, and Rylin felt herself flush a bright agonized red. Telling Cord the truth meant admitting how she'd felt about him last year: that she'd gone all the way to Dubai chasing him. Yet some part of her insisted that she owed Cord an explanation, no matter how much it stung her pride.

"I saw you with Avery. In Dubai," she said quietly.

Rylin watched as he sorted through the implications of her words. "You saw Avery kiss me?" he demanded at last.

Rylin gave a miserable nod, not trusting herself to speak. Even though it was months ago—even though she was with Hiral now, and it shouldn't matter—Rylin felt the shame of that night stealing over her, as sticky and suffocating as ever.

She'd gone to Dubai buoyed by a ridiculous hope that she could find Cord and tell him how she felt. That they could start over. She'd looked for him that whole night, but when she'd finally found him, it was too late. He was with Avery. Kissing her.

"Nothing ever happened again between me and Avery," Cord said slowly. "We're just friends."

Rylin had figured that out eventually, once Avery left for Europe and started dating that Belgian guy or whoever he was. She felt a little foolish. "You don't owe me an explanation," she said quickly. "It was all so long ago, it doesn't matter anyway."

"Except that it clearly does matter." Cord's eyes were unreadable. "I wish you'd said something," he added softly.

Rylin felt her blood hammering underneath her skin. "Hiral and I got back together," she felt a sudden need to say.

"Hiral?"

Rylin knew what Cord must be thinking. He was remembering what Hiral had done last year when she'd been working for Cord. "It's different this time," she added, not sure why she was explaining herself to Cord anyway.

"If you're happy, Rylin, then I'm happy for you."

"I am happy," she agreed, and she meant it; she was happy with Hiral. Yet somehow the statement had come out a bit defensive.

Cord nodded. "Look, Rylin, can't we start over?"

*Start over.* Was that even possible after everything they'd been through? Perhaps it wasn't a start-over as much as a start-from-here. It sounded nice, actually.

"I'd like that," Rylin decided.

Cord held out his hand toward her. For a moment Rylin was startled at the gesture, but then she tentatively reached out and shook his hand.

"Friends," Cord declared. Then he reached for the VR goggles to begin his section of the lab.

Rylin glanced over at him, curious at something she thought she'd heard in his tone, but his expression was already hidden behind the bulky mask of the goggles.

# LEDA

**LATER THAT AFTERNOON,** Leda turned down the hallway toward the main entrance of the Berkeley School. The other students moved in coordinated flocks around her like uniformed birds, all wearing the same navy pants or plaid pleated skirts. Leda watched as they formed into groups, only to exchange a few snitches of gossip before breaking off again. The halls were thick with that frantic back-to-school hum, everyone rapidly recalibrating their relationships after three months apart.

Thank god *some* relationships didn't change, she thought gratefully as Avery emerged from a classroom across the hall. Avery had no idea just how much Leda had needed her.

She was oddly glad that Avery had insisted she come to Cord's the other night. Leda hadn't exactly been the life of the party—it all felt so garishly loud and bright, and she kept worrying that the darkness would open up within her again, like an earthquake that might erupt at any moment. But nothing all that bad had happened. Actually, Leda realized, it had felt *good*, doing something almost normal again.

"Come with me to Altitude?" Avery asked, falling into step alongside her. "There's a new thermo-shock yoga class I want to try. Super hot for the stretch, freezing for the cooldown."

"I have some studying to do tonight," Leda said, adjusting her crossbody bag over her shoulder.

"Our first day back? We don't even have any homework yet!"

"It's my SAT tutor. I need to push my score above a three thousand." Leda was applying to Princeton. Her mom had gone there, and lately, Leda had found herself trying to be more and more like her. It was a new impulse, given that she'd spent the first eighteen years of her life trying to be the opposite of her mom.

"You're welcome to come with me, if you want the extra practice," she added, but Avery shook her head.

"I'm not taking the SAT. Oxford doesn't recognize it."

"Oh, right. Because of *Max*," Leda said lightly as they walked through the school's massive stone gates and out into the fabricated sunshine. Though Leda had to admit that she'd been pleasantly surprised by Max. He wasn't at all what she'd expected. She couldn't imagine being attracted to him herself, with his shaggy hair and eclectic Euro style; the way his attention flitted between distraction and sudden, intense focus. But she sensed something fundamentally warm and sturdy about him. He was the type of boy you could trust with your best friend's heart.

"I wanted to go to Oxford before Max, remember?" Avery insisted, though a goofy smile played around her lips at the mention of him.

Leda froze at the unusual sight of two police officers lingering just past the school's entrance. Their relaxed poses didn't fool her one bit. They were watching the ebb and flow of students around the edge of the tech-net, looking for someone in particular.

Leda knew, with an instinctive animal certainty, that they were here for her.

One of the police officers—or maybe they were detectives?—met her gaze, and the flash of recognition in his eyes confirmed her suspicions.

"Miss Cole?" he asked, stepping forward. He was pale and plump, with a curling dark moustache and a name tag that said OFFICER CAMPBELL. In contrast, his partner was a young woman named Kiles; tall and willowy with a dark bronzed tan.

"That's me," Leda said reluctantly.

"We were hoping you would come down to the station, answer a few questions for us."

"Leda . . ." Avery whispered, and bit her lip in alarm. Leda held her head high, ignoring the frantic pattering of her heart. On some level she had known that this day would come.

She just didn't know which of her many transgressions she had to answer for.

"What is this regarding?" Leda was proud of how cool and unconcerned her voice came out. But then, Leda had plenty of practice at pretending not to care about things that actually mattered.

"We'll fill you in at the station," said Officer Kiles. Her eyes cut significantly to Avery. Through the haze of her panic, Leda felt a sharp curiosity. Whatever this was, it was confidential.

"I'm sorry, but you can't just question my friend without reason," Avery cut in. She had that stubborn, protective look she'd inherited from her father. "Do you have any paperwork?"

Kiles swerved on her. "Avery Fuller, right?"

The fact that they knew her name didn't subdue Avery one

bit. She was used to being recognized, especially these days. "If you think I'm going to let you drag my friend off without any formal request—"

"We're not *dragging* anyone. We were hoping that Miss Cole would come voluntarily," Kiles said smoothly.

"It's okay, Avery," Leda cut in, though she was touched by Avery's defense of her. She knew what would happen if she told the police no. They would just go get whatever paperwork they needed, meaning she would still end up there *in*voluntarily. And with far fewer niceties.

"I'm happy to come," she told the officers, trying to project more confidence than she felt.

———

"How are you doing, Miss Cole?"

Leda barely refrained from rolling her eyes. She'd always hated that question. It reminded her far too much of what her therapist would ask.

"I'm fine, thank you." She knew the police didn't actually care how she was doing. The question was a vacuous courtesy or perhaps some kind of test.

She tucked her heels behind the legs of her dented metal chair and glanced impassively around the interrogation room. She didn't see the telltale shimmer in the air, like a self-contained heat wave, that usually indicated a security cam—but that didn't mean anything, did it? Surely the police were recording her some other way. Or would they need her parents' consent for that, since she was still a minor?

Across the metal table, both police officers blinked at her, revealing nothing. Leda kept her lips pursed, content to let the silence swirl around her.

"Are you aware of why you're here?" asked Officer Campbell.

"I'm here because you asked me," Leda said crisply.

Campbell leaned forward. "What do you know about Mariel Valconsuelo?"

"Who is that?" Leda asked with more force than she should have.

"You don't know her?" Campbell laid his palms on the table, causing a holographic insta-screen to flare to life before him. Leda craned her neck, but from her perspective the holo was just a flat, opaque rectangle of pixels. He tapped the screen to input a series of commands, and a hologram burst to life, visible to all of them.

It depicted a Hispanic girl around Leda's age, with curling dark hair and conspicuous eyes. There was something fierce and determined in her features. She wasn't smiling, the way most people did in their official ID photos.

It was the face that, along with Eris's, had haunted Leda's nightmares for the past year.

Suddenly Leda was back in Dubai, terrified and helpless on that beach, and Mariel was looming over her, her gaze sharp with hatred. *You killed your sister, Leda,* she'd spat. A light from the dock had illuminated Mariel from behind, limning the edges of her form, making her look like some kind of avenging angel in her black bartender's outfit. An angel sent from hell, to hold Leda accountable for all the ugliness in her heart—

"It looks like you might recognize her," Kiles said pointedly.

*Shit.* Leda tried to get a hold on her emotions. "Maybe I've seen her around? She seems familiar, but I don't know why."

"Mariel worked as a waitress at Altitude Club," Campbell offered in a condescending tone. As if Leda was supposed to seize gratefully on that fact and thank him for it.

"I guess that explains it." Leda shrugged, but the officer wasn't done.

"She was also at the launch event for the Mirrors in Dubai.

She was part of the Altitude Club staff that the Fullers brought over to work the event." His eyes were twin globes of watchfulness. "According to her family, she was also dating Eris Dodd-Radson, before Eris's death."

Leda was very quiet and still. She tried to breathe silently, in and out through her nostrils, deliberate yoga breaths. She waited for the other shoe to drop.

Officer Kiles was the one who broke the silence. "You didn't meet her in that context? As Eris's girlfriend?"

"Eris didn't exactly gush about her relationships with me." That, at least, was true. "I didn't know Mariel."

"*Didn't* know her?" Kiles repeated. "But apparently you know that she's dead?"

God, what was *wrong* with her? "She's dead?" Leda lifted her eyebrows, as if she couldn't be bothered to know what had happened to Mariel. "I only used the past tense because Eris is dead. As you may be aware, I was actually on the roof of the Fullers' apartment when it happened." *The worst day of my life.*

Leda wondered, again, how Mariel had died. She hadn't been able to find that information on the i-Net, and it wasn't as if the obituary said what had happened; they never listed the cause of death. Presumably that was in poor taste.

Campbell leaned his elbows onto the table, trying to impress upon Leda how much sheer physical space he occupied. "Mariel drowned. Her body was found in the East River."

Leda's mind lurched violently to one side, as if yanked by a thin thread of memory, but it snapped off and floated away before she could be certain of it. She felt cold all over.

Mariel had ended up with the death she'd tried to give Leda. There was a dark irony there, as if this were some kind of poetic justice administered by the gods.

"What does this have to do with me?"

The two police officers glanced at Leda, then at each other, then at Leda again. They seemed to come to some unspoken understanding, because Kiles leaned forward with what she probably assumed was an encouraging expression. "You may not have known Mariel, but she certainly knew you. She was gathering information about you before she died. She had a file on you and your movements."

Of course she did. Mariel had been planning her revenge on Leda, for what Leda had done to Eris. But the police didn't know that—right? If they did, wouldn't she have been brought here a long time ago?

Leda did her best to act afraid, which wasn't difficult given that her nerves were stretching tighter and tighter over the empty pit of her panic. "Are you saying that Mariel was *stalking* me?" she demanded.

"That is what it looks like, yes." There was a pause. "Do you have any idea why she might do that?"

"Isn't it obvious? She was grief-stricken over the loss of Eris and wanted to feel close to her. So she turned to Eris's friends."

It was a gamble, but it was the best Leda could come up with on the fly.

There was a silence heavy with meaning, as if all the air in the room had gone stale. Finally Campbell lifted his brows. "You see, until now, we thought Mariel's death was accidental. But we recently uncovered new evidence that suggests it might have been the result of foul play. So we've reopened the case as a murder investigation."

Mariel had been *murdered*? But who would do such a thing, and why? Leda blinked, panicked that the subject of her thoughts was somehow visible.

"We're trying to understand what was going on with Mariel before she died. Especially since she had been dating Eris."

Officer Campbell lifted an eyebrow to underscore the strangeness of it, that two young women should die under unexpected circumstances, so soon after dating each other.

"What kind of new evidence?" Leda asked as innocently as she could.

"That's classified."

Leda's mind echoed with a strange, unsettling silence. It was a silence that rang with chilly finality, like the weight of a gravestone, as if the entire current of the East River was pressing down on her chest, forcing the air from her lungs. *They might find out.*

If the police were investigating Mariel, they might somehow discover Leda's relationship to Eris—and worse, the fact that Leda had accidentally pushed her. . . .

"Mariel was very fixated on you," Kiles was saying. "I don't think it's just because you were friends with Eris. Do you know of any other reason she might have been watching you?"

"I don't know," Leda said defensively, wishing she could put her hands over her ears to block out the terrifying silence. Fear and alarm were swirling wildly through her.

"Perhaps you—"

*"I don't know!"*

The words burst out of her like bullets and rebounded sharply around the room. Leda put her hands firmly on the surface of the table to hide their trembling and stood.

"I have made every effort to be cooperative," she said clearly. "But this line of questioning is useless. I didn't know this Mariel person and have no information about what happened to her. If you need to get in touch with me again, please do so through my family's lawyer. Otherwise, I believe we're done here."

Leda stormed away, half expecting one of the detectives to stop her. But neither of them said a thing.

Outside the station, she leaned against a wall for support, her mind spinning through the implications of what had just happened.

The police were reinvestigating Mariel's death. They had already discovered the connection between Mariel and Leda. How long would it take before they found out the reason Mariel was stalking her: that Leda had pushed Eris off the roof?

And that wasn't the only thing that Mariel had known before she died. There were also the other secrets: Rylin's, and Avery's, and Watt's. The secrets that Leda told her in a drug-fueled haze. If the police kept digging, they might discover Mariel's connection to the others too. They were in danger, and it was her fault.

She was going to have to see them again, she realized. All of them. Even Watt.

# WATT

*I'm not nervous,* Watt insisted, then realized that he was perched on the very edge of Avery Fuller's couch. He scooted back against the pillows self-consciously.

*Okay,* he told Nadia. *Maybe a little nervous.*

When Leda flickered him last night, Watt had practically slid out of his desk chair in shock. He almost thought the message was some kind of twisted practical joke from Nadia. He hadn't been expecting to hear from Leda anytime soon—really, anytime *ever*—given the bleak finality of their good-bye last year.

Then Watt realized that it was a group message, and the other two recipients were Avery and Rylin. *We need to talk—in person,* Leda had written. *I think we're all in danger.*

And despite the gravity of the situation, despite the fact that he should probably be concerned about whatever Leda had discovered, Watt couldn't help feeling a fragile hope ballooning in his chest. He was going to see Leda again.

He'd shown up early to Avery's apartment, hoping that he might catch Leda for a moment alone; after all, *she* was the one who'd summoned them all to this group meeting. But she hadn't yet arrived. Watt just sat there silently, ignoring Avery's pointed glances, trying to figure out what the hell he was going to say. How did you greet the girl you loved when you hadn't seen her in eight months—when her last words to you were *If you care about me at all, you'll leave me alone*?

He cast his gaze nervously around the room, all brocade carpets and blue-patterned wallpaper and carved antiques that looked as if they'd been shipped straight from Versailles. For all Watt knew, maybe they had. He'd forgotten how imposing it was simply to *get* this high: switching on the 990th floor to the private elevator that opened onto the Fullers' landing, then stepping through that massive two-story entryway. He'd felt a bit like Hercules climbing the staircase of the gods to Mount Olympus.

Now here he was, in the fabled sky island, the bright human aerie perched atop the greatest structure in the world. Watt glanced out the floor-to-ceiling windows, the flexiglass so impossibly clear that it looked like it wasn't there at all. He felt like he could stretch out his hands and brush the sky. What was it like for the Fullers, having no neighbors except those below them? Didn't it feel strange that their only connection with the rest of the city was the opening to their private elevator shaft?

His head darted up at the sound of the doorbell, but then he realized that of course Leda wouldn't need to ring the doorbell at all. She was on the preapproved entry list here.

"I thought we were done with all this." Rylin Myers sank into the opposite armchair.

"I thought it was over too. A long time ago." The sleeve of

Avery's sweater dress fell forward as she reached for a glass of lemon water. A platter of snacks was arranged on the coffee table before them, completely untouched.

How like Avery to provide refreshments at a time like this. Yet Watt couldn't help thinking that it was oddly comforting, as if Avery's unobtrusive hospitality was helping diffuse the tension.

He'd almost forgotten that when he first met Avery, he'd thought he was infatuated with her. But after dating Leda—after realizing what it *really* felt like to fall for someone—Watt knew that all he'd felt for Avery was a crush. He and Avery were much better off this way, as occasional friends.

He heard footsteps again, and before he could figure out what his first words to her would be *(Something witty, Nadia, help!)* Leda stepped into the living room, knocking all the air from the immediate vicinity.

She was even thinner than before, draped in a black turtleneck sweater, and her hair was cut short. It drew attention to the stark architecture of her face.

Leda's eyes automatically rose to meet his. For a moment there was no one in the room but the two of them. Watt swallowed against the maddening flood of old tendernesses and love and frustrations that rose up in him.

She was really here. For the first time in months, she was *here*, and Watt couldn't believe it; he felt as if he'd taken an adrenaline boost, slapped a million caffeine patches over every last inch of his skin. It was as if he'd been in a trance these long months without Leda, and seeing her again had struck him violently back to life.

"I would apologize for being late, except I think you're all early," she said smoothly, taking a step forward. Watt had forgotten the way she moved, as if every motion began in her warm, dark eyes, and flowed unbroken all the way to her ballet flats. She sat down next to Avery and crossed one leg over the other, only the slight jangling of her foot betraying her anxiety.

"We're early because your message was so terrifying and vague!" Rylin cut in. "What's going on?"

"The police are investigating Mariel's death."

There was a beat of collective silence at Leda's announcement. Avery twisted her hands in her lap. Rylin's eyes were wide with horror.

*Nadia*, Watt thought fiercely, *what do the police know so far? And why weren't we keeping tabs on this?*

*I'm sorry. But you know I can't hack the police department. They back up those files using location-specific hardware protections.*

Leda explained that police detectives had called her in for questioning because they were reopening the investigation into Mariel's death—this time as a homicide case. The cops had clearly found a connection between Leda and Mariel, but they didn't seem to understand it yet.

Avery clutched a chenille pillow to her chest. "Did you tell them about Dubai?"

"You mean, did I tell them that Mariel tried to *kill* me? I don't think it would make me look very good in a murder investigation. All I said was that I have no idea what happened to her."

"None of us know anything!" Rylin burst out. "So we're fine, right? That's the end of it?"

"Except that Mariel knew our secrets," Watt said, speaking up for the first time.

All three girls whirled around to face him. Avery's and Rylin's eyes were wide and startled and thick-lashed; but Leda just met his gaze evenly. She'd clearly already been down this line of thought.

"She knew our secrets," he repeated. "There's a clear

connection between Mariel and us. Now that the police are digging into her death, it's only a matter of time before they figure it out. After all, they already found Leda."

Leda gave a terse nod of agreement, her dangle earrings brushing forward over the collar of her sweater.

"Are you saying that we're *suspects*?" Rylin demanded.

Watt knew what she meant. If Mariel had been gathering files on all of them, it could look like they'd killed her to cover up what she knew. It was proof of motive, if nothing else.

"There's no way," Avery insisted. "We didn't even know Mariel. Why would *we* be suspects?"

"Because the police seem to be questioning motive rather than means," Watt explained. "They obviously don't know who killed her, so they're trying to figure out who might have *wanted* to kill her and working backward from there. And if they make the connection between Leda and Eris's death—"

He didn't need to finish the sentence. If the police learned the truth about Eris's death, the fact that Leda had blackmailed them all to keep it hidden, then they would clearly try to find out what that blackmail had entailed. Which would lead them straight to everyone's secrets.

Avery gasped. The sun cast the shadow of her eyelashes on her cheekbones. "You're saying that if the cops keep investigating, they might discover what Mariel had on all of us," she summarized.

Silence hung in the air. Watt imagined he could see it, as if all their unspoken fears had been made tangible, swirling like snowflakes.

"Now you see why I wanted to meet up. I had to warn you guys," Leda said miserably.

"I still don't get it. If they have no clue who might have killed Mariel—if their only option is to guess at motive and work backward—then why did they reopen the case at all?" Avery asked.

"They must have some new evidence," Rylin posited. "Something that made them think it was murder without suggesting who did it."

Leda bit her lip. "The police told me how she died," she said softly, and they all looked up, because that information definitely *hadn't* been in the obit. "Mariel drowned in the East River."

"She drowned?" Avery repeated. "That sounds like an accident to me. What new evidence could they possibly have found to prompt a reopening of the investigation?"

The room erupted into a storm of theories.

"Maybe they found new security footage of someone pushing her, but can't see who it is?"

"Or maybe they found a weapon, and realized that someone used it to attack her."

"But how would they know that weapon was used on Mariel? DNA?"

"Why can't they just use location data to see who was there that day?"

"Location data isn't stored for more than forty-eight hours, you *know* that. It was a landmark Supreme Court case—"

"Maybe they found a record of a security breach somewhere along the river but can't tell who it was?"

*"Enough!"*

Leda had begun pacing back and forth like a caged lioness. When she reached one end of the carpet, she would turn automatically and start back in the other direction. Watt had forgotten that about her: the way she was always doubling and twisting on herself, as if it were impossible for her to ever fall still.

"I didn't call you guys here to instigate a blind panic, okay? Especially since you might not even be involved! Mariel was obsessed with *me*. This is my problem. That doesn't necessarily mean it's all of yours. I only wanted to warn you, just in case," she added a little less vehemently.

"It's my problem too, Leda. If they find out about—" Avery faltered. "It wouldn't be good, if anyone learned what Mariel knew about me."

Rylin nodded. "Same."

*Nadia, did we ever find out what Leda had on Rylin?*

*She stole drugs*, Nadia informed him.

Watt didn't have to ask Avery's secret, because he already knew what it was. Her relationship with Atlas.

He glanced over at Leda. Her secret—the fact that she had killed Eris, no matter that it was an accident, and had then tried to cover it up—was as dangerous as his. Maybe even the worst of all.

"We're all in this together," he said, which was true. The three other people in this room had once been strangers, but now their lives were inextricably bound with his.

"I have to go," Rylin said abruptly. "Keep me posted if anything happens. And be careful."

Leda was still pointedly refusing to look at Watt. "Thanks for letting us meet here, Avery."

Watt nodded good-bye to Avery before following quickly on Leda's heels. "Leda," he called out, but she just kept walking down the Fullers' long entryway, her footsteps quickening. Her heels echoed on the white marble tiles with their black border.

*She's avoiding you*, Nadia pointed out unnecessarily.

Watt started running. "Leda!" he tried again, not that it would be any use—the elevator doors were opening, and she was hurriedly retreating inside.

He just barely managed to squeeze into the elevator before the heavy brass doors shut behind him with a resounding click. He didn't have much time. Just the length of a single elevator ride, to convince the girl he loved that they had to see each other again.

"Hey, Leda." He said it nonchalantly, as if he hadn't just chased her down a hallway after a discussion about a *murder investigation*. As if it wasn't a big deal that they were alone in the same space for the first time in months. Close enough to touch. Breathing the very same air. "We need to talk."

"I don't think that's a good idea."

"Not about *us*." Watt attempted to force a beat of normalcy into his voice, which was pretty much impossible. "I meant about this Mariel stuff. I want to help."

"Thanks, but I'll be fine. I only wanted to warn—"

"Warn us, yeah, I got it." Watt leaned forward, bracing his arm against the elevator's wall so he effectively boxed Leda in. "You need my help, Leda."

"No, I *don't*," she insisted, ducking under his arm and retreating to the opposite side of the elevator. "Besides, Watt, this isn't something you can hack your way out of."

"Sure it is," Watt said automatically, though he wasn't actually sure where he would start. "Unless you already hired another hacker? Tell me who it is, so I can sabotage them." He meant it as a joke, but the delivery was all wrong.

"I can't afford to be spending time with you," Leda said quickly. "It's too risky—it could spark all my problematic behaviors, and if I spiral out of control again, my parents will send me to boarding school. I don't want to risk it, okay?" A vein pulsed in her throat.

"Look, I'm sorry that I'm some kind of human trigger." Watt sighed. "But you should know that I'm going to keep working on this either way. You're not the only one who has a lot to lose, if those secrets get out."

"I really am sorry. I never wanted you to get involved." Leda seemed a bit softer. She'd been all sharp angles when he first stepped into the elevator, but now some of those angles were sanded down.

"I am involved, like it or not," Watt said, trying to focus on his words and not how maddeningly close she was. "We can work separately on this, or we can combine forces. You know what they say, two brains are better than one." In this case, maybe three were better than two, if you counted Nadia.

They reached the 990th-floor landing with a soft click, and the doors hissed open. Leda didn't get out yet.

"All right," she said, as gloriously prideful as ever. "I guess we can work together on this. You can be useful when you want to be."

Watt knew that was the most eloquent request for assistance he was likely to get. Leda Cole *never* revealed vulnerability, and she never asked for help.

He felt a flush of eager excitement. No matter what she said—no matter the circumstances in which they were seeing each other again—he refused to believe that they were over. He was still Watt Bakradi, and she was still Leda Cole, and they deserved another shot.

He was going to take advantage of every minute he got to spend with her. Whatever it took, Watt swore, he would win Leda back.

# AVERY

"THANKS FOR COMING with me," Avery said softly, as she and Max walked down the high-ceilinged gallery of the Metropolitan Museum of Art.

"Of course I came. I've missed you," Max replied, even though he'd seen her only two days ago. He reached up to adjust his skinny linen scarf, which was covered in a scrolling red batik print. "Besides, the point of me staying in New York was to see all the places that matter to you, and this one is clearly high on the list."

Avery nodded, a little surprised that Max didn't realize how shaken and unsettled she felt. He seemed to think that this was just a spontaneous museum outing. But Avery had come here to clear her head. She was still reeling from that unexpected meeting yesterday, and Leda's revelation that Mariel's death was now under investigation. Now that her family's entrance to the roof was closed, the trapdoor in their pantry sealed off, the Met was the only place Avery felt like she could escape.

The museum rose alongside the bubble of Central Park, its iconic pillars overlooking the diamond of the softball fields and the famous pale-pink ice rink that was always frozen, no matter the season. Supposedly the rink had been meant to change colors, but it froze at this shade of pink the week the park opened—and in that typical New York way, now no one would ever dream of changing it.

Avery took a deep breath. You could taste the difference in the air, in here: It was completely sterile to protect the art from oxidation or corrosion. The whole entrance to the museum felt oddly like a vacuum chamber, as if you were stepping into space, some grand new universe of artistic beauty.

"How was your first week?" she asked Max, trying her best to sound normal.

"It was incredible. Dr. Wilde is an even better lecturer than I expected! She's actually agreed to read my thesis herself, instead of assigning it to a TA."

Avery smiled. "That's fantastic, Max."

"And last night I went to a party in my hallway," he went on, his eyes dancing. Max remained amused by the way American college students partied in whatever spaces were available to them, their parties spilling out into study rooms and dorm kitchens. "You're going to love my neighbors, Avery. One of them is a sculpture student named Victoria who specializes in spun-wire." He stumbled over the phrase, as if scared that he didn't know what it meant, then declared, "I told her all about you."

Avery reached to twine her fingers in his. "I can't wait to meet them."

Max had moved into one of the Columbia dorms on the 628th floor. Avery was secretly glad that he hadn't asked to stay at the Fullers' apartment. Her parents would never have allowed it. They had three guest suites, but no one actually *used* them, not even Avery's grandparents when they came to visit. The rooms were just additional square footage meant to display Mrs. Fuller's extensive collection of antiques, each surface carefully arranged with ceramic Staffordshire dogs or terra-cotta Chinese figures or blue-and-white Delft candlesticks. Each room had been featured in *Architectural Digest* or *Glamorous Homes* at least once. Besides, Avery had thought, it would be kind of weird having her boyfriend live down the hall from her *and* her parents.

She didn't exactly have a good track record of dating boys who lived on the thousandth floor.

But to her relief, Max seemed absolutely thrilled to be living in a tiny dorm room. He kept talking about what an authentic, important part of the study abroad experience it was, to be immersed in school life. Already it sounded as if he'd made friends with everyone in his hall, and found the nearest coffee shop and twenty-four-hour diner.

They headed down the Impressionist wing. Light spilled through the enormous floor-to-ceiling windows, illuminating the broad canvases with their loose, spontaneous brushstrokes. Avery had always loved the Impressionists, if only for their manic obsession with color. None of their works had a drop of white or black paint. If you looked closely, you would realize that even the shadows, even the *eyelashes*, were done in greens or purples or shades of bronze.

"You okay?" Max asked gently.

*I'm worried about an investigation into the death of a girl I barely knew, because it might uncover my secret relationship with my adopted brother. Oh, and also the fact that I lied about my friend Eris's death.*

She couldn't say any of that, of course. Max wouldn't understand, wouldn't *love* her anymore, the moment he knew about her history with Atlas.

"Stressed about the election?" he guessed, and she almost laughed. In her worry about the police investigation, she'd half forgotten that the mayoral election was next week.

"I turned in my Oxford application last night. I guess that's put me on edge," she offered. *Among other things.*

"You'll get in," Max assured her.

Avery nodded, but she still felt nervous. It seemed as if more was riding on this application than just her college plans—because if she got in, then she and Max would probably be together for at least two more years after this one. And who knew what that might mean?

"How was school today?" Max pressed.

Avery thought of Leda, who still had a haunted, hunted look about her that made Avery's heart break. She thought of how empty everything felt without Eris. "You know, typical high school drama," she evaded.

Max grinned. "Actually, I don't know. I went to the Homburg-Schlindle Academy for Boys. Very little room for drama."

"No drama!" Avery gasped in mock horror. "How on earth did you entertain yourselves?"

"Fistfights, mostly."

"Right, of course." She tried unsuccessfully to imagine Max getting into a fight with someone. More likely he'd challenged anyone who bothered him to an epic chess match.

A pair of girls walked past, probably around fourteen. They were both wearing blouses stitched with buttons: along the collar, the wrists, even the hemline. Each row had at least one button that didn't match the others.

The girls smiled shyly when they saw Avery, then tipped

their heads together to whisper, gliding quickly past.

"You did that!" Max exclaimed in a low voice.

"I don't know," Avery hedged. The whole thing made her feel kind of weird.

Max just laughed. "You started this button frenzy, you might as well take ownership of it. Though I suppose I *am* the muse behind it all," he couldn't resist adding. "It's a good thing I have such abysmal fashion sense."

"Right," Avery replied, playing along. "Otherwise where would I get my inspiration?"

They kept walking down the hallway, past Impressionism and into the early modern portrait galleries. Avery's eyes skimmed over each canvas in turn, pausing over their familiar compositions. Max pretended to be looking at the paintings, but Avery saw that he was really looking at her.

"Which is your favorite?"

She shook her head. "I couldn't pick a favorite."

"Of course you can," Max insisted. "Pretend the museum is burning down and you only have time to save one thing. Which is it?"

For some reason, Avery didn't like these what-if games. It wasn't the first time Max had asked this sort of question; he was always trying to summarize his surroundings, organize things into clearly discernable categories and keep them there. He wanted to know Avery's favorite painting, so if someone asked him about Avery's art history classes, he could say, *Yes, that's what she studies, and she loves* this *work of art most of all.*

Art history wasn't about ranking or maximizing things. It was about thoughtfulness, and appreciation—the search for a cohesive thread among all the wondrous things people had created through the centuries, in an effort to *say* something, to feel a little bit less alone.

"Maybe . . . *Madame X*." Avery nodded toward the famous portrait of the enigmatic woman in the slinky black gown. There was something subtly fragile about her, as if her real self was nothing like the face she presented to the world.

"Cool choice. Though she isn't anywhere near as beautiful as you," Max said. He had completely missed her point.

*Atlas would have understood*, Avery caught herself thinking, and instantly chastised herself for the thought. It wasn't fair of her to expect Max to know her the way Atlas did. Max had met her less than a year ago, while Atlas had known her most of her life.

Max reached into his pocket for his tablet, which had started buzzing. He still refused to wear contacts—which was one of the many things Avery loved about him.

"A couple people from my dorm are seeing a holo tonight," he told her, looking up. "Want to go?"

"Sure," Avery said easily. Sitting in a dark, anonymous theater sounded nice right now.

As they headed back toward the museum's main entrance, they had to walk through the antiquities gallery. Its shelves were crowded with countless small broken things, items of jewelry or eating utensils, now reduced to fragments of discolored clay.

"I never liked this room." Avery paused before a few shards of something that were labeled, simply, USE UNKNOWN. "People created these things, probably to help themselves *survive*, and now we don't even know what they were for." There was something eerily sad about it all. It made her wonder what people would say about modern devices, centuries in the future—if a scientist would someday excavate her beauty-wand and wonder what its purpose was.

"What does it matter what these things were for?" Max shrugged. "It's interesting to study, but it doesn't have any real impact on the present. The most important thing is to focus on making the world a better place right now, while we're still in it."

Avery was momentarily struck by how uncannily like her dad Max sounded.

"And, of course, spending time with you. That's my main focus," Max added, with a smile that wiped away any hesitations. She leaned up to brush her lips against his.

"Mine too," she said emphatically.

# CALLIOPE

**CALLIOPE TWISTED BACK** and forth on the circular podium, utterly disgusted with what she saw reflected in the mirror.

She was wearing what had to be the most appalling bridesmaid's dress of all time. It was a horrific confection of tulle and satin, with a square neckline and enormous puffed sleeves that tightened at the elbows and extended to the wrists. Layers of tulle were bunched over and over on the voluminous skirt. As if that wasn't enough, the dress came complete with a *cape*, which tied around the neck with ribbons.

The only part of Calliope not covered in all these swaths of fabric was her face. She felt as if she were wearing curtains.

On the podium next to her stood Livya, sinking underneath the same monstrosity of a dress. She looked pale and washed out, as always, her hair falling in thin listless strands around her heart-shaped face.

"What do you think, girls?" asked Elise. Calliope didn't miss the way her mom's eyes darted anxiously toward Nadav's mother, Tamar, her future mother-in-law, who was seated in a nearby armchair, her hands clasped primly in her lap. She'd been the one to select these dresses.

"They're great," Calliope said weakly. Honestly, she hadn't known there was a garment on earth that could make her look this ugly. There was a first time for everything, she supposed.

"I think they're divine," Livya gushed, moving past Elise as if she weren't even there and heading straight to her grandmother. She planted a kiss on the old lady's cheek. "Thank you, Boo Boo."

Calliope refrained from rolling her eyes at the absurd nickname.

They were in the wedding boutique at Saks Fifth Avenue, which, perversely enough, was no longer located on Fifth Avenue at all, but on Serra Street, toward the center of the Tower. The fitting room looked like a wedding cake come to life, with its peach velvet settees, white plush carpets, even a tray of little iced petit fours arranged on the sideboard.

Most striking of all, though, were the mirrors. They were ubiquitous, so that a girl could see herself from every conceivable angle, and perhaps a few inconceivable ones too.

Normally, being places like this—cool, expensive boutiques full of beautiful things—calmed Calliope. It was something in the proud look of them, the expectant hush as their doors swung open and you saw all those beautiful rich things arranged within. But today her surroundings seemed to be mocking her.

Livya sank into an armchair next to her grandmother and began tapping furiously at her tablet, her face sour. The dress poufed comically around her, making her look like a human-sized loofah with skinny, protruding arms. Calliope would have laughed at the sight, except that she sort of wanted to cry.

"Elise," said Miranda, the bridal sales associate. "Do you think we could make a final decision on color? The superlooms are fast, but I'm getting concerned about timing."

The sample dresses that Livya and Calliope were wearing had been spun from smartthreads: the playful, cheap-looking material patented thirty years ago. The final dresses that they wore at the wedding would be real fabric, of course, because who would actually want their bridesmaid dresses to change color? These smartthread models were for sales purposes only.

No one had asked Livya to move, yet she stood with an audible, resigned groan and stepped back onto the podium alongside Calliope. She kept her arms crossed over her chest, as if to convey how utterly pointless she found this entire exercise.

"Let's start with the purples." Miranda reached for her tablet. A colorful bar on one side depicted all the colors of the rainbow, red bleeding through to yellow and then purple again. As Miranda's fingers moved slowly down the palette, the fabric of Calliope's and Livya's dresses shifted accordingly, deepening from lilac to violet to a dark wine color.

"I need to see it with the flowers," Elise said eagerly, turning to a marble console table along the edge of the room. It was littered with sample bouquets that their florist had sent over, everything from simple all-white arrangements to vast multicolored sprays of foliage. The room smelled pleasantly like a garden.

They tried various combinations, switching the gowns to gold and navy and even a dark red. A few times Elise began to smile, only for Tamar to emphatically shake her head. Then Elise would give an apologetic shrug and say, "I guess we aren't quite there yet. Let's try another?"

Finally Miranda let out a breath. "Why don't we take a break?" she suggested. "We should do a fitting on your gown anyway, while you're here."

Tamar cleared her throat bitterly. "And the mother of the groom's dress too, of course," Miranda hastened to add.

"All right." Tamar rose, stiff-backed and slow. She was wearing an embroidered navy dress with a matching pillbox hat, her curls frozen in an immovable hairsprayed helmet. Elise offered to help her up, but Tamar shooed her away imperiously. When she waved her claw, the jewels on her rings—she had at least one on each finger—flashed ostentatiously.

When they had all disappeared into their fitting rooms, Calliope crouched down to snatch Miranda's tablet from where it lay on the nearest table. Her brows lowered in concentration as she scrolled back and forth along the color bar, sending their dresses to fiery red and back again.

"That's really irritating."

Calliope shot bitterly through a few more colors before lowering the tablet to her side. "I'm sorry," she muttered. She wasn't accustomed to Livya talking to her, at least not when they were alone. They never spoke at school, and at home they limited themselves to a stark three-word vocabulary, volleying "heys" across the apartment before retreating to their separate rooms. It was like a silent contest for which of them could speak less.

"No, you aren't."

"*Excuse* me?"

"You aren't sorry." Livya's eyes widened beneath their colorless lashes. "It's rude to tell lies. Don't say you're sorry if you don't mean it."

"I have no idea what you're—"

"You can drop the act with me. It doesn't look good on you anyway," Livya snapped, all the sticky, syrupy sweetness gone from her voice.

Calliope squared her shoulders. Her reflections in all the countless mirrors did the same, tipping up their chins with quiet, unmistakable pride. "I have no idea what you mean," she said coldly.

"Of course. You're just a sweet little philanthropist from nowhere, aren't you?" Livya tilted her head. "You and your mom must have made *such* an impact through the years, traveling all over the world, saving the planet. Remind me again, why are none of your friends coming to the wedding?"

Calliope reached down to re-fluff the tulle in her bell-shaped skirt, to avoid looking at her future stepsister. "It's a long way for many of them to travel," she recited, the lie that she and her mother had told over and over these past months. "Besides, most of them can't afford it."

"What a shame. I was so looking forward to meeting them," Livya said, not at all convincingly. "You see, my dad has a hard time trusting people. Most of the women who've dated him in the past were just in it for the money. One of the things he loves most about your mom is how truly selfless she claims to be. That all she cares about is saving the world. That she would never use him like that."

Calliope heard the challenge in that statement—in Livya's use of the word *claim*—but she decided it was safer to let it lie. The fine dark hairs on the back of her arms prickled.

Girls like Livya would never understand. When they wanted something, all they had to do was hold out their hand and ask their parents for it, pretty please. Calliope had been forced to flirt, plot, and manipulate for every nanodollar she'd ever spent.

"You know," Livya went on, almost conversationally, "I saw the strangest thing in our apartment earlier this week. I could have sworn that I saw someone sneaking out late, on a week-night, wearing a slutty silver dress."

Calliope could have kicked herself. She'd grown sloppy, play-ing the same role for far longer than was good for anyone. This was exactly why their cons usually had a four-month time limit: The longer they stayed in one place, the greater their risk of being found out. No matter how convincing a story you wove, eventually the lies and blank spaces would begin to catch up with you. Eventually you would slip up.

"You might want to be careful, taking too many practice SAT tests in a row," Calliope replied with remarkable self-possession. "It sounds like you're beginning to hallucinate."

"Right. Because a girl like you, out to dig wells or save the fishies or whatever it is you and your mom care about—a girl like you would never sneak out," Livya said sweetly.

"Exactly." Calliope had pulled the tablet back up and was scrolling viciously through the color bar, faster and faster, changing the shades of their dresses so rapidly that it was becoming nauseating.

Just then, Elise's and Tamar's footsteps sounded from the dressing room. Calliope quickly lowered the tablet to her side, leaving their gowns at a pale dove gray.

"Oh! This is it!" Tamar crowed as she sailed into the room wearing a webbed purple thing with long sleeves that tapered to a point over her wrists. In Calliope's opinion, it made her look even more witchlike than ever.

Tamar turned to Miranda peremptorily. "The dresses will be perfect in this soft gray. It's a fall wedding, after all."

"How lovely!" Elise exclaimed, good-natured as always. She tried to hug her future mother-in-law, who just stood there in stiff-backed silence.

Then Elise stepped forward and wrapped an arm around each of the teenagers, pulling them closer, as if they were all one happy family. "My two girls," she said quietly.

"Your dress is stunning, Mom," Calliope replied. Elise's gown had long sleeves and a high neck, but instead of looking dowdy it was elegant and demure, a swirl of hand-stitched lace scattered with tiny crystals that caught the light.

Livya cut in, not to be outdone. "You look absolutely perfect, Elise," she simpered, in her prim, kiss-up voice—no trace of the threatening creature who had been there a moment previously.

Calliope looked up to where their three reflected faces hovered together, illuminated by the ambient light. Her eyes met Livya's in the mirror. The other girl was staring at her hungrily, looking suddenly like a predator, alert and watchful for the slightest sign of weakness.

Calliope held her gaze, refusing to blink.

# LEDA

**LEDA TRAILED DOWN** the unfamiliar street after Watt, wondering what exactly she'd gotten herself into.

He'd flickered her earlier this afternoon that he needed to show her something, about Mariel. *Meet me at the Bammell Lane monorail station at nine*, he'd insisted.

Leda had taken a slow yoga breath, trying to settle her mind. She wasn't ready to see Watt again, to let him disturb the fragile equilibrium she'd worked so hard to maintain. But even worse than her fear of facing Watt was her fear of what would happen if this investigation dug up the truth.

And honestly, Leda was already pretty unsettled. Ever since that questioning at the police station, she'd been having the old nightmares again, even worse than before—because now the images of Eris's death alternated with flickering visions of Mariel, drowning, reaching for Leda with icy, implacable hands. Leda would gasp, fighting her off, but Mariel kept dragging her down. . . .

*Okay. I'll be there*, she told Watt.

When their monorail car uncoiled itself from the city and began to snake through the air, Leda couldn't help looking down at the surface of the East River. A few boats sliced through the water on silent motors, the *V*'s of their wakes disappearing in the darkness.

It seemed terrifyingly cold, the light of the quarter moon breaking and fragmenting on the river's choppy surface. Leda shivered and moved unconsciously closer to Watt, trying not to think about her nightmares.

The streetlamps flickered to life around her, their light falling in golden pools onto the pavement, which glittered with the telltale sparkle of the magnetic shavings that kept hovercraft aloft. Not that any hovercraft were zipping past. Brooklyn had been slowly draining of people for years, now that it went dark around noon, thanks to the hulking shadow cast by the Tower.

Leda couldn't quite believe that she was here, with Watt, standing next to him again after all these months. It felt oddly surreal, like she'd slipped through the meshes of reality only to find herself back where she'd been a year ago. She kept stealing small glances at him, as if to compare *this* Watt with the one she remembered—his hair a little thicker and more unruly, his eyes as bright as ever.

He caught her staring and smiled. Leda bit the inside of her cheek, flushing with mortification.

"Where are we going?" She felt a desperate need to say something, anything, as if the silence was becoming infused with layers of meaning she didn't know how to interpret. "Or do we not have a destination at all? Are we just wandering aimlessly out here in the wilderness?"

"Right, because Brooklyn is definitely the wilderness," Watt deadpanned.

"It might as well be!"

"I promise it will be worth it," he assured her. "Just trust me."

Trust Watt? That felt hard to do, given all the broken promises that lay between them. Leda turned away, to keep from looking into his eyes.

Two girls stood at a small bitbanc kiosk on their right: one of those touch screen stations where people might check their balance or make transfers, if they didn't have contact lenses. It took Leda a moment to realize that the girls weren't using the kiosk at all. They were preening and applying lip gloss, watching their reflections on the sliver of curved security mirror above the interface. One of them met Leda's eyes in the mirror and politely stepped aside, as if to make space.

"Last mirror before José's," she explained and then smiled.

"Um, thanks," Leda mumbled. What was José's?

"We'll see you in there," Watt replied. Leda couldn't help noticing the warm way both girls were staring at him. For some stupid reason it irritated her.

She followed Watt onto the stoop of an old brownstone. Heavy, dark curtains hung in the windows, making the face of the building look lifeless or even sinister, as if the windows were empty blank eyes. The door's paint was peeling, and there was a notice tacked to it that read FORECLOSURE. NO ENTRY.

"Watt . . ." Leda began, but the protest died on her lips as he pushed the front door. It gave way easily.

Leda squeezed behind him, blinking at the faded wallpaper. Standing in the middle of the cramped entryway, before a wooden staircase, was a tall white guy who looked about their age. Leda heard the unmistakable sounds of laughter and music drifting down from the second floor. She shot Watt a confused glance.

"Do I know you?" the bouncer demanded.

Watt didn't miss a beat. "Hey, Ryan. We're friends of José's. Is he here yet?"

"He's coming later," Ryan replied with a shade less hostility, though he still stood determinedly between Watt and Leda and whatever was at the top of that staircase. "It's forty nanos each."

"Fine. Confirm transfer," Watt muttered. He locked gazes with the bouncer and nodded, to move forty nanodollars from his bitbanc into Ryan's. Leda started to do the same, but Watt nodded again to cover her payment, and Ryan stepped aside to let them pass.

"What are we doing here?" Leda hissed as they made their way up the stairs.

"I'm hoping that we'll get some answers about Mariel—about what she knew and who she told," Watt explained. "She used to come here a lot."

"Of course she did," Leda said darkly. She stumbled over a protruding nail and cursed under her breath. "Who *wouldn't* want to pay for the privilege of traipsing around an old tear-down?"

"It's okay to be afraid," Watt said softly, reaching out to steady her.

Leda brushed his hand aside. She felt suddenly angry with him, for knowing her so intimately. "Who is José?"

"José has been doing this for a while now: setting up parties in abandoned homes, then charging people for entry. He also happens to be Mariel's cousin," Watt replied as they reached the top of the stairs, and Leda fell silent.

The second-floor living room had been utterly transformed. Temporary drink stations were set up on either side of the room. Music spilled out of small egg-shaped speakers. Dim lighting emanated from glo-bulbs, the disposable orbs of light that were powered by self-contained nanowires, though they only lasted several hours. *Because the electricity must have been cut off with the foreclosure*, Leda realized. Clever.

But most striking of all were the dozens of young people packed into the space.

They were all good-looking in a fierce, edgy way, with angular inktats and 3-D skin appliqués. Leda saw lopsided hemlines, micro-miniskirts paired with kneesocks, vinyl dresses that flashed in bright, eclectic colors. One girl was wearing a dress that consisted of nothing but plastic squares linked together by tiny metal rings. Several of them looked up, murmuring at the arrival of Leda and Watt.

Leda felt strangled by a sudden, sticky fear. "I can't do this. I thought that I could but I can't; I *barely* made it through Cord's the other day. I'm not ready for this." She winced, shrinking in on herself, but Watt reached to grab her above both elbows.

"What happened to the Leda Cole I used to know?" he asked, his voice low and urgent. "That girl wasn't afraid of anything."

*That girl was afraid of* everything, Leda thought. *She was just better at hiding her fear.*

"I'm right here with you. I won't let anything bad happen, I promise," Watt added.

Leda knew that was an impossible promise. But she thought suddenly of Dubai—of how she'd been lying helpless by the water and Watt had come to save her, riding a stolen hoverboard at breakneck speed. She remembered how reassuringly safe she had felt the moment she realized he was with her.

"Okay. We can stay," she said reluctantly and cast another glance around the room.

Leda quickly lifted her flowy black shirt and tied it into a knot on one side, making it into a midriff top. She ran her fingers through her short, dense hair to loosen its curls. Then she reached into her pocket for her shiny red paintstick and swiped it over her lips.

"You don't have to stare," she told Watt, discomfited. "I'm just trying to fit in."

"I'm not—I'm sorry—I mean, if I'm staring, it's just because you're so beautiful," Watt said haltingly.

Leda caught her breath and quickly shook her head. She refused to let Watt dredge up any of those feelings. They belonged to the *old* Leda, and she and the old Leda had long since parted ways.

"Seriously, Watt. You say one more thing like that, and I'm gone," she told him, ignoring the slightly mutinous cast to his expression. "Now, what's our plan?"

"We should to talk to José when he gets here. Mariel was pretty close with him; he might have a sense of what Mariel knew."

"How are you going to find out? Break into his contact lenses? Or steal his tablet?"

"I thought we could try *talking* to him. As a smart girl once told me, not every problem needs to be hacked," Watt told her.

Leda flushed at the memory. It was something she'd said to Watt the very first night they kissed. "This isn't a very sophisticated plan."

"Sometimes simplicity is the key to success," Watt countered, and shrugged. "Want to play beer pong while we wait? With soda, of course," he amended, and gestured toward the far wall, where several beer pong tables were powered by graphene charge-packs. A group of older guys clustered around the tables, pounding on the surface and hollering at something that had happened in the game.

Leda's throat felt sealed shut. No way in hell was she playing beer pong with Watt. It was too *convivial*, too relaxed, when she needed things between them to be strictly professional.

"Or we can keep staring at each other in silence," Watt went on cheerfully.

Leda felt her old competitive instinct rising stubbornly to the surface. "I would love nothing more than to beat you at beer pong," she snapped. "Except that none of the tables are free."

"Not a problem," Watt said easily. "Grab a pitcher and meet me over there?" He started toward the group of guys before she could argue.

Sure enough, when she returned a minute later with a plastic pitcher of lemonade, Watt was leaning with proprietary ease on a table. "How did you clear out the frat rats?" Leda asked, reluctantly impressed.

"I scared them away."

"Right, because you're *so* intimidating." Leda rolled her eyes. "More like you used Nadia to hack their accounts, and sent them fake messages from the people they like."

"A magician never reveals his secrets," Watt said mysteriously. He poured the lemonade into their cups, which were made of a metal so thin that they felt lighter than paper. Then he pressed a button and the cups leapt instantly into the air, lifted by the table's powerful magnet, arranging themselves in a triangular shape perpendicular to the ground. Tiny bubbles of suction prevented the liquid inside from spilling.

"Did you know that when they first invented this game, there were no force fields?" Watt weighed one of the white pong balls in his hand, tossing it back and forth. "Apparently people had to constantly run around chasing their Ping-Pong balls when they overshot."

"Quit stalling, Watt."

He laughed and tossed the ball at a sharp angle. It bounced off the force field along the side of the table and clattered to the surface.

Leda felt an involuntary smile spreading over her features. She held out her hand and the Ping-Pong ball floated into her palm, responding to the powerful 3-D sensors as if by magic.

"Don't be too hard on yourself. Rebound shots are an advanced move." She flung the pong ball deliberately against the force field. It collided with an audible sizzle, then clattered directly into one of Watt's cups.

"Impressive." He lifted the cup in a salute before tipping it back. Leda rolled up her sleeves and reached for the pong ball again, grinning wickedly.

"Ready to concede yet?"

"Not a chance."

As they settled into the game, Leda felt her heartbeat relaxing, the tense knot in her stomach beginning to slowly uncoil. Strangely enough, she and Watt had never actually gotten to just *hang out* before. They had either been plotting against each other or plotting together against someone *else* or sneaking around, hooking up in secret. By the time they finally admitted how they felt, it was too late: Leda had learned the truth about Eris and fallen off the deep end, only to realize that she couldn't let herself be with Watt.

Still, it was nice, pretending to be normal. If only for a moment.

Leda immediately went stone-faced. What did she think she was doing? She shouldn't be relaxing around Watt, letting him make her laugh. She couldn't afford to let him get close again, no matter how easy it—

Watt abruptly dropped the Ping-Pong ball and swiped his hand over the surface of the table, abandoning the game. "José is here."

Leda turned, and saw at once who Watt was talking about.

José moved through the room with unmistakable authority. He looked several years older than they were: stocky, with a close-cropped dark beard. Red and black inktats curled around his bicep to disappear beneath the fabric of his shirt.

She hurried after Watt, who had already moved to stand on the edge of José's circle of admirers. Eventually José turned to them with a slightly puzzled, but polite, expression.

Watt cleared his throat. "Hi, José. We were hoping to talk to you for a minute. Alone," he added when José didn't say anything. "It's about Mariel."

José made a small gesture with his hand, and the group of people around him instantly melted into the party. He led Leda and Watt to a side room, empty except for a small baby pool, where a few girls were splashing barefoot in the few centimeters of water. They took one look at José and retreated.

"You were friends of Mari's?" José asked, drawing out the question to show that he didn't believe them.

Leda decided it was safer not to lie. "We were friends of Eris's, actually," she cut in.

"I see. You're a highlier," José said laconically, as if that explained everything. His eyes traveled up and down Leda's outfit, glittering with amusement, before turning to Watt. "You are, but not your boyfriend."

"He's not my boyfriend," Leda said impatiently, ignoring the strange pang she felt at that statement. "We're here because we wanted to know more about Mariel. She came to these parties a lot, didn't she?"

José's expression darkened. "If you think that I don't regret that night every minute of every damn day—I should never have let her walk home alone when she was so obviously messed up. . . ." He faltered and looked away.

*Oh*, Leda realized. Maybe Mariel was last seen at one of these parties before she died. "It's not your fault. She had a lot going on, before it . . . happened," she ventured, wondering if the statement was too bold.

"Of course she had a lot going on. She'd just lost her girl-friend!" José burst out, then sighed, deflating. "She really loved Eris, you know."

"I know," Leda said softly, and even though it was woefully inadequate: "I'm so sorry."

"I can't stop blaming myself," José went on, more to himself than the two of them. "I keep thinking about her, wondering what she would be doing right now if I had insisted on walking her home that night. I'm almost tempted to go steal her diary, just to read her last few entries. Hear her voice again."

Leda's gaze whipped up. "Diary?"

"Those last few months, Mari had started carrying around a paper notebook. She never left home without it," José said, and shrugged. "She said she loved how old-fashioned it felt."

Leda exchanged a loaded glance with Watt. Did Mariel actu-ally care about things being low-tech—or had she been trying to hide from Watt and his quantum computer, which she'd known about ever since the night in Dubai? If so, it worked. Watt and Nadia might be able to hack anything that ran on electricity, but neither of them had known about this notebook.

"You never saw what Mariel was writing in there?" Watt asked, and Leda could have kicked him for his lack of tact.

José looked offended. "I would never violate her privacy like that. Why are you so curious about it?" His eyes narrowed. "What did you say your names were?"

There was a beat of hot, shifting silence. "We were just leav-ing," Leda said quickly, and turned away. Watt followed close on her heels.

As they walked back to the monorail station, the air tore bitterly through her thin jacket. Leda realized that she was trem-bling. Watt slipped his arm around her, and this time, she didn't protest.

# RYLIN

**"CAN YOU PICK** up more of the caramel-flavored caff packs while you're out?" Chrissa asked, interrupting the languid silence of their apartment. She was lying facedown on her rumpled bedcovers, her chin tucked on her crossed arms, her eyes half closed as she supposedly studied for a history test on her brand-new contacts. Though Rylin suspected she might actually be cruising the i-Net. Or napping.

"No way. I refuse to support your caffeine addiction." Rylin crouched before their shared closet, searching through the litter of debris on the floor for her buckled motorcycle boots.

Chrissa pushed herself up onto her elbows to shoot her older sister a glare. "*My* caffeine addiction? You're the one who keeps sneaking those packets to school!"

"Only because the cafeteria refuses to serve anything except organic, vitamin-infused, 'meditative' water products," Rylin confessed, and grinned. "Fine. I'll grab another box."

"Why are you and Hiral going to the mall today, anyway? It's such a zoo on Sundays." Chrissa wrinkled her nose a little at Hiral's name. She didn't like that Rylin had gotten back together with him, even though Hiral had done his best to try to win Chrissa over—brought her banana ice cream, fixed her earbuds when they broke, listened to her incessant talk about the girl on her volleyball team she was crushing on. And still Chrissa didn't approve of him.

Rylin tried not to let her frustration show. "Why can't you accept that I'm with Hiral, and stop acting weird about it?"

"Weird? What am I doing that's weird? You're the weird one," Chrissa said evasively, to which Rylin rolled her eyes. She tried to remind herself that Chrissa was young and immature; but it hurt, the way she kept broadcasting her disapproval.

"I know you don't like Hiral," Rylin said quietly. "You still blame him for what he did last year, back when he was dealing. Which isn't exactly fair, since I'm the one it impacted, and I forgave him a long time ago."

"That's not true," Chrissa argued, "and it's unfair of *you* to accuse me like that. I would never hold Hiral's past against him."

"Then why—"

"I just thought you outgrew him, is all," Chrissa said baldly. She flicked off her contacts, to level her bright-green eyes at Rylin. "But since he clearly makes you happy, I'll shut up about it."

Rylin didn't know how to answer that. She focused on pulling her boots on over her socks, which were printed with tiny watermelons. "Anyway, I'm not going to the mall with Hiral, I'm going for class," she said tersely.

"For *class*?"

"For psych class," Rylin admitted, knowing exactly what was coming.

"*Oh,*" Chrissa said meaningfully. "With Cord."

Rylin had already told Chrissa that Cord was her lab partner. She'd tried her best to sound unconcerned, as if the whole thing were no big deal, but Chrissa knew their history and probably saw right through her.

"We have to run a field study examining social mores in a crowded location," Rylin tried to explain. "The mall seemed like the easiest place."

"Social mores? What does that even mean?"

"Behavioral norms. The things people do automatically, subconsciously, because that's how everyone else does it."

"Mm-hmm." Chrissa refrained from commenting on the fact that Rylin was going to the mall—on a weekend—with her ex-boyfriend.

Rylin felt plenty guilty without Chrissa's help. She couldn't stop wondering if it was wrong of her to have hidden this from Hiral.

She had *meant* to tell Hiral that Cord was her lab partner; she really had. Last night, when Hiral came with her to Lux's birthday party, she had planned on telling him. But she kept putting it off. By the time they were walking home, holding hands, eating doughnuts from their favorite late-night food cart, she'd decided against it. Between her schoolwork and his work schedule—he was on the late shift again, which ran into the early hours of the morning—she barely saw Hiral these days. Why ruin a perfectly good night by bringing up her ex-boyfriend?

Besides, she and Cord were actually starting to get along during psych class, to relax back into something that resembled friendship, at least within school bounds. It wasn't romantic, Rylin kept telling herself.

And the more time that went by without her mentioning it to Hiral, the less it seemed like a big deal.

After all, she was keeping a much bigger secret from Hiral: all the drama over the Mariel investigation. Mariel had known that Rylin stole drugs. If that secret somehow came to light through the police investigation, it wouldn't take long for the cops to realize that Hiral had been involved too. He was the one who'd sold the drugs for her.

Hiral had worked so hard to put all of that behind him, and Rylin had no desire for it to resurface now. She knew it wasn't easy—god, even last night she'd seen their old friend V approach Hiral at Lux's party, throwing an arm easily around Hiral's shoulders as he whispered something. Probably offering him a hit of his latest drug. But Hiral just shook his head, ignoring him.

When she arrived at the main entrance of the mid-Manhattan Mall, a teeming monstrosity that spanned the entire 500th floor, Rylin was startled to find Cord already waiting for her. He was standing near the doors, his arms crossed, wearing an oversized sweatshirt, mesh athletic shorts, and rubber flip-flops.

"What on earth are you dressed as, a basketball team's waterboy?"

Cord gave a bright, unselfconscious laugh. "Is it too much? I raided Brice's closet. I didn't want to look absurd."

"Then you've failed miserably." *He would have looked perfectly fine in his usual T-shirt and dark jeans,* Rylin thought, confused. It took a moment before she realized why he'd wanted to dress up—or rather, dress exaggeratedly down. "Is this your first time going this far downTower?"

"Absolutely not. I've been to Central Park lots of times."

Rylin blinked to hide her consternation, though she should have guessed. Even when they were together, Cord had never come down to her apartment. Their entire relationship had begun, thrived, and ended within the confines of his 969th-floor apartment.

"I'm happy to buy something else, if you're embarrassed to be with me," Cord offered. "You look nice, though."

Rylin laughed. "That's just because this is the first time in months that you're seeing me in something that isn't a school uniform," she pointed out.

Cord gave a puzzled frown, as if he hadn't quite thought of that, and didn't especially like the realization.

They swept through the main double doors into a department store, and Rylin was immediately assaulted by the sensory overload within. There was just so *much* of everything—stacks of black cyra tops, row upon row of upcycled denim, not to mention the soaring walls lined with women's shoes. There were stilettos and slingbacks and boots, some color-shifting to match your outfit, others self-repairing so they never showed a scuff mark. Most were lined with the new piezoelectric carbon soles, which converted the mechanical energy of walking back to electricity and fed it directly into the Tower's main grid.

Chrissa had been right: The mall was overcrowded today. The breathless conversations of the other shoppers washed over Rylin as if she'd been in an echo chamber. Adverts instantly popped up on her contacts—*Jeans just 35ND for one day only!* or *Don't forget to vote in the municipal election this week!* She quickly disabled the contacts, slightly relieved by the newfound clarity of her vision. She'd had them for a year now, since she started at Berkeley, but she still wasn't used to how crowded they got in public places.

"I think I should buy you this." Cord held up a soft green tank top that said CAN'T I JUST WATCH THE SCHOOL VIDS FROM MY BED?

"I don't think it matches the school uniform," Rylin jested, though she hadn't missed the fact that Cord offered to buy it for her, rather than suggesting she buy it for herself. And did he even understand what the shirt meant? He'd probably never watched a school vid in his life. Up at Berkeley, the courses were taught exclusively by live professors.

They headed through the department store's far doors and into the mall proper, toward the massive bank of elevator pods at the center of its cathedral-like interior. The elevator pods looked like nothing so much as a strand of delicate opaque pearls, constantly detaching and reattaching as they moved throughout the mall along their fiber-cable necklaces. They would float up, sporadically stopping and starting as new people got on or off, and then finally drift back to earth.

Elevator pod technology was nothing new. It had been invented before hovercrafts sometime in the last century and wasn't useful on any kind of large scale, certainly not for the Tower itself. But in self-contained spaces like malls or airports, it was still the cheapest and most effective way to move people short distances.

"Ready?" Cord asked, starting toward the nearest station.

Because of the way the tech worked, pulling them along on that nanofiber, the pods themselves only opened from one end. And for some reason that Rylin had never paused to question, everyone always entered the pod and then turned around to face the entrance, waiting expectantly for the sliding panels to open again.

For their experiment, Cord and Rylin were going to board a crowded car and then face the back instead of the front, to see how people reacted. It had been Rylin's idea, actually. She liked to think that it was brilliant in its simplicity.

The moment they stepped onto the station, the smartmatter beneath their feet registered their weight and summoned a pod. Cord tapped at the screen to mark their destination as the highest level of the mall, a full thirty floors above them. Then they both stepped inside.

Rylin started to turn unthinkingly toward the curved flexi-glass door. As the pod clicked shut and jerked into the air, the surface of the mall fell away before them, making the shoppers look like a swarm of ants.

"Forgetting something?" Cord asked behind her, amused.

Rylin quickly shuffled to face the back, resisting the urge to turn back and look at the view. "You know," she said, "when Lux and I were little, we used to ride this up and down for hours."

It had been like a free carnival ride, the novelty of which never wore off. Rylin used to secretly imagine that she was the president, riding in her private hovercraft up to the White House—until she learned that the White House wasn't even a tower, but a flat, squat building. It still didn't make sense to her. What good was it to be the leader of America if you didn't have a decent view?

"That's funny," Cord said, though Rylin heard the note of disbelief in his voice. Of course he hadn't spent his childhood riding elevator pods; he'd probably been playing a full suite of holo-games on his expensive immersion console. "Who's Lux?" he added.

Rylin blinked. "My best friend." It was easy to forget how little Cord really knew her. But then, he only ever saw her at school or on other upper floors.

Before Cord could respond, their pod lurched sideways to pick up someone else. Rylin and Cord stayed where they were, facing the featureless back wall, as a pair of older women stepped inside.

There was a palpable moment of silence. The women had turned to face the curved flexiglass doors at the front, but Rylin felt their necks twisting, their gazes boring into her. The pod resumed its motion.

"Tanya, I've been meaning to show you this," one of the women said to the other, pulling out her tablet. She held it in such a way that it was angled toward the back wall, forcing herself and her friend to look in that direction. Rylin saw their feet edge slightly backward. She felt strangely triumphant.

Slowly, by degrees, the women turned to face the same way as the two teenagers. It happened in minuscule increments, the curve in their spines so subtle that it would have been undetectable to someone who wasn't looking. But by the time the elevator pod pulled to another stop, near the top of the mall, the women were also facing backward.

The doors opened again and a boy, around twelve or so, stepped on board alone. He didn't even hesitate, just kept on facing the back as if that was what he did every time.

Rylin lifted her eyes to meet Cord's. He gave an exaggerated wink, forcing her to stifle a giggle.

Finally they reached the top floor, where a colonnaded walkway circled the center of the mall. Rylin hurried toward a display of activewear bracelets. She was laughing now, a full-bodied laugh that began deep in her belly, revealing the twin dimples on her flushed cheeks.

"Did you *see* that? Those women totally caved to our social pressure!"

"And the effect clearly magnifies with more people. That boy didn't hesitate at all," Cord agreed. The fluorescent lighting caught the warmth in his light blue eyes.

"Just think of how much faster they would've turned if you weren't dressed so ridiculously," Rylin couldn't resist adding.

"Absolutely," Cord agreed, with mock solemnity. "We both know that you were the success factor in this experiment."

"Does that make you the complicating factor?"

"More like the comic relief."

They stepped back into the elevator pod, once again facing the back. Rylin held her breath as they pulled to a stop about halfway down. She and Cord exchanged a complicit glance, both of them still smiling.

"Rylin?"

She turned around to see Hiral standing there, holding a bright-red shopping bag. His eyes darted from her to Cord and back again.

Rylin realized with a start how it must look to him, that she was out with Cord, in secret. She felt a twisting pain in her chest. "Hiral! We, um, we're running an experiment for psych class," she stammered. "We're violating social norms and then recording people's reactions. We stand backward on the elevator pod! It's absurd, really, what people do—"

"I don't know if we've met before," Cord interrupted, holding out his hand. "I'm Cord Anderton."

"Nice to meet you, Cord. I'm Rylin's boyfriend, Hiral," Hiral countered. Rylin noticed with dismay that he wasn't looking in her direction. "That's really interesting, what you're doing for school."

The air seemed to condense around them, filled with palpitations of awkwardness. Shit. The only two boys she'd ever been with—the only ones she'd ever really cared about—and here they both were, standing together in a tiny pod suspended in midair. Rylin was hyperaware of every gesture, even of the sound of her own breathing, which seemed loud and rattling in the bubble of space.

"Why don't you join us, Hiral?" Rylin heard Cord offer. She glanced over at him in alarm, wishing he hadn't said that, but apparently he wanted to watch the world crash and burn.

Hiral didn't answer at first. He didn't need to. Rylin could read the emotions darting over his face: his confusion and wounded pride, but also his reluctant desire to understand what the hell was going on.

She realized that Cord had the right idea. If Hiral stayed, he would see that Rylin hadn't been doing anything wrong—that this was just for class, and didn't mean anything.

"That would be fantastic! Social pressure becomes increasingly effective the more people you have," Rylin said, babbling. "We could use the help, if you're not busy."

"I don't mind helping," Hiral ventured warily. "What do we do?"

Cord began to explain the experiment. Rylin nodded in vigorous agreement, though her eyes had zeroed in on Hiral's shopping bag. It was from Element 12, an upscale jewelry store. She felt even more miserable. Hiral had gone out shopping, most likely for a present for *her*, and here she was, hiding the fact that she was spending time with her ex.

Dimly she realized that the pod was pulling to a stop. The three of them all whirled around to face the back. Sure enough, a couple a few years older than them stepped on, and unquestioningly kept on facing the back of the pod. Rylin let her eyes dart toward Hiral. He seemed incredulous.

When they disembarked at the bottom, Hiral shook his head. "I never realized how quickly people change their behavior. And for no good reason."

She wondered if he was talking about her.

"We have to do that at least thirty more times if we want valid results. You don't have to stay, though," Rylin hastened to add.

"That's okay." Hiral now he met her gaze. "I'm happy to stay."

Rylin nodded, not trusting herself to break the tentative truce that seemed to have woven itself around the three of them.

# CALLIOPE

**CALLIOPE GAVE A** private, self-satisfied smile. She was about to go on a date with Brice Anderton.

At least . . . she *thought* it was a date. She wasn't totally sure, which to Calliope's mind was reason enough for going. It was rare indeed that a boy's intentions confused her.

She hadn't expected to hear from Brice again, after she ran into him at the ComBattle. But to her surprise, and unexpected delight, he had flickered her earlier to ask if she was free tonight.

"Sure," Calliope had replied saying the words aloud to send as a flicker. Her mom and Nadav were meeting with a wedding vendor, leaving her home with Tamar and Livya. And Calliope felt confident that she could shake the two of them.

Then came Brice's reply. *Thanks. I'm backing a new business venture. I'd love to hear your thoughts on it, as a potential target customer.*

Business venture? Calliope should have been irritated, yet all she felt was intrigued.

She slipped out of Livya's bedroom—they were sharing now, since Nadav's mom was still in town—and paused to glance both ways. All clear. She crept down the hallway on quick, silent feet, holding her breath.

"Where are you sneaking off to?" Livya cried out, emerging from the darkened living room. Her pale face was illuminated with an ugly, twisted glee. *Oh my god*, Calliope thought wildly, had Livya been *waiting* for her, just hoping to catch Calliope in some misdeed?

"To school." Calliope inwardly cringed. She should have thought of a better lie.

"School," Livya repeated, with marked skepticism.

"I have a review session for my calculus class. Basic stuff. I'm really struggling with the material." For a moment Calliope thought she'd laid it on too thick; but to her relief, Livya gave a self-righteous smirk. She clearly relished the idea of Calliope taking remedial calculus.

"Good luck studying. Sounds like you need it," she simpered and stepped aside.

On the corner of their street, Calliope paused to yank her enormous sweater over her head, revealing a cap-sleeved shirt with appliqué floral embroidery. Then she logged on to her contacts to summon a hover, leaning one hand on a wall for balance as she traded her plain black flats for studded heels. She instantly felt more like herself again.

When she arrived at the address Brice had given her, she was surprised to see that it was a shopping district on the 839th floor. Brice was waiting at the end of the promenade, before an industrial-style storefront that Calliope had never noticed.

THE CHOCOLATE SHOP, read the massive block letters above the entrance.

"Thanks so much for coming." He held open the door for her in a show of unnecessary chivalry.

"If you'd told me we were buying chocolate, I would have come sooner," Calliope said lightly.

She had been to countless chocolateries, all over the world. The cozy Middle Eastern ones, with colorful throw blankets and spicy Turkish coffee; the Parisian ones, with herringbone china and hot chocolate so thick it was more like pudding. But Brice's chocolate shop felt startlingly like a science lab. Everything was done in an imposing white and chrome, all the surfaces sterile, with scattered touch screens. Behind the titanium counter Calliope saw test tubes and vials, labeled with things like SUCROSE and EMULSIFIER and VANILLIN.

"Let's place your order," Brice said with a lazy smile.

He placed his hand on the counter, but it didn't call up a menu, as Calliope had expected. Instead, a slot opened on the counter to dispense a single white pill, almost like a breath mint. "Just take that," he said, placing it in her palm.

"Oh, come on," Calliope laughed. "Don't you think I know better than to accept drugs without knowing what they are?"

"It isn't a drug," Brice protested as one of the shop's staff finally appeared from behind the counter, a young man with auburn hair and a stark white lab coat.

"Brice! So good to see you, as always. Sorry for the delay." His eyes flicked to the tablet on the counter, and he nodded. "I see you've already got your colloidosome tablet."

"My what?" Calliope demanded.

"You put it on your tongue, and it makes a taste profile of your palate," the lab technician, or whatever he was, informed her. "The tablet itself is harmless, but it's coated in nanostructures that record the chemical compounds of your individual taste buds and transmit them to our main computer. We'll use that information to design you the perfect personalized chocolate."

"I don't need that. I already know what I like," Calliope said firmly. "I love caramel, and raspberry, but I *hate* chocolate covered in salt. I mean, honestly, salt belongs on margaritas and nowhere else. . . ."

She trailed off, realizing that both men were watching her expectantly. *What the hell?* she figured, and put the tablet on her tongue. It tasted like nothing at all, like air; and before she knew it, it was gone. She smacked her lips, puzzled.

"Interesting. You have less of a sweet tooth than I would have guessed, given that you claim to like caramel," the chocolatier said, almost to himself, "with incredibly strong quinine receptors. Let's see . . ." He moved from one beaker to another, humming slightly.

"*Claim* to like caramel?" Calliope whispered with mock outrage.

"You'll see," Brice assured her. "I bet you right now that this is the best chocolate you've ever tasted."

Calliope lifted an eyebrow. "Oh yeah? What are the stakes of this bet?"

"Dinner," he said smoothly. "If it's your favorite chocolate in the world, you go to dinner with me."

"And if it isn't my favorite?"

"Then I'll go to dinner with you." He grinned.

"Interesting terms," Calliope murmured as the dispenser spat out a perfectly round truffle, with no designs of any kind.

"Here," Brice said, reaching for the chocolate, "let me."

Calliope started to protest, but before she could say anything, he'd popped the truffle into her mouth.

Her eyes fluttered closed as it melted on her tongue, dissolving all thought. She couldn't have said what it tasted like exactly; it wasn't any flavor she recognized. All she knew was that it was utter bliss, as if all her taste buds were firing at once.

"Oh my *god*." She opened her eyes, only to see that Brice was right there before her.

"Sounds like you liked it." Brice turned back to the chocolatier. "Peter, we're going to need a dozen more of those."

"I'll throw in a few of your custom blend too, Brice," Peter offered, evidently pleased by Calliope's reaction. "I still have it on file."

They settled at a table by the window. A moment later, Peter appeared with their tray of chocolates and several glasses of sparkling water.

"I can't get over these," Calliope said, reaching for another truffle. "I mean, I transmit some tongue data, and now it supposedly *knows* me?"

Brice leaned back, studying her. "All it knows is your palate. I, however, would like to get to know you."

"What do you want to know?"

"Anything. What kind of music you listen to. What magical power you would pick, if you could have one. Your greatest fear."

"That started shallow and got serious fast," Calliope pointed out.

"Well, I never know how long I'll get before you disappear on me." Beneath the seeming lightness of Brice's tone, Calliope heard a note of something else, something that made her shiver a little in anticipation.

She opened her mouth to spin another lie—and paused. She was sick of hiding behind layers of pretend.

"You're going to laugh, but my favorite band is Saving Grace."

"Wait—the Christian band?"

"I didn't realize they were a Christian band when I started

listening! I just liked their music," Calliope said defensively. "And all the songs are about love!"

"Yeah, *divine* love." Brice sounded amused. "I had no idea you were so holy."

"Trust me, I'm more of a heathen. As for a magical power . . ." Calliope reached for another truffle. She didn't usually like questions like this, ones that dealt in fantasy. Perhaps because her life already felt like make-believe. "The ability to transform into a dragon," she concluded.

"A dragon? Why?"

"So that I could fly *and* burn things. Two powers in one."

A smile tugged at the corner of Brice's mouth. "Always bargain shopping, aren't you?"

"What about you—what power would you pick?" she asked, genuinely curious.

"The ability to turn back time," Brice said quietly, his eyes drifting toward the window. Calliope fought back the urge to reach across the table for his hand. He must be thinking of his parents.

"What's your mom like?" he asked after a moment. "You guys are really close, right?"

Calliope was startled by the insightfulness of the question. She'd never been on a date where a guy asked about her relationship with her mom. Then again, she'd never been on a date where she didn't have an ulterior motive.

"My mom is my best friend," she admitted, feeling a little dorky as she said it. "She's hilariously witty, and upbeat, and smarter than people give her credit for. And she has such a sense of adventure."

"She sounds like you."

Calliope flushed and kept going. "We used to have this tradition, that whenever we had a big decision to make, we would go to afternoon tea, no matter where we were in the world. It was our signature thing."

"That makes sense," Brice replied, instantly understanding. "You wanted to keep doing something British even when you were traveling. A link to where you came from."

Calliope twirled her straw in the cup of sparkling water. This was all veering dangerously close to the truth, and yet she didn't feel as afraid as she should. "Do you and Cord have any traditions like that?"

"Skydiving and strip clubs," Brice said evenly, then laughed at her reaction. "I'm kidding. Despite what you've heard, Cord and I aren't all that bad. So where is your favorite place for tea in New York? The Nuage?"

"We haven't had time to go out for tea much these days. My mom is so busy, with all the wedding planning," Calliope said, sighing.

"Wow. You sound utterly thrilled."

Calliope couldn't hold it in anymore. She'd been feigning excitement about this wedding for months, nodding and smiling and reciting the same tired sentiments over and over. "It's going to be *miserable*," she said baldly. "And boring. And I won't have a single friend there—"

"You'll have me," Brice interrupted, and Calliope was startled into silence.

"I was invited," he went on, his eyes brushing hers. "I do some business with your stepfather. I guess he felt obligated to invite me, as a courtesy. I wasn't planning on coming . . . but now I'm wondering if I should."

Calliope's heartbeat picked up speed. "Maybe you should."

"Hey," Brice realized, "you never answered my third question. What's your greatest fear?"

For years, Calliope had thought that her greatest fear was

getting caught and going to prison. Now she wasn't so sure. Maybe it was more terrifying to live a life that wasn't yours.

"I'm not sure," she evaded. "Do you know yours?"

"Like I would tell you that, and give you a weapon you could use against me," Brice said lightly. But Calliope didn't laugh. It was too close to something that she and her mom would have really done not that long ago.

She opened her mouth to say something—just as Brice leaned in to kiss her.

He tasted like heat and like the magic chocolate, and without quite knowing how it happened, Calliope was tipping forward and grabbing at his sweater. She knew this was reckless; it was dangerous, but like all dangerous things, it had a deep, thrilling undercurrent that was richer and better and more *alive* than anything safe.

———

Later that evening, as they walked along the promenade of the shopping center, Calliope paused before an enormous fountain. Her eyes drifted to the wisher station a few meters away. "I haven't seen one of these in ages."

A couple of children were clustered around it, begging their parents to let them buy a wisher—the small round disks designed to be thrown into a fountain, accompanied by a wish. These were expensive wishers, so Calliope knew they would produce a special effect when they collided with the water: a cloud of dark ink, or a miniature whirlpool, or a temporary light effect that mimicked a school of fish.

Apparently, in the days before currency was digital, people actually threw money into fountains. It sounded to Calliope like something unbearably lavish, something only the wealthiest people on earth would have done—to be so rich that you literally tossed your money away for your own amusement.

"Want one?" Brice asked, following her gaze.

"It's okay—I didn't mean—" Calliope stammered, but he'd already scanned his retinas for the purchase.

"Come on," he urged, giving a surprisingly boyish smile. "Everyone should make a wish every now and then."

Calliope curled her fingers around the cool metal disk, burnished the color of copper. She wondered which kind it was. You never knew until you threw it into the water.

*I wish that I could find my way forward. That I could feel like myself again*, she thought fiercely. Then, with a wordless sort of desperation, she threw the wisher into the water. It instantly erupted in a shower of bubbles.

"What did you wish for?" Brice asked.

Calliope shook her head, smiling at the silliness of it. "I can't tell you! If you tell, it never comes true."

"So the wish *was* about me!" Brice proclaimed, causing Calliope to shove him in halfhearted protest.

As they turned away, the stream of bubbles was still floating cheerily to the surface.

# AVERY

**THE MORNING OF** the New York municipal election, the thousandth floor erupted in a firestorm of frenetic energy.

Pierson Fuller stood at the center of it all, talking at twice his normal speed with the cluster of assistants and political strategists who surrounded him. His cheeks were ruddy, and he kept fidgeting with his blazer in a way that reminded Avery of an overgrown schoolboy. He didn't even glance up as Avery walked past—but her mother did.

"You can't wear that to the polling station. It'll look terrible in the photos." Elizabeth's eyes widened reproachfully.

*Good morning to you too, Mom.* Avery gestured at her plaid skirt and white shirt in mild disbelief. "This is my school uniform," she pointed out unnecessarily.

"And it's not photogenic," her mom said crisply. "Go put on one of those dresses I tagged in your closet, then you can come back after you vote and change for school."

"Let her wear the uniform; it's fine," her dad said, and turned to Avery. "You're okay with doing a few interviews after you vote, aren't you, Avery?"

"I guess," she said hesitantly.

"That's my girl. You know my stance on all the main issues, don't you?" Her father reached for his tablet. "Actually, I have a summary page I'll send along. Very short and simple."

*We wouldn't want my poor brain to be overwhelmed by anything too complicated, would we?* "I think I've got it," Avery assured him. She tried to remind herself that he was under a lot of pressure, that he didn't really mean anything by it.

"I know you do. Just be charming and keep smiling and stick to those talking points. They'll love you!" Pierson exclaimed. Avery noticed that the one thing he hadn't said was *Be yourself.*

As always, there was a hover ready and waiting at the exit of her family's private elevator shaft—but to Avery's surprise, it wasn't empty.

"Max! I didn't know you were coming with me." She slid into the seat next to him and keyed in the address.

"And miss the chance to watch the American democratic system at work?" he exclaimed, though it was evident why he had really come. He knew that Avery was dreading this day, and he wanted to support her.

Max kept up a steady stream of chatter as the hover sank into one of the vertical corridors that ran through the Tower. "I'm fascinated by the way Americans insist on meeting somewhere to vote in person. In Germany, you know, voting is considered a private thing. We all vote online." He gave a sheepish grin, his hair falling forward into his eyes. "But of course you Americans prefer voting together, all in the same place. The same way girls always go to the bathroom together, like animals that have to band together for security."

"I don't do that," Avery protested, though she was smiling.

"Which is one of the many reasons I love you," Max said firmly.

Their hover emerged onto the 540th floor, the location of the largest midTower polling station. Technically Avery could vote anywhere in New York City—people weren't assigned locations to vote, not anymore, since the whole process was linked to retinas and fingerprints. Still, most people voted at their nearest station, for convenience's sake. Which meant that voting was at least somewhat segregated by neighborhoods.

Her dad had asked weeks ago if Avery wouldn't mind voting at the midTower station. It had probably been his campaign manager's idea: a last-ditch Election Day publicity stunt. Using Avery as a living, breathing commercial for her father.

People were already queued up and down the block before the community center, a sense of anticipation gathering in the air like a storm. Avery heard one group murmuring about health care, another online security, and yet another the environment. It struck her what a tricky game it was, politics—trying to please everyone, when everyone wanted such different things.

"That's her!" A girl elbowed her friend, both of them staring as Avery started toward the back of the line. The whispers instantly multiplied. Everyone was suddenly blinking, probably taking snaps. "Wonder who she'll vote for," more than one of them said sarcastically.

*And so it begins again*, Avery thought, her stomach twisting at the unwanted attention. Max trotted alongside her. He'd started talking loudly about his research, probably in an attempt to distract her.

She'd only made it a few meters before a young man in an

official-looking vest came forward. "Miss Fuller!" he said officiously. "Please come with me. You're a press case and can skip the line."

"No, thank you. I don't want special treatment," Avery assured him.

"Don't be silly. We always do this for the candidates' families," the polling attendant insisted, reaching for Avery's elbow to steer her through the crowd. The people in line cast her dark looks.

Avery tried to keep the smile on her face, but it was dimmer now, mechanical beneath the spotlight of attention.

The polling attendant led her through the main doors of the community center, which was decked out in swaths of New York decorations. Across the room, a few simulated windows depicted the chill of a gray autumn day.

"I'll wait for you right here," Max told her. "Good luck." He paused at a wall of election stickers—the kind that fastened themselves to fabric on a time release, much better than the old pins people used to stab their clothes with. Most of the stickers said I VOTED! "Can I take one of these even if I didn't vote?" Avery heard Max asking, and almost laughed. Of course Max wanted to feel included.

At the wall of retinal scanners, she lifted her gaze and focused on not blinking. There was a momentary instant of darkness as the low-energy beam licked over her eye, gathering all the rich data from her pupil, exponentially more data than what was encoded on a fingerprint. AVERY ELIZABETH FULLER appeared on the screen before her, along with her New York State ID number and birthdate. She had turned eighteen over the summer, and this was her first time voting.

A cone of invisibility descended on Avery from above. Not real invisibility, of course, just simple light refraction technology, the kind used mainly in recreational toys or in schools on test days. Genuine invisibility was available to only the military. Avery knew that her body was still in full view of everyone outside the cone, though watery and hazy, as if seen through a rippling surface of water.

A holo materialized before her, projected by one of the computers along the ceiling. NEW YORK CITY MUNICIPAL MAYORAL ELECTION it said in block letters. Beneath were the names of the candidates: PIERSON FULLER, DEMOCRATIC-REPUBLICAN PARTY, and DICKERSON DANIELS, FEDERALIST PARTY, along with a string of minority-party candidates Avery had barely heard of. Beneath each person's name appeared his or her headshot. There was her dad, smiling and waving in his little square of high-res insta-photo; and next to him Dickerson Daniels, wearing his signature red bow tie. Avery reached up to touch her index finger to the circle marked with her dad's name.

But her hand didn't seem to be working properly, because for some reason, it had hovered over Dickerson Daniels's name instead.

She didn't want her dad to be mayor.

She didn't want four years of this media circus, this endless public scrutiny. She didn't want to keep being summoned to appear in preapproved dresses, to smile and nod on command like a marionette. She wanted to be *herself* again.

If Daniels won, wouldn't people eventually lose interest in her? Her life would go back to the way things had always been. People would stop staring at her in public places, except for the occasional fashion blogger trying to chronicle her outfits. Most of all, her *parents* would go back to normal. They would stop obsessing over every last detail of their family's appearances, and go back to stressing about other things, like making even more ridiculous amounts of money.

A cold sweat had broken out on Avery's brow. Several minutes must have ticked by. Had she been in here too long? Would people notice? The faces of her father and Daniels kept smiling cheerfully and waving at her from their squares of holo. Her hand wavered, and she began to lean in, toward Daniels.

But at the last moment, Avery's rigid lifelong training kicked in, and she pushed the holo-button marked with her dad's name—jerkily, as if she hadn't fully committed to the decision and part of her was still resisting it.

The box glowed a bright green, confirming her vote, and then the screen repixelated into the election for treasurer.

Avery bent over to catch her breath, her hands on her knees. She felt as if she'd just fought a battle within herself, and had the oddest sense that she'd lost.

Finally she pulled herself together and cycled through the other items: everything from city council to town clerk to library trustee. The holographic ballot rolled itself up with a flourish, and the invisibility cone dissolved into thin air. Avery reached up to smooth her hair as she stepped away, producing a vague, distracted smile for the various hovercams aimed in her direction. There was a whole swarm of them now, clearly sent by her parents, whose PR team was probably already blasting the pics to the feeds.

As she walked toward the line of press contacts waiting for an interview, the cold metallic eyes of the cameras and the organic eyes of humans followed her every move.

---

"Fifteen minutes left!" one of the campaign aides cried out as the hum of excitement reached a fever pitch.

It was later that night, and Avery was home on the thousandth floor, where her father had set up a makeshift campaign headquarters in what he and her mom called the great room. It was the room they usually used for parties, almost the size of a ballroom, and empty of furniture. Right now the room was packed, seething with volunteers and publicity assistants and their parents' friends. A stage had been set up along one side, with enormous touch screens above it, depicting the citywide votes in glowing bars of red and blue. The data was being fed into the system in real time, as the last few citizens made their way to the polling stations.

Unless something drastic happened in the next ten minutes, it looked as if Avery's father was about to win.

"Avery," her mom hissed at her elbow. "Where have you been? You missed photo call!"

"I'm sorry, Mom." Avery had purposefully shown up late, her one small willful act of rebellion. But she was here now, and wearing the dress her mom had picked out: a bright crimson shift, since red was the signature color of the Democratic-Republicans.

"Avery, smile!" her mom admonished. "The cameras—"

"Right," Avery said wearily, grinding her teeth into a smile. The cameras, of course. Waiting, poised to take snaps, to document the perfect lives of the perfect loving family.

"Excuse me," she added, and turned away blindly, only to collide into Max.

"I was just looking for you." His hands settled warmly on her shoulders.

Avery closed her eyes and let her head fall against his chest for a moment, drawing upon Max's unwavering, steady strength. He smelled like laundry detergent and spicy deodorant.

"Thank you," she whispered into his sweater.

"For what?"

"For everything. For being you."

"I'm not very good at being other people," Max said lightly, but Avery could tell he was concerned about her.

She stepped back and let out a strangled laugh when she saw his sweater. It was a bright Christmas red. "Did my parents tell you to wear the party color?"

Max didn't deny it. "I'm good at following orders. And, you know, I have good reason for wanting the Fullers to like me," he told her, his hands still on her shoulders.

"Do you, now?"

"Yes." Max smiled. "You see, I'm in love with their daughter."

"Ten seconds!" cried out one of the campaign staffers. Everyone in the room quickly joined in, counting down as if it were New Year's. On the podium, Avery's father began adjusting his tie, preparing for his victory speech; her mother stood at his side with a proud, placid smile.

It all felt suddenly overbright and loud to Avery, with a slight glossy tinge of unreality, as if the whole thing were a holo show viewed from a distance. As if it had nothing to do with her.

The room erupted in cheers, and she realized dimly that her dad had won. If only she hadn't voted for him, after all.

"Thank you, thank you!" her father boomed. "Thanks to my entire staff for your tireless, instrumental work on this campaign. I couldn't have done it without you.

"We should remember that only a few decades ago, confidence in New York was in short supply. We were a city displaced, the laughingstock of the global community as we moved all Manhattan's residents out of their homes, and began the world's most ambitious construction project to date. . . ."

*Of course*, Avery thought. Her dad never turned away from an excuse to talk about the Tower, and his role in it.

"Thanks to everyone in this room for your support, your donations, and, of course, for your votes!" Everyone laughed dutifully, and Avery's father cleared his throat. "And most of all, I would like to thank my beloved family for their never-ending support."

There was another smattering of applause. Max took a respectful step back, creating a halo of space around Avery, who felt the full onslaught of everyone's stares. A mass of zettas—the small hovercams used by paparazzi to take pictures of celebrities—coalesced into a cloud around her. Avery resisted the urge to swat them aside; that would only result in a bunch of unflattering snaps.

Avery knew that her parents loved her, but at times like this, it was hard to feel like anything but an employee of the family company, a standard-bearer of the Fuller name. A beautiful, golden, living prop, which her parents had custom-ordered nineteen years ago for precisely this purpose.

"*All* my family," her father added.

Something in his voice made Avery look up, and then she couldn't look away.

He stepped out onto the stage almost casually, as if they'd been expecting him. Which they had, Avery realized. This was another PR stunt, just as elaborate and staged as her midTower vote this morning.

He looked different. Of course he did, Avery thought. This whole time, she had been imagining him just as she last saw him—preserved in the cryo chamber of her memory—but life wasn't like that. Life left its mark on you.

He was wearing dark-wash jeans and a white button-down, no trace of red in sight. His light brown hair was cut shorter than Avery had ever seen it. It highlighted the bold, strong lines of his face, his long nose and square jaw, making him look older.

His eyes met hers, and he glanced from her to Max, a million emotions darting over his face too quickly for Avery to make sense of them.

"My son, Atlas!" Pierson Fuller cried out. "Who, if I'm not mistaken, delivered the final vote!"

"Though not the deciding one." Atlas smiled, and the room erupted in laughter again.

Her father was saying something else—that Atlas would be here until the inauguration to help Pierson get his business affairs wrapped up, since he wouldn't be able to touch any of his personal assets while in office. But his words were lost over the roar of noise. Everyone seemed to be flooding forward, exclaiming over Atlas, congratulating Avery's father, popping bottles of champagne.

"I can't wait to meet your brother!" Max said, and glanced at Avery. "Did you know he was coming home?"

Avery's mouth formed the word *no*, but she wasn't sure she actually spoke it.

She couldn't move. She knew she needed to do something, to walk forward with a smile and introduce her adopted brother, who also happened to be her secret ex-boyfriend, to her *current* boyfriend. But she was planted in place.

The sheer reality of him, of his presence here after all this time away, struck Avery with a blind, blunt force. Her entire world felt upended.

Why hadn't anyone warned her? Why hadn't *Atlas* warned her? Clearly this plan had been in place for a while. Did they want it to be a surprise for her . . . or had she been right last year, when she worried that her father suspected what was really going on between them?

Avery couldn't quite believe it. After all this time—after she had finally moved on from him—Atlas was back.

# LEDA

**LEDA PULLED HER** feet up onto the cream-colored couch that dominated her parents' living room. It was scratchy and stiff, not particularly inviting, but still her favorite place in the apartment. Probably because it was right at the center of things.

She was home alone tonight, watching an old holo, letting its familiar dialogue lap pleasantly against her mind. At school earlier, Avery had asked if Leda wanted to come to some campaign event that Avery's parents were forcing her to attend, but Leda had refused. Max would be there to keep Avery company, and besides, it didn't sound like fun.

She found herself wondering what Watt was doing tonight, then scolded herself for thinking about him. And yet . . . she had *liked* spending time with him the other day. Even if that time was spent at a random party in Brooklyn, investigating the death of a girl who'd known their darkest secrets.

They had been flickering back and forth ever since, discussing what to do about Mariel's diary. They both assumed that it was in the Valconsuelos' apartment, but couldn't agree on their next step. Watt wanted to break into the apartment and try to steal it, which Leda insisted was too risky. What if instead they pretended to be friends of Mariel's, she suggested, and concocted some excuse for needing to search her room?

Every time she tried to bring it up, though, Watt would inevitably pull the conversation off-topic: to ask Leda whether she missed him *(no)*, whether she thought he needed a haircut *(still no)*, what class she was in *(stop hacking my school tablet; I'm trying to focus)*. When he interrupted her SAT tutoring session, Leda demanded in mock frustration that he hunt down the SAT answers to make it up to her.

*And deprive you of the joy of knowing that you beat everyone all on your own? Absolutely not*, Watt had replied. Leda shook her head, fighting back a smile.

At least she no longer dreaded falling asleep. She was still having the nightmares, but they were shallower, easier to wake herself up from; especially now that she was waking up to a series of waiting flickers from Watt. There was something comforting in the knowledge that he was on her side. For the first time in months, Leda no longer felt alone.

A buzz sounded through the apartment, and Leda's head shot up. It wasn't the delivery she'd ordered from Bakehouse; that would have scanned automatically into the kitchen. She pulled her hair into a messy bun and went to answer the door.

Watt was standing on the other side, holding a massive double-handled bag with the Bakehouse logo. "Delivery for Miss Cole?"

She gave a strangled laugh. "Did you just hack my *delivery bot*?"

"I was in the neighborhood," Watt told her, which they both knew was a lie. "And don't worry, I've hacked far worse."

Leda realized belatedly that she was wearing her oversized school sweatshirt and artech leggings. "Sorry. I would have dressed up, but I wasn't expecting company. Then again, I don't know if you count as company when you show up uninvited."

"In some cultures, it's rude to insult people who show up on your doorstep bearing food."

"Except that you're acting like a human delivery bot, bringing me food *I* ordered."

"You're calling me a human bot? Rude again." Watt's dark eyes were bright with laughter.

"It's not rude if it's accurate." Leda reached for the delivery bag and paused, trying not to make her next words sound like a big deal. "You might as well stay, since you're already here. I always over-order."

"I'd love to," Watt said, in a show of surprise, though Leda knew this was exactly what he'd hoped for.

Watt followed her back into the living room and set the Bakehouse bag on the coffee table, scattering the disposable boxes over its imitation mosaic surface. His eyes flicked to the holo, and he grinned. "You're watching *The Lottery*?" he teased. Leda started to turn it off, but Watt threw a hand out in protest. "Oh, come on! At least wait until they win!"

"That's not until the very end," she reminded him, a little surprised that he'd even seen this holo. It was something she and her mom used to watch, back when Leda was really young.

"Good thing we have all night," Watt replied. Leda wondered what he meant by that.

She stretched across the coffee table to reach for a pizza slice, only to frown at it in confusion. "This isn't my pizza."

"I adjusted the order. You're welcome," Watt said cheekily.

"But—"

"Don't worry—your weird veggie pizza is still here." He slid a box toward her. "But seriously. Who orders pizza without pepperoni?"

"You're insufferable. You know that, right?"

"Takes one to know one."

Leda rolled her eyes and took a bite of her favorite goat-cheese-and-asparagus pizza. She felt oddly glad that Watt had decided to show up tonight, whatever his reasons. It was nice having him around. As a friend, of course.

She shifted to look at him, suddenly curious. "How do you do it? Hack things, I mean?"

Watt seemed surprised by the question. "A lot of it is Nadia. I couldn't do it nearly as quickly without her."

"You *built* Nadia," Leda reminded him. "So don't try to pass off the credit on her. How do you do it, really?"

"Why do you want to know?"

"Because." Because she wanted to understand this part of Watt's life, this thing that he was so startlingly talented at. Because it was important to him.

Watt shrugged and wiped his hands on one of the synthetic napkins, then pushed aside the takeout boxes to clear a space on the coffee table. He tapped at its surface, the false mosaic quickly melting away to reveal a touch screen. "Can I get into your room comp system?"

"I didn't mean—you don't have to hack something right this minute," she spluttered, confused.

"And miss the chance to show off for you? Never."

"Grant access," Leda said, a little flustered, and the room comp automatically admitted Watt to its system.

He lifted an eyebrow, his fingers poised over the touch screen.

"So who'll it be tonight? One of your friends? That German guy Avery is dating?"

Leda imagined asking Watt to hack Calliope's page on the feeds, or Max's, or even Mariel's, which was still saved to the i-Net auto caches. Not long ago, she would have unhesitatingly jumped at the chance to learn more secrets. That was how she and Watt had been brought together the first time: by snooping and spying on people.

But Leda had learned the hard way what happened when you went digging for secrets you were never meant to learn.

"Show me how you accessed the Bakehouse order," she said instead.

Watt rolled up his sleeves. Leda found her gaze lingering on his bare forearms. "This one is easy," he boasted. The holo-monitor before them danced rapidly from one display to the next as he synced up her family's system with whatever he used. "There aren't many authenticity certificates, so I don't even have to go through side channels."

Leda watched in fascination as his fingers flew over the surface of the table. There was something captivating about the sight of him, sitting there, relaxed and blazingly confident.

She'd forgotten how sexy Watt was when he was hacking things on her behalf.

"How did you get so good at computers? I mean, it's a whole other language," she asked, with reluctant admiration.

"Honestly, computer language makes more sense to me than verbal language. At least its meaning is always clear. People, on the other hand, never really say what they think. They might as well be speaking in hieroglyphics."

"Hieroglyphics wasn't a spoken language," Leda said faintly, though she was caught off guard by the insight.

Watt shrugged. "I guess I always hoped that if I studied

151

computers, I might make a difference; make the world better, even in some small way."

*Make the world better*, Leda thought, surprised by his earnestness. Maybe Dr. Reasoner had been wrong when she insisted that being around Watt would resurrect the old, dark Leda.

Maybe he wasn't such a trigger after all.

Watt met her gaze and she flushed, reaching down to smooth the napkin on her lap. She felt as if she were all energy, a bundle of raw, restless movement. As if her body were throwing off real, sizzling sparks.

Her pulse picked up speed. Watt was so close that she could trace the bow-shaped curve of his lips—those lips she had kissed so many times. She couldn't help wondering, a bit jealously, how many other girls had kissed him since then.

Watt leaned closer. Something was unfurling in the space between them, and Leda didn't know how to fight it anymore, or maybe she just didn't want to. . . .

As she tipped her head back to kiss him, Watt pulled away.

Leda's breath caught. She felt torn between relief and a wild sense of disappointment.

"Leda." Watt was looking at her in a way that made her blood pound close to the surface. "What do you want, really?"

Such a simple question, and yet it wasn't simple at all. What *did* she want? Leda imagined opening her brain, unspooling all her tangled thoughts like a skein of woven cloth, trying to make sense of them.

For so much of her life, she had wanted to be the best. The cleverest, the most successful, because of course she could never be the prettiest, not with Avery around. That was why she'd first hired Watt, wasn't it? So she could gain the next step on her ever-ascending staircase toward whatever she was chasing?

Now all Leda wanted was to be safe from the darkness within

herself. And that meant staying away from Watt. Or at least, she had thought it did.

"I should go," Watt said before she could answer.

"Watt—" Leda swallowed, not quite certain what she was about to say; and perhaps he knew that, because he shook his head.

"It's fine. I'll see you later." His footsteps echoed on the way out her front door.

Leda collapsed back onto the couch with a defeated sigh. Her eyes drifted toward the bag of takeout, and she reached for it listlessly, only to realize that there was another box at the bottom, still sealed shut. She pulled the box onto her lap and peeled it open.

It was a slice of chocolate cake, with thick cream cheese icing smeared all over the top. Her absolute favorite, the cake that Leda's parents ordered every year for her birthday. But she hadn't ordered it tonight.

*Watt.* She shook her head and reached for the tiny foldable fork with a private smile.

# RYLIN

**AS SOON AS** the three-tone chime sounded the end of the school day, the Berkeley hallways flooded with students. Everyone herded toward the main front doors, where they would pour themselves into waiting hovers or pause at the edge of the school's virtual tech-net, muttering furiously into their contacts as they replied to their queue of messages. Standing there, they looked like the edge of an undulating human bubble.

Rylin walked into the mounting tide of students, toward the science building. She had missed psychology class earlier and needed to make up the lab if she didn't want to fail.

This morning she had messaged Berkeley to tell them she wasn't feeling well. She had her tampered mediwand all prepped and ready to use—she and Chrissa had rigged it years ago to mark them sick whenever it scanned—but the Berkeley administrators didn't even request proof of her supposed illness. They just took her word for it, which sparked a feeling of guilt Rylin hadn't anticipated. She did her best to push that guilt aside and focus on Hiral.

She hadn't seen him since last weekend at the mall—which had gone much better than Rylin expected. Hiral had stayed to help her and Cord run the experiment, and then they had all gotten *milkshakes* together at the famous blend-bar in the food court. To Rylin's surprise, and delight, it had seemed as if Cord and Hiral were getting along. Or at least they were pretending to, for her sake.

But since that day, Hiral had been mysteriously absent. He kept saying that he was busy, that there were "things" he needed to "take care of," but he didn't volunteer any details, and Rylin didn't press for them. She didn't get the sense that he was angry with her about Cord. Actually . . . Rylin couldn't help being unpleasantly reminded of his behavior the last time they dated, when he'd started dealing drugs with V.

He wasn't doing that anymore, she reminded herself. She *knew* that he wasn't. What Chrissa said last weekend was just messing with her head.

So today Rylin had decided to take the morning off and steal a few hours with Hiral before his late work shift. She'd cooked breakfast tacos and curled up with him in bed, her arm thrown across his chest, her head nestled into his shoulder. And even though he'd smiled and said all the right things, Rylin still couldn't shake the sense that he wasn't wholly there with her, in the moment, but somewhere far away.

She turned now into the psych classroom, where Professor Wang was standing behind her desk, shuffling a few items into her forest-green shoulder bag.

"Hi, Professor. I'm sorry I missed class earlier; I wasn't feeling well." Rylin's eyes roved over the equipment arranged on her lab console, patches and wires covered with the little red hearts that marked them as medical devices.

The professor brushed aside her excuse. "Another student missed class today as well, so you won't have to perform this lab alone. It's much better when these questions come from a human instead of a computer program." She gave a brisk nod. "Here he is now."

Cord strode into the room, grinning even wider when he saw Rylin at their usual station. "Rylin. I guess we're both stuck doing penance this afternoon."

Professor Wang snapped her bag shut with a decided click. "Yes, the irony wasn't lost on me, that the two of you missed class on the same morning," she said coolly.

"Lucky us," Cord said lightly. "I guess it's true what they say, that timing is everything."

The professor glanced impassively from Rylin to Cord, and Rylin couldn't help feeling that in that single moment, she'd grasped their entire history. After all, she did study people for a living. "You two know the drill by now. When you're finished, submit your results electronically. I'll see you in class tomorrow." She crossed the room and pulled the door shut behind her.

Cord immediately rounded on Rylin. "So, Myers, spill. Where were you this morning?"

"I was sick." She didn't exactly want to tell Cord that she'd been in bed with Hiral. "What about you—were you playing hooky?" She tried to deliver the phrase the way Cord always did, but couldn't quite manage his insouciance.

"I was," he said levelly, his gaze fixed on her. "You should come with me next time. It's been a while."

Rylin flushed and tapped quickly at the tablet to avoid having to answer. "Playing hooky" was what Cord called it when he went to his dad's old garage in West Hampton and raced illegal driver-run cars along the Long Island Expressway. He'd actually taken Rylin there once last year to show her just how heart-stoppingly fast those cars could go. They'd ended up driving to the beach and building a sandcastle like children.

Then they'd slept together for the first time—right there on the beach, in the middle of a rainstorm, because they couldn't wait another minute to get their hands on each other.

She wondered if Cord was thinking about that day too, only to remember that *she* shouldn't be thinking about it. They were friends, and nothing more.

Friends who happened to have a romantic history.

"Lie detector lab," Rylin read aloud, letting her hair sweep forward to block her face. "Students will use somatic feedback and biosensors to determine when the other is telling an untruth. The average person . . ."

Rylin trailed off there, and perhaps Cord was reading the same thing at the same time, because he didn't ask her to continue.

*The average person tells a lie at least two times per day. Being deceitful—to protect ourselves, to protect the feelings of others, or to promote our own interests—is so common that we even have a saying: "To lie is human." Yet most people can detect falsehoods in others with less than 30 percent accuracy. In this lab, we will re-create a version of the conditions used by law enforcement in official lie-detection procedures. . . .*

"I nominate you as the first victim," Cord declared. Rylin didn't protest. She felt a cold dread twisting in the pit of her stomach, like some scaly creature stirring to life. If she got called in for questioning about Mariel's death, would the police do something like this? It wouldn't matter, she told herself; she didn't know anything about what had happened to Mariel.

But what if they discovered what Mariel had on Rylin—that

she had been stealing drugs? Maybe she could deny it, Rylin thought wildly; after all, it was her word against a dead girl's.

If nothing else, maybe this lab would give her some useful practice at lying under pressure.

She held out her wrists, letting Cord swab them with an antiseptic pad, deliberately avoiding making eye contact with him. He peeled the backs from a series of sensor patches before placing one on each of her wrists, and another at the center of her forehead. His touch on her skin was very precise and methodical.

*The average person tells a lie at least two times per day.* How many times had Rylin lied so far today—to Hiral, to the school, to Chrissa? And those were just the *recent* ones. As she began to tally up all her mistruths and half-truths, Rylin felt a little sick.

She'd lied to Hiral about Cord, and to Cord about Hiral, and to the police about what happened to Eris. She'd lied to Chrissa too, in an effort to keep her safe. And most of all Rylin had lied to herself, when she absolved herself from all of it. She'd told herself over and over that she didn't have a choice. Didn't she?

The biosensors kicked on, and Rylin's vitals were suddenly depicted on the tablet before them, pink and yellow lines tracking her elevated heart rate, capillary dilation, and sweat levels. The official government machines were exponentially more accurate than this, she knew; those also tracked rapid eye movement and neural firings in the brain.

"Your heart rate is already a little elevated," Cord pointed out, a curious note in his voice. "Let's start with a couple of control questions. What's your name?"

"Rylin Myers." The lines stayed horizontal.

"Where do you live?"

She had a feeling he wanted her to say *New York* or *the Tower*, but Rylin couldn't resist. "The thirty-second floor."

Cord nodded, his lips curling a little at the edges. "Where are you applying to college next year?"

Rylin tried to sit up straighter, to see the questions written there on the tablet, but Cord had angled the screen away from her. Was that really one of the lab prompts?

"NYU," she said slowly. "I'm applying other places, but NYU is my top choice. It has the strongest holography program in the country. Besides, I don't want to leave New York, not when Chrissa still has two more years of high school."

She didn't mention Hiral, though he was another reason for staying in New York. He kept saying how proud he was that Rylin was applying to college, studying something she loved. Though he did clam up a little whenever she mentioned it.

But even if she did get into NYU, Rylin wasn't sure how she would pay for it. She'd been surreptitiously applying for holography scholarships, leadership scholarships, anything she could think of. Not that she especially wanted to share this with Cord, who'd never faced a financial problem in his life. He wouldn't understand.

"You'll get into NYU," Cord declared. "After the faculty see *Starfall*, there's no way they won't admit you."

"You watched *Starfall*?" She hadn't told anyone at school about her film. How did Cord even find out about it?

"Of course I did. I loved it," he told her. Rylin felt oddly touched.

"Though I have to ask," Cord went on, "which character was based on me? The neighbor, or the new guy at the end of the film?"

Rylin rolled her eyes, fighting a smile. Of course Cord would think that he was in the movie somehow. "Where are you applying to college?" she asked, realizing that she didn't know.

"I'm not sure. I think I'll just file the Common Application a bunch of places and see who takes me." He gave an uncertain shrug. "I still have some time to figure it out."

Rylin felt a little catch in her chest, because she recognized Cord's confusion for what it was: the feeling of not knowing what to do, what step to take next, when you had no parents to advise you. It was the terrifying feeling of making a monumental life decision and knowing that whether you failed or succeeded, you would do so wholly on your own.

"Sorry, we'll keep going." Cord slid his finger along the screen to reveal the next question. "How many times have you been in love?"

"*What?* What kind of question is that?" she spluttered.

"I don't know, Rylin, it's right there on the instructions!" Cord held out the tablet as evidence; and sure enough, there it was, written in the signature bold-faced type of the lab program. "Probably just Wang trying to get a laugh out of a bunch of seniors," he added, but Rylin had a different theory.

"Or she wrote a specific set of lab questions just for us. To punish us for missing class."

"It does sound like something she would do. She's got a bit of a masochistic streak."

Rylin let out a strangled half laugh. She couldn't help it: This was all so bizarre, being here with Cord, trying to be *friends* with him despite constant reminders of their awkward, tangled history. "She's probably filming us right now!"

To her relief, Cord burst out laughing too. "You're right. We're probably test subjects in some experiment of hers!"

The laughter seemed to loosen something between them, and Rylin's chest eased up a little. But she still hadn't answered the question. The lab wouldn't let them move on until she did.

"Two," she heard herself say, her voice almost a whisper. Cord's head whipped up in surprise.

She didn't need to clarify what she meant. She had been in love twice—with Hiral, and with Cord.

"Rylin," Cord said softly, and leaned forward to brush a hair back from her cheek.

She stayed very still. She knew she should pull away, should tell Cord to stop—

The door swung open with a violent clatter, and Rylin tore herself away, the air rushing into her chest. Her eyes darted guiltily to the doorway. It was only one of the cleaning bots.

"Look, Rylin," Cord began again, with a bursting sort of desperation. "I wasn't joking earlier, when I told Professor Wang that timing is everything. Our timing has never been right."

"And you think it's right *now*? Cord, I'm dating someone else!"

"I know that! Am I wrong, or is there something still between us?"

"You're wrong," Rylin said, her breath coming in fast, frantic bursts. "There's nothing between us."

Cord looked pointedly down at the tablet, where Rylin's biolines were roiling and fluctuating, colored a bright, erratic red.

Rylin said nothing. She just ripped the patches from her body and ran toward the door. She didn't need to be an expert in psychology to interpret those spiking, wild lines.

They meant that she had lied, when she said there was nothing between her and Cord.

———

Later that evening, Rylin sat at her kitchen table, her head in her hands. Chrissa had volleyball practice, which meant that Rylin was alone with an uneaten plate of spaghetti and her self-recriminatory thoughts. What the hell had she been thinking, acting that way with Cord, letting him almost *kiss* her? And why had the tablet marked her words as a lie, when she felt certain that she meant them?

She wondered if she had been lying to herself. If, on some level, she believed that there *was* still something between her and Cord.

Rylin was so lost in thought that she almost didn't hear the knocking at her front door.

"Hey," Hiral said when she opened the door. "Are you busy?"

"Not really." Rylin stepped inside, and he trailed along after her.

"I just wanted to say how great this morning was."

"I know. It was great," Rylin said quickly. She reached up to touch her necklace, the one Hiral had gotten her at Element 12 last week. It felt impossibly heavy on her skin, like a broken promise. This morning, when they'd been curled in bed—before that weird make-up lab and that heated moment with Cord—felt impossibly distant.

Hiral let out a breath. "I wanted to talk to you about next year." From the way he said it, halting and uncertain, Rylin thought she could guess what this was about.

She took a step forward, closing her hands around his. "You're worried about NYU, aren't you? You think that if I get into this holography program, I'll get all wrapped up in it and won't have any time for you." She winced, realizing that it was already close to the truth, now that she had to cut *class* just to see him. "Hiral, I promise that won't happen."

"I know, Ry. And I'm so proud of you for applying to college. But . . ." He paused. "I just wondered—you haven't even submitted your NYU application yet, have you?"

"No." Rylin wasn't sure where this was going.

"Maybe we should go away instead, after you graduate high school. We could leave New York, like we used to talk about! Go to South America—or maybe Southeast Asia, somewhere far away and low-tech. Where we can be together with just the sunshine and the clean air and each other, like we always wanted."

Was that really what she'd said she wanted? Rylin barely remembered the things she and Hiral used to talk about, years ago. She tried to imagine doing what Hiral said—leaving New York, getting out of the city and starting over—and drew a blank.

So much had happened this past year to change her. Rylin had discovered new depths within herself, new goals, because of Berkeley and holography . . . and Cord. She had learned to let herself actually *hope* for things again, which she hadn't done since before her mom died. Because if you didn't hope, or care, you weren't in danger of being hurt.

But hoping for things also magnified your joy when they actually came true.

"Hiral, I'm glad you're thinking about the future—"

"Because you never expected me to?"

Rylin winced. She hadn't meant to sound condescending.

"I'm sorry." Hiral reached below her chin to tip it up so that Rylin was looking into his eyes. "All I want is a future with you. But being in New York is tough for me, because of everything that's happened. Because of who I used to be."

There was a current of significance to his words that made Rylin's stomach drop. "What's going on, Hiral? Is there something you want to tell me?"

"No," Hiral said too quickly.

Rylin looked directly into his warm brown eyes, the eyes she thought she knew so well. She didn't need a biosensor to tell her that he was lying.

"What about you, Ry?" he asked, turning her own question on her. "Is there something that *you* want to tell me?"

Rylin wondered if Hiral had guessed about Cord—if he could see her guilt written there on her face. Maybe she should confess everything, clear the air between them of secrets.

"No," she whispered instead.

She couldn't bring herself to tell him about Cord. Whatever was bothering him, Hiral clearly had enough to worry about as it was. Her moment with Cord was nothing, just an almost-kiss. There was really nothing *to* tell.

But deep down, Rylin knew that was another lie to be added to her ever-growing tally.

# CALLIOPE

**CALLIOPE HAD BEEN** to a lot of weddings for an eighteen-year-old. Dozens, really, all over the globe, in connection with some con or another. She thought fondly of the year that she and Elise had run wedding cons almost exclusively. "People tend to let their guard down at weddings," her mom had explained with palpable excitement. "Emotions run high, everyone drinks too much, and especially among the super wealthy, they try to outdo each other with over-the-top jewelry." It made weddings a great place for some high-class pickpocketing.

Today, though, Elise was subdued. She'd barely spoken through their interminable hair and makeup appointments, through all the time they spent hooking and fastening her into her enormous white dress, pushing each tiny silk-covered button patiently through its matching loop. Calliope wondered if she was having second thoughts. If she regretted seeing this con all the way through.

They were standing now in the Temple Brith Shalom, up on the 918th floor. An enormous chuppah rose overhead: a floral canopy, with roses twining up its sides to spill over the top in glorious profusion. Calliope knew that the flowers would all be donated to the hospital once the wedding was over. Practically everything at this wedding was marked for donation—the roses, the leftover food; even Elise's dress was going to a drive for underprivileged brides. Calliope secretly hoped that the leftover booze would be donated to high schoolers with strict parents—the kids who didn't have a liquor cabinet to raid for their parties.

Under the chuppah, Elise and Nadav stood before a plump rabbi, who held a hand toward them in silent blessing. Calliope stood to one side with Livya, each of them wearing their enormous tiered bridesmaid dress and holding a spray of white flowers. Hundreds of faces were lined up in the pews of the synagogue, their expectant smiles blurring indistinguishably together. Calliope kept glancing out there, trying unsuccessfully to find Brice in that sea of people. She hadn't been able to see him since their date at the chocolate shop; their entire household had been on wedding-stress lockdown all week. But it hadn't stopped her from messaging him whenever she knew Livya wasn't watching.

At the thought of Brice—of the way he'd kissed her, warm and certain and tasting of chocolate—a secret smile played around her mouth. Livya noticed it and shot her a dark look. Calliope quickly lowered her head, trying to arrange her features into a more pious expression.

"Welcome. We are gathered here today to witness as Nadav and Elise take the first steps of their new life together," the rabbi intoned. He wasn't even using a mike-bot, Calliope realized, yet his booming voice projected throughout the temple. Very old-school.

"The love that they share is a love for the ages, a love built on selflessness. Nadav and Elise were first brought together through their shared love of philanthropy. They each put the needs of others before their own needs."

*How lovely*, Calliope thought ruefully. If only it were true.

"Before they step into the chuppah, I would like to invite Nadav and Elise to participate in the ceremony of the *bedeken*, or veiling, in which the groom covers the bride's face. This is to signify that his love is for her inner beauty, and not her outer appearance."

Livya coughed under her breath, just once. Calliope pretended not to hear.

Nadav tentatively lifted the lace veil over Elise's head. It fluttered in opaque folds before her. Calliope felt an odd stab of panic, seeing her mom faceless like that. It could have been anyone getting married up there.

"And now the *hakafoth*, or circling. The bride will walk around the groom seven times as a symbol of the new family circle that she is creating with him."

Calliope watched as the ghostly form of her mother began to loop around the edges of the chuppah's platform, her skirts swishing behind her. Nadav was beaming with a bright, eager joy.

*A new family circle.* Calliope stole a glance at Livya. The other girl's upper lip was curled into a sneer, her nostrils flaring, the type of face you make when you smell something rancid.

"And now, let us extend a blessing to this beloved couple," the rabbi intoned, before launching into a traditional Jewish prayer in Hebrew. Everyone seemed to be reciting the words; Calliope pretended to mumble along.

She couldn't help thinking of the last wedding she'd been to—at a family estate in Udaipur, with gold-plated invitations and thousands of candles hovering in the air as if by magic, the scent of them heavy in the air. Now *that* wedding had been fun. Calliope remembered drifting around the enormous grounds, a flower twined in her hair, pretending to be first one person and then another, turning her various accents on and off as needed, like a faucet. There really was nothing like the thrill of anonymity. Of stepping into a party as a blank slate and letting the situation dictate who you might become.

As she stood here now, staring out at the sea of faces watching her, all she could think was how surreal it all felt.

She was dimly aware of her mom slipping a ring on Nadav's finger and reciting the words of the marriage vow: "With this ring, you are my husband, and I love you as my soul." Then Nadav was saying the same thing, slipping an enormous pavé band onto Elise's finger; and they were kissing, and the temple had erupted in applause.

"One last tradition! The breaking of the glass," the rabbi proclaimed, holding up a hand for silence. An assistant handed the rabbi a wineglass wrapped in velvet—the old-fashioned kind of glass, which could break, not flexiglass. "The breaking of the glass is a reminder that marriage can hold sorrow as well as joy. It represents the couple's commitment to stand by each other forever, even during the difficult times."

Calliope felt a shiver of premonition. Forever was a long time for anyone to promise. And she and Elise had broken so many of their promises before.

Elise and Nadav set the glass on the base of the chuppah and each placed a foot over it. Then, at the same time, they both put their weight on their heels, shattering it into countless tiny shards.

———————

"Calliope! I've been looking for you."

Calliope turned around slowly, taking a few steps away

from the dance floor. They were finally at the reception, at the Museum of Natural History, where she had been waiting with an eager, half-painful sort of anticipation for Brice to find her.

"At least, I think it's you. Are you in there, beneath that fluffy mushroom cloud of a dress?" he added, and made a show of squinting at her. He hadn't shaved, in blatant disregard for black-tie etiquette, but the shadow of dark stubble looked good on him. Calliope found her eyes dragging along his jawline, wishing she could reach out and touch it.

"I didn't really have much choice. I was . . . talked into this dress. Very forcibly," she told him.

"I'd rather talk you out of it."

"Once you do, we can burn it afterward."

"Don't do that! Where else will we find a flammable camping tent?"

As she laughed appreciatively, Brice put an arm on her elbow and steered her wordlessly toward the dance floor.

The museum's famous holographic whale glided in lazy circles above them. On the stage, an eighteen-piece band played soft jazz music. A trail of antique iron candelabras led out onto the terrace, where heat lamps floated like miniature suns.

Calliope knew that she should step away. She'd felt Livya's gaze on her all night, just daring her to make one false move, one mistake that would blow her cover. Livya would never even talk to a boy like Brice, let alone dance with him.

"Has the wedding been as utterly boring as you expected?" he asked as they moved toward the middle of the dance floor. He danced the way he talked, his movements bold and confident.

"Not anymore," Calliope murmured, and smiled. "I'm glad you came, Brice."

"So am I." His hands skimmed lower, to play with the enormous bow sewn onto the back of Calliope's dress.

"Stop it!" she whispered, smacking his hands away. "You're going to get me in trouble."

"I hope I do. When most people say trouble, they're usually talking about something exciting," Brice replied, though he resettled his palms much higher.

"I know," Calliope said helplessly. "But I'm not supposed to be . . ."

"Dancing?" Brice tried to spin her, and the rustling folds of her dress almost caused him to trip. He let out a laugh. "Whoever designed this bridesmaid dress didn't want you to dance, that's for sure."

The music crescendoed louder, as the band suddenly launched into one of those wild top-forty songs that everyone loved. Calliope risked a glance at Nadav, who was talking to someone she didn't recognize. His jaw had tightened; he'd probably told the band not to play music like this, yet they were doing it anyway. Near him, Livya stood like a pale, thundering column, her judgmental gaze scouring the dance floor.

Calliope knew that she couldn't join in, at least, not the way she wanted to. Because the girl she was supposed to be—sweet, modest Calliope Brown—wouldn't dance to music like this, her hair flying and boobs bouncing. Not that you would even notice her boobs bouncing right now, buried as they were beneath a million flounces of fabric.

"Come on!" Brice exclaimed, jumping up and down along with everyone else. Calliope wondered, with a sneaking suspicion, if he'd been the one to request this song—maybe even bribed the band to play it. Because he suspected that it would break her out of her rigid, forced role.

And he was right.

She let her head tilt back, her hair falling from her updo to hang loose around her face, and let herself dance. She danced as if she were alone, unapologetically and unabashedly, smiling so wide that her jaw hurt. Brice took her hands and jumped alongside her, both of them shouting the words to the song—

"Calliope!"

Livya was pushing through the dance floor toward her. "Your mom is looking for you. She's ready to cut the cake."

Calliope instantly stopped jumping. She took a quick, even breath and reached up to tuck her stray hair behind her ears. "Thanks for coming to get me," she said. "Let's go."

She shot an apologetic look at Brice, who nodded in understanding. "Bring me back a slice," he replied, with a touch of mischief.

Calliope noticed that Livya pointedly refused to look in Brice's direction. She just turned back toward the front of the room, where Elise was standing next to an enormous tiered cake.

"Calliope," the other girl said as they walked, "I know you're new here and can't be expected to know everything about everyone." *Try me*, Calliope thought, *I bet I know fifty times what you know.* "But Brice Anderton is bad news."

*Good thing you aren't the one he was flirting with.* "Bad news?" Calliope repeated, all innocence.

"I just want you to be careful. A nice girl like you should stay far away from boys like that. Boys with *reputations.*"

This was the part where Calliope should back down. But part of her felt sharply resentful. Who was Livya to say what she could or couldn't do? "He doesn't seem that bad to me," she protested.

Livya gave a smug smile. "I'm just looking out for you. After you disappeared the other night—"

"Disappeared?" Calliope asked blankly.

"I checked with your calculus professor, and she said that there wasn't any review session that evening. Where did you *really* go?" Livya pressed.

Calliope didn't answer. All the bright, breathless joy she had felt with Brice seemed to vacuum away, leaving nothing but a dull sense of anger.

Livya laced her fingers deliberately in Calliope's. To all the onlookers, it probably looked sweet, that the two girls were holding hands. But Livya's nails were pressing into the soft flesh of Calliope's palm like a row of tiny claws.

Calliope had never hated a role so much as she did now—god, not even that time she'd had to work as a nurse and wash out bedpans to try to sneak her mom into that Belgian hospital. At least then she'd been able to *say* what she wanted.

She wished she could break out in screams, tear her hand violently from Livya's. Instead she forced herself to swallow it back. *This isn't real*, she assured herself. *I'm not really this cold, unfeeling person. I'm just playing a part. It isn't real.*

"Thank you for the advice," she said woodenly.

"Of course. I'm your stepsister, Calliope. I'm family now," Livya simpered, that ugly smile still pasted on her face. "And I would do *anything* to protect my family."

Calliope couldn't let a threat like that go unanswered. "So would I," she replied and smiled right back at her.

# AVERY

**"THANKS AGAIN FOR** tonight," Avery told Max, lingering on the landing to her family's private elevator. She wasn't quite ready to go inside.

She didn't want to risk seeing Atlas.

Avery still couldn't believe that he had moved back into their apartment. He had unpacked in his old room and was heading off to work every day with their dad, slipping nonchalantly back into his old life as if no time at all had passed since he left for Dubai. As if nothing had changed.

Except that everything had changed, Avery thought furiously. *She* had changed. And it wasn't fair that he was suddenly here, when she'd gone to such painful lengths to move on from him.

"Are you okay, Avery?" Max asked, sensing her hesitation.

"I just wish that I could stay with you tonight," she said, and meant it. Avery had slept over in Max's dorm room the past few evenings. She wished she could keep staying there indefinitely—but her mom had made a pointed comment about it this morning, and Avery didn't want to push her luck.

"Me too." Max pulled her into a hug, tucking his chin above her head. "I'm sorry this election stuff has been so intense. I never realized how much it would affect you. We aren't so obsessed with the candidates' families in Germany."

"That sounds nice." Avery smiled. "Maybe next time my dad can run for mayor of Würzburg."

In the week since her dad's election, her parents had become more committed than ever to maintaining their image as New York's first family. "New York royalty," the feeds kept calling them. Even worse, they had dubbed Avery the so-called princess of New York.

Her inbox was now flooded with interview requests—which she found ludicrous, given that she wasn't an authority in anything except, perhaps, being a teenager. Or hiding an illicit romance from her parents.

Yet bloggers suddenly wanted her to weigh in on everything from her favorite face cream to her most-anticipated fashion trends. When Avery tried to decline the interviews, her parents were horrified. "You're the youthful face of my administration! Tell them whatever they want to know!" her dad cried out, and signed her up to talk to anyone who would listen.

Meanwhile, Avery's follower count on the feeds had skyrocketed from a few thousand to a half million. She'd tried to make her page private, but her parents adamantly refused. "We can hire an intern for you, to post and reply to things," her mom offered. Avery had thought she was joking.

"I'll see you later," she murmured and gave Max one last kiss. Then she stepped into the elevator that rose toward their foyer, holding her breath.

As the door slid open, Avery saw with a sinking feeling that she hadn't waited long enough. Atlas was home.

He stepped out of the kitchen, the shadows falling softly over the planes of his face, so familiar and yet so changed. The silence fluttered between them like a curtain.

"Hey, Aves," he ventured.

"Hey." All she was willing to give him was that single word.

She was acutely aware that this was the first time she and Atlas had been alone together since he came home. She had seen him, of course, but always with her parents or Max there as a buffer.

"I was just about to make pasta. Want some?" Atlas offered into the silence.

"It's almost midnight," Avery croaked, which she realized wasn't an answer. She felt like a newborn, discovering her vocal cords for the first time.

"I was at work late."

Avery wondered, suddenly, if he'd stayed at work late on purpose—if he was avoiding home for the same reason she was. Because he didn't want to run into her.

She followed him warily into the kitchen, lingering near the doorway as if she might make a quick escape at any moment. "Since when do you cook?"

Atlas smiled, the old half smile that Avery used to love, but it didn't reach his eyes. "Since I live alone in Dubai and got sick of takeout. Though pasta isn't exactly complicated."

She watched as Atlas flash-cooked the noodles, chopped tomatoes, shaved down a hunk of cheese. There was a strong, lean grace to his movements that seemed new to her. She felt the same way she'd felt the last time he returned home—like he'd traveled across some unknown distance, had seen and done things that would forever set him apart from her.

And just like last time, she felt an instinctive urge to draw near him. As though, if she got close enough, she might understand some of what he had done.

"What was it like?" Avery leaned forward onto the counter, pulling the sleeves of her sweater toward her wrists.

"Loud. Busy. Not that different from New York, except way hotter outside the towers."

"Not Dubai." She shook her head. "I meant—being away."

"You went away too, if I recall," Atlas pointed out.

"It's not the same." When Avery traveled, she took her identity with her; she never stopped being Avery Fuller. She was jealous, she realized, of Atlas's anonymity.

"That reminds me. I have a present that I've been meaning to give you," Atlas said abruptly, wiping his hands beneath the UV sanitizer beam. Before Avery could react, he'd disappeared down the hall toward his room.

Moments later he returned, holding something bulky behind his back. "Sorry I didn't wrap it," he apologized, and handed Avery a multicolored bundle.

She unfurled it before her, and her breath caught in her chest.

It was a square of handmade rug, about the size of the coffee table in their living room. A vibrant swirl of colors, blue and yellow and orange threads all woven into an intricate pattern that kept revealing more details the longer you looked at it. Avery saw peacocks, miniature trees, fiery sunbursts, and in the center, a radiant white lotus floating against a turquoise pool. The border was edged in gold stitching.

"Atlas," she said softly, "this is breathtaking. Thank you."

"I know it's not a real magic carpet, but this was the closest I could find."

She looked up sharply. "You remember that?" Avery used to ask Santa for a magic carpet every Christmas. She'd wanted one so desperately that her parents ended up commissioning an engineer to build a child-sized one, with metallic-woven fabric that lifted her a whole four centimeters above the ground, like a hover. They never understood why Avery hated that thing.

This was much more what a magic carpet should feel like.

Atlas was watching her closely. "Where would you go, if it were really magic?"

"I don't know," she admitted, and smiled. Her fantasies of magic carpet rides had never gone past the part where she left the thousandth floor. "I guess I was always more excited for the flying than for the destination."

"I know what you mean."

Avery glanced again at the carpet, the beautiful woven richness of its fibers. "Thank you," she repeated, taking an unconscious step forward, and realizing a beat too late how close Atlas's face was to hers.

That was when he leaned in to kiss her.

Some part of her saw it coming, and yet Avery couldn't pull away. Her body seemed to have momentarily shut down. She couldn't move, couldn't think, couldn't do anything except stand here and let Atlas kiss her. His mouth on hers struck something deep within her, like a bell.

And for a single forbidden moment, Avery felt herself kiss him back.

Then her nerves came violently to life again, and she stumbled away, her breathing ragged. "Atlas! What the hell?" She wanted to scream, but their parents were home, so somehow—using every last shred of her willpower—she kept her voice at a low hiss. "You can't do that, okay? I'm with Max now!"

It felt to Avery like the very air was charged, like the old Tower air before they adjusted the oxygen levels; as if a single spark might burst into flames, and destroy everything.

"I'm sorry. I guess I was . . . Never mind. Just pretend it didn't happen."

"Pretend it didn't *happen*? How do you expect me to do that?"

"I don't know," Atlas said bitingly, "but you've been doing a fantastic job of it so far."

"That's not fair." Avery noted with a wild sort of hysteria that she was still holding the rug in one hand. She brandished it before her like a weapon. "You're the one who ended things with *me*, remember?"

"I'm just saying, you've done a great job pretending that you and I never happened. You have everyone convinced, even me." He kept his gaze on her, steady and unblinking. "When I saw you with Max, I almost thought that I'd made the whole thing up. That it was something I'd dreamed."

"That isn't fair," Avery said again. Tears pricked at the corners of her eyes. "You can't do this, Atlas. You literally destroyed me. I was so broken, I thought it would be a lifetime before I could put myself back together. And then I met Max . . ." She trailed off, taking a shaky breath. "You can't resent me for being happy with him."

He winced. "Aves, I'm sorry. Of course I want you to be happy. I didn't come here to break up you and Max."

"Then why the hell did you just kiss me?"

Atlas's grip tightened over the edge of the counter. "Like I said, forget it. Chalk it up to a stupid mistake, okay? I promise it won't happen again. What more do you want from me?"

"I want you to forget that anything ever happened between us, okay? Because I have!"

He took a step back, retreating across the distance her words had created. "Consider it done."

Back in her bedroom, Avery couldn't resist unfurling the carpet near her windows. She had to admit, her room needed this—it was all neutrals, ivory and gray and the occasional soft blue. The carpet was a glorious oasis of color in a sea of boringness.

Trust Atlas to bring her the most thoughtful present in the world, then ruin it by turning her emotions upside down.

She sat down on the magic carpet and closed her eyes, wishing it would take her anywhere but here.

# WATT

LEDA KEPT GLANCING nervously over her shoulder as they turned onto Mariel's street. "I can't believe we're doing this. Actually, I can't believe *you're* doing this. I don't really have a choice, but you . . ." She glanced over at Watt, seeming disconcerted. "There's no reason you should be doing this for me."

Watt thought it was pretty obvious why he was here: He would take any opportunity to spend time with Leda, in any context. Even if it meant asking questions about a girl's murder.

He hadn't seen Leda since he dropped by her apartment with the Bakehouse order. They had been flickering back and forth all week, discussing what to do about Mariel's diary—studiously avoiding any mention of their almost-kiss on Leda's couch. Watt was so glad that Leda was still talking to him, he had even agreed to her initial idea: that they should just show up at the Valconsuelos' apartment and *ask* to be let inside.

"We're here," he realized, pausing at the door marked 2704.

The Valconsuelos' apartment was on the 103rd floor, on a street called Baneberry Lane. It was only a hundred and forty floors below where Watt lived with his family, but the difference was palpable. Down here the streets felt less like streets, and more like wide hallways that happened to be floored in carbon-composite, lined with metal studs. The overhead lights were fluorescent and distinctly unforgiving. Even Watt, who hadn't known Eris very long, had trouble picturing her here. It made him cringe to think of what it must be like for Rylin, down on the 32nd floor.

"Okay," Leda said in an oddly small voice. She poised her finger on the doorbell—and held it there, uncertain. Watt understood her reluctance. This felt much more serious than sneaking into a party.

Wordlessly, he put his hand over Leda's to help press the bell. They heard the sound of it on the other side of the front door, echoing through the apartment. Leda pulled her hand out from beneath Watt's, though he couldn't help noticing that it wasn't all that quickly. The thought made him smile, in spite of everything.

The door swung open to reveal a woman in a cozy purple dress. Her hair rose to a widow's peak at her brow, and her brown eyes crinkled with lines, the pleasant sort of lines that came from a lifetime of smiling. But she wasn't smiling right now.

"Can I help you?"

"Hi, Mrs. Valconsuelo. We're friends of Mariel," Watt said quickly.

For a moment Mrs. Valconsuelo simply stared at them both, as if trying to place them.

*She doesn't believe you,* Nadia told Watt. *Her nostrils are flaring, her hands tensing, the classic signs of mistrust.*

Nadia was right; they should have known better than to try

to lie to a mom. Moms had a bullshit meter that was hard to sneak anything past.

"I should have said that we were friends of Eris. I only met Mariel once," Watt amended, and nudged Leda sharply in her side. She blinked, seeming jarred to life.

"We're so sorry to bother you. Eris"—Leda faltered for only a fraction of an instant over the name—"had something of mine, something she borrowed, and I've been trying to track it down. It seems as if Eris might have lent it to Mariel. I wouldn't ask, except it's something important."

"What is it?" Mrs. Valconsuelo asked.

Leda's chin tipped imperceptibly higher; the face she made when she was about to lie. She was so tremulous, so fiercely vulnerable, Watt marveled that Mrs. Valconsuelo didn't see it.

"A scarf," Leda decided, and Watt felt a pang of sympathy for her, because he knew exactly which scarf she was thinking of. The one that Leda's father had given Eris, which started the entire cascade of misunderstandings. "It has sentimental value, otherwise I wouldn't ask."

"I understand." Mrs. Valconsuelo stepped aside to let them in.

An oppressive silence hovered in the apartment. Watt could tell that it wasn't normally this quiet; this was the type of apartment that should be ringing with laughter. The silence was a stranger here, lurking around every corner with heavy footsteps, as uninvited and unwelcome a guest as he and Leda.

They followed Mariel's mom down the hall to a door that was covered in loud, brightly colored stickers. Mrs. Valconsuelo kept her eyes deliberately averted from her daughter's bedroom. "Feel free to look around. Everything is the way she left it, except for whatever the police might have moved when they came by." With that, Mrs. Valconsuelo hurried back down the hall, as if she couldn't get away from the painful memories fast enough.

So the police had already been here. Whatever they found, if they found anything at all, Watt and Leda could assume that the police had already seen it. At least this way, they would know what the police knew.

They exchanged a glance and stepped into the dead girl's bedroom.

The overhead lights, sensing their movement, flicked on. Dust motes hung suspended in the air. The room was much as Watt had expected: a narrow bed with a multicolored quilt; a small desk with a cream-white top and embedded touch-controls, easily the most expensive thing in the room. A chair was tucked to one side, only slightly visible under the mountain of jackets flung casually over its back. It felt oddly as if Mariel had just walked out and might return again at any moment.

"Should we divide the room in half?" Watt suggested, passing off Nadia's idea as his own.

"Good thinking. I'll start with the closet."

They moved quickly through the room, searching beneath the mattress, inside drawers, in the closet. Watt noticed that Leda wasn't moving very fast. She kept running her hand over the quilted bedspread or picking up an item of clothing and setting it down again.

*I wish we could figure out Mariel's death*, he thought to Nadia, in a burst of frustration. No matter how many times he reasoned through it, Watt couldn't shake the sense that he had all the right pieces to the puzzle—that the answer to Mariel's death was somehow right before him, and he just wasn't seeing it. Was it really a murder? If so, who had done it and why? What evidence did the police have suggesting foul play?

*You aren't here to solve her murder*, Nadia reminded him. *Just to find out what she was doing before she died. Whether the police might have found the connection between her and you.*

Nadia was right, of course. But part of Watt still wished he could solve it. Maybe if he found out who killed Mariel, he could give the answer to the police and make the whole investigation go away.

"This feels weird," Leda said at last, holding up a framed instaphoto.

"I know." Watt had been thinking of Mariel only as the girl who attacked Leda in Dubai. But standing in her bedroom, surrounded by all the accumulated clutter of her life, Mariel felt much less like a goddess of vengeance, and much more like a teenage girl. A misguided girl who was desperately hurt by the loss of the person she'd loved.

"No, you don't know. It isn't *your* fault," Leda replied, her voice breaking. Watt glanced over in surprise. She was still holding the framed instaphoto, staring at it furiously, as if it might reveal some new secret. It was a photo, Watt realized, of Mariel and Eris.

"It's all my fault," she said again fiercely. "If I hadn't pushed Eris, none of this would have happened! Mariel and Eris would still be together, and Mariel would never have followed us to Dubai—you and *I* would still be together—"

Leda crumpled a little, still holding tightly to the frame. Watt hurried forward and folded her in his arms. She didn't lean in, but she didn't push him away either. "It isn't your fault that Mariel tried to enact some kind of Old Testament vengeance on us," he told her. "Stop trying to carry all the guilt in the entire world by yourself. There's enough blame to go around, I promise."

A breath shuddered through Leda's thin body. Watt fought back the urge to hug her tighter. "Why do you keep *doing* this?" she demanded.

"Doing what?"

"Being so nice, acting like you still care about me."

"Because I do still care about you. You know that."

"Well, you shouldn't," she said tersely, taking a step back. "I'm no good for you, Watt."

"Stop saying that. I know you, Leda, the *real* you—"

"That's just it! You know me too well! You know the real me, the me that no one else has seen. You're the only person I ever told about me and Eris being related," she added quietly.

Watt was strangely touched by that. "I do know you, Leda," he said softly. "I like to think I know you in a way that no one else does. That I can see a core of goodness in you that the rest of the world is too hurried or careless to see."

Leda looked up. There was a new softness at the corner of her lips and eyes. Then her gaze drifted past Watt, and she cried out in sudden excitement.

"Watt, look!" Leda stepped forward to pull a notebook from a shelf behind him. It had a tattered black-and-white cover, like the notebooks Watt had used back in elementary school.

"What are you two still doing here?"

Mariel's mom stood in the doorway, a hand on one hip. "Can I help you find your *scarf*?" she asked pointedly. They had clearly overstayed their welcome.

Somehow Leda concealed the notebook behind her back. "I couldn't find my scarf. Maybe Eris never lent it to Mariel after all. I'm sorry to have bothered you."

"Thank you," Watt mumbled, and hurried with Leda out the Valconsuelos' home.

The moment they turned the corner, Leda began to flip open the notebook. Nadia sent off sirens in Watt's mind, not that he needed them. He quickly reached over Leda to slam the spiral shut. "Not here!" he hissed, his heartbeat skipping. "Not in public!"

Leda gave a reluctant nod. "Should we go to my place?" she asked impatiently.

"Mine is closer."

They took off, racing toward the upTower lift, then sprinting the two blocks to Watt's apartment. He heard muffled noises emanating from the kitchen but charged on past, dragging Leda to his bedroom and pulling the door shut behind them.

Even in the midst of everything, Watt felt strangely relieved that his room was clean, if cluttered. His desk was scattered with pieces of computer hardware, which were reflected on the flat-screen monitor tacked to the wall. Clothes on hoverbeams clustered near the ceiling like a woven storm cloud.

Leda flopped onto Watt's mattress with familiar ease, scooting over to create space for him. He sat gingerly next to her, on the edge of the bed, feeling oddly afraid that he might spook her. Then he looked on, his heart pounding, as Leda began to read.

The journal tracked Leda's movements—obsessively. Leda turned page after page of Mariel's cramped, spidery writing, recounting where Leda was going, and when, and with whom. Mariel had obviously been stalking her.

No wonder the police had questioned Leda, if they saw this notebook.

Watt fought back a dull sense of horror. He should have *protected* Leda from this; but then, how could he have known? He and Nadia couldn't access anything that wasn't tech-based. Recording things this way, by hand and on paper, provided more security than any firewall.

Leda pursed her lips and flipped toward the back of the notebook. Watt froze at the sight of his own name.

"These are the entries after Dubai," Leda breathed, in evident horror.

Here, Mariel had written about all of them, not just Leda. The section on Avery was the biggest—unsurprisingly, since Eris had died at Avery's apartment. Watt frowned, reading how

Mariel had painstakingly tracked Avery's movements from Eris's death onward. She'd taken notes about Avery's dad's campaign, Avery's public appearances, even the few pics that Avery had posted from her semester in Oxford.

There were fewer notes about Rylin and Watt, but then, there was much less about them in the public domain.

*There's nothing here to incriminate you,* Nadia assured him, and Watt realized in a daze that she was right. His chest brimmed with hope as Leda turned to the final page.

It was like some kind of inspiration board: Mariel had written all four of their names in heavy, fat-tipped marker, with arrows scrawled across the page, connecting each of the names to one another. The lines overlapped and twisted like snakes, with biting comments written along each arrow, such as *ATLAS* connecting Leda to Avery; or *DRUGS* connecting Rylin to Leda.

Then Watt saw the arrow linking himself to Leda and felt dizzy. *NADIA* was written there, in Mariel's scrawling, angry letters.

*It's really not that bad,* Nadia chimed in, tracking the movements of his pupils. *If anything, it looks like Nadia is just the name of a girl that got between you and Leda.*

Leda glanced up. Her hands were curled tight around the edges of the journal. "This is freaking me out. All these obsessive notes, this speculation about how we're connected, it looks as if Mariel was searching for a weak spot. Trying to plan how she could break us apart!"

"That's exactly what she was doing," Watt agreed. "But it doesn't matter. Leda—we're okay."

"Okay? Our names are all *over* this notebook, and we know the police have seen it!"

"So what? There isn't anything here they can build a case on. It's just a bunch of cryptic shorthand notes. All they know is that Mariel was stalking us." Watt grabbed Leda by the shoulders and looked directly into her eyes. "She didn't write down our secrets, or the fact that you pushed Eris. That's the important thing. Even if they want to question us about Mariel's death, so what? None of us were involved. They won't find anything."

"She didn't write down our secrets," Leda repeated hesitantly. "You're right. There's nothing here that can incriminate us."

"We're safe, Leda. We're actually safe."

She tilted her head thoughtfully. Her newly short hair curled around her ears, curls that Watt used to wrap his hands in, when he would tip Leda's head back to kiss her. Then, to Watt's surprise, she began to laugh—a joyful, relieved laugh, deeper and heartier than you would expect, given how small she was. Watt missed that laugh.

He would have fallen in love with her right then, all over again, if he didn't already love her with every atom of his being.

"We really are safe," she said wonderingly.

Something in Leda's voice gave him pause. She was different, Watt thought, trying to pinpoint what exactly had changed. Then he realized—her force field was down.

All this time, Leda had been holding herself at arm's length, at a stiff and safe distance from the world, and most of all from him. But now her shield was lowered, her electric fence switched off, every last barrier between the two of them zapped into oblivion. He felt as if he was looking at Leda for the first time in months.

Watt held his breath as she leaned in to kiss him.

The kiss was like a jolt of nitrogen, of electricity, dancing down every last nerve ending in his body. Her hands closed over his shoulders, slipping under the edges of his sweater, and where her bare skin touched his it felt somehow significant, like the imprint of her hand would be forever tattooed there. Leda's pulse was as erratic as his.

It astonished Watt how utterly *right* everything suddenly felt. Why had he wasted all those months spinning madly like a top, trying so desperately to forget Leda, when just touching her made the world seem so simple?

When she finally pulled away, Watt felt dazed. "I thought . . ."

"I changed my mind. Girls do that sometimes, you know." Leda smiled softly and leaned in to kiss him again.

# RYLIN

**"INBOX," RYLIN MUTTERED** yet again as she headed warily toward the monorail stop. Her contacts obediently pulled up her messages, but as before, there was nothing new from Hiral.

It was Thursday night, when Hiral would normally have been at work. Except that he had sent a cryptic message that afternoon, asking if Rylin could come meet him here.

She couldn't shake the sense that there had been something strange about Hiral's mood this past week. He'd been dodging her messages, had barely even looked her in the eye when she brought his favorite muffins over one morning before school. Whatever was on his mind, he clearly didn't want to share it with her.

Though she wasn't exactly sharing everything with him right now, either.

She turned onto the platform and saw him there, wearing a simple gray sweatshirt and jeans, a backpack slung carelessly over one shoulder. Maybe he'd packed a picnic, planned some kind of surprise excursion to the outer boroughs, Rylin tried to tell herself. She didn't quite believe it.

"Hey, you." She rose up to kiss him.

"Thanks for coming," Hiral said gruffly and shoved his hands in his pockets. "I'm glad you made it."

"Of course I made it," she replied, but Hiral didn't return her smile.

Rylin's eyes flicked up to the departures board, and a new dread twisted in her stomach. This monorail only went to the airport. "Hiral," she said slowly, "what's going on?"

"I'm leaving." He seemed to be speaking in as few words as possible, as if each syllable caused him unthinkable pain.

"Leaving? What are you talking about?"

"I wasn't going to tell you, except I had to say good-bye."

"Good-bye?" Rylin stumbled back a step, toward a vending machine illuminated with a coffee icon. The bitter scent of coffee grounds emanated from its surface. Her sense of foreboding had stretched itself into something much greater, something Rylin knew she wouldn't be able to fix.

"I'm leaving New York for good. I took a job on Undina, harvesting algae. My flight leaves in two hours," Hiral said quietly.

"What the *hell*?" Rylin cried out, her throat raw. "You decided to leave, with no input from me? We aren't even going to discuss this?"

Hiral frowned in confusion. "We did discuss it, and you made it clear that you didn't want to leave."

"That was barely a conversation!" This couldn't be happening. Was Hiral, the boy she'd known her entire *life*, really turning his back on everything?

"I'm sorry I didn't warn you, but I thought this was the right thing to do."

The monorail pulled up in a sudden and violent rush of air,

lifting Rylin's ponytail from the back of her neck. Hiral turned to watch its arrival, his eyes following its progress along the track, before turning back to her.

"So you're giving up," Rylin said slowly. "You didn't even give me a chance to fight for us."

"Rylin," he replied, "do you even *want* to fight for us?"

"Of course I do!"

The doors opened and people poured out of the monorail, flooding past Rylin and Hiral toward wherever they were headed. Rylin barely registered them, even when they bumped right into her. Her eyes were locked on Hiral's.

"I don't think that's true," he said heavily. "I think you know that we're over, just like I do."

"No! You don't get to just *decide* that we're over!" she cried out, attracting a few stares from passersby. Why was Hiral just standing here, looking at her with such defeated resignation?

Rylin was getting pretty sick of the boys in her life making decisions without bothering to consult her. They kept kissing her when she didn't want to be kissed, or *not* kissing her when that was all she wanted; hitting on her and breaking up with her; forcing her to steal drugs and sell drugs and then forgive the whole thing; pulling her this way and that until she was stretched unbearably thin. When did Rylin get to make up her own mind, for once? When would she get a damned say in any of it?

Hiral didn't get to just take their relationship into his own hands, with no thought for her. "You can't do this. You can't just walk away after everything we've been through," she insisted, with less vehemence.

"It's *because* of everything we've been through that I have to walk away. Because you deserve better!" Hiral exclaimed. "I'm sorry I didn't tell you my plan, okay? But I was worried that you might try to convince me to stay—and if you did, I knew it would be hard for me to say no to you." He let out a long breath. "I really need to leave."

"Why?"

Passengers began to board the monorail car, bringing with them their suitcases or babies, their regrets or hopes. Most of them were grinning with visible excitement, as if they couldn't wait to reach their destination, wherever it was.

Hiral hesitated. "I was in trouble. Last year before I was arrested, I ran up some debts with V and his supplier, a debt that I never really paid off."

Even though she was wounded and stung, Rylin felt her blood prickle on Hiral's behalf. "Never paid off? *You* were arrested and they weren't! How is that fair?"

"Who said any of this was fair?" he demanded. Rylin could tell that he hated to admit this to her. "I owed those guys a lot of money. I tried to pay it off bit by bit, but it wasn't fast enough for them. They kept pressuring me to deal again. They said if I didn't get the money, they would frame me, send me back to jail—and this time I wouldn't be found innocent. I would go to prison. For years, maybe."

"Oh, Hiral," Rylin breathed, reaching for his hands. "Why didn't you tell me?"

"I wanted so desperately to be worthy of you, Rylin. More than anything I wanted to hold myself to the promise I made you when we got back together. I swore that I wouldn't hurt you ever again."

The monorail was still waiting there, hushed and expectant, its eerie lights reflecting around the curved inside of its surface. Rylin felt a stab of panic. Those doors would only stay open another minute.

"We can figure this out," she said impulsively.

Hiral shook his head, gently detangling her hands from his.

"Your place is here, Ry. With Chrissa, going to college, studying holography. Becoming the person you deserve to be."

And Rylin knew that he was right, no matter how much it hurt.

He gave a brave smile. "Besides, I think I'm going to like Undina."

Rylin tried to picture Hiral there, in that enormous modular floating city located off Polynesia: living in employee housing, spending his days scraping algae from massive nets, his hair sun-kissed and shaggy. Making friends with all the other young people—there were thousands of them; Undina had a bottomless demand for labor. And it was its own sovereign nation, with no citizenship requirements: the natural destination for anyone who wanted to start over.

Anyone who wanted to leave their old life without a backward glance.

She realized, with a pang of regret, that he wasn't changing his mind. "I love you," she whispered.

"I know that you do. And I love you too. But I also know that I'm not enough for you."

The train's lights began flashing; it was about to pull out of the station. Hiral shot Rylin an anguished glance. "I hope I see you again someday," he said quickly. "But even if I don't, I'll always be thinking of you."

"Hiral, I—" she stammered as he pulled her close to kiss her one last time. Then he sprinted through the closing train doors.

Rylin's vision became blurry. She watched Hiral wave at her through the flexiglass as the monorail swooped off into the night, and he became just another silhouette in the window. Then he was gone.

It was a long time before Rylin finally made her way back home.

# WATT

**"I'M REALLY GLAD** you decided to stay." Watt leaned against the door, reluctant to say good-bye to Leda. He didn't want her to leave, didn't want this charmed moment between them to be over.

"I know. But I really have to go," she said, and smiled. There was a new bloom of color to her cheeks, a translucent liquid glow shining through her skin. When she was like this—when she was *happy*—Leda was more magnetic and beautiful than anyone in the world.

"Leda—"

She turned to him expectantly, and Watt swallowed. His throat felt dry.

"Thank you for trusting me again. For letting me back in."

Leda sighed and sank back onto his bed. She pulled up one leg to cross it over her ankle, seeming lost in thought. "Did I ever tell you why my parents sent me to rehab?" she murmured.

Watt shook his head.

Leda bit her lip and looked down, hunching her shoulders forward as if to ward off a blow. "After I learned that Eris was my half sister, I went to a really dark place, until one night I overdosed. I don't even remember what I took—I didn't actually think it was that much, but anyway . . ."

Leda's voice sounded haunted at the memory. "When I finally woke up, I was on top of my bed, fully dressed. I guess I'd cut myself at some point, because there was blood all over my shirt and on my hands. I didn't remember anything, Watt." She stared determinedly down to avoid looking at him. "I had no idea where I had been the past twenty-four hours."

"Leda. I'm so sorry." Watt remembered the hollow, haunted look in Leda's eyes when she'd come back from rehab and broke up with him. He had never realized how drastically she veered off the deep end.

*Watt*, Nadia's words cut into his consciousness. *You need to find out when this happened.*

He was so deeply shocked by Leda's story that he didn't even question Nadia. "When was this, Leda?"

"I don't know. A couple of days before I went to rehab. The first week of February, I guess?"

*Mariel died that week*, Nadia reminded him, very gently. *Leda has a block of time that she can't account for—after which she woke up covered in blood—during the same few days that Mariel was killed.*

There was a sudden ringing in Watt's ears, as if the entire world had spun wildly on its axis and then ground to an abrupt halt. *No.*

"Watt? What is it?"

Leda had gone on a horrific drug-fueled spiral after learning

196

that Eris had been her half sister—which was right around the time that Mariel had died.

Maybe Watt had seen this coming, in a blind, subconscious way, as if the truth were around a corner that he refused to turn. He thought of all those times he'd paused, thinking over Mariel's death—all those unsettling moments when the story hadn't quite fit, and how his mind lingered over it, puzzling out the pieces. The answer had been there, but Watt never saw it because he didn't *want* to see it.

*No*, he told himself again. He hadn't seen it because it was impossible. Leda was many things, ruthless and willful and passionate, but a cold-blooded killer wasn't one of them. He'd seen Leda push Eris; he knew she'd never meant to kill her—that it was an accident.

But now that the doubt was in his brain, he couldn't prevent it from worming even deeper. Wouldn't Leda do anything to protect the people she loved? If she thought Mariel was coming after her—if she thought Mariel was going to destroy Avery and Rylin and Watt—she might have killed Mariel in the middle of her wild, drugged-out bender and then blacked it out, her own mind shielding her from what she had done.

*Nadia*, he thought silently. *Are you saying that Leda might have killed Mariel and doesn't remember it?*

*I'm just pointing out the pieces of evidence, Watt. I'm not drawing any conclusions.*

Watt felt nauseous, but he had to ask.

"Leda. Do you think that *you* could have killed Mariel?"

# LEDA

**"WHAT ARE YOU** talking about?" Surely she had misheard.

"Mariel died the very same week that you were . . . unaccounted for," Watt said haltingly. "When we got back from Dubai, when you bought all those drugs."

"You think I faked an overdose so I could *kill* Mariel? You think I've been lying about it all this time?" she cried out, sitting up angrily.

"No, no," Watt scrambled to say. "I'm not suggesting that you *planned* to kill her. But maybe you were so messed up that you didn't even realize what you were doing. You might have run into her outside the Tower and remembered what she'd tried to do to you, and you were so afraid that you pushed her into the water. Or maybe she attacked *you*," he added, his eyes lighting up; he seemed to prefer that idea. "She could have come at you, trying to finish what she started, and you killed her in self-defense! You just don't remember because you blacked it out."

*No*, Leda thought wildly. It couldn't be.

Every one of her nerves was strumming at its highest, sharpest pitch. She put her hands on her knees, feeling dizzy. A horrible chthonic monster had stirred in the depths of her mind, a terrible, faceless fear—what if Watt was *right*?—but she wouldn't look at it right now; she couldn't or she would start screaming. She would face it later, when she couldn't see Watt's eyes.

"Leda, it's okay. Whatever happened, it'll be okay." Watt reached a tentative hand toward her, but Leda whirled on him. She was never fiercer or more cruel than when she felt cornered.

"How dare you?" she breathed. "You, of all people."

"Leda, I'm trying to help!"

"You told me earlier today that you see a goodness inside me that the rest of the world is too careless to see," she reminded him, her voice breaking. "And yet you think I'm capable of *killing* someone."

"I just wanted to ask if it was possible," Watt said helplessly. Leda threw up her hands.

"Why are you even asking me? I clearly have no idea; according to you, I've forgotten the whole thing. Ask the computer you keep in your brain. That's how you solve all your problems anyway!"

Watt flinched at that, but Leda hardly noticed; she was trembling.

"Don't worry. I'm leaving," she announced in a chilly, remote voice that didn't belong to her at all.

A small, foolish part of her hoped that Watt might run after her. But he just let her storm away in silence.

Somehow Leda made it home and into her own bed. She felt cold all over, the way she had felt in Dubai when Mariel left her to drown, as if fingers of ice were creeping up her spine. Her breaths came shallow and ragged.

Everything swirled through her mind at once, and she closed

her eyes, trying to make sense of it.

Could she have really killed Mariel and blacked it out?

Leda cast her mind back to that night. She'd been so devastated after Dubai, all she had wanted was to forget that she had killed her half sister. To wipe that knowledge brutally from her mind and start fresh.

*What a reckless, stupid thing to have done*, Leda thought. Forgetting never fixed anything. She remembered something Eris used to say when she drank until she blacked out. *If you don't remember it, it doesn't count.*

But this wasn't a drinking game or a sloppy dance-floor makeout, something to wince and laugh about the next day. If this had really happened, it was murder.

Was she capable of that—of *killing* a girl in cold blood? Even a girl who hated her and left her for dead?

Whatever she'd done that day, Leda only remembered it in flashes. She remembered being in class, thoughts of Eris chasing one another desperately around her mind . . . escaping to the park to meet her dealer, Ross . . . the hollow look of her eyes in a mirror somewhere, as she fumbled in her bag for another pill . . . lights, pulsing and sharp, as if at a club . . . Everything else was a sticky, dark blur.

Every instinct in Leda screamed at her not to push further. She was afraid of the truths she might find buried there. Still, she tried to dredge through her mind for the missing memory.

She imagined seeing Mariel outside near the river. Screaming at Mariel, pushing her into the water. Leda pinched her fingernails into the soft flesh of her leg until it brought tears to her eyes, *willing* herself to remember, but her mind remained stubbornly blank.

She so desperately wanted it to be impossible. But wanting to believe things wasn't enough to make them true.

Leda wished she could cry. It seemed almost worse this way, as if her grief lay in some foreign land, far past tears. A bottomless grief, opening like a dark chasm within her. She kept blinking, not sure if her eyes had dried out.

She collapsed back onto her coverlet and just lay there, staring numbly into the darkness, for what might have been an hour or might have been a minute, the way that time warps in strange ways when you're in pain. The house felt utterly still, and the stillness settled on Leda like a fine, cold mist. It chilled her to the bone. She felt miles away from any other warm, living thing; even though her parents were probably right here in the apartment, a few dozen meters away.

What stung the most was the fact that the accusation had come from Watt. Just when Leda had changed her mind, had decided to take a chance on him again, he'd proven that all her fears were right.

He knew what she was capable of and didn't hesitate to assume the worst of her. And really, could she blame him?

There was a gentle knocking at her door. "Leda, sweetie. Are you up?" her mom called out from the hallway. It seemed to Leda that her mom's voice emanated from another world, a world where Leda wasn't a hideous murderer.

If only her mom could take her to that world, so she could escape the horror she was currently living.

"Where were you?" Ilara asked.

"I was out. I think I'm getting sick," Leda replied, deliberately vague. Her mom started to come inside, but Leda raised her voice, sharpening it like a weapon. "Please, just *go*."

To her relief, Ilara didn't ask any more questions, and retreated.

It was for the best, Leda told herself. Confronting the monster within herself was a task that could only be done alone.

# CALLIOPE

**CALLIOPE SAT CONTENTEDLY** on the floor of her mom's closet, watching through half-lidded eyes as Elise packed for her honeymoon.

She had always found it oddly soothing, watching her mom pack a suitcase. It might have been the way Elise picked up various items—a flowy crepe de chine skirt, a pair of cropped jeans, a dangly pair of earrings—and sorted them into careful piles. The way she wrapped them, in delicate no-wrinkle paper, each shoe lovingly tucked into a padded bag. There was something comforting and ritualistic about it all, especially since packing a bag usually meant their con was drawing to a close. It was the last mile marker before they left town for good.

Calliope yawned and stretched her legs out before her. There was a linen-tufted bench that ran the length of the closet, but she didn't want to sit on it; the oyster-colored carpet was so soft and fluffy. She found herself surprisingly glad that Elise and Nadav had decided to wait a few days before leaving on their honeymoon. It was nice to have a moment alone with her mom.

Calliope just wasn't used to watching her mom actually *get married*. Although she'd been engaged fourteen times, Elise usually skipped town long before the actual ceremony, with the ring and any other gifts she could take with her. Only once before had she actually gone through with the wedding—to a Polish lord, with real papers of nobility—and Calliope felt certain that Elise had done it because she wanted to secretly call herself a lady for the rest of her life. It was the ultimate f-you to her old boss, Mrs. Houghton.

"Don't forget swimsuits," Calliope reminded her mom, trying to be helpful.

"I won't need a swimsuit, sweetie."

"There isn't even a hot tub in the Gobi Desert?"

"It's northern Mongolia," Elise corrected. "To visit the woolly mammoth reculturation center. We'll be volunteering on the steppe, helping dig up the permafrost that obstructs their grazing sites."

God, her poor mom had given that speech so many times, she practically believed her own con. "Sorry you couldn't convince Nadav to take you to Bali, or the Maldives." If her mom was going to actually be married to this guy, at least she should get a beach vacation out of it.

"Oh, I don't mind. And we're going to Japan for a few days afterward to relax."

"Japan, to *relax*? You hate it there!"

"Japan can be relaxing. All those zen gardens and tea ceremonies."

Calliope was surprised how hurt she felt at the idea of her mom having tea without her. "You made us leave Japan early the one time we went," she reminded Elise. "You said it was loud and chaotic, and impossible to navigate unless you speak Japanese."

"Nadav speaks Japanese."

It was the weirdest thing, but her mom actually seemed *excited* about this honeymoon. Maybe she was just ready to get away from all the madness of the wedding, and her ice queen of a mother-in-law. Calliope didn't blame her.

She felt guilty all over again for the sacrifice she had asked her mom to make: agreeing to stay here in New York, to trade their nomadic existence for a settled family life. Surely by now Elise was getting restless. Wasn't she counting down the days till it was all over?

Wasn't Calliope?

She thought briefly, longingly, of Brice—but then she remembered Livya, and that ominous threat she'd made at the wedding. There was no way Calliope would ever really get to date Brice, not with her new stepsister breathing down her neck.

*It doesn't matter*, she told herself, trying not to feel disappointed. Her flirtation with Brice had been just that—a flirtation. It hadn't meant anything.

Calliope stood up and wandered over to the marble-topped dresser where her mom was sorting a stack of ivory pajamas. She cleared her throat. "Mom, I don't know if this is worth it anymore."

"What do you mean, sweetie?"

"It's my fault that we're here. I'm the one who wanted to stay and actually live somewhere for once, play out this con for another year. But it's getting ridiculous. New York isn't worth this. *Nowhere* is worth this. We aren't even having any fun here—we're stuck pretending to be prim and proper and boring, just to maintain your meaningless relationship with Nadav!"

"It isn't meaningless," Elise said quietly, though Calliope didn't hear her at first.

"You shouldn't have to suffer through that awful honeymoon. Why don't we just leave? Besides, it's getting too risky. I think Livya—"

Elise took Calliope's hands in hers. "I don't want to leave," she said quietly.

Calliope blinked, stunned, as the truth hurtled inescapably toward her. It couldn't be.

"Surely you don't— I mean—" she stammered.

"I love him."

Calliope thought back to all her mom's girlish exclamations of delight, the starry-eyed way she'd looked at Nadav during the wedding. Had those smiles been real? "After all the times you told me *never* to let myself care about a mark?"

Her voice had risen too loud, but Elise didn't chide her. "I love Nadav," she stated simply. "This marriage is real. It isn't just a con to me, not anymore."

*This is just a job*, her mom used to say, in clipped, unsentimental tones. *It's temporary and unpredictable. Caring about people will only hurt you. Don't let it happen.* And now Elise, arguably the world's greatest con artist, was violating her own cardinal rule—and for who? A nerdy cybernetics engineer.

Calliope stared wonderingly at her mom, suddenly realizing just how drastically Elise had changed.

Of course, Elise had changed constantly over the years. As they moved from place to place, playing out their various cons, she'd been forced to keep altering her appearance: widening and then re-thinning her nose, changing her hair and eye color, tweaking the curve of her chin. She was always beautiful, yet each time her mom emerged from surgery with a new face and new irises, Calliope had to get used to her all over again.

This was completely different. This time, Elise had actually become someone new.

"How . . . ? I mean when . . . ?"

Elise sank down onto the bench with a sigh, pulling Calliope to sit next to her. "I don't know," she confessed. She looked suddenly girlish and innocent, the light gleaming on her pearl stud earrings. "Maybe it's that I've been with him for so long, much longer than I've been with anyone else. But I really care about him."

"Even though he thinks you're a goody-goody philanthropist?"

"Yes, even though he thinks I'm a goody-goody philanthropist," Elise repeated, in such a matter-of-fact tone that Calliope couldn't help laughing. She laughed at the sheer unlikely madness of it all, and after a moment Elise was laughing too.

"I don't understand," Calliope said at last. "How can you love him when you aren't even yourself with him? I mean, he thinks you actually *want* to spend your honeymoon volunteering, scooping up woolly mammoth poop!"

"I've had plenty of beach vacations in my life. I don't really need another one," Elise said, in a way that made it seem as if she truly didn't mind at all. *That must be real love*, Calliope thought wonderingly—being able to efface your own desires for the person you care about.

She wondered if she would ever feel that way about anyone. Brice's face rose stubbornly into her consciousness, but she quickly forced it away.

"It's really worth it to you?" she asked. "Staying in New York is worth playing this role forever?"

"Nadav is worth it," Elise corrected. "New York was always your thing. I like it here, but I wouldn't really care where we were, as long as I was with him."

It was so outlandish that it had to be true. *Wow*, Calliope thought again in silent shock. Sweet, fumbling Nadav: so well-meaning but gruff. Who would've guessed that Elise would end up falling for him?

"If you really love him, I'm happy for you," she decided, and was gratified by her mom's smile.

Then Calliope remembered what Livya had said to her at Saks and again at the wedding. Her heart sank.

She glanced down at her hands, clasped in her lap, her fingernails filed into careful half-moons and utterly devoid of polish—because of course nail polish, even nude colors, wasn't in character. "I think Livya suspects something."

"What do you mean?" Elise asked carefully.

"She confronted me while we were dress shopping and at the reception. She suggested that we're gold diggers, and that we aren't who we say we are." Calliope paused to let her well-trained eidetic memory kick in. "She said that most of the women who've dated Nadav in the past were just in it for the money, and that one of the reasons he loves you is because of how selfless you claim to be."

Her mom listened to this with surprising calm. "Any girl would say that about a stranger marrying her wealthy father. It doesn't sound like Livya really knows anything."

Calliope winced. "She did catch me sneaking out. Twice." She refrained from mentioning the fact that it was to see Brice.

"Then you can't sneak out again," Elise admonished. "Not with Livya watching us so closely. We can't afford to do anything suspicious."

Elise didn't have to spell it out for Calliope to know what she meant. Nadav's moral code was severe and uncompromising. If he learned the truth about them—that they were high-class grifters who'd left a string of broken hearts in their wake; that Elise had, in fact, first targeted Nadav for his money—he wouldn't just send them packing. He might very well send them to jail.

"Promise me you'll behave. Don't risk everything just because of some boy," Elise pleaded.

And even though she'd been telling herself that it meant nothing, that it was just a flirtation, Calliope bristled at her mom's words. "He isn't just some boy."

"I'm sorry, sweetie. But no more sneaking out, no more acting sarcastic or opinionated. Just keep your head down and act like the sweet, selfless girl that I told everyone you are," Elise asked. "It'll all be over in less than a year when you graduate. Then you can go off and be whoever you want to be. Please, for my sake, promise me."

Calliope sighed in resignation, watching as her reflection in the mirror did the same. For once, the sight didn't make her smile. "Why did you tell Nadav that we were philanthropists, again?"

"Because it was so clearly his type," Elise said softly and sighed. "I'm sorry this is such a mess. To think that of all the people we've conned, he is the one I ended up staying with."

"More like, of all the roles we've played, this is the one we ended up stuck with," Calliope exclaimed. "Why couldn't you have pitched us as something else? Eccentric heiresses to a shipping fortune, or bohemian artists, or what about French nobility? I loved that time we were comtesses."

"You were an appalling comtesse," Elise declared, and they both smiled wistfully at the memory.

"Poor Nadav, in love with a made-up character."

"Maybe I can change," Elise said with surprising vigor. "Maybe I can *become* the person he's fallen in love with, if I give it enough time."

Calliope wasn't sure that was the best foundation for a relationship, but what did she know? She'd never exactly had a real relationship either.

"Besides," Elise went on, "this way if you go to college next year, you'll actually have somewhere to come home to."

"College?" Calliope had never really considered it.

"What else are you going to do, start running cons by yourself?" Elise shook her head. "I don't want that for you."

Calliope didn't want that either. Yet she couldn't really picture herself in college, at least not in classes. Lounging around a coffee shop and scouting out boys, maybe. Flitting around parties and breaking hearts, definitely. Joining a sorority, rising to the top of its hierarchy, and ruling it with an iron fist, for sure. But actually going to classes and studying to *become* something? Calliope wouldn't even know where to start.

"I'll give college some thought," she said vaguely.

"Knock, knock," Nadav said, pushing open the closet door. Calliope barely refrained from rolling her eyes. Of course Nadav was the type of person who said *knock, knock* instead of just knocking.

"Are you almost packed? Oh, hi, Calliope," he added.

"I was just giving my mom some fashion advice," she said, standing up quickly.

"Good. I'm glad someone is doing that, since I'm definitely not qualified." *Another lame dad joke.* Nadav's gaze drifted to Elise, and he flashed an indulgent smile. "I just wanted to remind you that our plane leaves at six."

"I can't wait," Elise said warmly. She was gazing at Nadav with such affection that the intensity of it almost knocked Calliope backward.

She and her mom had lived so many lives through the years, casting off their used identities each time they moved, like last season's discarded clothing. But Nadav brought out another side of Elise: the happiest side of her, maybe even the best side. And if this was what her mom wanted, then Calliope would do everything in her power to help her get it.

She didn't even know Brice that well, so she wasn't sure why she was so disappointed to lose him. But it didn't matter. She wouldn't see him again.

She had to give him up, for her mom's sake.

# AVERY

**AVERY WAS SHOCKED** at the crowd that had showed up to watch the Fuller siblings' showdown. Though technically, she supposed, the showdown was only half theirs.

She'd never competed in Altitude Club's annual young members' tennis tournament before. She'd always found the whole thing showy and false, much more about the after-party than the tennis. It was all white pleated skirts and high, bouncing ponytails and passed cocktails—an excuse for the young members to carry their unused rackets in a false show of athleticism. But a few weeks ago, at Altitude brunch, Max had seen the tournament advertised on the flickering display screens.

"Mixed doubles! Come on, we're a great team."

"I don't really want to," Avery hedged. She thought longingly of those golden summer afternoons back in Oxford, when she and Max would play against their friends on the clipped emerald courts of the public park. The games were loose and carefree.

They never even kept score—the only thing they counted were the number of Pimm's they had consumed—and when they got tired of playing, they would settle on the grass with a basket of cheese and baguettes, to feast in the glorious liquid sunshine.

"You love tennis," Max had insisted. "What do we get if we win?"

"Nothing! Just our names on a plaque outside the locker room."

"You're telling me that you have the chance to win *eternal glory* and you're passing it up? Frankly, I'm shocked," he professed, which coaxed a smile from her.

"All right, fine," Avery had proclaimed, throwing up her hands in mock surrender. She knew that Max was just trying to distract her from all the stress of the election and college applications. It was sweet of him, although misguided.

At least she was heading back to Oxford soon. Avery had been invited to interview there, which was a good sign; only the top applicants were asked to interview on campus. And Max would be coming back with her for moral support.

It would be a weekend away, she kept telling herself, just like old times. She needed that. She could use a reminder of what she and Max had been like this summer, before he came to New York with her—before the election, before Atlas came home. Before he kissed her.

She hadn't realized that Atlas was planning on entering the tennis tournament too. But he did, partnering with his old friend Sania Malik, the same girl he'd taken to the Under the Sea ball last year, when he was trying to hide his secret relationship with Avery. In a strange turn of events, Sania was in Max's class at Columbia, and they were *friends*, which made this whole thing even weirder.

Avery kept hoping that Atlas and Sania would fall out of the competition. But to the entire club's surprise and delight, both of the Fuller pairs kept winning, climbing up their separate brackets until now they were facing off in the finals.

Now, standing against the baseline, Avery lifted her hand to shade her eyes. She'd never seen the stands of Altitude's Centre Court so packed; but then, people always did love a good family rivalry. Especially when that rivalry was in the family of the newly elected mayor.

She saw a lot of her classmates, though there was no sign of Leda. Every time Avery had tried to meet up with her lately, Leda had proclaimed that she was busy. Avery just hoped that busy meant *happy* or *with Watt*. If so, then Avery would gladly stop pestering her.

She clenched her palms tighter around her racket. Max glanced back over his shoulder and winked at her. "You've got this," he said softly. They had won the first set 6–4, but this one was much closer. Atlas and Sania seemed to have finally found their rhythm.

Avery nodded and looked across the court—directly into Atlas's eyes.

Something in them made her catch her breath. A look, a plea, something so fleeting that Avery couldn't even begin to make sense of it, just as the ball abruptly collided with the court near her feet. She blinked, startled. She had lost the set.

The announcer called their five-minute changeover period. On the other side of the court, Max was already grabbing his electrolyte drink, chatting easily with Sania. Avery watched in dazed fascination as they leaned in and snapped a selfie, as if this whole thing were casual, good-natured fun.

She stalked over to the hydration station on their side and grabbed a water. Atlas gave a rueful smile, nodding to where their parents sat in the bottom row of the stands, surrounded by eager well-wishers. "Mom and Dad clearly think this is hilarious," he remarked.

Something about the comment rankled Avery. "It *is* hilarious," she said tersely. "You being here, playing tennis against me, as if we're any old brother and sister who happened to make it to the finals. The new mayor's kids' epic showdown. What a hilarious joke," she spat, twisting angrily at the cap of the water bottle.

Atlas seemed saddened by her outburst. "You're the one who said to forget that anything ever happened with us. To act like normal siblings."

Normal siblings. As if they could ever go back to that.

"I'm sorry, I just . . ." she said helplessly as the buzzer sounded.

It wasn't *fair* of Atlas to do this to her. She'd been doing just fine before he came back to town and threw everything into disarray. Why couldn't he have stayed on his side of the world?

But she hadn't been fine, a small voice inside her whispered. She hadn't been fine since the moment she set foot back in New York, and all her old problems came rushing back to meet her.

There was a slight buzz near her head as Avery lined up along the baseline. Another zetta, hoping to get a good shot for whoever was watching on the feeds. *All right*, she thought, suddenly angry. If they wanted to see flawless, famous Avery Fuller, she might as well give them a show.

Avery tossed the ball into the air and incinerated it with her serve. The shot whipped past Sania before the poor girl could react. Avery felt oddly gratified by the startled expression on Atlas's face.

She kept on playing like that, fueled by a hot, queasy adrenaline. She played so fiercely that she was no longer thinking, not about Atlas or Max or her parents' laughter or the blurred, painted faces of the crowd. It felt good to shut down her brain like this, to become nothing but a bundle of fast-twitch nerve endings in a shiny package.

She won one game after another with almost no assistance from Max, who tried a few times to make a shot or two, only to interfere with the blaze of her warpath. Eventually he stood aside and just let Avery play the game herself. Across the court, Sania had done the same.

But that was how she'd wanted it, wasn't it? A singles match, her versus Atlas?

She won the remaining games one after the other, stacking them neatly in a row, until suddenly it was match point. When the ball came toward her, Avery barreled it across the court at full force. Atlas barely managed to hold up his racket, sending the ball straight into the net.

Avery forced her lips to curl into a smile. She walked up to the net to thank Sania and Atlas, trying to ignore the bright, hot yells of the crowd.

Atlas didn't say anything when they shook hands. He barely touched her at all.

"Damn, you really turned up the heat out there! I don't think I've seen that side of you before." Max threw an arm around Avery's shoulders and leaned in, his breath warm in her ear. "It was kind of a turn-on, seeing you get that competitive."

Avery nodded and smiled mechanically. Max probably still thought that he'd helped take her mind off things. She didn't have the heart to tell him that she only felt worse.

People began swarming onto the court in congratulations, a million grinning faces seeming to leer up at her. A white tent had been set up nearby—only at Altitude did they feel the need to pitch a tent indoors—where pink champagne was being passed on engraved trays.

Avery couldn't help looking over at Atlas.

When their eyes met he gave a sad smile, and the sight of it turned Avery's victory to ashes in her mouth. Unlike everyone else here, Atlas knew her. He *knew* what that display on the court had meant, how strangely unsettled Avery was feeling. And he knew that he was the reason.

Avery couldn't take his eyes on her anymore. She rose on tiptoe to kiss Max, letting her racket clatter dramatically to the ground as she wrapped her arms very publicly around him, drawing out the kiss much longer than she needed to.

When she finally stepped away, her eyes darted reflexively to Atlas. He was retreating toward the Altitude Club exit. She realized, with a flush of shame, that it was exactly what she had intended.

"Ready to go in?" Max asked good-naturedly, with a nod to the party.

Avery nodded, holding tight to his hand like a lifeline. She *needed* Max right now, to reassure her that she was still here, still herself. That she was the Avery Fuller he knew and loved, and not the broken girl who Atlas had left in his wake all those months ago.

# LEDA

**EVERYTHING FELT WRONG** to Leda these days.

She stumbled through the world at the center of a cloud of wrongness, which seemed to pervade everything, closing its fingers stealthily around her throat. The ground felt unsteady beneath her, like the surface of a ship, like melting quicksand.

It was the same as last year, when she came back from Dubai with the knowledge that Eris had been her half sister—except that this time it was *worse*, because this time Leda had no idea what she had done. Could she have truly killed Mariel and blacked it out? Why did the world keep doing this to her, piling one brutal revelation atop another until she couldn't stand it?

All she wanted was to forget. To fight back against the dark cloud with a cloud of her own.

So at lunch on Monday, instead of sitting with Avery in the cafeteria, Leda retreated to the secret garden.

The garden wasn't actually secret; that was just what the

elementary school kids called it. Tucked along the inner border of campus, it stretched long and narrow behind the lower school cafeteria, fed by enormous sun-bulbs overhead. It was technically part of Berkeley's sustainability initiative, to keep the school up to oxygen input-output codes. But Leda had also found that it was the easiest place on campus to be alone—especially when what you wanted to do alone was smoke up.

Autumn had always been her favorite time of year in the garden. In the spring it was too pastel, and in the winter it was even worse, with all those white-and-red candy cane plants and holographic gingerbread men running around for the little kids. But right now the garden was a rich explosion of fall colors, not just brown, but reds and oranges and occasionally a smoky forest green. The leaves crunched pleasantly underfoot. Balloon pumpkins—which had been genetically engineered to be less dense than air—floated at waist height, tethered to the ground by their gnarled green stalks. As Leda walked, the pumpkins bobbed a little in her wake.

She turned the corner, past the massive golden beehive and a burbling fountain, to station herself beneath an air vent. It was barely perceptible from the ground, since the ceiling was nine meters high—you had to be really know what you were looking for to even notice that it was up there.

Leda's hands shook as she fumbled in her bag for her gleaming white halluci-lighter, the tiny compact pipe that you could smoke almost anything in. Her chest felt like a bundle of twitching wires. She touched the pipe to the heat pad on the edge of her beauty-wand, gently toasting the weed within. Nothing fancy, just your usual marijuana-serotonin blend, because god help her, she needed a little kick of happiness right now.

Leda inhaled deeply, letting the smoke curl delicately into her lungs, suffusing her with an instant warmth. Suddenly, she wished someone were here with her. Not Watt—she was still stung by his accusation, and hadn't answered any of his pings since she'd run away from his room. She didn't know when she would be able to face him.

Still, she wouldn't hate having *someone* here right now, just to hear another voice. She was always at odds these days; when she was alone she wanted to be with other people, and when she was with other people she just wanted be alone.

Footsteps sounded on the flagstones. Leda quickly twisted her arm behind her back to hide the halluci-lighter, cursing, because the smell was definitely still there—

Then she saw who it was, and let out a disbelieving laugh.

"Since when do *you* skip lunch to come smoke?" she asked Rylin, a challenging edge to the question.

Rylin strode over and reached for Leda's halluci-lighter. She took a single slow breath, with the cool composure of someone who had done this many times before, then nonchalantly exhaled the smoke into a perfect green O. *Totally badass*, Leda thought grudgingly.

"I don't know if it counts as skipping lunch if I actually came here to eat," Rylin replied, holding up a recyclable go-bag from the cafeteria. She settled on the lower step of the fountain, her plaid skirt fanning out over her lap, and unfolded the waxy sandwich paper.

Leda smiled in spite of herself. Even though they went to the same school, she hadn't seen much of Rylin this year, except, of course, for that emergency meeting at Avery's. She found herself wishing that they had stayed better friends after that brief truce in Dubai. Leda would never have admitted it aloud, but she saw something of herself in Rylin's no-nonsense attitude, her deeply private nature, her impatience with the world's conventions.

She sank down next to Rylin and tucked her legs behind her mermaid-style, still clutching the halluci-lighter in one hand. When Rylin wordlessly held out half her sandwich, Leda took it with a nod of thanks. She hadn't realized how hungry she was.

They sat for a while like that, the silence broken only by the crunch of the crispy pretzel bread, the occasional listless puff of the abandoned halluci-lighter. Leda offered the pipe to Rylin again, but to her surprise, the other girl shook her head.

"Smoking isn't really my thing anymore, after . . ."

"After Cord broke up with you for stealing his drugs?" Leda prompted, then cringed at the callousness of the wording. "I didn't mean—"

Rylin waved away the apology. "Yeah, that. Also, after my ex-boyfriend got arrested for dealing."

"Sorry. I had no idea." Leda twisted the halluci-lighter back and forth in her hands.

Rylin glanced over. "Are you okay, Leda?"

The simplicity of the question nearly broke Leda's self-control. People didn't do that often enough—just look at each other and ask *Are you okay?*

"Did you bomb the SATs or something?" Rylin guessed.

"The SATs?" Leda's college applications felt oddly detached from her, as if they had never really belonged to her in the first place. So much of what she had wanted before felt that way now. Watt's revelation seemed to have cleaved the world into two universes: the one where she was just Leda, and the one where she might be a killer.

No, she corrected, *might be a killer* was the wrong way to put it. She already knew she was a killer. She had killed Eris.

But instead of confronting what she'd done, Leda had tried to bury it every way she knew how—by blackmailing people to keep the secret for her, by doing drugs until she blacked out. She had turned forcibly away from the truth, even when the truth literally dragged her to the brink of death.

"Is it about the Mariel investigation?" Rylin tried again.

Leda glanced over at her. Strangely, she wasn't afraid of discussing this with Rylin. They were already so inextricably bound together, each in possession of the other's secret. And Rylin—more than Avery with her picture-perfect life; more even than Watt, who walked around with a computer in his *brain*—would understand what it felt like to be lost.

"Sort of," Leda admitted, and tossed the pipe aside. "I've done some really shitty things, you know."

"News flash, Leda, we all have."

"But these are mistakes I can't undo! I can't make it right! How do you live with yourself after something like that?"

"You live with yourself because you have to." Rylin stared into the refracted blue surface of the fountain. "You forgive yourself for what you've done. It can only kill you when you try to run from it. If you just look it in the eye and face it, it becomes part of you, and it can't hurt you anymore."

Leda looked down. She had folded the empty wax paper over and over, into a tiny triangle. "You have a sister, don't you? What's it like?"

"Having a sister?"

"Yes."

Rylin bit her lip. "A sister is a built-in best friend. She knows me better than I know myself, because she's lived my life alongside me, and helped me through the best and the worst of it," she said. "We fight, but no matter what I say, I know that Chrissa will always forgive me."

Rylin's words fell into Leda's mind, and burned where they landed. That was what having a sister *should* be like. And instead, Leda had killed hers.

"I have to go," Leda said abruptly. There was something important she needed to take care of.

But before she reached the entrance to the secret garden, Leda paused. "One more thing," she added. "What were you doing hiding down here during lunch instead of sitting with Cord?"

"I—I have a lot going on—" Rylin stammered.

"I've seen you two dancing around each other all year. Can you please give it a shot? For my sake, if nothing else." Leda smiled. "I could really use something to root for."

---

Later that afternoon, Leda took the monorail to Cifleur Cemetery, in New Jersey.

It was cold out, the Tower looming over the water like a dusky shadow. She paused to look in the floral vending machine at the cemetery's gates, but everything inside felt too trite, all white wreaths tied with satin bows. Leda quickly logged on to her contacts and ordered something that was much more Eris: a profusion of oversized vivid blooms, with a few incandescents tucked in, twinkling like fireflies. The flowers appeared by drone-drop within minutes.

Leda had been to Eris's grave only once: the day that Eris was buried. She realized with a mortified pang that this visit was overdue.

"Hey, Eris," she began, her voice ragged. This stuff didn't come easily to her. "It's Leda. But, um, maybe you knew that already."

A hologram flared to life before her, and Leda stumbled back a step. It was an image of Eris, standing before her headstone, waving and smiling like a prom queen greeting her subjects. Leda assumed the holo was voice-activated, by the use of Eris's name.

She took a breath, trying to get over the weirdness of seeing hologram-Eris here. "I brought you some flowers," she said, setting down the bouquet. It had a heady, dusky scent that Eris would have liked. Actually, knowing Eris, she would have plucked a rosebud from the arrangement, tucked it behind one ear, then promptly forgotten all about it.

It would have been Eris's birthday that week. Leda wished so fervently that she were still here. Leda would have thrown her a party, complete with those bubbles of champagne Eris had loved so much—hell, an entire *blimp* full of champagne.

She knelt awkwardly before the headstone, as if she were in church. Her eyes darted over every last detail of holographic Eris, desperate to find something they had in common, some proof of their shared DNA.

She remembered the day she'd first met Eris. It was in seventh grade, back when Leda was still silent and invisible, before she'd mustered up the confidence to approach Avery. Leda and Eris were both in the children's theater club, which was performing *The Little Mermaid*. Eris, unsurprisingly, had been cast as the mermaid.

Half an hour before their first show, Leda was checking the prop table backstage when she heard Eris's voice emanating from a dressing room. "Is anyone out there? I need help!"

"What is it?" Leda pushed open the door, only to find Eris standing inside, completely topless.

"I can't get this to fasten." Eris held out her glittery shell bra, utterly unselfconscious. Even back then she was all curves and smiles. Behind her glimmered a holographic tail, projected from a single-process beam on the back of a headband.

"I'll find you some insta-stick." Leda had darted out of the closet, painfully aware of her bulky sea anemone costume.

As the years went by, the two girls saw each other more, drawn together as they were by the common thread of Avery.

But Leda had never really understood Eris. Eris seemed to flit around like a firefly, always coming up with some wild and impractical idea, dragging her friends on adventures from which she alone bounced back unscathed. She fell recklessly in and out of love, laughed when she was happy, dissolved into public tears when she was upset. It had seemed so foolish to Leda, who did everything in her power to *conceal* what she was feeling. But she saw now that it was brave, in its own way—wearing your heart on your sleeve like that.

What would things have been like if Eris hadn't died? If instead of pushing her, Leda had taken her hand and actually *listened*? Perhaps they would have joined forces and gone to talk to their dad together. Perhaps by now they would be doing all those things Rylin had talked about—supporting each other, trusting each other, sharing their fears and secrets.

Accident or not, Leda had killed her half sister, then forced all the witnesses to help cover it up. What kind of sister did that?

"Eris. I'm so sorry. I never meant to hurt you. I can't believe that I'm here and you aren't. I wish . . ." Leda faltered, because there were so many things she wished, she could never list them all. "I wish we could start over."

She had tried so hard, for so long, to avoid thinking of what she'd done to Eris—to amputate that part of herself and start over. But the damage was still there, buried deep within her like scar tissue. Real grief left that kind of mark on you.

The only way to heal from grief like that was roughly: step by clumsy step, as you muddled your way back toward some form of peace, or redemption, or forgiveness, if you were lucky enough to get it.

Leda couldn't change what had happened, couldn't bring Eris or Mariel back to life. She could only do the best she could from now on. Whatever that was.

The holo seemed to flicker for a moment, almost as if it were nodding. Leda couldn't look at it anymore; she waved her hand through it to dispel it. Now it was just her, alone in the hushed shadows of the cemetery. Which she deserved.

Leda closed her eyes and kneeled before Eris's headstone, her head bowed in prayer. It had been a long time since she prayed like this.

But if anyone needed a prayer right now, it was her.

# CALLIOPE

**"WE MISS YOU** girls!" the holographic image of Elise exclaimed, from where she was projected over the coffee table like a ghostly apparition—if ghosts appeared in high-res safari attire. She and Nadav were at the woolly mammoth camp in Mongolia, bundled up in scarves and dirty hats, grinning ear to ear.

At least these daily pings from the happy couple would end soon. Calliope couldn't take them anymore.

"We miss you too! It looks like such rewarding work." Livya edged imperceptibly farther from Calliope on the couch, wearing her school uniform and her usual sticky-sweet smile.

"It's so cool of you guys to use your honeymoon as an opportunity to give back, rather than to celebrate yourselves," Calliope gushed, never one to be outdone.

"I know. It was all your mom's idea." Nadav exchanged a smile with Elise. "She has the biggest heart of anyone I've ever met."

*Only if her heart is in proportion to her cleavage,* Calliope thought, trying to amuse herself. *Then it is definitely big.*

"Livya," Nadav went on, "is your grandmother there?"

"She's right here! Say hi, Boo Boo," Livya simpered, reaching for the vid-cam and angling it toward Nadav's mother.

"Hello, Nadav. I hope you don't get sick in that freezing weather," Tamar said implacably. She didn't even bother to acknowledge Elise.

Tamar would be staying here, living in Calliope's room, until Nadav and Elise returned—she was literally babysitting the two eighteen-year-old girls. Calliope thought the whole thing was ludicrous. Even worse was the fact that she now had to share a room with her stepsister. That first night, Calliope had taken one look at Livya's queen-sized bed and decided instead to inflate the insta-mattress, mumbling that she snored. No way in hell was she sharing a *bed* with Livya. She would probably wake up with a knife in her back.

Even though they slept in the same room, Calliope and Livya had barely spoken since the wedding. They behaved like a pair of queens presiding over warring dominions from a joint palace.

"Have a great night, girls!" Nadav butted his face before the projector so, from their end, he seemed to hover before them like a disembodied head.

"Be safe!" Calliope waved good-bye just as a flicker came through on her contacts. *Are you still under house arrest?*

It was from Brice.

Calliope quickly turned aside and logged on to her tablet. No way could she answer this as a flicker. Livya would hear her whispered reply and know precisely what she was up to.

*Unfortunately,* she typed back.

Brice had flickered her a few times since the wedding, and each time, she'd pretended that she was grounded. It made her sound completely lame and high-school, but it was essentially the truth.

Calliope couldn't bring herself to reply the way she knew she should, the way Elise would want her to—with a snide dismissal, making Brice think that she no longer cared about him. Because she did care about him.

Even if she couldn't see him, at the very least she could keep *communicating* with him.

*Don't forget our bet. You owe me dinner,* Brice replied.

Calliope bit back a smile, which would certainly have given her away. *We never technically made that bet. I don't recall shaking on it.*

*A verbal agreement is binding in the state of New York.*

*In that case, I owe a lot of people a lot of things that I never delivered on,* she couldn't resist answering.

*Don't change the subject,* he chided. *Your mom and Nadav are out of town. It's just dinner. What do you have to lose?*

Calliope hesitated, her tablet pulled close to her chest. She knew she was playing a dangerous game. If she wasn't careful, someone would post a snap of them—or worse, mention to Nadav that she had been out with Brice. But how would that happen? Brice and Nadav didn't have any friends in common. It wouldn't do any harm, would it, as long as Livya and Nadav never found out?

She stood up and started toward the living room door.

"You're going out." Livya's voice was trenchant with accusation.

Calliope tossed her hair over one shoulder in cool unconcern. "I'm going to the hospital to read in the children's wing. You're welcome to join me," she added. It was risky, but Calliope knew that Livya had her violin tutor tonight.

"Maybe next time. If there is a next time," Livya replied in a tone that indicated her clear disbelief. Calliope didn't let it slow her down.

————————

She had never been to the Captain's Bar at the Mandarin Oriental before. Which was unusual, given that Calliope prided herself on knowing all the hotel bars in every city she had ever visited. But this wasn't her typical sort of bar. She cast a low, pioneering glance around its deep leather couches and burnished silver mugs, covered in warm shadows. In the corner, a woman in a black gown sang a throaty ballad, something poignant and full of longing.

Yes, everything was high-end and expensive, but definitely not young or glamorous. This was the type of bar intended for serious conversation or serious drinking, or both.

She positioned her elbows on the varnished surface of the bar and took another sip of her champagne, waiting for Brice. He had flickered to tell her that he was running a few minutes late. Not that Calliope really minded. There was something fun about sitting alone at a bar—the way her feet dangled over the edge of the barstool, making it feel as if she were floating. The soft layers of noise, the choreographed dance of the bartenders moving back and forth. The bubbles in her champagne glass rose in an eager stream to the surface, reminding her of the bubbles from the wisher. She felt incognito in a pleasant, tingly way.

"Sorry I'm late." Brice slid onto the barstool next to her.

"I don't mind. I actually like sitting alone at hotel bars."

"Because of the excellent people watching?" Brice nodded at their mostly empty surroundings.

Calliope shrugged. "No one expects anything of you at a hotel—no one cares who you are or where you came from. I've always thought of hotel bars as miniature foreign embassies. A place you can seek asylum, if you need it."

"I can't imagine you needing to run from anything," Brice joked, at which Calliope fell silent. She had run away from every place she'd ever visited, hadn't she?

Brice waved over a bartender. "Two ginger smashes," he ordered, and pushed Calliope's champagne to one side. "If you're coming to the Captain's Bar, you should do it right."

Calliope tossed her head, letting her earrings dance. "I believe it was Napoleon who said that champagne is never a bad idea."

"You're quoting a notorious dictator. Why am I not surprised," Brice deadpanned, and Calliope laughed.

Their drinks arrived in a pair of enormous silver tankards. They were a deep amber color, made with crushed ice and a stick of ginger wedged at the top.

Calliope leaned forward to take a sip of the cocktail. It was sweet and spicy all at once. "Did you know these mugs are actual sunken treasure?" she heard herself say. "Apparently they sat for centuries on the ocean floor before the Mandarin retrieved them from the wreck of a Spanish galleon."

"What a fantastic story. It would be even better if it were true." Brice lifted an eyebrow. "You're very good at making up stories."

Calliope felt instantly foolish. She shouldn't be doing this, letting her compulsive lying streak get the better of her. She was more of a professional than that.

"I was thinking we could do dinner at Altitude, if that works for you," he went on, after a moment.

Calliope bit her lip. Altitude was one of the places that she and Brice definitely could not go. Far too many people there knew the Mizrahis—people who might casually remark to Nadav or Livya that they had seen Calliope out with Brice.

She opened her mouth to deliver some excuse, to say that

she'd already been to Altitude twice this week and was sick of it. But the words congealed in her throat.

"Actually, it would be better if we didn't."

Brice tapped his fingers lightly on the table. His hands looked strong and surprisingly callused. "Okay," he said levelly.

"It's just—my family doesn't want me seeing you. They don't want me doing anything like this, really," she added, gesturing to her outfit, a low-cut black halter dress and startling red paint-stick. "They want me to be more like my stepsister."

"And since when are you the type of girl who does what she's told?"

"It's complicated."

"I just don't understand why you're trying so hard to be someone you're not," he insisted.

"You wouldn't understand." *You don't know what it's like to constantly play pretend. To trade in falsehoods—false identities, false alarms, false hopes—all to gain something that you aren't even sure you want anyway.*

"Explain it to me, then." Brice studied her, his deep-blue eyes shadowed with a question, and Calliope realized with a start that he might, possibly, care about her. She felt thrilled and terrified at once.

"My mom fell in love with Nadav, and it turns out he's really strict. I don't want him to realize that I'm not the girl he thinks I am, and regret marrying my mom," she said haltingly. "I just want them to be happy."

"He's so strict that he won't even let you go on dates?" Brice asked, incredulous.

"Not with you," Calliope said, then immediately worried she'd gone too far.

"Once again, my reputation precedes me." Brice said it

jokingly, but underneath, Calliope heard a vein of sadness. "Where did you say you were going tonight, rescuing puppies at the animal shelter?"

"Close. Reading to children at the hospital." Calliope realized, as she said it aloud, how ridiculous it sounded. But how else could she have gotten out of the apartment?

"Did your mom date anyone else, before Nadav?" Brice asked.

*You have no idea.* "A few people," Calliope evaded. "No one very serious."

"What happened to your dad?"

She looked down into her drink, idly stirring the surface with the stick of ginger. "We don't really talk about him. He left when I was a baby."

"You aren't curious about him?"

"No," she said defensively, then sighed. "I used to be, though. When I was little, my mom and I played this game—every time I asked her where my dad was, she gave a different answer. One day she would say that he was a doctor and was busy curing some terrible disease. The next day, that he was an astronaut living in the colony on the moon, or that he was a famous actor, busy filming his next movie."

"Now I know where you get your flair for the dramatic," Brice said with false lightness.

"There was always a different answer, no matter how many times I asked the same question. But none of those million answers were true. I guess eventually I stopped caring. What did it matter, anyway? We were perfectly happy without him, just the two of us. Except it isn't just the two of us anymore," she added in a softer voice.

"I know the feeling," Brice said quietly. "I'm very used to it being just the two of us—just me and Cord. Which was why I refused to let our aunt and uncle from Brazil adopt us after my parents died."

"You did?" Calliope hadn't known that.

"Yeah," Brice said gruffly. "They wanted us to leave everything behind, move to Rio. But we didn't need them, you know? I could tell, even back then, that Cord and I were just fine on our own."

Of course the Andertons could afford to take care of themselves financially. And yet Calliope's heart went out to them, two boys trying to live on their own, with no adult guidance. No amount of money could make up for that.

"I didn't mean to upset you about Nadav," Brice apologized. "I think it's great that you care so much about your mom's happiness."

"Thanks." Calliope was suddenly afraid that she'd said too much. She kept offering these real, unvarnished reactions to Brice, allowing a dangerous amount of her real self to bleed through. It just felt like such an unexpected relief, lowering the weighty shield of her public persona and actually telling the truth for once.

"I guess I didn't understand why you were trying so hard to be anonymous, when you could be the one and only Calliope Brown." Brice gave a verbal flourish to her name, like a sportscaster, and she broke into a smile. "How did you end up with a name like Calliope, anyway?"

"I— My mom wanted me to be a goddess," Calliope replied, almost slipping up, because *Calliope* was a name she had chosen for herself. Her real name she kept secret, as if it were imbued with some intrinsic and mystical power.

"In that case, it fits you perfectly."

They sipped their drinks for a while longer, letting the

sounds of the bar settle over them, talking about slightly less loaded topics—Brice's work and the recent mayoral election. Eventually Calliope realized that her mug was empty.

"So, not Altitude," Brice declared. "Where should we go for dinner, then? Maybe Revel?"

Calliope started to nod, but some perverse instinct made her pause. "Actually, I was hoping we could try Hay Market."

Brice laughed. "Hay Market has a two-month waiting list. I don't think we'll get in, even if I try to bribe the maître d'."

Calliope knew that. Hay Market was the hottest new restaurant in the Tower, which was exactly why she had picked it. She wanted to walk into a glamorous, exclusive restaurant on the arm of a dangerously good-looking boy—a boy she was starting to like far too much.

And she was in the mood to show off a little.

"You'll get in because you're with me," she promised.

Brice opened his mouth to protest, but Calliope lifted a finger to her lips, already pinging the restaurant. "I'm going to need a table for two, right away. Under Alan Gregory," she said, settling into the con with familiar ease. Her voice had instantly transformed into something clipped and businesslike, utterly unlike her typical low, throaty tones.

Ah, it felt so good to tell these small lies, to dance lightly around the edges of the truth. To force the world to bend to her will, just a little bit.

"He'll need the full tasting menu, of course," she said, over the hostess's stammered protests. "No, not the window. The table by the fireplace. Thank you."

Brice shook his head, his eyes glinting with admiration. "You never do anything halfway, do you?"

"Would you still be here if I did?"

"Dare I ask, who is Alan Gregory?"

"The *London Times* food critic," Calliope declared with a self-satisfied smirk.

Brice was intrigued enough to slide off his barstool and follow her toward the door. "And what happens when the chef comes out and realizes that I'm not Alan Gregory?"

"I guess he'll have to be happy with Brice Anderton," Calliope replied, the old theatrical smile creeping onto her face. "I know I am."

# AVERY

**"I'M SORRY OUR** date night ended up becoming a fashion show," Avery apologized, stepping into yet another gown—her fifteenth, if she hadn't lost count.

"Trust me, watching you get dressed and undressed dozens of times is a pretty good date night." Max looked at her with unabashed approval, and a warm flush traveled from the base of Avery's spine up to her cheeks.

"Can you zip me up?" She gestured behind her, and Max obediently pulled up the zipper.

They were in Avery's bedroom, which had been completely taken over by racks of black-tie gowns: her various options for the inauguration ball later this month. Almost every designer in America, and a good number of international designers, had sent over a sample dress for her to try.

Avery wasn't used to "trying on" dresses this way. Normally when she shopped, she projected clothing designs onto a holographic scan of her body; and then if she liked it, the garment was made to order. This was different, because she hadn't ordered a single one of these dresses. The designers had custommade them for her on spec, each hoping that theirs was the gown she would pick.

And Avery had to make up her mind now, because tomorrow a photographer was coming to the thousandth floor to photograph her. Apparently she would be the central image of next month's *Vogue* download.

She turned toward the wall of her bedroom, which she'd clicked over to mirror mode, and studied the dramatic runway gown that now spilled over her. It was a bright, fluorescent orange.

"I look like a safety sign." Avery gave a strangled laugh.

"The most beautiful safety sign in the history of intersections." Max wrapped his arms around her to hug her from behind. His eyes were warm, catching the scattered light.

"Thank you, Max. For everything," she said softly. He had been a source of steadiness throughout the turmoil of the campaign.

She was glad that he would be there next week, when she interviewed at Oxford. She could use a little of his unflappable calm.

"I love you," she said impulsively and spun around to kiss him.

She kissed his cheeks and his forehead and the spot in the cleft of his chin that was darkened by a shadow of scruff: a rainfall of little kisses at first. Then she was kissing his mouth, and his arms had curled around her back, and it wasn't so light anymore.

The sound of footsteps outside Avery's door forced them quickly apart. "Mom?" she asked, hesitant.

The footsteps paused. "Did you need something?" she heard

Atlas say, and her chest constricted, because she hadn't meant to invite Atlas in at all.

"It's fine. Sorry, I—"

But Max had jumped up, throwing open Avery's door with an eager grin. "Atlas!" he exclaimed, oblivious to the tension between them. "I didn't realize you were back! How are you?"

Atlas looked distinctly uncomfortable. He'd jetted off to San Francisco earlier this week, ostensibly for business, though Avery felt certain that it was to get away from her. She hadn't even seen him since their showdown at the Altitude tennis courts.

She made a slow half turn toward the doorway, the voluminous orange skirts swinging widely around her like a bell.

"Hey, Max," Atlas said evenly; and because she had known him since they were children, because she could read every last shred of emotion in his expression, Avery knew the meaning that Atlas was trying to convey with those two words. They were a peace treaty with her.

Max glanced back at Avery. "Do you mind if I head home now, Avery? I have so much studying to do before exams. Not that I didn't enjoy the fashion show, but we both know I'm useless at this. You're in much better hands with Atlas."

"Of course I understand. Good luck." She leaned forward to plant a kiss on the corner of Max's mouth, deliberately ignoring Atlas. "Let me know if you want me to come by later for a study break." There were volumes of innuendo in the way that Avery pronounced *study break*.

"Sounds great," Max said with a wicked grin. Then he was gone, and it was just Avery and Atlas alone in her bedroom.

"You don't have to stay," she said quickly. "I'm sure you have more important things to be doing right now."

"I don't mind," Atlas replied. Avery thought she heard a hint of challenge in that statement, but couldn't be sure.

She glanced away. Her reflection bloomed like a flower from the mirror-screen, garish and repulsive, covered in all those yards of heavy orange fabric. She felt suddenly desperate to get out of the dress, as if it were literally crushing her. Avery reached behind her back to fumble for the zipper pull but couldn't twist her arm to reach it. She let out a cry of desperation—

"Hey, it's okay," Atlas murmured, pulling down the zipper. He was very careful not to let his skin brush hers.

As she turned back around, Avery saw a flash of pink on the flesh of Atlas's inner arm, and gasped.

"What?" he demanded.

"What happened?" Without thinking, Avery reached out to trace the scar, an angry red half-moon near Atlas's elbow. He held very still as her fingers brushed over the mark.

She knew his body so perfectly, even after all this time. She had long ago memorized him—every last one of his scars and freckles, on every last inch of his skin. But she didn't recognize this one.

"I burned myself," Atlas said quietly.

Suddenly Avery realized what she was doing, touching Atlas in this intimate way. She caught herself and retreated. Her gown was still hanging open at the back; she crossed her arms over her chest. "They don't have derma-repair in Dubai?"

"Maybe I wanted to leave it. Maybe I think it looks badass," Atlas said lightly.

Avery rustled into her closet to take off the offending gown, slipping into a robe and sweatpants before returning to the bedroom. Atlas was still there.

"Are you okay, Aves?"

Hearing the familiar nickname made her oddly sad. She swallowed. "Do you remember those forts we used to build when we were little?"

She and Atlas used to construct elaborate forts in the living room, pushing the furniture together, topping it with piles of pillows and sheets. If their mom caught them, she would invariably freak out—*Do you know how expensive these silk pillows are? Now they will all need to be dry cleaned!*—while Avery and Atlas looked at each other and giggled. When they disappeared into those forts, it felt as if they were able to escape from anything.

"What made you think of that?"

"I just wish that I could go hide in one of our forts right now, to get away from all this." Avery cast out her arms, indicating the rows of couture dresses, which were all designed specifically for her body and yet felt unbearably suffocating.

Atlas met her gaze in the mirror. "I don't think I realized how much you hated that Dad is the new mayor."

Avery struggled to find the right words. "It's too much attention. I feel like I'm caught in limbo, like I have a constant pit in my stomach. No one sees the real me anymore, not even our parents," she said helplessly. "Sometimes I think I'm going to snap in two."

"You know you're much stronger than that," Atlas said quietly.

"It's just that sometimes I think of the version of me that Mom and Dad do see, sparkling and perfect, and I wish I *could* be that girl. Instead of the flawed person that I really am."

"Your so-called imperfections are the best part of you."

Avery didn't know how to answer that, so she didn't say anything at all.

"Our parents never saw me for me either, you know," Atlas went on after a moment. "Through the years, they've looked at me and seen a lot of things—a PR stunt, a way to keep you happy, maybe even an asset to the business—but not *me*, the way that I really am. Trust me when I say that I know how it feels to want to live up to the version of you that Mom and Dad built in their heads. I might even want it more than you," he added, and the angles of his face changed, became sharper, "because this wasn't always my life."

Avery was startled into silence. Atlas so rarely talked about how it had been for him, before he was adopted.

"When Mom and Dad brought me home, I thought I was the luckiest kid in the entire world. I kept worrying that they might wake up one day and decide that they didn't want me after all, and return me like a pair of shoes."

"They would never do that." Avery ached at the thought of Atlas, young and uncertain, afraid of such a thing.

"I know. But unlike you, I remember a time *before* I had their love. Which is why I hate disappointing them. They expect so much, but they have also given me everything." He sighed. "That was part of the reason I stayed away so long last year—just to see how it felt, being myself without being a Fuller."

"And how was it?" Avery couldn't quite imagine who she would be if she weren't Avery Fuller. If she could just walk through the world unremarked upon, like any other unremarkable person.

"It felt like a haze had lifted. Like everything was much clearer," Atlas told her and smiled. "Aves, promise me that you won't worry about Mom and Dad. That you'll do whatever is right for you. I mean, for you and Max," he added awkwardly; and the moment between them was abruptly broken.

"Sorry, I should get going." Atlas reached up to run a hand through his hair, making it stick up at funny angles. "I'm not any help with this. Besides, you know that it doesn't matter what you wear. You could show up to that party in a plastifoam box and you would still look perfect."

Before she could find some way to answer, he was gone.

The ripples of his presence seemed to lap through the room like waves, crashing over her.

Why did Avery have to struggle to make herself understood to everyone else in her life, yet Atlas always seemed to *get* her on an instinctive and elemental level? Why couldn't she make the rest of the world see her the way that Atlas did?

She collapsed onto her four-poster bed and stared blankly up at the ceiling, which was decorated with a hologram of her favorite Italian mural. Its pixels constantly shifted, so slowly as to be imperceptible, brushstroke by brushstroke; as if an invisible artist was suspended up there, always repainting it into a new arrangement.

She wished she were still angry with Atlas. Because whatever this was, it felt immeasurably worse.

# RYLIN

**RYLIN LEANED BACK** in the swivel chair and stretched out her legs, frowning up at the holo she was slowly stitching together. She had been here in the school's edit bay all afternoon. Right now, it was the only place she could try to make sense of all the unresolved questions in her life.

She still felt blindsided by Hiral's abrupt departure. And she missed him. As a boyfriend, yes, but also as a person in her life. It saddened her that after everything they had been through—the death of Rylin's mom, Hiral's dropping out of school, his arrest and subsequent release—that it had ended like *this*, with a brief and unceremonious good-bye at the monorail.

She couldn't help thinking that Chrissa had been right all along. Rylin had been so certain that she and Hiral could have a fresh start. But their secrets and lies had caught up with them once again.

This weekend, while she sorted through the bruised

confusion of her thoughts, Rylin had found herself reaching for her silver holo-cam. Before she quite knew what she was doing, she'd started filming.

She filmed Chrissa, and Hiral's family. She scanned insta-photos from the early days of their relationship—a painstaking process, adapting those into holographic 3-D images; she'd been forced to borrow Raquel's transmuter at the library. She surreptitiously filmed young couples at the mall and old couples on the Ifty. She wandered out onto the 32nd-floor deck and filmed the sunset, the vibrant orange clouds lined with deep dusky purple, like a quiet sigh.

As she sorted through all her raw material in the comforting darkness of the edit bay, Rylin began to see this impromptu film project for what it was. Somehow she was crafting a memoir of, or maybe a tribute to, her time with Hiral. This holo was her way of mourning their relationship, all the good as well as the bad.

She kept remembering things, small incidents she hadn't thought of in years. Like the first time she'd tried to bake a cake for Chrissa and burned herself on the stove, and Hiral cradled her hand to his chest with a cool-pack while feeding her raw batter with a spoon. That time they were stuck on the monorail together, during the Tower's one and only blackout, and they held tightly to each other's hands until the lights flashed back on.

It felt somehow easier to make sense of their relationship like this—as vignettes, as a series of disconnected and highly visual moments—than to confront it in its entirety. Maybe when she finished she would send it to Hiral. He would understand what it meant.

She was still filtering through the footage when the door to the edit bay slid open.

Rylin squinted into the brightness. Somehow she wasn't all that surprised to see Cord—as if she'd felt his presence even before he walked in, like a slight shift in temperature.

He had taken off his tie and unbuttoned the collar of his shirt. It made him look rumpled and sloppy and so unabashedly sexy that Rylin caught her breath.

"What are you doing on campus so late?" She wasn't used to seeing Cord here in the edit bay.

"Actually, Myers, I was looking for you. I tried pinging you a few times, but it kept going straight to message, which meant that you were either still inside the tech-net or off-planet. I figured this was more likely."

Rylin didn't answer. Her heart had given a funny sideways lurch, anticipation searing up and down her body. She had tried so hard not to think about Cord after this breakup with Hiral. She needed time to process everything that had happened, to focus on herself. It had been a while since Rylin was single. Maybe she could use the time alone. She certainly didn't want to be *that* girl, the type who Ping-Ponged instantly from one boy to another.

Cord took a step closer and clasped his hands behind his back, adopting the formal sort of pose in which people studied art. His gaze lifted to the holo that flickered before them. "Is Lux starring in this one too? What is it?" he asked.

*Just a memorial to my newly ended relationship.* Rylin stood up slowly—to see it from his angle. "A new project. It's about . . . endings," she explained as the hologram zoomed in on a couple's clasped hands.

"Endings?"

"Hiral and I broke up. He left New York, actually."

Cord slowly crossed the distance between them. He stood

245

distractingly close, so close that Rylin could see herself reflected in the pale blue of his irises, could trace the faint shadow along his jaw.

"I don't really believe in endings," he said laconically. "At least, I don't believe in calling them endings. There's something too depressingly final about it."

"What would you call them?"

"Opportunities. A value change. The beginning of something new."

Rylin's eyes fluttered shut. She shivered hot and cold at once.

"Rylin," Cord said, "I'm not going to kiss you."

She recoiled a step, stiff with wounded pride, but Cord's expression gave her pause. "I want to—I really do," he croaked. "But I refuse to be that asshole who makes a move on you when you're fresh out of a relationship."

Their gazes met for a long, dark, hot moment. Sound seemed to dissolve into silence. Rylin's thoughts, her blood, seemed to move with a poignant slowness.

She rose on tiptoe to kiss him.

She was startled by the tender brush of longing she felt as Cord's mouth touched hers. She tried to kiss him lightly, but it had been too long; they both fell forward into the kiss. Rylin pulled him instinctively closer. She felt dizzy with it, drunk with it, that Cord was here and real and hers.

But was that a good thing?

She had been here before, and it ended badly then, and why on earth did she expect it to be different this time?

Even though it cost every last ounce of her resolve, Rylin tore herself brutally away from the kiss.

"Cord," she whispered, trying to ignore the way his hands felt, still clasped around her back. "What are we *doing*?"

"Making out, until for some inexplicable reason you forced us to stop," he said and began to lower his mouth to hers. Rylin took a step back.

"You and me, together again? This is crazy." No matter how much she wanted him, Rylin knew that she couldn't go through it a second time: all the countless small wounds they'd inflicted on each other, all the misunderstandings and hurt and loss. Wasn't that the definition of insanity, to do the same thing over and over and expect a different result?

"Of course it's crazy. I'm crazy about you, Myers. I have been since that first day you stormed into my apartment last fall." When she didn't smile at that, he let out a breath. "What is it? What are you afraid of?"

She leaned her forehead against his chest to avoid having to look into his eyes. "That we're being foolish. That nothing has changed, and we'll just hurt each other all over again."

"We both made mistakes last time, Rylin. I know now that I should have given you a chance to explain yourself that night. I should have realized how much I loved you before it was too late." He bit back a sigh. "Eris told me to, you know."

Rylin's head shot up at that. "Eris?"

"The night she died. She told me that you were the real deal—that I should fight for you."

"She didn't even know me," Rylin protested weakly.

"Eris made a lot of snap judgments," Cord said, as if that explained everything. "She said that she could tell what you meant to me from the way I was looking at you."

"Oh," Rylin breathed. She probably should have felt weirded out by that, but for some reason it was nice—to know that Eris, a girl Rylin hadn't even known, had believed in her and Cord.

And Leda believed in them. Rylin remembered what she'd

said the other day, about needing something good to root for. As strange as it was, that thought warmed Rylin too.

"Rylin, I swear to you that if you give me another chance, I won't make the same stupid mistakes. I can't promise that I won't make *other*, equally stupid mistakes," Cord added ruefully, "but I'll try my best."

Rylin gave a cautious smile. "That seems fair. As long as we don't repeat the old ones."

"God, I've missed you." Cord began to kiss her again, a rain of small warm kisses, each one punctuated with a sentence.

"I missed your laugh." *Kiss.* "The way you call me out on my bullshit." *Kiss.* "That turquoise bra you secretly wear under your dark clothes, just because you can get away with it." Rylin opened her mouth to protest, but she couldn't say anything, because Cord was already kissing her again and listing more things; and so she gave up and tilted her head back. Her pulse was going haywire, her entire body humming sharply to life.

"I missed that look you get on your face when you're filming, your nose all crinkled." *Kiss.* "The way your hair falls out of your ponytail and hangs around your face, just like this, when I kiss you."

Rylin started to reach her hand up to fix it, but Cord shook his head. "No, leave it. You look beautiful."

She smiled up at him in the shadows. "Getting me alone in a dark room and showering me with compliments? If I didn't know better, Cord Anderton, I would say you're attempting to seduce me."

"Is it working?" he asked, and Rylin laughed, circling her arms blissfully around his shoulders.

They kissed more slowly this time as the tattered lights of the hologram flickered over them.

# WATT

**"TURN LEFT HERE,"** Nadia whispered into Watt's eartennas. Normally he would have let her direct him visually, with glowing arrows inscribed over his vision, but right now he wanted to soak in every last detail of MIT's campus. Tall stone buildings stretched on either side of its paved streets, which were still wholly pedestrian; Cambridge had refused to ever tear them up and embed the magnetic flecks needed to keep hovercraft aloft. The bright winter sun danced over the white dome of the main building, its rows of elegant pillars standing guard over the quad. Watt was surprised how much he liked the old-fashioned classical architecture. Something about its brutal orderliness appealed to him. This, he thought, was where real learning happened.

The invitation to interview at MIT had come just two days ago. So far it was the only thing that had pulled Watt out of his dazed state—after he had somehow, inexplicably, screwed things up with Leda yet again.

But then, he had wanted MIT long before he even knew who Leda was.

He'd taken the Hyperloop this afternoon from Penn Station. Watt had never ridden one of the high-speed maglev trains before, and spent most of the ride staring out the window at the blurred sides of the tunnel, marveling at it. They'd been going almost a thousand miles an hour, yet there were no bumps or turbulence or discernable changes of speed. It hadn't really felt as if they were moving at all.

*Here goes nothing,* he thought now, and walked up the steps of the admissions building into an anonymous waiting room. Half a dozen sets of eyes immediately darted toward him, sizing him up.

The other applicants looked just *like* him, Watt noted in sudden panic, except that they were all wearing suits, even the girls. Watt glanced down at his own interview ensemble, a wool-blend blazer and button-down paired with khakis, and felt instantly self-conscious.

*I'm the only guy here not in a tie!* he thought frantically to Nadia. He should have asked Leda what to wear. Except, of course, Leda wasn't talking to him anymore. Might not ever talk to him again, after what he'd accused her of.

*Leda will forgive me again, won't she?*

*I don't know, Watt,* Nadia replied. *I don't exactly have a data set for this.*

Watt nodded—realizing a beat too late that he probably looked as if he was bobbing his head for no reason. He'd promised himself that he wouldn't think about Leda. It would only make him even more unsettled and anxious than he already felt.

The tension in the room was stretched impossibly tight, like a cord about to snap at any moment. Watt perched on an unoccupied corner of the couch and cast a surreptitious glance around the room at his competition. The other students were all hungry and beady-eyed, exuding that ruthless confidence that comes from being the top of your class—from being the biggest fish in your own personal pond, from always *winning*.

Watt didn't feel quite so confident anymore.

He waited while a few other names were called—Anastasia Litkova, Robert Meister—shifting his weight nervously, plucking at the threads of the couch. Nadia offered to run a few questions with him, but Watt thought it would only make things worse. Finally a young man in a maroon sweater vest peered in and announced, "Watzahn Bakradi?"

"That's me!" Watt said quickly, stumbling in his eagerness to get up. A girl in a tailored navy pantsuit rolled her eyes at him and went back to muttering some kind of focusing mantra under her breath.

Watt followed sweater-vest guy down a dim hallway, his footfalls absorbed by the thick carpet, and emerged into an austere, brightly lit room. He was relieved to see a single wooden table with two chairs. At least this wasn't a panel interview, with multiple admissions officers grilling him at once.

"Watzahn. I must admit, I've been looking forward to this interview," said Vivian Marsh, the head of admissions at MIT. She had deep-set eyes and straight chestnut hair that just brushed her shoulders. Watt had met her once, last year, after an information session at his high school.

The door behind them clicked as the admissions assistant stepped out of the room, leaving Watt and Vivian alone.

Watt pulled out his chair and took a seat. The surface of the table was empty, except for a pencil and paper arranged by his chair—was he expected to take notes?—and a funny instrument near Vivian, a container that was fat on both sides but narrow in the middle, and filled with sand.

*That's an hourglass. An old-fashioned way of marking the pas-sage of time*, Nadia informed him, just as Vivian reached for the hourglass and tipped it over. The sand began to stream back through, to spill into the other side. "Just to make sure I don't run over our half hour," she explained, but Watt recognized the hourglass for what it was—an intimidation technique.

He sat up a little straighter, trying his best not to be intimidated.

"Your grades are very impressive," Vivian began without pre-amble. Watt was about to say *thank you*, but before he could she had steamrolled onward. "You wouldn't be here if they weren't, of course. So what else?"

"What else?" Watt repeated dumbly. *Nadia! Help!* He and Nadia hadn't practiced anything vague or open-ended like this. He was ready to rattle off answers to all the usual questions, like *Why do you want to go to MIT?* or *What are your greatest strengths?* But *What else?*

Vivian leaned forward a little. "Watzahn, there are thou-sands of applicants with GPAs like yours. And most of those applicants are leaders of, or at least participators in, multiple extracurricular activities—which means they have experience delegating tasks, working with teams to create a final product. But all I see here is that you joined the math club last year," she said, her eyes glazing over a little as she reviewed his file. "What do you do in your spare time? What makes you *tick*?"

*Oh, you know, the usual. Operating an illegal computer, taking on some hacking jobs for extra cash, investigating the death of a girl I barely knew. Trying to win back the girl I love.*

"I'm really interested in computer engineering," he attempted.

"Yes, you wrote about that in your essay," Vivian said impa-tiently. "But why you? What makes *you* especially qualified to build a quantum computer?"

Watt glanced at his contacts, where Nadia was helpfully listing all his strengths. "I'm able to get deep into the code without losing sight of the big picture. I'm creative but also analytical. I'm patient, but I know when to be quick on my feet, and spontaneous."

"Why don't we see some of that quick thinking at work. I'm going to give you a little mental-math problem," Vivian decided. "Are you ready?"

Watt nodded, and she continued. "A standard golf ball is forty-eight millimeters in diameter. A New York elevator car measures twenty meters high by three meters wide by four meters tall. How many golf balls—Don't you want to write these numbers down?" she broke off, gesturing to the paper and pencil.

Oh, right. Normal people probably needed to do that. Watt considered doing as she said; but then, what good was it to be normal? MIT wasn't interviewing for *normal*.

"Three million two hundred thirty nine thousand and ninety-nine," he said instead. "That's what you were going to ask, right? How many golf balls can fit in the elevator car?"

*Thanks, Nadia*, he thought in relief. Finally, an interview question he knew precisely how to answer.

It took a moment for Watt to realize that Vivian didn't seem all that impressed.

"Who told you?" she demanded. "Someone told you that question ahead of time. Who was it?"

"What? N-no one," Watt stuttered. "I just did it in my head."

"No one is that fast," Vivian snapped, and Watt felt like a complete idiot, because of course she was right. No *human* was that fast.

"Here," he said, "I'll walk you through my mental math." He sketched all the numbers out for her—it was a simple multiplication problem, really; the trick was remembering to subtract the golf balls that you'd double- and triple-counted, on the sides and corners of the imaginary cube. But Vivian still looked livid.

"We have no tolerance for cheaters at MIT. Should you ever get a chance to work with quantum computers, you'll see how incredibly powerful they are." *You have no idea*, he wanted to say. "Their processing capabilities truly defy comprehension. Do you know what quantum computers are used for in today's world?" she finished abruptly.

"The Department of Defense, NASA, financial institutions—"

"Exactly. Which means that they traffic in incredibly sensitive information: people's identification numbers, bank passcodes, issues of national security. Data that cannot be compromised at any cost. Don't you see why the individuals who work with them need to be of unimpeachable integrity?" Vivian shook her head. "I would never allow someone who cheated anywhere *near* a quantum computer."

"I didn't cheat," Watt said again, though of course that wasn't true. He'd cheated simply by bringing Nadia into this interview. "I'm just really good at mental math. It's why I joined the math club," he added hopelessly, fighting off a sinking sense of despair.

"I hope so. Because if I thought you had done anything morally questionable, I wouldn't have invited you to campus today."

Watt tried not to squirm. He'd done plenty of morally questionable things—lying about Eris's death, breaking into the police files about Mariel, not to mention building Nadia. He hoped his face didn't betray how much his heart was pounding. Suddenly all he could hear was that soft, inescapable hissing sound of the sand falling through the hourglass, each grain of it marking a moment less of this single crucial interview.

"Now, moving on," Vivian said smoothly. "What's your favorite book?"

Favorite book? Watt hadn't actually read a full-length text

for himself since he was thirteen. He just had Nadia compose summaries for him.

*Pride and Prejudice*, Nadia suggested, and Watt vaguely remembered that he was supposed to have read it for English class at some point, so it was clearly a good option. He went ahead and said it.

"Really," Vivian replied woodenly. "Jane Austen."

Nadia had pulled up a synopsis of the work, but Watt had a sickening sense that Nadia's prompts weren't really helping him. He tried to talk over the new, unformulated fear that was clogging his throat, making his brain slow down. "I love that book, the way that Darcy is so prideful and Elizabeth is prejudiced," he babbled—but wait, was that wrong? "And of course she is also prideful, and he's prejudiced," he added miserably.

Vivian stared at him for another beat. The disappointment was clear in her eyes. "I think we're done here," she said quietly, reaching for the hourglass. "You're free to go."

Watt finally found his voice. "This isn't fair. I'm applying for a computer science degree. What do you care what I *read*?"

"Mr. Bakradi, half the students who come in here tell me that *Pride and Prejudice* is their favorite book. You think that's an accurate indication of the population, or do you think it's because I listed it as my favorite book, at the top of my public profile on the feeds?"

*Oh, crap.*

"I don't want to know my own favorite book; I want to know yours!" She let out a frustrated breath. "It's clear to me that you're smart and good with numbers, but that isn't enough to work with quantum computers. The whole point of the interview was for me to get to know you as a person. I wanted to see some individuality, some *texture*. I wanted someone who will put himself out there, not cut corners and try to tell me what I want to hear. I'm sorry this didn't work out, but you'll find the right place." She smiled—a thin, watery smile, the first time she'd smiled during the whole interview. "Can you have Harold send in the next candidate?"

Watt didn't move. He couldn't move. Perhaps he hadn't heard her properly. Surely this wasn't over.

*Watt*, Nadia prodded. When he still didn't react, she sent a little zap of electricity down his spine, and it forced him into action.

Somehow, amid the great roar of the entire world crumbling to pieces around him, Watt managed to thank Vivian. In the waiting room, the heads of all the other candidates darted up eagerly, counting the minutes, realizing that he must have failed. Their eyes stayed locked on him as he walked past, as if they were predators stalking a wounded prey, watching it leave a bloody trail behind it.

Watt found his way blindly to a bench outside, his head sinking into his hands. His chest was constricting strangely. It felt difficult to breathe.

*I'm so sorry, Watt. I thought this was the right approach—it's widely accepted in the research that people* prefer *to see themselves reflected in interviews, that similarity begets liking—*

*It's not your fault.* Watt could hardly blame Nadia for that disastrous tailspin of an interview.

No, Watt knew that this was his fault, and his alone.

*I wanted someone who will put himself out there*, Vivian had said. *Not someone who will tell me what I want to hear.* But that was how Watt had always gotten by—gaming the system and telling people what they wanted to hear, whether it was teachers or girls or even his parents. That was what he used Nadia for. And what was so wrong with it, anyway?

Had Nadia become too much of a crutch? He'd gotten so

accustomed to her; she was the lens through which he observed, analyzed, responded to the world. Watt realized that he could hardly remember the last time he'd had a conversation without Nadia softly helping, prompting him on what to say, or looking up references so he didn't seem foolish. Except, perhaps, with Leda.

Maybe he should stop relying on Nadia and open up a damn book.

Watt sat there for a long time, in the cold winter sunshine, watching the clouds chase one another across the burnished blue sky. He knew he should go back to New York, but he wasn't ready. Because once he left campus, he would have to come to terms with the fact that he was seeing it for the last time.

Coming to MIT had been his dream for most of his life. Somehow, through his own foolishness, Watt had lost hold of that dream. And it had taken less than thirty minutes' worth of sand in an hourglass.

Maybe there was such a thing as being too smart for your own good.

# AVERY

**THE OXFORD DEAN** beamed, cheerful and red-cheeked, as he held open the door to his study. "Miss Fuller. Thank you for sharing your thoughts regarding the Romanesque influence on twenty-second-century supertowers. I must say, this was one of the liveliest interviews I've had in years."

"The pleasure was all mine, Dean Ozah," Avery assured him. She turned outside, pulling her plaid jacket closer over her shoulders. When she saw the figure lounging past the dean's front gate, she gave a small, private smile.

Intermittent sunlight filtered through the branches and onto Max's face, highlighting his bold cheekbones, his prominent nose. With that floppy dark coat and windswept hair, he looked like a sentinel from some historical novel. It had been the work of a single morning, she thought wryly, for Max to revert to his disordered Oxford self.

"Avery! How did it go?" he exclaimed, hurrying forward. His

eyes burned into her, as if he was trying to read the transcript of the interview on her face.

"Not to brag, but I think I crushed it."

Max reached for Avery's hands to twirl her in a clumsy dance move. "Of course you did!" he proclaimed, so loud that Avery had to shush him. "I knew you would!"

Avery let him lift her into the air, spinning her around so the hood of her coat fell back over her shoulders. She collapsed against his chest in laughter. Max reached out to tuck a loosened strand of hair behind her ear, making Avery feel beautiful and windblown. "I'm so proud of you," he added and reached into the pocket of his jacket, grinning. "Good thing I brought something to celebrate with."

He pulled out a crumpled paper bag from her favorite bakery. "Pumpkin or buttercream?"

"Buttercream," Avery decided, reaching for the scone. Its sugar crystals glittered like diamonds in the cold afternoon light. This was so typically thoughtful of Max. "I love you," she said quickly through a flaky mouthful of scone.

"Were you talking to me or to the buttercream?" Max teased. "You know what, actually, don't answer that."

As they walked back toward town, Avery told Max about the interview in more detail. She had been in her element, talkative and eager and just a teensy bit provocative; and the dean had absolutely loved it. They'd discussed everything from the future of academia to medieval illuminated manuscripts to where you could find the best lamb tandoori in Oxford. Avery felt certain that she could go to Oxford if she wanted to.

*If* she wanted to go? Where had that stray thought come from? Of course she wanted to go.

The setting sun bronzed the air, casting the city in a cheerful glow. Avery tried to shake her inexplicable sense of unease. The interview was finally over and she was here with Max, eating scones, in a city that she loved. Best of all, she was out of New York, away from the inauguration plans, the prospect of constantly seeing Atlas. There were no zettas buzzing around her face, no one stopping her on the street to ask for an interview. So why did she still feel on edge?

"Where should we go?" she asked. Maybe if she kept moving, she would shake off this strange restlessness. "Want to meet up with Luke and Tiana?"

"We can," Max said nonchalantly. "But there's somewhere I want to take you first."

He led her along the bustle of Main Street, down a quieter avenue that Avery had never noticed before. A magical hush seemed to fall over them. The street was lined with an array of small buildings in charming colors. The cobblestones were so bright they seemed to sing beneath her feet.

Max led her up a single flight of stairs to a heavy, carved door that was flanked by a pair of brassy light fixtures. "After you," he said.

Avery tried not to look too knowing as she started up the steps. One of their friends must have moved here, and Max had asked them to help organize a surprise party for her. A little presumptuous, given that she wasn't technically admitted to Oxford, but Max was always ready to celebrate things that hadn't happened yet.

She paused to arrange her features into a suitably surprised face, and pushed at the front door. It swung open easily at her touch.

The *Surprise!* she expected didn't come. Avery blinked, puzzled, and stepped into the entryway.

It was a charmingly old ramshackle apartment, with scuffed

wooden floors and faded yellow walls. There were a few stray pieces of furniture, a heavy rug and a bookcase covered in a fine film of dust. She walked past the narrow kitchen to a small patio out back, where a single folding table and matching chairs had been arranged.

"What do you think?" Max followed her outside.

Avery turned around slowly, taking it all in. "Who lives here?"

"*We* do. I mean, if you want to," Max amended hastily. "I put in an offer this morning."

Avery felt suddenly light-headed. She sank into one of the metal folding chairs.

"Max," she said helplessly, "we don't even know if I'll get in. . . ."

"Didn't you just say that you crushed the interview? You'll get in," he declared. "I figured it makes sense for us to buy a place instead of paying rent; we'll be in Oxford for the next four years at least, while you're at university. Maybe longer, if I get into the PhD program, or if you decide to go to grad school."

"I'm not sure I want to get a PhD," Avery protested.

"Why not? You're smart enough to," Max declared. "This is a great place for us, Avery."

"It is," she said softly, glancing around. This apartment seemed so . . . *Max*. But she wasn't sure it felt like her.

"I know it's a little unfinished. It needs some rugs and art. Which is where you come in," Max said and smiled. "But can't you picture us here, curling up in the living room to grade papers? Having friends over for dinner? Standing out here on a warm summer night to watch the fireflies? You can almost see part of the river, if you look that way," he added, pointing eagerly.

Avery felt as if the air in her lungs was trapped. Max was only two years older than her, yet he was so much surer of himself. He had his whole life—or rather, both their lives—completely planned out.

Max seemed unnerved by her silence. "Unless you don't *want* to live here. I mean, if you aren't ready yet. . . ."

Even though she felt frozen by an inexplicable sense of panic, Avery recoiled from the prospect of hurting Max. Her face unfolded into a smile. "Of course I want to live here," she assured him, and paused as another idea occurred to her. "Did you say that you bought this place? Max, please at least let me pay for half of it."

"It's okay. I have some money saved. I *wanted* to do this, for you. For us." Max leaned forward with a quiet intensity. "I love you, Avery Fuller," he began, and even though they were both sitting—even though he wasn't on one knee—Avery had the sensation that what he was about to say was something akin to a proposal.

"The last year with you has been so perfect. *You* are perfect. You're like a dream that I've been longing for my whole life and never thought I would find. And now that I've found you, all I can think about is how much I want to be with you always."

Avery felt that flutter of panic again. "I'm not perfect, Max." It wasn't fair of him to ask that of her, to build her into some untenable ideal in his mind and then inevitably be disappointed when she failed to live up to it. No relationship could withstand that sort of pressure.

Atlas had always known better than to use the word *perfect* with her.

"Right, no one is perfect. You're just as close as it is humanly possible to be," Max replied, not understanding her meaning; and for some perverse reason Avery needed him to understand. The way Atlas always had.

She also knew that she shouldn't be thinking of Atlas right now.

"I'm not perfect," she repeated. Something in Max's eyes frightened her, though she wasn't sure why. "I'm impatient and defensive and petty, and I'm not worth that kind of blind devotion. No one is."

His face had gone pale. "What are you saying? Are you telling me not to love you?"

"No, I just . . ." She let her head fall forward into her hands, fighting off a nameless sense of dread. "I don't want to disappoint you."

"And I don't want to disappoint *you*, Avery. But I'm sure I will, a thousand times, and I'm sure you'll disappoint me too. As long as we're honest with each other, we can get through anything."

*As long as we're honest with each other.* Avery pushed aside the tiny voice that was reminding her of all the things she hadn't told Max: The truth about Eris's death. The investigation about Mariel. Her relationship with Atlas.

But none of that mattered anymore, she reminded herself. Those secrets all belonged to the old Avery, and she had left the old Avery behind in New York. She was starting over.

Max reached into his pocket.

For a single, paralyzing moment Avery thought he was pulling out a ring, and her heart skipped and skidded wildly in her chest because she had no idea what she would do if he did.

Then her breath let out, because it was only a set of old-fashioned brass key-chips, for automatic entry into the house. Max looked up and met her eyes. She wondered if he'd heard the relief in that sigh.

"I love you," he said simply. "All I want is to make you as happy as you make me. I want to see your first smile of the day when you wake up, and the last one before you go to sleep. I want to share my fears and my hopes and dreams with you. I want to build a life with you." He slid one of the pair of key-chips toward her across the wrought-iron table.

"I love you too," Avery whispered, because she did.

"Are you *crying*?" Max lifted a hand to her face, capturing the single tear that had escaped to run down her cheek. "I'm sorry, I know the apartment is kind of a fixer-upper. If you hate it, we can pick another one," he hastened to add, and Avery shook her head.

She wasn't sure why she was crying. She loved Max. They fit together so easily, without conflict or friction or obstacles. He made Avery the best version of herself. So why wasn't her love for him as free and unencumbered as his was for her?

Why wasn't she as blazingly certain of what she wanted as he seemed to be?

"I'm crying because I'm so happy," she said and leaned over to kiss him, wishing it were that simple.

# LEDA

**THAT SAME EVENING,** Leda was sprawled on her bed, idly flicking through the feeds on her contacts, when a flicker from her mom appeared. It was addressed to Leda and her dad. *I'm stuck at work, don't wait for me for dinner!*

Leda's mom, a corporate lawyer, had been working a lot of weekends recently. With Leda's older brother, Jamie, away at college this year, that meant that Leda and her dad were often home alone—and ever since Eris's death, they hadn't been on the best of terms. They'd gotten in the habit of both claiming to have "a lot to do" and wolfing down their food as quickly as they could before fleeing in opposite directions.

It saddened Leda. There had been a time, not long ago, when she felt incredibly close with her dad—when on nights like this, he would have looked at her with a guilty smile and asked if she wanted to go to their favorite Italian place around the corner, instead of staying at home. They would linger over double dessert, exchanging stories from the day, strategizing whatever problem was bothering Leda.

In the wake of Eris's death, Leda hadn't known how to face her dad. Their relationship had become strained, and they drifted ever further apart. Now they met and spoke with the impersonal, courteous disinterest of strangers passing in the street.

But this time, Leda wasn't going to ignore her mom's message the way she always did.

She may not have figured out the truth in time to repair her relationship with Eris, but it wasn't too late for Leda and her dad.

She headed down the hall to his home office and paused at the door. A chorus of voices talked over one another on the other side; he must be on a vid-conference. She tapped at the door anyway.

"Leda?" she heard her dad say, breaking off from his call. "Come in."

Matt Cole's office was delightfully cozy, all bold colors and deep wood furniture. A glazed redwood trunk, hovering in the air in suspension, served as the desk. Before the antique étagère flickered a holoscreen, squared off into eight boxes, each containing the disembodied head of someone else on the vid-call. Leda wondered which of them were in Asia, or Europe, or South America.

"I'll need to see a revised deck by tomorrow morning. Thanks so much, everyone," her dad concluded and sliced horizontally into the air to end the conference call. "Hey, Leda," he said, turning hesitantly toward her. "I just have a few more things to wrap up before dinner."

"Actually, there's something I wanted to talk to you about."

Leda glanced at the sleek black chair before the desk but

dismissed it as too businesslike, the type of place she would have sat if she were one of her dad's clients. Instead she headed to the pair of armchairs nestled in one corner of the office.

Her dad followed with cautious footsteps. Leda took a seat, curling her bare feet into the heated carpet and reached for the framed instaphoto on the nearby table. It was her mom's wedding portrait.

Ilara looked incredible in her wedding gown, a minimalist sheath of ivory silk crepe. Its neckline swooped down in a dramatic V, but she could pull it off. She was as thin and small-chested as Leda was. She looked so *happy* in this photo, Leda thought, her eyes dancing with a light, almost playful joy.

"What is it, Leda?"

She set the photo back down, her heart hammering in her chest. She knew this was the right thing to do, yet she was still afraid. Once she said these words, she could never un-say them.

"I want to talk about Eris. I know that she was my half sister."

Her dad seemed utterly lost for words. His eyes had drifted from Leda to the image of her mom, still smiling blithe and unaware in the hammered pewter frame.

"Oh, Leda," he said at last. "I'm so sorry. I never meant to hurt you."

*But you did*, Leda thought, though it seemed unnecessarily cruel to say. *You hurt all of us.* That was always how it happened, wasn't it? No one ever set out to hurt the people they loved, but they ended up doing it all the same.

"How did you find out?" he asked.

Leda remembered lying on the sand in Dubai, shivering and dizzy; Mariel's face etched eerily against the darkness as she announced that Eris had been Leda's sister. "It doesn't matter," she said. "But it wasn't until after Eris died. I wish I had known earlier. It would have . . . changed things, between us."

Her dad leaned forward, his hands gripped tightly around his knees. "I didn't know for years, Leda. I had only just found out; Eris's mom told me a few months before Eris died." He spoke with a rapid urgency, as if it were critical that Leda believe him in this.

"You should have *told* me, before—" *Before I misjudged things and pushed Eris away, too hard. Before I lost my chance to actually get to know her—as a sister.*

"I'm sorry," he said again, helplessly. Leda saw the grief in his eyes. It was real.

Her throat felt swollen. "I miss her," Leda said quietly. "Or at least, I miss the chance with her I never had. I wish I could remember something more personal than her smile, but I don't have much else. So I try to concentrate on that. Eris smiled all the time, not fake smiling the way most people do, but a real smile."

Leda lifted her eyes to her dad. He was very still and quiet. "Or the way she used to dance. Eris was a terrible dancer, you know, all arms and elbows—a complete klutz, with no rhythm. It should have been funny, but it wasn't, because it was Eris. When she was on the dance floor, no one could look away."

Her dad's face was ashen, his eyes gleaming with unshed tears.

"I hold on to these memories," Leda forced herself to continue. "The easy, superficial ones, because those are all I have. That, and the memory of how she died."

"Leda," her dad said brokenly, throwing his arms open; and Leda moved forward into the hug. They stayed like that for a while in a silence that was thick with regret. Leda felt her dad's tears, which startled her; she wasn't sure if she had ever seen her father cry. It struck something deep within her.

She let him cry like that, his tears soaking her sweater, feeling as if she had become the parent, as if she were the one taking care of him. A strange catch released in her chest. At least they were no longer pretending to be okay when they weren't.

"Does your mother know?" her father asked at last.

"I haven't told her, if that's what you mean. It isn't my secret to tell." Leda looked piercingly into her dad's eyes. "I think you should, though."

"Why? It will just hurt your mom, and it won't change anything. Eris is gone. And Caroline and I—we were over a long time ago," he hurried to say, naming Eris's mom.

Leda understood the impulse. It was devastating, showing the worst parts of yourself to the people you cared about. Knowing that they would never look at you the same again. And yet—"Doesn't it weigh on you, keeping a secret like that?"

"There are times, Leda, when the truth can do more harm than good. When sharing a secret is much more selfish than keeping it," her dad insisted. "I know it's not fair to put you in the middle like this, and I'm sorry. Someday, when you do something you wish you could undo—something you regret, something that changes you forever—you'll understand what I mean."

Leda knew exactly what her father meant, far more than he could ever guess.

# CALLIOPE

**IT WAS VERY** early on Monday, and already Calliope was slipping out of the Mizrahis' apartment.

She couldn't take another morning there. Elise and Nadav had come back from their honeymoon last week, in a show of hand-holding, smothering affection. Calliope was happy that her mom had found love, she really was, but that didn't mean she wanted to be witness to that love all the freaking time. But Nadav was obsessed with family togetherness, even more now that they were officially a family. Every meal, every conversation, every last school function—they all suddenly became family events, which meant that Calliope was expected to be there, smiling that dumb pasted-on smile. She felt stifled beneath it all.

Her only escape was going out with Brice. Calliope knew she shouldn't be seeing him anymore, yet she couldn't *not* see him. She told Elise and Nadav that she was continuing her volunteer work at the hospital. So far it seemed to be working as an excuse, even if Nadav did occasionally insist on dropping her off there. Calliope would just smile and walk inside, then slip out a few minutes later.

Still, every time she came home from seeing Brice—after those brief few hours of actually being herself—Calliope would return to the Mizrahis', to the role she hated so much. At least now she was sleeping in her own room again, even if there was that creepy painting of the dead deer hanging on the wall.

This morning, when she woke up hours before her alarm, Calliope felt a sudden, almost panicked desire to get out. She needed a morning to herself, to hell with the consequences. She messaged her mom and Nadav that she had to meet a classmate early for a school project, then slid into raspberry-colored jeans, a thin black top, and dangly earrings, weaving her hair into a messy fishtail braid. Like hell was she wearing her school uniform right now.

She went straight down the E line to Grand Central, and felt better the moment she walked through its massive carved archway.

Calliope had always loved train stations. There was something inherently soothing about them, especially this early in the morning, when they were inhabited by a strange, almost subdued silence. Vacuum-bots moved across the floor in stately isolation. Warm muffins began to emerge from bakeshops, the scent of them wafting out into the corridors. Calliope headed to a coffee dispenser and placed her order for an iced hazelnut latte, her footsteps echoing in the vast space.

As in the original Grand Central, the floors were laid with a creamy, distinguished-looking Italian travertine. Doric columns soared up at the corners of every intersection. Directional holograms flickered throughout, helping travelers find their way to the countless lift lines, monorails, helipads, Hyperloop subsea trains that all met here, in a ruthlessly efficient tangle. This was the center of the spiderweb knitting the city, the entire *world*, together.

Calliope realized that she was just in time for the sunrise. She took a seat in the Metro-North corridor, turning expectantly toward the massive windows along the eastern wall.

It had been a long time since she saw the sun rise, even longer since she'd actually woken up for it. Usually when Calliope witnessed the dawn of a new day, it was because the previous day hadn't actually ended.

She leaned back in her chair, watching the sunrise as if it were a private performance intended just for her. And for a moment it felt that way: as if the sun, or perhaps the city, was showing off for her benefit, reminding her how wonderful it was to be young and alive and in New York. There was something delicious about being awake while most of the city was still asleep. It was as if Calliope alone presided over the sacred mysteries of the city.

The station began to stir to life around her. The first trains were arriving from the European seaboard, the early morning commuter trains for people who'd wanted to squeeze the last few hours out of their weekends in Paris or London. Announcements began booming louder and more frequently over the speakers, creating a sense of continually cresting excitement. An indefinable magic seemed to cling about it all— but then, transportation was the only real magic left on earth, wasn't it? The ability to go anywhere, become anyone, simply by purchasing a ticket.

Maybe Calliope loved train stations because for most of her life, they had been her escape mechanism.

She was startled by the sight of a familiar figure in the crowd. It was Avery Fuller, walking hand in hand with that lanky

German boyfriend of hers. They seemed to be returning from a weekend away, just in time for school. Calliope watched as Avery hugged her boyfriend; then they turned in opposite directions, each of them apparently going to a different lift line.

Calliope realized with a start that Avery was headed right toward her. She quickly arranged herself just so, as if she was on display—the iced coffee held casually in one hand, one leg folded over the other—and directed her profile toward the sunrise. She expected Avery to glide on past without speaking, or maybe even to say something snide.

What she didn't anticipate was that Avery would pause. "May I?" she asked, gesturing to the neighboring seat.

Calliope gave an unconcerned shrug. She'd never been one to back down from a confrontation, or whatever this was. But behind her steely facade, her heart was hammering. She and Avery hadn't exactly talked since last year, when Calliope had confronted her after the Dubai party, and told Avery that she knew about her and Atlas.

"Are you headed somewhere?" Avery asked, her printed faux-leather suitcase hovering uncertainly behind her. Her hair, which fell loose around her shoulders like in a shampoo advert, gave off a lively light. She looked expensive and cool in her simple white shirt and jeans, not at all creased or disordered, the way Calliope always appeared post-travel. Calliope resented her for it, a little.

"I just came here to think." Perhaps it was the early hour, or the strangeness of Avery Fuller deciding to sit and chat with her for no apparent reason, but Calliope was feeling honest. "I actually like train stations. All these people going different places, hurrying toward destinations I'll never know . . ." She trailed off. "It makes me feel calm when I'm agitated."

Avery stared at her with naked curiosity. "It's your Tiffany's."

"My what?"

"The place you go to feel calm," Avery explained. "Haven't you read *Breakfast at Tiffany's*? Or seen the holo?"

"Never heard of it," Calliope said dismissively.

To her surprise, Avery laughed. It was a clear, self-assured laugh, the kind of laugh that made you want to sit up straighter and join in.

Calliope cast a puzzled glance in Avery's direction. "Where are you coming back from?" she ventured.

"I was in Oxford for my college interview. My boyfriend went with me. But I had to get back for this week. . . ."

Oh, right. Calliope remembered that the inauguration ball was this weekend.

As the train station filled up, more and more people seemed to be noticing Avery's presence. Calliope watched as the whispers gathered and spread, spiraling out like a hurricane with Avery at its epicenter. She saw the hard, impassive look that settled on Avery's face, and came to a startling realization.

Avery Fuller didn't enjoy being the center of attention.

"It must be liberating," Avery said softly, as if reading her thoughts.

"What?"

"Getting to do what you want, *be* who you want." Avery shifted abruptly toward Calliope, her cheeks a soft pink. "What's it like, traveling the world that way?"

Was Avery Fuller, the girl from the thousandth floor, actually asking her what it was like to be a *con artist*? "I'm sure you've traveled all over the world," Calliope replied, disconcerted. "I mean, you just came back from a weekend in England."

Avery waved that aside. "I'm traveling as myself, and usually with my parents. Which comes with its own set of expectations.

What's it like to become a new person whenever you go somewhere new?"

All of Calliope's senses were on high alert. She had never, *ever* talked about this with anyone. It was so taboo it felt like blasphemy.

She wiped her palms on her jeans. "Why do you want to know?"

"I'm just curious," Avery said, and Calliope heard the edge beneath her words. *Even Avery Fuller doesn't always know her own mind*, she thought wonderingly. Even Avery Fuller occasionally felt torn between two different paths, two different versions of herself.

Calliope cleared her throat, not wanting to get this wrong. "It is liberating sometimes, but also lonely. Every time I go somewhere new, I have to let go of whoever I was last time, and become the person that the situation calls for. I'm constantly pushing restart on myself."

"Doesn't anyone ever recognize you?"

Calliope looked up sharply, wondering if Brice had said something to Avery, but the question didn't seem prompted by anything in particular.

"Sorry," Avery breathed. "I guess what I mean is, what do you change about yourself? Just your accent?"

Calliope flashed suddenly to all those hours of practicing accents with her mom. She used to stand before Elise, her hands folded, like an actress at an audition. *Tell me a story*, Elise would command, and Calliope would launch into some inconsequential anecdote about what she'd eaten for breakfast or how she wanted to cut her hair. *Toulouse!* Elise would exclaim, and then *Dublin! Lisbon!* Each time she named a city, Calliope had to switch to that accent seamlessly, without breaking stride in her narrative.

"It's the accent, sure. But it's as much about confidence, and how you carry yourself. You, for instance, have the posture of a girl who's used to being at the center of the spotlight, in every room you've ever been in. No offense," she added quickly.

Avery nodded slowly. "What if I wanted to carry myself differently?"

"Slouch. Don't make eye contact with people; use your peripheral vision instead. Shrink in on yourself, and de-emphasize the physical," Calliope told her. "It's surprisingly easy to keep people from looking at you. I bet you've just never really tried."

Avery seemed to think that over for a while. "You're very brave," she said at last, and Calliope couldn't have been more shocked if Avery had begun stripping off all her clothes, right there in the train station. Brave? She was selfish and impulsive, but never had she thought of herself as brave.

"I guess it's only brave if you succeed. It's just reckless if you fail."

"But when have you ever failed?" Avery asked.

Calliope blinked. *I've failed in New York, by living as someone I'm not*, she wanted to say, but then she thought of Brice and brightened a little. He knew the real her, whoever it was, buried beneath all those layers of lies.

"I've had my moments," she evaded, but Avery didn't really seem to be listening anymore. She was looking back out at the sunrise, thoughtful.

"See you in class later," Avery said abruptly, standing up. "I'm sure we'll both be exhausted."

"I've had later nights—and earlier mornings. And I'd venture to say you have too." Calliope was pleased to see that she had coaxed a smile from Avery. For a moment, it felt as if they were almost friends.

As the other girl walked off, Calliope turned away from the

sunrise to watch the anonymous sea of people moving through the train station: all the greetings and good-byes, the laughter and tears, the commuters chattering on various pings, the travelers standing in pools of isolation. She was very accustomed to being alone. But it suddenly struck her how many other people there were in this vast city, also alone.

# RYLIN

**"YOU *ARE* ALLOWED** to take me out in New York, you know." Rylin pulled aside the curtain of their enclosed private deck to gaze at the view.

"Where's the fun in that?" Cord laughed, seeming unconcerned.

They were on the evening cruise of the *Skyspear*: the most luxurious, and most famous, of the space tourism vessels now in operation. Though this hardly counted as space, Cord insisted. They would remain at an altitude of three hundred kilometers the entire time, never leaving the comforting band of Earth's low orbit.

"I mean, you don't have to always be making big romantic gestures with me," Rylin insisted. Last year he'd whisked her off to Paris, and now this?

"Maybe I like big romantic gestures," Cord replied.

"I know. But next weekend, let's cook tacos and watch a holo.

Something more . . . low-key," she finished, and smiled. "I guess I feel silly being on a flight to nowhere."

They had taken off from New York a few minutes ago, in the late afternoon, and would land back in New York just two hours after departure, having circumnavigated the entire globe. They had already technically reached orbit, which meant that they weren't burning any more fuel. The *Skyspear* worked like a high-speed satellite, propelled by the slingshot effect of Earth's gravity.

Their "viewing suite," one of several dozen in first class, was essentially a private living room, containing a stone-colored couch and a pair of armchairs. No bed, Rylin had noted right away, in a confusing combination of relief and disappointment.

The real showstopper was the flexiglass that lined most of the floor and one entire wall. Rylin could scarcely look away. It was heart-stopping but exhilarating, watching the view unfurl beneath them. The entire world felt like a secret, wild and full of promise, revealing itself only to her.

On the edge of the glittering patchwork quilt, a golden crescent of sun just tipped over the planet's curve. That was one of the highlights of this evening cruise: that they would fly straight into the dawn and through to the other side. Rylin wished she'd brought her vid-cam.

"This isn't about the destination, Rylin. It's about the journey." Cord came to stand behind her, wrapping his arms around her and resting his chin on her shoulder.

But Rylin felt as if most of her life had been about the journey, rather than the destination. Now she finally had a sense of purpose, and she didn't want to make any moves unless they were in the right direction. She didn't need to slow down and enjoy the ride. She wanted to get where she was going, and then enjoy being there.

"Besides, I wanted to do something special tonight. Isn't it nice, being so far from New York?" Cord gestured down to the city, which was already a tiny, pulsing firefly receding behind them. "Really puts things in perspective."

"The world does look small from up here," she agreed.

"The world *is* small."

"Maybe to you!" Rylin spun around, her breath catching at how close Cord was. Her blood felt as if it had rushed to her fingertips, her lips. "To me, it's enormous."

"For now. It's my goal to change that."

Rylin hesitated. She knew she should probably say something, point out that Cord was trying to throw money at their relationship again, just as he had the last time. But she didn't want to ruin the moment. She liked Cord for *Cord*, not for the expensive things that came along with dating him.

"You have that wrinkled-nose, lost-in-thought look." Cord smiled. "Whatever it is, you don't have to take it so seriously."

"Maybe you don't take things seriously enough." Rylin meant it as a joke, but her delivery wasn't quite right. Cord looked hurt.

"I take *you* seriously," he countered.

"Sorry." Rylin glanced back down at the view, still pensive. "I wish my mom were here. She would have loved to see this."

"Really?" Cord sounded skeptical, as if he couldn't picture Rylin's mom up here—which he probably couldn't, she realized. He had never known her mom as anything except the maid.

She tried not to sound defensive. "She loved adventures. She was the one who always dreamed of getting to see Paris."

Cord seemed to have nothing to say to that. He never did, Rylin thought in chagrin, not when the conversation got heavy like this. For someone who'd suffered plenty of losses of his own, he wasn't very good at talking about them.

He settled down on the couch, letting her study the view in

silence. Eventually Rylin came to sit next to him, leaning her head on his shoulder. "Tell me everything I missed this past year," she demanded.

"Where should I begin?"

"At the beginning," Rylin teased, and Cord smiled.

"Fair enough. I guess the first story is what happened to Brice on the way to Dubai. . . ."

Rylin tipped her head back, listening to Cord's smattering of anecdotes from the past year: the trip he and Brice took to New Zealand, the time his cousins came to visit from Rio and overstayed their welcome, the prank Cord pulled on his friend Joaquin. She listened, and yet she didn't actually care that she had missed any of these things.

Cord had a tendency to focus on the big, epic moments, things like this *Skyspear* cruise. But a relationship wasn't made or broken on the dramatic stories. It was built the rest of the time, during the drowsy late-night conversations, the laughter over a bag of pretzels, the quiet study sessions after class. *That* was what Rylin loved.

She realized that Cord had finished talking, and was looking at her in a way that brought color to her cheeks. "I've missed you, Myers," he said. "This might sound weird, but I missed having you to talk to more than anything else. There were a lot of things that I only talked about with you."

Rylin reached for his hand. She knew what he meant—that underneath the romance, they had also been friends. "I missed talking to you too." She really had missed him, she thought, even when she was with Hiral.

She wondered how Hiral was doing right now. Maybe his floating city was big enough to be visible from this high up.

"Look." Cord nudged her gaze toward the window, where golden flames licked above the horizon.

Rylin gasped. They were flying directly into the sunrise.

Banners of fire spun out into the darkness. It was dazzling, blinding; Rylin wanted to tear her eyes away but she couldn't, because there it was, the sun, the closest star within reach. Her whole being felt flooded with a rush of glorious lightness. To see the face of the sun, she realized, was a lot like falling in love.

"You know," Cord said with a mischievous smile, "the natural state of low orbit is actually zero-g. The gravity in this thing is optional."

"Is it?" Rylin felt a delicious shiver trail down her spine. She could guess where this was going. "I've never kissed anyone in zero-g."

"Neither have I, but there's a first time for everything." Cord reached for the touch panel on the wall and tapped the gravity controls to off.

Rylin didn't realize how tightly she'd been clenching the armrest until the gravity had melted away, and she was drifting upward. She quickly let go. How ridiculous of her to be nervous; this wasn't exactly her first time with Cord. But she couldn't help the way she felt.

She floated upward, her hair waving and floating about her in a dark cloud, as if lifted by her heartbeats. Cord had maneuvered himself to her side; he stretched out his hand, reaching for her, and when her fingers laced with his he pulled her to his chest.

They were fumbling and awkward at first, getting used to the lack of gravity. When she lifted Cord's shirt over his head and tried to toss it aside, it didn't stay put the way it would have normally, but kept hovering alongside them like a troublesome gnat. Rylin swatted at it. Suddenly she was laughing, and Cord was laughing too; and she knew with an unshakable certainty that this was right.

And then they were no longer giggling, because their mouths were pressed together, all the awkwardness between them dissolved. Rylin wondered why she had ever doubted them. How could she when her skin was on fire, when Cord's skin was her skin and they were tangled like this, hot and slow and elemental all at once?

Their ship kept on orbiting farther into the sunrise, the dawn bathing their bodies in a warm golden glow.

# LEDA

**LEDA COULDN'T STOP** thinking about Watt.

It was the strangest thing, but her anger toward him was deflating. It felt like an artifact left over from long ago; like something that belonged to a harder, more bitter Leda, the Leda who was still feuding with her parents. Who had never visited Eris's grave.

Leda no longer believed that Watt was some kind of human trigger for the darkest side of her. Not anymore. Maybe because she had confronted her darkness—had looked it squarely in the face and wrestled it away—and now there was nothing left for her to fear.

She wanted to talk to Watt, to tell him that she had confronted her dad about his affair with Eris's mom. That her family was reforging itself into something new and whole again. That if there was hope for her family, then maybe there was hope for Leda too.

She wanted to recount it all to Watt, to share her victories and her defeats with him—because unless he knew about them, none of it felt quite real.

At some point Leda had come to rely on Watt, and she couldn't bear the thought of losing him again.

And so Friday night, the day before the inauguration ball, Leda decided to ping him. But Watt didn't pick up. He didn't answer her flickers either.

When Leda rang the doorbell to his apartment, Watt's mom answered. She blinked, unable to mask her surprise. "Hi, Leda. I'm afraid that Watzahn isn't here."

Leda stuffed her hands into her pockets, surprised that Watt's mom remembered her. She felt suddenly nervous. "Do you know where he is?"

"I'm not sure," Shirin admitted. "I'll let him know you stopped by."

As she turned away, Leda remembered something Watt had told her once—that when he felt truly upset, there was one place he liked to go, to be alone. She logged on to her contacts to find the address and let their embedded computer calculate the fastest route. Then Leda set off, following the directions overlaid onto her vision.

The Game Preserve was an eclectic spot a few floors upTower. It was set up like an old-timey arcade, with a bright tile floor and neon tube lights snaking along the ceiling. Nostalgic rock music blasted through the speakers. The entire space was crowded with a haphazard collection of old vid-game consoles, shooter games and space-invader games and even the kind where metallic claws grabbed at stuffed-animal prizes. Along the far wall were the more expensive holo-suites: the small rooms you could rent out, complete with headsets and haptic gloves, for one-on-one virtual reality. Leda saw a few gray-haired men sitting over coffees, playing 3-D chess on a touch-board.

She swerved down one aisle and then the next, knowing precisely what she was looking for. When she found it, she smiled in involuntary relief.

Watt was ensconced in a plastifoam gaming console shaped like an old wooden pirate ship, complete with the signature skull-and-crossbones insignia. He leaned over the ship's studded wheel, furiously tapping a serious of commands, as the holoscreen before him depicted a row of enemy cannons. Leda was amused to see that Watt's avatar was a woman with long red hair, in a very historically inaccurate dress and high boots.

"Playing as the pirate queen, I see," she remarked, sliding onto the seat next to him.

Watt dropped the controls in shock. "Grace O'Malley has the best weapons," he croaked after a moment. "It's all about strategy."

He stared at her curiously, almost warily. The lights of the game played over his face, making it seem as though he were underwater. "How did you know I was here?"

"You told me last year that *Armada* was your favorite game," Leda reminded him.

Watt didn't look so good. He was wearing ratty jeans and an old sweatshirt, but it was more than that. There was something dispirited about him, as if he were a muted, crushed version of himself.

"Watt," she started to say, but he was talking at the same time, his words falling clumsily over hers.

"I owe you an apology. I should never have accused you of— I just—"

"Let's not talk about it," Leda pleaded. Her chest throbbed with confused emotion, and she scooted closer to Watt. "I've been thinking a lot lately. And I'm finally starting to . . ." *Make things right* was what she wanted to say, but it didn't quite fit. "Move past it."

"I'm glad, Leda."

Watt reached tentatively for her hand, and Leda laced her fingers in his. The holographic waves crashed over them, almost soothing in their repetitions.

"I lost MIT," Watt said after a moment.

Leda's head darted up. "You lost *MIT*?" No wonder he seemed so defeated.

Watt's jaw hardened, his gaze clouding over. "I botched the interview. They asked me to leave."

"Oh, Watt. I'm so sorry." Leda knew the words were inadequate; but what could you say to someone who'd just lost their lifelong dream?

"It was my mistake. I tried too hard to be something that I'm not." Watt sighed. "On top of losing you, it felt like more than I could handle—that I had somehow screwed up everything in my life through my own foolishness."

"Watt, you haven't lost me," Leda assured him. "I just needed some time. I'm scared of myself . . . of what I might have done. But I don't want to push you away."

She looked over at him. The blood rushed to the thin skin over the bones of her chest; she felt her heartbeat echoing in the space within her ribs. There were no secrets between them, she realized, dazed. Nothing between her and Watt except for space.

Then his arms were around her, and she was pressing her mouth to his, certain that she would never get enough of him.

They fell back against the holo-console and it erupted into a dozen displays at once, like fireworks. Watt broke away. "Sorry," he mumbled, but Leda just laughed. She didn't care.

She realized that all she wanted was to be alone with Watt,

away from everything. Somewhere they could shut away the world, if only for a little while. "Do you want to get out of here?" Leda twisted at a coil of her hair, suddenly nervous. "My parents are away. I mean, if you want to."

"Yeah. Of course," Watt stammered, as if half afraid she might change her mind.

"Okay." Leda reached for his hand again and gave it a squeeze. There was that impish smile she loved, curling up at the corners of his mouth.

When they were back upTower, through the front door of her family's place and up the stairs to her room, Leda pulled the door shut behind her.

To think that at this time last year, Watt had been nothing to her but the person who filled her hacking requests. Now he was her co-conspirator, her partner in crime, the boy she loved. Watt had slipped into her life and under her skin, and Leda was so very glad of it, even though she knew it was what he'd intended all along.

Well, if she was going to do this, she'd damned well better dive in headfirst.

# WATT

**WATT HADN'T BEEN** in Leda's bedroom for almost a year.

It was different, he thought—hollower, with new blank spaces on the walls and shelves. Leda had meant it when she said she had tried to sweep away all the detritus of her former life.

But she was still Leda, still the girl he loved, standing before him—slight and trembling, yet not fragile at all. Watt knew the implacability of her strength, like a blade that was whip-thin but sharp.

"Leda," Watt said softly. "We don't have to, um . . ."

In answer, Leda grabbed Watt's shirt to pull him closer, and kissed him.

They fell backward onto her bed in a feverish tangle. Leda fumbled with the hooks and fastenings of Watt's jacket, tossing it aside. He reached behind her to pull the zipper of her dress. "Here, let me," Leda said impatiently, tearing herself away from him just long enough to shimmy out of it. It fell onto the floor with a hiss.

Then she was facing him in nothing but her wispy bra and underwear. Watt felt his heartbeat echoing in the space between them.

He reached up tentatively to trace her smile. He adored Leda's mouth, the eager fullness of it. He adored everything about her: the arch of her neck, the softness of her arms, the way she fit so perfectly tucked into his chest. Everywhere they touched seemed to explode in a white-hot friction.

Watt regretted every moment of the last year he hadn't spent with her. He regretted every kiss that he had ever given to anyone who wasn't Leda, because he knew now how much a kiss could mean.

He loved Leda—for her wildness and her inner fire and her fierce, stubborn pride. He loved that she was more ruthlessly alive than anyone he had ever met. He wanted so desperately to tell her that he loved her, but he didn't dare, because he was terrified it might send her running. Instead he kept kissing her, again and again and again, trying to pour his love into the kisses.

He hoped, desperately, that she loved him too.

---

Early the next morning, Watt leaned on one elbow, glancing down at Leda with unadulterated wonder.

She shifted on the pillow, which was warm and slightly perfumed from where she'd slept. The dim light gleamed on her earrings, which Watt realized were shaped like a pair of tiny crescent moons. He wondered if they had some meaning: if Leda had bought them on a trip, maybe, or if they'd been a gift. He felt hungry for every last detail about anything that mattered to Leda.

He fought back the urge to reach out and touch her, to check that she really was here. That last night wasn't just a dream.

Watt realized with a start that she was awake, her eyes fluttering open to shine in the darkness like a cat's.

"Watt," she breathed, and he leaned in to kiss her.

"I hate to say this, but I should get back."

"I didn't think you were the type to run off," she murmured, teasing.

"Trust me, the last thing I want is to leave. I just don't want to be the guy who gets you in trouble with your parents."

"You're right." Leda let out a breath and sat up, letting the sheets spill forward off her shoulders. "Watt?"

He paused at the door to look back at her. "Yeah?"

"Will you go to the inauguration ball with me tonight?" She gave a hesitant smile. "I know we've had a few ups and downs at formal events, but I thought this time . . ."

Watt grinned, pretending to deliberate. "I'm not so sure. I mean, last time you only invited me because you wanted access to Nadia."

Leda rolled her eyes. "You know that's not how it—"

"But I can't say no to you, Leda," Watt finished. "Of course I'll be there."

The whole way home, he kept Nadia off. She had powered herself down while he was with Leda, the way she always did when Watt was with a girl, and for some reason he wasn't ready to break the silence.

Which was why he didn't get any warning that there were police officers at his apartment.

———

"As I told you, my son is out at a friend's house." Watt's mom had planted herself sturdily in the doorway, her voice lifted in outrage. Before her stood a pair of police officers: a squat man with a moustache and a bright-eyed woman who couldn't be much older than Watt.

*Quant on*, Watt thought furiously, watching as Nadia ran facial-reg on them. She quickly put name-identification boxes below their faces: Harold Campbell and Lindsay Kiles.

"It looks like he's back now," Officer Kiles said flatly as Watt approached the door. She lifted an eyebrow, as if to question why he was showing up so very early on a Saturday morning, looking distinctly rumpled and stale.

Officer Campbell butted in. "Mr. Bakradi, we were hoping you would come answer a few questions for us."

"Absolutely not," Watt's mom insisted. Her hands were planted on her hips, her jaw set in a grim line.

Watt felt bewildered, and a little afraid. *Nadia, what's going on? I thought the police didn't have any concrete evidence.* All they knew was that Mariel had been stalking them, which didn't prove anything.

Nadia seemed as nervous as he was. *I'm trying to see what this is about, but as I've said before, I can't hack the police's system without being on-site.*

Watt wondered if Rylin and Avery would be questioned too, or if this was just about him—about his hacking. Or worse, about Nadia.

"It's okay. I'm happy to come, if I can be of any help," Watt said as politely as he could, ignoring the angry protests of his mom. He ran a hand through his unruly hair before following the officers back toward the main thoroughfare.

He felt a stab of dismay at the sight of the blue police hover pulled up at the corner. For some reason he'd expected that they would take public transit. It didn't exactly inspire a lot of confidence, being forced to ride in the back of that hover, where the doors didn't open from the inside. It felt as if things had gone in fast-forward, that he had already been tried and found guilty.

Watt lifted his hand to the bump where Nadia was located, to reassure himself that she was still there—a risky gesture, but he tried to make it look as if he were scratching his head. At least he would have Nadia with him during the questioning, he thought, with a fevered gratefulness.

But the moment he followed the detectives into the station's interrogation room, Nadia set off an alarm bell in Watt's mind. *There's an infrared sensor in here to detect active tech.*

*That's for tablets and contacts! It's okay, my brain is* supposed *to show up hot,* Watt assured her, because the thought of doing this interrogation without Nadia made him want to throw up.

*Not safe. I'm going cold,* she told him, and with that she shut herself off.

Shit. Watt would actually have to go through with this alone.

He took the metal folding chair across the table from the detectives. Should he sit up straight or slouch? Maybe lean an elbow on the table? He needed to strike the right balance between nervousness and confidence; because wouldn't an innocent guy be somewhat blasé about all this, knowing he had done nothing wrong? Or would an innocent person be quaking with fear?

Why couldn't he make even a decision about his *posture* without Nadia's input?

Officer Campbell spoke first. "Mr. Bakradi. Did you know a girl named Mariel Valconsuelo?"

"I don't know who that is," Watt replied, perhaps a bit too emphatically. If there were infrared sensors in here, were there also lie detectors? But the detectives couldn't run a real lie analysis without putting biosensors on him, could they?

Campbell nodded at his colleague, who tapped a screen, causing a hologram of Mariel to flare to life before them. She looked angry and uncompromising, her head tilted upward, as if it was a terrible imposition that she was being asked to take an ID picture.

"Mariel was dating Eris Dodd-Radson before Eris died," Officer Campbell said significantly. Watt didn't answer.

The officer lifted an eyebrow. "You didn't ever meet Mariel?" she asked again.

"Not that I can recall."

"Before she died, Mariel was gathering information about you."

Watt tried his best to act shocked by that revelation. Officer Campbell leaned farther forward onto the table, as if determined to occupy more space. "You don't have any idea why?"

"Maybe she had a crush on me?" The moment he saw the officers' faces, Watt knew that irreverence hadn't been the right way to go.

"I can assure you that she did not," Kiles cut in drily. Watt bit the inside of his cheek. Nadia would have kept him from saying that.

The officer waved, and the hologram grew watery and dissolved like rapidly melting snow. "How do you know Avery Fuller?" she went on, abruptly changing tack.

"Avery is a friend," Watt said warily.

"Just a friend?"

Did they know he'd taken her to that University Club party, last year? "I wanted it to be more but, you know, Avery is basically unattainable," Watt quipped, and he could swear he saw a ghost of a smile on Campbell's face.

Officer Kiles was less amused. "What about Leda Cole? Are you 'just friends' with her too?"

"What does my love life have to do with this, exactly?"

The young officer stared at him levelly. "I'm trying to understand how you became so intertwined in it all."

Watt understood the subtext. How had Watt, a seemingly ordinary downTower guy, become entangled in the lives of girls from the 103rd to thousandth floors?

"I guess it just . . . happened," Watt said inadequately.

The detectives exchanged a ponderous glance. Finally Officer Kiles lifted her hand, palm up, in an ambiguous gesture that might have meant good-bye or might have simply implied a lack of trust, as if she didn't quite buy Watt's story.

"Thank you, Mr. Bakradi. You're free to go. For now," she added ominously.

Watt didn't need to be told twice. He stood as quickly as he could and hurried toward the door. Before he could reach it, though, Officer Kiles asked him one more question.

"By the way, Mr. Bakradi—do you know anyone by the name of Nadia?"

Watt felt a sudden chasm opening inside him, a black hole of fear so immense it seemed to have a gravity all its own.

For a single breathless moment, he considered confessing. Trying to cut a deal in exchange for telling them everything—that Mariel had been stalking all of them, that Leda had accidentally killed Eris, that she might have killed Mariel too, but he wasn't sure; he couldn't be sure of anything anymore. Before Watt got tangled up in all this, the world had seemed so simple, so *binary*, divided crisply into black and white, 1s and 0s. Now he knew nothing for certain.

But everything in Watt recoiled at the thought of hurting Leda. He stumbled back a step, hoping his face didn't look as stricken as he felt.

"I don't know anyone named Nadia."

The instant they were outside the police station, he turned Nadia back on abruptly and filled her in on everything that had happened. *We're in trouble*, he concluded, with a heavy, sinking feeling.

*They don't know anything except that the name Nadia was scrawled in that notebook*, she reminded him.

*But what if there's other evidence? I'm terrified that they're going to keep digging and digging, that they won't rest until they find* something. *And we both know there's a lot to find*, he thought helplessly.

*I'm so sorry*, Nadia replied, which was ridiculous, since none of this was her fault. It was his.

Watt knew what he had to do.

There was only one way to find out for certain what the police knew or why they had questioned him this morning.

*I'm going to hack the police station*, he decided.

Nadia's response was a swift *NO*, written in flashing red letters so large that they obstructed Watt's vision. He ignored her.

It had been a long time since Watt had to go all James Bond and sneak Nadia somewhere for an on-site hack. Actually, the last time he'd done it was the day he met Avery—when he was working for Leda, trying to figure out who Atlas liked. It felt like a million years ago.

But Watt wouldn't feel safe until he knew for certain what the police knew. And the only way he could find that out was from inside their infrastructure.

*Absolutely not, Watt! It's too dangerous*, Nadia replied, and he could hear her silently shouting. *This isn't a tollbooth. This is the NYPD headquarters we're talking about!*

But Watt couldn't handle this state of uncertainty anymore. *It's the only way for us to find out the truth*, he insisted, trying to ignore the way the hairs on the back of his arms lifted with fear at the prospect.

*I refuse to approve of this! If you get caught, you could end up in prison!*

He set his jaw, determined. *And if they know the truth about you, I'll definitely end up in prison.*

She stopped arguing after that, because they both knew that Watt was right.

# AVERY

**"I'LL GET IT!"** Avery proclaimed when the doorbell sounded on the thousandth floor.

"Avery, *stop*! It's the reporter," her mom admonished, with a disappointed shake of her head. "And put your shoes back on."

*Right, because god forbid anyone find out that we walk around our home barefoot.* "It isn't the reporter; it's Max," Avery argued, though she dutifully pulled on the low-slung heels her mom had picked out. They matched her plum-colored dress, with a narrow waistline and cap sleeves. Which her mom had also picked out.

"You invited *Max*?" Elizabeth heaved a loud sigh. "Avery, this was supposed to be an intimate family brunch. With a photo shoot."

Avery felt a stab of resentment. She knew exactly why her mom didn't want Max here. Her parents genuinely liked him, but they had done their best to keep him away from anything election-related. Because Max, with his shaggy hair and mismatched clothes and dry sense of humor, didn't fit the image Avery's parents were trying to construct of their perfect all-American family.

"Yes, I invited Max," Avery said curtly. She had been dreading this meal all week and wasn't about to face it without Max.

Their brunch guest was a reporter from *Modern Life*, one of the most followed news sources on the feeds. He was currently writing a profile about Avery's dad, one of those cozy at-home pieces about what the newly elected mayor of New York was like "behind the scenes." It would be posted to the feeds later today, just in time for the inauguration ball.

Avery knew she was expected to sit there and smile like the well-behaved, photogenic daughter everyone thought she was. To tell a charming story that helped cast her dad in a relatable light. To act elegant but approachable.

She strode quickly down the entry hall, her multiplied reflections floating in the mirrors alongside her. Her footsteps echoed on the newly polished floors. Their housekeeper, Sarah, was preparing a "home-cooked" meal of omelets and pancakes, and Avery's mom had deliberately left the kitchen door open, so everything smelled lightly of sugar and domesticity.

"Hey, there," she exclaimed as she opened the front door for Max. She had offered several times to put him on the approved-entry list, but he unerringly refused. *And deny myself the pleasure of seeing your beautiful face each time you let me in?* he'd asked, to which Avery had no response except a smile.

He stood there now in a button-down shirt and khakis, his dark hair slightly less mussed than usual, a bouquet of fresh lilies in his outstretched fist. When Avery started to reach for them, Max laughingly shook his head.

"These aren't for you; they're for your mom," he said. How typically thoughtful of him.

"You didn't bring anything for me?" Avery teased.

"Just this." Max leaned forward to kiss her, sending shivers down the length of Avery's body.

"Thanks. I needed that."

"Remember," he murmured into her ear as they walked through the apartment with fingers laced. "You won't have to deal with any of this stuff next year. You'll get to run away with me to Oxford and leave it all behind."

"I know," Avery said, but her statement lacked its usual conviction. It wasn't Max's fault, she assured herself. Just that she was young and still entitled to change her mind about things . . . to live in the dorms, for instance. . . .

"Max!" Her father strode into the living room, closely followed by Avery's mom, who gave a tight, mincing smile. Atlas was already sprawled on the couch, a coffee in hand. He stood up to greet Max, not quite meeting Avery's eyes.

"Mr. Fuller. Thank you so much for inviting me this afternoon," Max said politely, and held out the bouquet of lilies. "These are for you, Mrs. Fuller."

"Thank you, Max. We're thrilled that you could make it," Avery's mom told him, and Avery wondered once again at what a good liar her mom was, because even she—who'd heard her mom complaining about Max a mere two minutes earlier—almost believed it. Elizabeth handed the lilies to Sarah, who whisked them off to deposit them on a table somewhere.

The doorbell sounded again. "That will be the reporter," Avery's dad said, looking around at each of them in turn like a general surveying his troops before a grand parade. "This is the biggest coverage of our family so far. Let's make sure it's positive, okay?"

The reporter's name was Neil Landry. He was only in his late twenties, with slick dark hair and an eager smile. Very charming and personable, exactly what you would expect from someone whose career consisted of constantly making and uploading vids.

"Mr. Landry. Thank you for joining us on such an important, exciting day." Avery's dad shook the reporter's hand with characteristic gusto.

"Please, call me Neil." His smile was almost as blinding as Avery's dad's.

"Only if you'll call me Pierson."

Avery's dad stepped behind the enormous bar, which was made of a slab of Carrara marble that, to his delight, had come from the twentieth-century headquarters of the New York Prohibition Agency. He opened a bottle of champagne for mimosas. "We're celebrating!" he exclaimed in an ebullient mood.

Avery smiled and nodded and tried to follow along. Everyone else seemed to be doing just fine, even Max, who was clearly making a valiant effort for Avery's sake. They all laughed, they flattered the reporter, they lobbed harmless jokes at Avery's dad. It was all a perfectly choreographed dance, and Avery knew her part. She just wasn't performing it.

Eventually they moved into the dining room, which was situated in a corner of the apartment, to take advantage of dramatic floor-to-ceiling windows on two sides. Even now the sun was honeycombing through the fluffy white clouds.

On the center of the table, where Max's arrangement of lilies should have been, was a small bud vase containing a single red rose. An absolutely perfect rose, every line of its petals curved just so, its color deepening in precise degrees from the edges toward its center. It was the Avery Fuller of roses, the kind of rose that had been genetically designed for this sort of showmanship. The kind of rose that could never exist in nature. Avery imagined the florist placing an order for this maddeningly perfect rose, thinking smugly that it reflected reality.

She had a sudden urge to rip it apart. Or better yet, to collect dozens of misshapen, twisted, spotted roses, and arrange them in an enormous bowl for her parents, as a gift. A reminder that nothing in the world is perfect. That imperfection can be celebrated too.

As Sarah brought in the first few dishes, Avery's mom met her eyes across the table and mimed sitting up straighter, her brows lowered in disappointment. Avery adjusted her posture. She hadn't even realized she was slouching.

Maybe what Calliope had said the other day was starting to get to her.

She just didn't feel up to it anymore. The constant pressure to get things right, to never make a single misstep. She twisted her superfiber napkin furiously in her lap. It was woven far too strongly to rip, so she just kept contorting it on itself, over and over.

"So, Pierson," the reporter said, as Avery's mom finished a story about how she and Pierson met at a church fund-raiser, which was so false that it was almost laughable. Avery knew that her parents had met through an i-Net dating site. "You said throughout the campaign that you would apply business sense to government. Is that still your approach?"

"Of course," Avery's dad said good-naturedly. "I want to run the city like a company. Make it efficient."

"And who will take over your actual company while you're helping this great city?"

"I have a very experienced board of directors in place. And my son, Atlas, is in town to help ensure that the transition goes smoothly."

Neil's eyes gleamed. "Atlas, you skipped college to go work for your father, didn't you?" Before Atlas could answer, he had rounded on Avery. "What about you, Avery? Are you going to join the family business someday?"

"I don't know," she said honestly. "I'm hoping to study art history in college. We'll see where that leads me."

"And this is your boyfriend?" Neil added jovially, his gaze sliding to Max for the first time. "What was wrong with all the men in New York, that you had to go get one abroad?"

Avery knew he was just trying to be witty, but she couldn't help reflexively looking at Atlas across the table, just for an instant.

"I guess I never found the right person in New York."

"Which worked out in my favor," Max cut in, trying to help. "I know how unbelievably lucky I am."

"I bet New Yorkers weren't too pleased with that!" the reporter boomed, his eyes still on Avery. Everyone at the table joined obediently in the laughter. "What do you think of what the press is calling you? The 'princess of New York'?"

Avery's hand closed around her water in its antique crystal glass, which was incised with a feathery, delicate design. She liked how fragile it felt in her hand. As if she could smash it against a wall and watch it fragment into a million beautiful slivers.

"It's a little silly," she admitted.

"Come on! What girl doesn't want to be called a princess?" Neil persisted.

To Avery's surprise, Atlas was the one who answered for her.

"I don't think 'princess' describes Avery," he said softly. "It implies that Avery didn't do anything on her own, that she's only worth knowing because of the family she comes from, while we all know Avery is remarkable in her own right. She's brilliant, and thoughtful, and the most caring and selfless person I know."

"What would you call her, then, if not a princess?" the reporter asked. Avery saw her dad listening, perhaps too intently.

"Unique," Atlas said quietly. "Avery is never anyone but herself. That's what the world loves about her."

Avery felt tears burning at her eyes. It wasn't lost on her that if someone was going to speak up on her behalf, it should have been her boyfriend.

The doorbell clanged, breaking the charged silence. Avery heard Sarah hurrying to answer it. There was the sound of low voices conferring and footsteps echoing down the hall. A moment later, a pair of police officers strode into the room.

Avery's blood drummed furiously in her veins. She felt suddenly light-headed, because she knew, with a rush of nauseating certainty, that this was about her.

"Miss Fuller?" asked the older policeman, a man with a curling moustache. "We were hoping you would come down to the station and answer a few questions for us."

"Excuse me, but what is this regarding?" her father cut in.

Avery knew that she should be afraid, but for some reason, the fear wasn't hitting her yet. Instead she felt a curious sense of detachment, as if she were floating somewhere near the chandelier.

"It's about the murder of Mariel Valconsuelo," answered the police officer; and that single word, *murder*, echoed through the room like a gunshot. Avery saw Neil Landry lean forward, his nostrils flaring in anticipation. Well, of course. Perfect Avery Fuller being questioned about a murder might be the start of a very good story.

The police officer folded his hat respectfully in his hands. "I do apologize for the inconvenience, Mr. Fuller. We would like to hear what your daughter has to say on this matter."

"Out of the question," Avery's dad said smoothly. "She can't talk, today of all days. It's the inauguration ball! If you really need Avery's testimony, you can come back with a subpoena."

Avery found her voice at last. "I don't mind," she whispered, and rose to her feet, still holding tightly to the napkin as if it were a good-luck charm. "I don't know anything about Mariel or about her death, but if there's any way I can be helpful, I am happy to try."

Pierson relented, though he still didn't seem pleased. "All right," he conceded. "But let me get Quiros for you. You shouldn't have to answer any questions without our lawyer present."

Avery nodded and followed the policemen out the door, trying to project a self-assurance that she didn't feel.

She had plenty that she wanted to keep hidden—about Eris's death, her relationship with Atlas, and most of all, what Mariel had done to Leda that night on the beach in Dubai.

Soon enough, everyone might discover that perfect Avery Fuller wasn't so very perfect after all.

# CALLIOPE

**CALLIOPE GLOWED WITH** palpable happiness as she walked with Brice into city hall, pulling her gown to one side so it wouldn't catch on her heels. It was a deep purple—the color of royalty, of course—made of a glorious lithe satin that clung to her waist before falling in dramatic folds down to her strappy black stilettos. Next to her, Brice looked brooding and aloof and devastatingly handsome.

"I'm so glad you decided that you could come tonight after all," Brice said warmly.

At first Calliope thought there was no way she could come to the ball. It was too high-profile and conspicuous, too flagrant a violation of the rules she should be living by; and besides, Nadav and Elise would be here. Yet in a shocking twist of events, Calliope's deliverance had actually come from Livya.

Livya had woken up this morning sick and clammy with a fever. She had begged her daddy to please stay home and take care of her. It made no sense to Calliope; everyone knew that room comps were equipped with a full suite of medical products, and could just as easily monitor a sick person or feed them soup. But of course, Nadav agreed to stay by Livya's side all night, like the smothering parent he was.

The moment she knew for certain that Nadav and Elise weren't coming, Calliope had messaged Brice. *I think I can sneak out, if you want to go to the inauguration ball.*

*Sneak out! For shame,* Brice had replied, and she could practically see the amusement glinting in his eyes. *I've been a terrible influence on you, Calliope Brown, and you should turn me away while there's still hope for you. If you can. I'm usually quite difficult to get rid of.*

*Don't even try to take credit for my behavior,* she had replied, smirking. *I was breaking rules long before I met you.*

She was glad, now, that she had decided to come. City hall took up multiple levels of the Tower, spanning the 432nd to 438th floors. It was a tangled warren of administrative offices and shabby board rooms, the entire thing dominated by an enormous domed foyer at its center, and its crowning glory: a curved observation deck that perched at the top of the dome, looking directly out at the sky.

This must be the very first black-tie function ever held here. The Tower itself was less than two decades old, yet these mid-Tower public spaces seemed to have aged more rapidly than the rest of the structure. There was already something faded and scuffed about city hall, as if it had been lived in too aggressively.

Tonight, though, the entire place was transformed into an enchanted fairyland. Every last centimeter was spangled and tech'd out to perfection: the flagstones of the foyer were covered in crimson carpets, printed in an interlocking *F* monogram. The walls had been lined in a hologram of waving gold banners, scattered with occasional vid-clips of Pierson Fuller. And flowers, there were so many flowers, piled into perfect globes that hovered over every table. As Calliope moved with Brice through the room, a progression of faces flashed past like lights flickering on and off; all painted with makeup and treated with DNA longevity treatments, all animated by the same weary excitement. It felt a bit like a wedding, as if Mr. Fuller was making a lifelong commitment to something. Probably to his own ambition.

To one side of the room, Calliope saw Avery talking to a group of reporters. She couldn't help thinking that there was a tempestuous heat to Avery's beauty tonight—as if beneath her bright-gold exterior, she was coming rapidly untethered.

A photographer walked past and lifted an image-renderer to snap a pic of them, but Calliope quickly ducked aside. She couldn't afford photographic evidence of her and Brice. She was risking enough just being here.

Though even if Nadav's friends did see her, Calliope wasn't sure they would actually recognize her. Wearing this dramatic low-cut gown, her hair tumbling sexily over one shoulder, Calliope looked nothing like the frumpy, morose creature she had been at her mom's wedding. She felt utterly like herself again.

When she left the apartment earlier, Nadav had been in the kitchen, overseeing the stove as it brewed a pot of soup for Livya. His head had instantly darted up at the sound of Calliope's footsteps. "Where are you headed?" he'd demanded.

"Volunteering at the hospital," Calliope said automatically.

"Again?"

"Yes, well, that's the thing about children. New ones get sick every day," Calliope had said evenly. Nadav just pursed his lips, ignoring the sarcasm.

She felt a sudden brush of guilt, remembering the way her mom had looked at Nadav during the wedding. *Don't risk everything just because of some boy,* she had begged.

Well, Brice wasn't just some boy.

"Cord is here," Brice said, interrupting her thoughts. Something in his tone gave Calliope pause; it sounded as if Brice wasn't all that happy to see his younger brother. Her eyes followed his, to where Cord stood with a beautiful half-Asian girl, her hair pulled into a simple low ponytail. She looked familiar. Hadn't Calliope seen her at school?

"Should we go say hi?" she offered, but Brice was already edging in the opposite direction.

"Not while he's with Rylin."

Rylin! That was definitely her name. "What happened between you and Rylin?" Calliope asked, curious. "Did you hit on her?"

"Worse. I got rid of her," Brice said bluntly. "I thought she was using Cord for the money, so I broke them up."

*Using him for the money.* Calliope shifted uncomfortably. There were dozens of boys who could, quite accurately, make the same complaint about her.

"Anyway," he went on, "their breakup clearly didn't stick. Now they're back together. And I'm the guy who tried to get between them."

"Rylin might forgive you. You both clearly care about Cord. If you tell her what you just told me, she might understand."

"Would you forgive me, if you were her?" Brice asked, and he had her there.

"Not at all. I like to hold grudges, though," Calliope said easily. "Rylin seems like she might be the forgiving type."

"She might," Brice agreed, "but then, I'm not really the apologizing type."

Calliope tilted her head, looking up at him. "Does that mean you won't apologize to me if you hurt my feelings?"

"I don't like this hypothetical scenario. Why are you assuming I'll hurt you?" Brice demanded.

*Everyone in a relationship hurts the person they're with eventually, even if they don't mean to.* But then, she and Brice weren't technically in a relationship. "Just trying to prepare myself," Calliope replied, trying to make it sound offhand. She was used to being the one who did the leaving, or the hurting; but then, she wasn't used to being the one who cared.

"Of course if I hurt you, I would apologize," Brice said, his eyes warm on her. "Think of yourself as the exception to my no-apology rule. You're the exception to every rule. You *are* a goddess, after all."

He grabbed a pair of champagne flutes and handed one to her as they wandered nearer the dance floor. Calliope took a small sip; it was expensive champagne, the kind that tasted like marzipan and fireworks. The kind that made you want to kiss whomever you were with.

She was glad she'd decided to come to this party, after all.

"Where do you think you're headed next year?" Brice asked.

"Next year?"

"To college. Are you thinking East Coast? California? Please don't say Chicago; it's too cold there," he added, half teasing.

Calliope felt as if the carpet with its scrolling interlocking *F*s had been yanked out from beneath her. She'd never been one for planning the future. She used to joke that she could tell you more about the next five minutes than about the next five years.

But ever since her mom brought it up, Calliope had been toying with the idea of college. She'd even met with one of the college counselors at school. His thoughts on her application had only served to dishearten her.

"I'm not sure where I'll get in. I'm not very good at standard-ized tests," she said vaguely. Not to mention her spotty school record.

"That's not surprising. You aren't exactly a standard person," Brice replied. "Still, I have no doubt that you're smart. Even if you currently use those smarts for nothing but sneaking into five-star restaurants."

Her contacts lit up with an incoming ping from her mom, but Calliope shook her head to one side to decline it.

"What do you want to study?" Brice pressed.

"I don't know. Maybe history or creative writing," she admit-ted. She *was* pretty good at inventing stories. "Why are you so curious?"

Brice stepped a little closer, as if to block her off from the dance floor, to obtain some small measure of privacy. "Because I like you, Calliope. I would like to keep seeing you, no matter where you end up."

Her mom pinged again. Again Calliope shook her head.

"I would like that," she told him, her smile growing wider.

She had never met anyone like Brice—had certainly never revealed so much of herself to anyone before. She should have felt nervous about how well he really knew her. It was as if every fragment of truth she had handed him was a bullet, a weapon he could choose to someday use against her; and Calliope simply had to trust that he wouldn't.

Her contacts lit up a third time, and Calliope felt a cold chill trace down her back.

"Sorry," she murmured with a little jerk of her head and turned aside to accept the ping. Her heart pounded in her rib cage.

"Hey, sweetie." Elise's voice was oddly strained and muffled. Calliope realized with a pang that she was hiding this ping from

Nadav. "Something has happened. It's Livya."

Maybe Livya was seriously ill. "Is she in the hospital?"

"No. Although that's where you are supposed to be, if you recall." Elise sighed. "You aren't reading to sick children, are you?"

"Look, Mom, I—"

"I thought I told you no side cons."

"This isn't a *side con*!" Calliope hissed, momentarily forgetting that she was in a public place. She cupped her hand around her mouth to hide her words. "I actually like him, okay?"

Elise pretended not to hear that. "Livya set you up, sweetie. I'm pretty sure she faked being sick to lay a trap for you and see if you would sneak out."

"Oh my god." Calliope staggered a step back.

"Please tell me you aren't at the inauguration ball."

Calliope couldn't answer, because she didn't want to lie to her mom.

"Leave right now," Elise said after a moment. "I'll cover for you until you're home."

And then she abruptly ended the ping.

Calliope shook her head. She should have seen this coming. She, who could always predict other people's reactions, who prided herself on her cool levelheadedness—how had she been outwitted by Livya Mizrahi?

"Everything okay?" Brice asked.

Calliope bit her lip. She let her eyes dart quickly around the room, taking it all in—the lights, the glittering gowns, the amphitheater of space filled with people. The echo of music and gossip and delicate martini laughter. And yet, just as she had at the train station last week, Calliope felt irrevocably distant from these people.

*I actually like him*, she had said to her mom, and it was true.

She really liked Brice, more than she had ever allowed herself to like anyone, and she liked the idea of continuing to see him into the future.

But Elise *loved* Nadav, and Calliope had promised not to screw it up for her.

"I'm so sorry. I have to go," she whispered, then turned to leave the party as quickly as she could.

# AVERY

"I'M PROUD OF my father for everything he's already done for the city of New York and everything he plans to do." Avery forced herself to smile, her mouth spitting out the pre-approved sound bytes from her father's PR team. "I know that his impact on the city will continue to be monumental."

"And yet you're planning to move to England?" the reporter pressed. A zetta hovered near Avery's mouth to capture her response.

"I'm hoping to attend Oxford, if I get in," Avery said, her teeth still clenched in that smile. She didn't really see what her college plans had to do with her father's inauguration. And how did they know about Oxford, anyway? Her application status was supposed to be confidential. One of her friends must have let the rumor get out—or worse, someone on the streets of Oxford had spotted her and recognized her. Which meant that Oxford wasn't nearly as removed from it all as Avery had hoped.

"New York would be devastated to lose you," the reporter simpered. She had bronzed skin and jet-black hair that was styled into shining waves. "Speaking of, here's your brother. Perhaps he can join you to—"

"Will you excuse me?" Avery said smoothly, ducking to one side. Like hell did she want to stand here and be co-interviewed with Atlas. After that interview at the police station this afternoon, she was already at breaking point. She hadn't told the detectives anything incriminating, but it had still rattled her.

The moment she got back home, Avery had immediately messaged Watt. For some reason she'd wanted to keep it between the two of them, rather than involving Rylin—or Leda. There was no predicting Leda's erratic behavior in situations like this. Besides, Avery couldn't shake the sense that Leda was still the one in the greatest danger.

She knew that Watt, no matter what, would have Leda's best interests at heart.

*I don't think they know anything—do you?* she had asked him. After all, the police weren't really accusing her of anything. It was more as if they were prodding her, fishing for something without fully knowing what it was.

*I'm working on it*, Watt had said obliquely. *I'll let you know what I find.*

Avery didn't know what he meant by that. She was afraid to ask.

She stalked now through the middle of city hall, which her dad had transformed into a gilded and hologrammed wilderness, filled with a herd of overdressed New Yorkers. Her parents stood near the stage, greeting people, smiling their empty politician smiles.

She glanced around, wondering where Max was, even though a strange part of her felt reluctant to see him. She kept replaying that moment in Oxford—when he gave her the key-chip to the apartment and imagined out loud the life they would build there. If he'd handed her the key to his heart, she couldn't have felt more guilty or undeserving.

Avery tried to set out looking for Max, but every few feet, someone stopped her. Lila Donnelly, who'd started the marathon on the moon, where everyone ran in weight-additive shoes to simulate Earth's gravity. Marc de Beauville, one of her father's greatest donors, who owned the midTower multilevel golf course. Fan PingPing, the Chinese pop star. They were all here, old money and new money, the curious and the bored, the businesspeople and the wide-eyed clusters of friends who had bought a ticket just because they had a weakness for glamorous parties.

She nodded at each of them, murmuring a few words of thanks before swishing past in her gown of gold tulle. It fell in frothy folds from her nipped-in waist, the edge of each tier lined in pale gold sequins and shimmering embroidery. With her hair pinned up in delicate curls and her mom's five-carat canary diamonds blazing in her ears, Avery knew she looked glittering and expensive. She hated it.

"Avery!" Leda pushed determinedly through the crowd toward her. "I've been looking all over for you."

"Hey, Leda," Avery managed, her smile still affixed to her face, but it felt a little wobbly. Leda wasn't fooled.

"What is it?"

"I can't *escape* him," Avery said helplessly. The words fell from her lips before she'd given them thought.

"But why would you want to?" Leda's eyes narrowed. "Is it the apartment thing?"

Avery's lips parted. Her mouth felt sandpaper-dry. Her eyes had darted reflexively toward Atlas.

Leda followed her gaze. Avery watched the comprehension

dawn on her face, that moment of tacit understanding mingled with shocked disbelief.

"Oh" was all Leda said at first. "I thought you meant Max."

Which was understandable, because she *should* have meant Max. If Avery was going to use a vague, antecedent-less *him*, it should have been her boyfriend she was talking about.

Neither of them spoke Atlas's name.

"Look, Avery," Leda said slowly. "You and Max are good together—calm, stable. No drama." Somehow, the way she pronounced it made it sound as though a world without drama was as dull as it was safe.

"Max and I have drama!" Avery protested. "And sparks and fireworks. Whatever you want to call it."

"Of course you do," Leda said, too quickly to be convincing. She heaved a sigh. "You've just been so happy lately with Max. I don't want you to lose that."

"You seem happy too." This time Avery's smile came out more genuine. "Is Watt here tonight?"

She didn't miss the telltale way that Leda's cheeks flushed at the mention of him. "He was supposed to be here, but he couldn't make it at the last minute. Something urgent came up," Leda said, and shrugged. "He told me not to worry."

Avery nodded. "I'm glad that you two are . . . you know."

"Yeah." Leda's eyes skimmed over the crowded room. "Can you believe that we're here? Senior year, at your dad's inauguration?"

Avery knew the feeling. Time kept slipping through her hands, too quickly for her to snatch it. "If only we could go back, do things differently. Fix all our mistakes."

"I wish," Leda agreed. "But I think the only thing to do is keep going forward, the best we can."

Maybe Leda was right. Maybe the secret to growing up was

turning away from the ugliest parts of yourself. Pasting a smile on your face, and pretending that *it*—the kiss, the confession, the night you watched your best friend die—never happened.

Avery wondered if maybe she *should* tell Leda that the police had questioned her today. She didn't want her to worry or spin out of control again. But maybe it was foolish to hide it from her. Maybe Leda had a right to know.

Avery started to open her mouth, uncertain how to bring it up, just as Max appeared at her side.

"Here you are," he exclaimed, dropping a kiss on Avery's brow. He looked crisply handsome in his tux.

"I was just going to go grab some dessert," Leda announced, taking her cue to leave. She shot Avery a meaningful look before swishing away. Avery watched her go, the exaggerated V of the back of her dress drawing attention to her tiny frame, the stark black-and-white pattern of her skirts.

"Sorry. I was doing interviews." Avery willed herself to seem normal, to refrain from looking in Atlas's direction. Because even now she knew exactly where he was. She kept trying not to, but she'd been following his movements all night out of the corner of her eye with that silent pulsing radar that operates just under the surface of one's mind.

She knew she shouldn't be thinking this way. She was with Max now—she *loved* Max. It was just that Atlas had been her first love, and when he was near her like this, all their secret history seemed to cloud over her head and suck the very air from the ballroom.

"No more interviews. I get you to myself from now on." Max reached eagerly for Avery's hand. The warmth of his skin on hers felt reassuring.

For a while she managed it. She moved through the room with Max, kept up a stream of small talk, chatting about all the things they were going to do in Oxford. When the band struck up a slow song, she let him spin her effortlessly over the dance floor, her feet moving through the steps with no input from her brain. She accepted a flute of champagne, but it tasted like nothing at all.

Avery felt his gaze like a brush against her lower back, as if someone across the room had whispered her name and it echoed all the way to her. She lifted her eyes and looked directly into Atlas's.

"I'm sorry." She broke away, tearing her hand from Max's. "I just—I need some air."

"I'll come with you," Max offered, but Avery shook her head frantically.

"I only need a minute," she insisted, more forcibly than she'd meant. And before Max could protest, she grabbed the skirts of her gown with both hands and fled toward the archway that led to city hall's single elevator. The New York princess, running away from it all.

The elevator door was tucked to one side, facing a row of offices that were currently empty of people. Avery knew that it had been crowded over here earlier: Groups of bored partygoers had stumbled up to look out at the observation deck, wandered around drunkenly, then come back down. But by now everyone had worked their way through another cocktail or two, and the dance floor was picking up speed; and besides, these people all saw the same view from their living rooms anyway, and from a much better altitude.

Now it was just Avery, standing alone, tapping viciously at the button to summon the single gray elevator.

When she emerged onto the observation deck, she let out a great rasping breath, as if she'd been swimming and had finally surfaced for air. The half-moon of the deck curved before her.

She took a step closer, reaching her fingers toward the flexiglass. The deepening winter twilight hovered outside the windows. She saw the ghost of her own reflection there, transposed eerily over the view.

Avery leaned her head against the flexiglass and closed her eyes, willing her heart to slow down. She knew she wanted to leave New York. But why wasn't she more excited about moving to Oxford with Max?

For so much of her life, Avery had let her desires be dictated by other people, without really questioning them. She knew how lucky she was to be living a life so many people would give anything for, and yet it hadn't been *hers*. She hadn't chosen it for herself. Her parents had literally custom-designed her to be the exact person they wanted. Avery had absorbed their beliefs every day until they became her own, until she didn't even know what she wanted anymore because it was all wrapped up in what they wanted *for* her.

She had thought that going abroad, studying art history, would be her way out of all that. Except Avery was starting to feel as if she had traded one set of expectations for another. She would be moving from the thousandth floor, and all the strings that came with it, to the life that Max wanted.

But was it the life *she* wanted?

She could see the years unfolding before her in sharp cinematic detail: filling that apartment with an eclectic collection of furniture. Staying there while Max got his PhD and became a professor and settled into a tenure-track position. A steady, thoughtful life filled with friends and scholarship and laughter and Max.

She loved Oxford, with its quaint charm, its cobblestones soaked with history. But it was hardly the only place she loved. Why should she limit herself to that single set of expectations when there was a whole wide world just begging to be explored?

Avery wanted to laugh too loudly. Drink too much beer. Smile so wide that her face hurt. Sing karaoke off-key. She wanted bright colors and raucous music and exhilaration and, yes, even heartbreak, if it came alongside love. Gazing out at the vast dark stretches of the city, Avery felt suddenly that New York—that Oxford—wasn't big enough to contain the sum total of all she wanted to live and experience and *be*. That it couldn't hold the volume of her unbridled, uncertain desire.

When she heard the elevator doors open behind her, Avery didn't turn around. It was probably Max.

"You okay?"

*Of course*, she thought woodenly. She had told Max to give her space, and so he had.

Atlas was the one who never did what she wanted him to.

"Why did you come up here, Atlas?"

"I was looking for you." His face in the moonlight was dark on one side and silvered on the other, turning his eyes to caramel.

"Congratulations," she said heavily. "You've found me. Now what?"

"Don't be like this, Aves."

She tried to sweep past him, but to her anguished surprise, he followed her into the elevator. She pushed the button to return to the main level of city hall.

"What do you want me to be like?" she demanded. Her voice was taut with tension. Couldn't Atlas hear it?

"Never mind."

She looked away from him, keeping her gaze stubbornly on the chrome doors of the elevator.

They were halfway down when the elevator jolted to a sudden, unexpected stop and the power cut out.

# WATT

**WATT STOOD AROUND** the corner from the New York Police Department headquarters, trying not to look conspicuous, but he needn't have worried. This was a busy midTower intersection, people shuffling past on their way to dinner or parties or wherever else they were headed this late at night. None of them even looked twice at him. Their eyes dilated and contracted as they shuffled through messages on their contacts, sleepwalking down the streets in little clouds of personal oblivion. At an intersection like this, it was easy to be invisible.

*We're doing the right thing, aren't we, Nadia?*

"What is the right thing, exactly?" she mused, the words echoing in his eartennas. "It seems like every human has a slightly different version of right and wrong."

Her words were oddly unsettling. Before Watt could reply, she went on, "You already know that I disapprove of this plan. It has too many risks, and far too little potential reward."

*It might save all of us!*

"Or it might result with you in prison. The only person in danger right now is Leda. You wouldn't even be involved, except for the fact that you're voluntarily involving *yourself*!"

*I was questioned this* morning*!*

"It's not worth putting yourself in unnecessary danger."

Watt shouldn't have been surprised. Nadia had been programmed to protect him, and thus always tried to lead him toward situations she could control, situations that were in his best interest. But Nadia didn't understand what it was like to love someone so much that their own safety became paramount to your own. Watt would do anything to keep Leda safe.

When he got home after the interrogation this morning, Watt had assured his parents that it was nothing of importance. To his relief, they believed him. He'd spent the rest of the day in a state of feverish anxiety: formulating his plan and building the zip-byte he would need to make it work.

He was going to hack the police station—tonight.

Watt felt a flash of regret that he wasn't able to go with Leda to the inauguration ball. But he couldn't pass up a chance like this. The NYPD was working on a skeleton crew right now, since the entire police department had been invited to tonight's gala as guests of the new mayor. Only the most junior officers were stuck here, working.

"You look absurd, you know," Nadia informed him, in a tone that implied an eyeroll.

Watt was wearing dark sweatpants and shoes, and a black long-sleeved T-shirt. *This is what people always wear in holos when they're about to do some kind of covert operation.*

"I hate to be the one to tell you, Watt, but you aren't a superhero. You're just a normal teenager!"

*You know that nothing about me is normal*, he reminded her, and rolled up the sleeve of his right arm. He was almost ready.

"Your heart is already racing, you don't need more stimulation!" Nadia argued, but Watt ignored her, slapping two caffeine patches on the skin of his inner arm, near his elbow. He felt an instant jolt of energy, as if his nervous system were an engine revving violently to life.

*I hate when you do that,* Nadia snapped, switching to transcranial mode. *It's like you hit me with a tidal wave.*

But Watt needed a tidal wave right now, needed every last shred of heart-pounding adrenaline he could muster up. Because his "plan" consisted largely of winging it. Nadia couldn't hack the police station until he'd infiltrated their system—which meant that she had no idea how many police officers were stationed inside or where they would be. The only thing she'd been able to find was an old map of the station from the Tower's original blueprints.

*Here goes nothing,* he thought, and strode to the back of the station with bold, confident purpose. There was a small entrance terminus back here, used primarily for delivery bots, with enormous tracks for the wheels of freight containers. Watt took a deep breath and crouched down to crawl through it.

*I can't believe no one has tried this before.*

*I think the police station isn't usually worried about people sneaking in. Their bigger problem is people attempting to sneak out.*

She had a point.

*This way,* Nadia urged, as Watt emerged into a hallway. He took off running, following the arrows that she laid over his vision. Down another hall, turn, through a suite of rooms; and suddenly he was dashing into the hot, stale closet where the police kept their tech servers. It was all alternating light and dark, no sign of life anywhere, as if he had emerged into some lunar landscape. The air smelled like daylight that had been trapped for decades.

The data storage room was just as Watt had hoped—backed up on hard drives, which were impossible to crack remotely, but doable if you were on-site and came prepared. Which Watt had.

He reached into his pocket to pull out the tiny, innocuous-looking malware he and Nadia had spent the afternoon working on: a zip-byte, he called it, because of its row of teeth. He clamped it directly onto a server box. It would dive into the police system, copy the file about Mariel, then disengage without leaving a trace that it had ever been there.

*Come on, come on,* he thought, as the zip-byte began to spin its code out into the NYPD system.

*Watt, someone's coming.*

Adrenaline spiked through his system. *Already?*

*I'm watching them on the security cams!*

Watt stabbed desperately at the server. "Come *on!*" he muttered, aloud this time, just as the zip-byte glowed the bright amber color that meant the upload was finished.

In a single motion Watt swiped it back into his pocket. He took a trembling breath, his heart hammering in his chest. Sweat dampened the armpits of his T-shirt. *Which way?*

*I'm sorry; this is my only option,* Nadia replied as the fire alarm went off.

Watt stumbled out into the corridor, which was flashing an angry red. The siren screamed overhead. He glanced left and right, his head pounding—there was a flash of heels coming from the left, which was enough to send him in the other direction. He hurried back toward the small freight door, realizing a moment too late that it might be locked during an emergency, but of course it wasn't. Several levels up, he thought he heard fire-bots scrambling to deal with the nonexistent blaze.

Watt crawled through the freight entrance and emerged running onto the street, melting seamlessly into the surging mid-Tower crowd, his ragged breathing and gleaming forehead the only indication that he wasn't just another commuter.

Thank god for Nadia, his own personal guardian angel.

He walked as fast as he could down the block, hands shoved into his pockets. Fear had lodged in his throat like a shard of ice. He couldn't believe that they had actually pulled it off.

There was an open plaza at the corner of the street, where people lounged around a cluster of benches: Saturday-evening shoppers holding hands, parents tugging their babies on magnetically tethered hoverstrollers. Watt sank onto a bench and clipped the zip-byte into his tablet.

It was a massive file, an aggregation of dozens of documents related to the death of Mariel Valconsuelo. The death certificate and coroner's report; transcripts of interviews with Mariel's parents and friends, and with Leda, Watt, Rylin, and Avery. Watt swallowed. He hadn't realized that Rylin and Avery were questioned too, though that made sense.

*How bad is it? How much do they know?* he asked Nadia.

Watt was going to read it himself too, eventually. Probably. But by now Nadia would have already scanned and analyzed the full contents of the file. After all, she could consume the entire dictionary in under half a second.

"Watt," she replied heavily. "I'm so sorry. It doesn't look good."

*What do you mean?*

"It seems the police have connected Mariel's death with Eris's. They know that something happened that night on the roof, that there was some kind of cover-up. Right now they're still trying to figure out why you all lied."

Watt felt cold and clammy all over. He ripped the caffeine patches from his arm, and his head instantly erupted into a splitting headache. He winced. *If they realize that Leda was blackmailing us, the next logical step is to find out what she had on us—why she was able to force us to hide the truth, and then we'll really be in trouble . . . Leda most of all.*

"Watt, you need to talk to them. To warn them."

Nadia was right. He had to talk to the others right away: to Avery and Rylin, and especially to Leda. They had to confer about what they would do next. The only way they could possibly emerge from this unscathed was together. If they all stuck to their stories, if they all guarded one another's backs, they might possibly have a shot.

*Where are they right now?* Watt demanded.

*They're all at Pierson Fuller's inauguration ball.*

Oh, right. Watt felt an odd sense of disbelief that events like that were still going on—that the world was still churning forward, when it felt as if it were tilting furiously off-kilter.

He stood up, took a deep breath and began to run, ignoring the alarmed stares of passersby. Thank god he'd bought that tux last year, in a ridiculous attempt to impress Avery. He was getting far more wears out of it than he had ever expected.

As he sprinted toward the downTower elevator, Watt had a curious and unwelcome sense of déjà-vu. This felt too much like last year, when he'd lost Leda at the Dubai party and found her precariously near death—or worse, like the night he'd raced up to Avery's roof, only to arrive just as Eris fell off the edge.

He could only hope that, this time, he wouldn't be too late.

# CALLIOPE

**WHEN CALLIOPE RETURNED** to the Mizrahis' apartment, she was greeted by a heavy and decidedly menacing silence.

She started hesitantly down the hallway, her footfalls vanishing into the thick carpet. Her reflection danced in the ornate mirror to her left, wearing the jeans and long-sleeved shirt she'd been wearing when she left, hours ago; she'd stopped back at Altitude to change out of her incriminating gown, which she'd left hanging in a locker there. She couldn't help thinking that she seemed unnaturally pale.

Nadav was seated in a high-backed chair in the living room, as if he were a judge about to deliver some kind of final sentence. He looked up at her arrival, but didn't speak.

Where was Elise? Maybe she was hiding from the confrontation, Calliope thought; maybe she figured that it was easier to swoop in later, to help advocate on Calliope's behalf.

Or maybe she'd decided that it was better for her marriage if she didn't weigh in on what her daughter had done.

"There you are, *Calliope*," Livya said smugly, turning the corner from her bedroom. She walked with small, mincing steps like a snail leaving a glistening trail of slime behind her. "We've all been so worried about you."

"I'm sorry," Calliope began. "I never—"

"You were at the inauguration ball, weren't you?" Nadav asked, and his words fell like sharp-edged stones into the screaming quiet.

It went against all Calliope's instincts to tell the truth in situations like this, but she also knew better than to tell a blatant lie when she'd been cornered.

"You're right," she admitted. "I was at the inauguration ball. I'm sorry I didn't tell you the truth about where I was going, but I was afraid that you would say no, and I had a good reason for wanting to go. The mayor's new public health team was there, and I've been trying to petition them about the hospital's emergency response teams—they don't have adequate equipment. . . ." Calliope was pulling this story out of thin air, but she had to admit it wasn't half bad; she was still a decent liar under pressure. "I went to the inauguration ball because it was the only way I could think of to actually talk with them face-to-face."

Livya rolled her eyes. "Cut the crap," she declared, and Calliope was gratified by the shock on Nadav's features. Neither of them had ever heard Livya curse before. She threw a great deal of enthusiasm into it, for someone so ostensibly sweet-tempered. "Why don't you tell the truth about where you were tonight? Or rather, *who* you were with?"

"I don't . . ." Someone must have told Livya, she realized with a sinking feeling. That room had been packed with hundreds of people, and any one of them could have casually mentioned the fact that Livya's stepsister was there with the older Anderton brother.

"She was out with Brice Anderton," Livya announced, turning triumphantly to her father.

Nadav seemed to find his voice again. "Calliope. You went out with Brice, even after I told Livya to warn you about him? Why would you do that?" He sounded more hurt than angry.

Calliope blinked, a little startled that Nadav had been the one behind Livya's ominous words at the wedding. "Because I *like* Brice. He isn't a terrible person. Please don't judge him based on his reputation."

"I just wanted you to be careful," Nadav said reasonably. "An older, more experienced boy like him, he might take advantage—"

"But, Daddy, Calliope is *plenty* experienced. If anyone was taking advantage, it was her," Livya cut in, and turned sweetly to Calliope. "You're sleeping with Brice because he's rich, right? But then, you learned from the best. Like mother, like daughter—"

"I'm not *sleeping* with him—" Calliope interjected, her hands balling into fists at her sides; but Livya just talked louder, almost shouting to be heard over her.

"I always suspected that you were a liar, and now I have proof! You're a lying gold digger, and I bet your mom is too!"

"What are you talking about?" Calliope asked, even as her stomach somersaulted in fear. Where *was* her mom?

Livya smirked. "Calliope, I was so *inspired* by your devotion to the hospital that I decided to make a donation in your honor, to the children's wing."

Calliope felt a cold dread gathering in her stomach.

"But when I called the hospital to make a donation, they had no idea who you were." Livya feigned confusion. "They had no record of all your *countless* volunteer hours."

Nadav frowned. Light from the windows streamed in great thick bars over the curlicues of the carpet, over the salt and pepper of his hair. "Calliope," he said heavily. "All those times you said you were going to the hospital, where were you really going?"

Livya cut in. "To go meet up with *Brice*! She's been putting on an act this whole time, don't you see? She doesn't care about philanthropy at all!" She rounded on Calliope. "I always thought there was something fishy about you. And it turns out I was right."

Calliope didn't argue, because for once, she couldn't think of a lie to tell.

"What's going on out here?" Elise glided calmly into the living room. She was wearing a simple white shirt with lace detail at the throat, making her look innocent and girlish. Calliope felt a measure of relief at the sight.

If anyone could fix this situation, it was her mother. There had never been a person alive, man or woman, that Elise couldn't calm down. She was the world's greatest living expert on bending people to her will.

"Elise," Nadav said, and Calliope knew what was coming: He would punish Calliope, deprive her of whatever remaining freedoms she had, and she would never see Brice again. Fine, she could take it; she would take any abuse right now to spare her mom. Calliope squared her shoulders and lifted her head, ready to plead for forgiveness.

She never expected what Nadav said next.

"Have you been lying to me?" He was looking not at Calliope, but at her mom.

Elise hesitated—only for an instant, but a crucial one, because in that instant her face revealed the truth. "What do you mean?"

"Were you honest with me about who you are? About your past? Or were you telling me what you thought I wanted to hear?"

Calliope saw her mom teeter uncertainly on the edge between a lie and the truth. She landed on the truth.

"I—I may have exaggerated our charity work," she stammered. "We didn't travel the world as roving philanthropists."

"So you moved here directly from London?" Nadav asked.

Elise was trembling. "We did travel the world for a few years. We just weren't volunteering."

"What were you doing, then? How were you supporting yourselves?"

Elise looked stricken. What they had been doing was shopping, eating at expensive restaurants, staying at the very top hotels, treating themselves to every creature comfort they could get their hands on. And they funded all of it by tricking people out of their money.

"We were seeing the world," Calliope explained. "My mom showed me all the historical and cultural sights, taught me to appreciate diversity."

Nadav ignored her. His eyes were still on Elise. "You made up all those years of volunteer work? Why? Was it just about the money?"

"Of course not!" Elise stepped forward to put a hand on Nadav's arm. He recoiled as if scorched.

"You're telling me you saw me at that party and lied about who you were because of my wit and personality? My money had nothing to do with it?"

Elise flushed. "Okay. I would be lying if I said the money wasn't part of it—"

"*Part of it?*" he said, caustically repeating her words.

"That was only at the beginning! Everything is different

now! I love you," she persisted, "so much. I had no idea that I could ever love someone this much."

"How am I supposed to believe anything you say?" Nadav's voice was very cold and deliberate, and it was far more terrifying than if he had shouted. "You just admitted that you were *lying* to me about who you are."

"I wanted to be someone you might fall in love with! Someone worthy of your love! I was afraid that you wouldn't love the real me. Don't you see?" Elise cried out. "Your love has actually made me better. I'm becoming that person, the woman you fell in love with. I'm right here."

Nadav stared at Elise in blank horror. He stared at her like a man broken: as if he wanted to strip away her charm and her beauty, layer by layer, so he might finally truly understand her, the way that he once believed he did.

"You lied to me. Every morning and every night, with every breath, with every moment of laughter. It was all a lie."

*"No!"* Elise's voice was ragged with desperation. "It wasn't a lie! I love you, and I know that you love me!"

"How can I love you when you're a complete stranger?" Nadav said heavily. "I invited you to share my life, and yet I feel like I'm meeting you for the first time."

Elise's eyes were wide and round with anguish. "Please. I'm asking for your forgiveness, and I'm asking for another chance."

Livya turned around to smile at Calliope, an empty, bitter smile that failed to reach her eyes. Calliope swallowed. She and her mom were as still as actresses frozen onstage before the lights go out.

Elise held out her hands, palms up, in a wordless gesture of appeal. "I love you," she whispered. "Please, I'll tell you the truth—we can start over—only please don't say good-bye, not like this, not after everything we've shared."

Nadav was pointedly looking away. "We're broken," he said quietly. "My trust is broken. I have no desire to sit here picking up the fragments and try to put them together again when we both know that it will never be the way it was."

Elise's frame shook with silent sobs. She'd screwed her eyes shut, as if by closing her eyes she might make this whole thing go away. Calliope couldn't remember the last time she'd seen her mom cry—really cry, not the fake tears she could summon on command.

"I'll leave the apartment to let you pack. You have twenty-four hours," Nadav announced. "Do not be here when I return. Either of you."

"Nadav," Elise pleaded, but his face seemed to have been carved from stone.

"You should be ashamed of yourself. Have you even stopped to think what kind of example you are setting for your daughter, marrying me for my money, lying about who you are?" He gave a defeated sigh. "Livya, let's go."

"With pleasure." Her eyes glinted with malice.

For a moment Calliope thought Elise was going to throw her arms around Nadav, beg him to change his mind. Instead she twisted her wedding ring off her finger and held it out toward him.

The flash of pain in his eyes struck the breath from Calliope's chest. "That was a gift. It's yours," he told her, and then his expression became hard and closed-off again, and he and Livya were gone.

Calliope felt the aftershocks of what had just happened racing through her body. She couldn't really breathe. "Mom . . ." she tried, at a loss for words. "I'm so sorry."

Elise reached up to wipe at her eyes, smearing makeup down her cheeks. "Oh, sweetie. This isn't your fault."

"It's *completely* my fault! You told me not to go out with Brice, and I did it anyway. If I had just listened to you, none of this would have happened."

"No, Nadav was right. I'm the adult, and I need to take responsibility for the life I've built for us. This day would have come sooner or later. I just always hoped it would be later." Elise sighed. "It's time for us to go, sweetie."

They were leaving New York. And this time, Calliope knew, they wouldn't be coming back.

# RYLIN

**RYLIN HADN'T PLANNED** on falling back in love with Cord so quickly.

She'd wanted to be thoughtful and intentional about it, instead of tumbling into their relationship all over again. But then, she hadn't exactly planned for it last time either. Maybe that was just the way love went—it was something that happened *to* you, and the best preparation you could hope for was the chance to take a deep breath before the wave of it crashed above you and you were in over your head.

"Thanks for coming with me tonight," Cord said as they walked together through the inauguration ball.

Rylin felt herself color under his gaze and reached down reflexively to smooth the skirts of her gown. It had arrived this afternoon in an enormous purple Bergdorf's box, complete with a satin bow.

"Absolutely not," Rylin had protested when the delivery

drone showed up. She wasn't going to let Cord start sending her extravagant presents. But Chrissa had insisted that they at least *open* it, and once Rylin had seen the dress—an architectural cream-colored strapless one, with silver splattered over it, as if someone had spilled a vat of liquid stardust on its smooth silk surface—she couldn't resist trying it on. It fit her exquisitely, the corseted torso giving way to a narrow floor-length skirt.

*One dress can't hurt*, she had concluded. After the day she'd had, being questioned by the police about Mariel's death, Rylin didn't have the strength to resist something this beautiful. Not that she'd told the police anything; she had nothing to tell, really. But the experience had still unnerved her.

She knew she should reach out to the others, to Leda and Watt and Avery, to ask if they had been questioned too. She told herself she would do it later. Right now, in this moment, all she wanted was to stand here with Cord, feeling beautiful.

"Promise you won't send me any more dresses," she pleaded, though she knew her words were weakened by the fact that she was standing here wearing one.

"Only if you promise to stop looking so gorgeous in them," Cord replied, and Rylin couldn't help smiling.

She glanced around the expanse of city hall, filled with stylish waves of people, teenagers and adults all wearing smart angled tuxedos or shimmering gowns. Holographic pennants snapped along the walls in a nonexistent breeze. She kept thinking that she didn't belong here, no matter how much she looked the part.

Then her eyes would slide back to Cord, and her blood would rise up light and buoyant in her veins, and Rylin knew that the setting didn't matter. She belonged with Cord, wherever that was.

"Will you come over to my apartment tomorrow?" she asked, reaching for his hand. She didn't mind being here, at a formal black-tie party, but it couldn't *all* be like this. When was Cord going to come down to the 32nd floor to meet her friends and Chrissa?

"Sure," he said easily. Rylin had the sense that he wasn't quite listening. But then he nodded toward the dance floor, and Rylin decided to let herself be distracted.

"Want to dance, now that I'm so good at it?" Cord grinned.

"I didn't realize you were ever bad at it," Rylin countered.

"I didn't realize either, until I started taking dance at school." Cord laughed as Rylin's eyebrows shot up. "You didn't know? This year I've been expressing my deep and unshakable love of dance through Dance 101: Introduction to Choreography."

Rylin stifled a snort. "You're a ballerina now?"

"The correct term is *ballet dancer*, thank you very much," Cord corrected. "This is what I get for dropping holography when all the other arts classes are full."

Rylin wondered if Cord had dropped holography because of her—because he didn't want to see her day after day—but it felt too self-centered to ask, and besides, it was all ancient history. "Don't worry," he went on. "I can't promise that I'll teach you *all* my epic dance moves, but at least one or two."

Rylin tilted her head in amusement. "What makes you think I don't have some epic dance moves of my own?"

They spun around on the dance floor until Rylin was breathless with exertion. Eventually the band paused to take a break. "Want to sit down?" Cord asked, leading her to a table where several of his friends were already clustered.

Rylin had met a lot of them last year, but they didn't seem to remember her, so Cord went ahead and reintroduced her around the table: Risha, Ming, Maxton, Joaquin. Rylin smiled, but the only one to smile back was Risha. Ming had a glazed-over look to her eyes, having evidently decided that it was more entertaining to read messages on her contacts. Rylin wondered if any of them even recognized her from school.

Oddly enough, she found herself wishing that Leda were here. At least Leda would have engaged with her.

"Cord, we've been looking for you. This party is unbearably lame," Joaquin announced.

Rylin was taken aback by the blasé attitude. This party was lavish and expensive and wasn't even age-scanning at the bar. What could Joaquin have to complain about?

"Can't you host the after-party?" Joaquin wheedled.

"I always host the after-party. Can't someone else step up to the plate for once?" Cord said easily.

The table erupted in an immediate chorus of excuses: "Don't look at me; you know my place is nowhere *near* big enough. We didn't even have room to host the soccer team!"

"My parents are cracking down on me ever since I got a D in calc this semester."

"I definitely can't host anyone, not after you guys threw up in the hot tub last time."

"That was fun, wasn't it?" Risha said almost wistfully.

"What about you, Rylin? Do you think you could get away with it?" Maxton had turned to her with a friendly smile. At Rylin's incredulous expression, he hurried to add, "We won't invite that many people. And we'll drone-drop all the booze, of course. All you'd have to provide is the space."

*Seriously?* Rylin wanted to ask, but she knew Maxton wasn't kidding. He had no idea who she was or where she lived. In his own way, he probably thought he was being inclusive by asking Rylin if she didn't mind hosting the after-party.

For a perverse moment she imagined saying yes, dragging all of these rich kids down to the 32nd floor to squeeze awkwardly around her kitchen table. Now *that* would be an experience.

"Fine, fine, I'll host," Cord cut in, reaching one hand across the back of Rylin's chair to give her a silent squeeze.

"I'm going to get a drink," she said faintly, to no one in particular, and started away from the table. She heard Cord follow quickly on her heels.

"Rylin, what is it?" he asked, reaching for her arm. She whirled on him, her cheeks flushing. "I'm sorry. Maxton didn't mean any harm by that question."

"I know," she sighed. "I just don't fit in with that group. Why do they need to have an after-party anyway? What's wrong with the very expensive, beautiful party we're at right now?"

"It's just how they are," Cord said with a self-deprecating smile, as if that explained everything.

"Exactly! All they ever do is talk about the next party. The next excuse to all get together and get drunk, and plan *another* expensive event." She let out a frustrated breath. "Don't you ever talk about anything else?"

"I know those guys can be kind of silly and immature, but I've known them my whole life. I can't just cut them out."

*Actually, you can*, Rylin wanted to say, but she bit back the words. There was no use fighting over this. "Let's just forget the whole thing."

"I promise this will be the last after-party I host," Cord assured her with a smile. "And tomorrow I'll make it up to you. We can go that brunch place with the raspberry biscuits you love. Or somewhere else," he said quickly, confused by her expression.

Rylin hadn't realized that he was still planning on having the after-party. Or that once again he would try to smooth over a disagreement with money and *things*.

"I'm going to get that drink," she said vaguely, starting back toward the bar, but he shook his head.

"No, let me. Please," Cord insisted. "You stay here and listen to the violinist. You'll really love her."

A violinist had stepped onstage, momentarily replacing the band. She perched on a delicate wooden chair, looping her feet under the bottom rung. And then she started playing, and Rylin forgot that she was sort of irritated with Cord, forgot about anything at all except the music.

It began low and plaintive, full of a longing so sharp that Rylin felt it like a pain between her own ribs. Dimly, she was aware of Cord retreating toward the bar, but Rylin stayed where she was, transfixed by the haunting, tragic music. It put into words what words failed to do.

She remembered the night this past summer when she and Hiral had gone to an outdoor concert together in Central Park. It had been Hiral's idea. *Maybe you'll get some inspiration for your holos*, he'd suggested. Rylin had been touched by his thoughtfulness.

She wondered what Hiral was doing right this moment. He was just so very far away. She felt a sudden urge to check on him, make sure that he was all right.

Rylin muttered to her contacts to do a quick i-Net search for Undina. She immediately landed on its home page, filled with sweeping photos of the ocean, the massive man-made city floating peacefully above it like a lily pad. Hiral was fine, she assured herself. He would be happy there.

Then a familiar name caught her eye. *Mr. Cord Hayes Anderton*. The next row, *Mr. Brice August Anderton*.

They were both listed on Undina's board of directors.

At first Rylin told herself that it was a mistake. This must be another Cord Hayes Anderton. Before she could help it, she'd tapped the link on Cord's name, to read how he and his brother had inherited their seats from their parents, who were founding investors in Undina. They were nonvoting members until they turned twenty-one, but the board was delighted to include them, in recognition of all that their parents had done. . . .

Rylin swiped her tablet off and leaned forward, feeling sick. Was Cord really on the *board* of Undina, the place Hiral was now working? Was that just an ironic cosmic coincidence, or did Cord have something to do with Hiral's departure?

She couldn't help remembering how unsurprised Cord had seemed when she told him that Hiral had skipped town. Come to think of it, hadn't Cord had been the one to come find *her* that evening in the edit bay? She'd never stopped to question why he was looking for her with such impeccable timing, but now she understood.

He had already known that she and Hiral were over.

When the violinist finally finished, and the room erupted in polite applause, Rylin felt as if she'd been torn from a dream.

Cord was walking toward her, a pair of drinks in hand. He saw Rylin and broke out into a wide, eager smile—until he registered her expression, and his handsome features creased in concern.

Rylin couldn't take it anymore; she stumbled blindly toward the exit, knocking past a waiter with a tray of champagne, letting the flexiglass flutes clatter to the floor. She didn't even care that the wine had sprayed up onto her skirt.

"Wait, Rylin!"

She whirled around. "Did you help Hiral leave town?" Her throat felt scratchy and dry.

Cord flinched beneath her gaze but didn't back down. "I did," he told her. "But please, Rylin, you don't understand."

Rylin felt numb with shock. The room seemed to spin around her, everything blurring together like a melting Surrealist painting.

"What part don't I understand? The part where you helped Hiral get out of the way, or the part where you hit on me two days later?"

Cord flinched at that. "I'm sorry I didn't wait longer, okay? I just missed you so much; I couldn't help coming to see you. That's why I said I wouldn't be the one to kiss you that day," he tried to add.

"Right. You showed such restraint."

"Rylin, you and Hiral were over!"

They had moved toward the front of the party, in the echoing entrance to city hall. Rylin saw an interminable line of hover-taxis already curling around the block outside.

"Hiral wasn't good for you, and you know it," Cord told her, and it was the absolute wrong thing to say.

"How *dare* you?" Rylin hissed. Anger and hurt crackled beneath her skin. "You have no right to do that, to keep making decisions on my behalf, okay?"

A couple brushed past them, studiously looking the other direction. Cord blinked, bewildered. "What decisions have I made on your behalf?"

"Breaking up me and my boyfriend, for starters! Making me come to this party, to hang out with your friends, in a dress you picked out." Rylin had thought this gown was a lovely romantic gesture, but suddenly she saw it in an uglier light. Had Cord bought it because he didn't want her to embarrass him by showing up in something cheap?

Cord seemed hurt. "I didn't realize I was forcing you to spend time with me. I thought you wanted to be here."

"I do want to be here, but, Cord, you never want to be down-Tower with me!"

"I just thought it was easier meeting up at my apartment. I have more space," he protested, and Rylin rolled her eyes.

"Right, because god forbid you have to come down to the squalor of the thirty-second floor," she snapped. "You never even told your friends that I'm not rich, did you? That's why they thought that I was one of them. Is it because you're ashamed to be dating me—the girl who used to be your maid?"

"I didn't bring any of that up because it isn't important," Cord said forcefully. "I care about you, Rylin. Where you come from isn't part of it."

"Except it is." Rylin felt angry with him, but most of all, angry with herself for being one of those people who make the same mistake over and over again. "I'm not some charity case, Cord. I'm a person—with feelings."

"Where is this coming from? I never said you were a charity case!"

"You didn't have to say it," Rylin told him, very quietly. Cord's face grew red in frustration.

"If you would stop being so damned prideful—"

"You're the one who kept this a secret from me!" Rylin's eyes burned. "I guess you have no idea how to build trust, because no one ever taught you."

"'No one ever taught you'?" Cord said bitingly, repeating her words. "That was cruel, Rylin. I would have thought that you, of all people, wouldn't jump straight to dead parents."

She recoiled, suddenly ashamed of herself. "I just meant that you always throw money at problems and expect them to disappear," Rylin said helplessly. "Even when that problem is an inconvenient boyfriend. I thought—" She ran a hand over her face. "I thought it would be different this time."

"I thought so too," Cord said wearily.

Rylin bit her lip until she tasted blood. She wanted to crawl out of her skin, to strip this expensive dress off her back and rip it to shreds. She felt disgusted with Cord and with herself.

She had been so angry with Hiral, for deciding that he would leave town without consulting her, for making it feel like he had made her choices *for* her. And yet Cord had been right here, doing the same thing the whole time.

"We should never have gotten back together," she said heavily. "We were right to break up the first time. We're too different, you and I."

She turned and walked away, her head held high, and only after she was on the lift back home did Rylin reach up to brush away the tears.

# AVERY

**THE INSIDE OF** the elevator car was completely dark.

"What's going on?" Avery blinked rapidly, then gave a series of voice commands to her contacts. They refused to cooperate.

"That won't work," Atlas said, hearing her struggle. "The elevator shaft is lined with magnets, which interferes with their frequency."

Avery pounded on the door. She knew it wouldn't accomplish anything, but it made a satisfyingly loud noise beneath her closed fist.

"Hey, hey. Calm down," Atlas said, reaching for her arm; and she realized how utterly absurd it was that she was standing here in her hand-stitched gown, pounding on the elevator like a Neanderthal.

"Sorry," she muttered, somewhere on the precipice between laughter and tears. If only she could see Atlas. The darkness felt pervasive in a heavy, palpable way, like it used to feel in Oxford. Real darkness, without the omnipresent urban glow.

"Maybe they're doing repair work somewhere nearby and damaged a power line," Atlas offered by way of explanation. "Or maybe the party is draining so much of city hall's electricity that it's overwhelming the grid."

"Someone will be here to let us out soon, though. Right?"

"I think so," he said unconvincingly.

Their breath came ragged and shallow. There seemed to be a strange hum of energy circling through the elevator car, crackling in the air: as if the entire world was waiting, breathless with expectation, for something to happen.

"I'm sorry." Atlas's voice sounded at once very close and very far away.

"This isn't your fault."

"Not for the power outage, for everything *else*. For coming back to town, upsetting you, interfering with your life—" He broke off impatiently. "I'm heading back to Dubai next week."

"You are?"

"Don't you want me to?"

Avery didn't answer. She was desperate for Atlas to leave, and yet she dreaded it. It was as if there were two warring halves of her, two versions of herself, and each of them wanted such drastically different things. She felt like she would break beneath the strain.

"I heard that you and Max are moving in together," Atlas went on.

"I don't know. Maybe." The apartment in Oxford felt suddenly as fanciful, as detached from reality, as something she had dreamed. Would she really live there?

"Maybe?" he repeated, puzzled.

347

"I'm not even sure I want to go to Oxford anymore," Avery admitted.

Atlas was quiet for a moment, digesting that. "It's funny," he said at last. "I was so surprised when you first announced that you were applying there. I had always pictured you doing something more adventurous. Like Semester at Sea. Or that school in Peru, the one perched on the edge of a mountain."

Avery should have known that Atlas would recognize her restlessness, her confused desire to get out of New York and figure out who she was. Atlas, the boy who gave her a magic carpet.

While Max handed her the key-chips to an apartment that came complete with a whole entire life.

Avery lowered herself to the floor, no longer caring about her expensive gown, and looped her arms around her legs to rest her forehead against her knees. "I wish you hadn't come home," she heard herself say. "I was doing just fine until you showed up and threw everything out of whack. You wouldn't understand, Atlas, you're so obviously *happy* in Dubai. But it was hard for me, for a long time after we said good-bye."

She heard him slide down to sit next to her. "I'm not actually that happy in Dubai."

Avery blinked. "You always seem happy when I see you."

"Of course. Because definitionally, you only ever see me when I'm with you. And *you* make me happy, Aves. Just being around you makes me happy."

The silence stretched between them like a rubber band at breaking point.

"Atlas," Avery whispered, then broke off. A million things swirled incoherently in her mind. But Atlas was talking again, his words tumbling rapidly over one another.

"Look, I didn't expect to say any of this tonight, but I can't help myself. Not anymore."

She felt him shift next to her in the darkness, a disembodied voice. Maybe it was easier for them to talk like this, she thought, without seeing each other's faces.

She wondered if he was going to kiss her again. She wondered what she would do, if he did.

"When I broke up with you in Dubai, I thought I was doing the right thing. I thought there was no way we could ever be together. But the problem is, there's no way I can be *without* you either. I ran away from you like a coward, and everywhere I went, you caught up to me. Everywhere I fled, I kept seeing you," he finished. "Every time, Avery, you happen to me all over again."

Avery knew she could make Atlas stop saying these things. One word from her and he would stop, and they would pretend it all away, just as they'd pretended away their kiss.

She opened her mouth, but no sound came out. Because she didn't really want him to stop.

Next to her Atlas was acutely still. "When Dad asked me to come back for the election, I told myself I wouldn't do this. I made a plan and I meant it, I really *did*, and it would all have been fine except we're here in the dark and now I have this chance to tell you, and I realize that I have to take it. It kills me every time I see you with Max."

His hand brushed hers, his pinkie finger curling imperceptibly around hers. Avery made no move to pull away. Where their skin touched, miniature fireworks erupted.

"I thought if I could just see you, make sure you were okay, I might get some kind of closure. I swore to myself I wouldn't kiss you again, and then I did." Atlas shook his head. "Obviously I can't keep my promises, even to myself. Not when it comes to you."

Tears slid down Avery's cheeks to splatter on the expensive golden fabric of her gown.

"Tell me right now that I shouldn't fight for you." There was a low, urgent note in his voice, as if he were staking his entire life on what she said next. "Tell me that you've chosen Max, and I'll back down, I swear it. You'll never hear any of this from me again. But I won't stop unless you tell me to. I had to say something—because I knew this was my very last chance, before I lost you forever."

Avery opened her mouth again to tell Atlas to stop, to tell him that she was choosing Max, that she *loved* Max. But she couldn't.

Max was wonderful, and he would make some girl very happy someday. That girl just wasn't her.

Avery knew, deep down, that there was really no choice. There never had been, for her. There was only one path forward, and he was right here in the elevator with her.

"Atlas," she said again, and now she was laughing through her tears. "Why is your timing always so terrible?"

Somehow she'd turned in the darkness and reached for his face, cradling it between both palms as if it was something infinitely precious, her fingers threaded in his hair.

Avery was done fighting this. She had tried so hard not to love Atlas, but her love had always been there, through all the long days they were apart, just waiting for this moment.

Tentatively, she kissed him. His mouth instinctively found hers. Their bodies, like their breath, folded quietly together in the darkness.

"I love you," she said wonderingly between kisses. "I love you, I love you," and Atlas was saying it back; and Avery knew this was wrong, that it was cruel to Max, but she couldn't find it in her to stop. They kissed as if there was no time left in the world for them, and maybe there wasn't.

"I missed you," she told him.

"I missed you every day, every *minute*, since we said good-bye," Atlas answered. "Didn't you feel me, loving you from across the ocean?"

Avery shifted, tipping her head to lean on his shoulder. She wondered how much time had passed since the power went out. It had probably only been half an hour and yet it had been a lifetime. Avery felt as if the entire world had reoriented in that half hour.

"Atlas. What are we going to do?" she asked, still holding tightly to his hand. "Nothing has changed since last year. All the reasons that we broke up are still there." *Broke up* wasn't the right term for it, she thought. It was more like they *broke apart*, as if tearing Atlas from her life had involved peeling off a raw exposed layer of flesh.

And now they were back. Despite all the mess, despite their parents and Max and the whole damn world, here they were all over again. It felt almost inevitable, as if there was no way they could have ended anywhere else except in this elevator car, right now, together.

"We'll figure it out somehow," Atlas assured her. "I promise."

For some reason his statement made Avery prickle with foreboding. "Don't make promises you can't guarantee you'll keep."

Atlas turned toward her, and even in the darkness Avery could feel the quiet intensity radiating from him. "You're right. All I can promise is to try."

They turned to kiss again; the silence groaned loud and thick all around them, and the minutes left to them, however many there were, ticked away too quickly. Each kiss felt imbued with significance. Each kiss was a promise that they would fight for each other, even though all the odds, the entire *world*, were arrayed against them.

Avery was still kneeling there, kissing Atlas—one hand wrapped around the back of his head, the other around his waist—when the doors to the elevator were forcibly pried open.

She felt the light flooding in, flashing on the backs of her closed eyelids, and she jumped apart from Atlas as if scalded. She tried uselessly to scramble to her feet.

Max was standing there, stricken. He had clearly seen the whole thing.

And far, far worse, Avery heard the unmistakable hum of a stray zetta. She watched, helpless to run after it, as the tiny remote-powered hovercam sped off. Its lens gleamed and then vanished into the distance.

# LEDA

**LEDA WAS GLAD** she'd come to the inauguration ball, if only for Avery's sake.

She hadn't realized how rattled Avery was by Atlas's return. Living under the same roof as her ex, being forced to see him every day—Leda should have realized that was a uniquely cruel form of torture. But then, Avery was so expert at disguising her true feelings from everyone, even from herself. Seeing her best friend tonight, the way she stood so proud and glittering in that ethereal gold gown, Leda's heart had ached for her. She recognized that bright remoteness for what it was—loneliness, and longing.

Leda leaned on a table near the dance floor, watching the party unfold around her. She felt more like herself than she had in ages. She knew she looked gorgeous in her gown, a close-fitting armor of structured black silk. Star-shaped diamonds blazed in each ear, setting off the dark curve of her neck. But it was much more than that. Leda was glowing from what had happened with Watt last night. She could still feel his touch on her, like an ink-tat that had marked her in new and indelible ways.

She wished he were here tonight. She'd tried not to be alarmed by his flicker earlier. *Something urgent came up. Everything is fine, but I can't make it. I'm so sorry. I'll explain later,* Watt had told her. She tried to take his word for it, but it was hard not to worry when she had no idea what he was up to.

A group of her classmates flocked to the dance floor; Leda saw Ming Jiaozu and Maxton Feld, and was that Risha with Scott Bandier again? How predictable. They caught her eye and tried to wave her over, but Leda shook her head. They were all happy to associate with her now, but none of them had been there when she crumpled to pieces last year. None of them were her real friends.

"Leda! We've been looking for you." Her parents approached, both of them grinning as if they'd gotten away with something illicit. It was an expression Leda hadn't seen from them in a long time.

"We're heading out to the Hamptons," her mom announced. She looked stunning in a pale apricot gown that set off her rich black skin.

"Right now?" It wasn't like her parents to do something so spontaneous. Which, Leda guessed, was probably why they needed it.

"Just for the night. It's not *too* late," Leda's dad said, his eyes sliding toward the edge of his vision as he checked the time. It was barely 10 p.m.

"I've been so wrapped up in work lately; your father and I could use a night away." Ilara reached out to tuck a strand of hair behind her daughter's ear. "Will you be okay on your own?"

"I'll be fine," Leda insisted, just as one of her mom's friends approached to ask Ilara a question, momentarily stealing her attention.

"I've been thinking about what you said last week," Leda's dad said abruptly, lowering his voice. "You were right. I need to tell your mother the truth. She deserves that."

Leda startled, then pulled her dad into a hug, so fierce that his head almost knocked against hers. "I'm proud of you," she proclaimed. "But—you're going to tell her tonight? In the Hamptons?"

"Is that a bad idea?" Her father looked sheepish, then shook his head. "Leda, whatever happens between me and your mom, I promise that I'll be here for you. I'm so sorry that you were caught in the middle of all this. I love you."

"I love you too," Leda said softly as her mom turned back toward them.

Ilara looped her arm easily in her husband's, still grinning widely. "We're going straight to the helipad. Are you staying, hon?"

Leda watched, speechless, as her parents slipped off into the crowd. Her father was brave enough to tell the truth: to confess what he'd done and face the consequences. While Leda persisted in hiding the truth beneath a mountain of lies and blackmail and secrecy.

If her father could tell the truth, then maybe . . .

She leaned her elbows onto the table, playing idly with the fake-fire taper on its surface. Its harmless flame flickered over her bare fingers. It warmed the nitinol ring on one hand. That was when Leda looked up—directly into Watt's eyes.

For a moment her breath caught. She'd forgotten how distractingly handsome he looked in his tux. The tailoring showed off the broad clean lines of his shoulders, set off the golden hue of his skin.

"You made it!" she cried out, rushing toward him, only to falter a little in her steps. Something in Watt's eyes quelled her excitement.

"We need to talk. In private," he croaked, his eyes darting around the party. "Are Avery and Rylin here?"

"I haven't seen them in a while," she said, fighting back her mounting sense of panic. "Why don't you tell me what's going on?"

They retreated toward the farthest edge of the party, where a pair of Chiavari chairs were tucked behind a towering display of flowers. Neither of them sat down.

"What's going on?" Leda demanded shakily.

Watt took a deep breath. "I hacked the police station tonight."

"What were you thinking? That's so dangerous!" Leda reached for him, grabbed him roughly by the lapels of his jacket, and shook him a little in panic.

"That tonight was a good distraction, since most of the police are at *this* party," he answered. "Also, I may not have been thinking clearly, since I went in for questioning this morning."

*"What?"*

He frowned. "I thought Avery must have told you. I was called in for questioning about Mariel. So were Avery and Rylin."

Leda could guess why Avery hadn't told her. Avery was trying, in her own sweet and misguided way, to *protect* her. But Leda expected more from Watt.

"You should have flickered me the instant that it happened. And you should have talked to me before you tried hacking the *police*!" Leda realized that her hands were still clutching tight to Watt's jacket, and she lowered them slowly.

"Don't worry, they'll never even know I was there. But we have a bigger problem." Watt averted his eyes from hers. "The police have figured out the connection between Mariel's death and Eris's."

Leda stumbled back a step, her whole body trembling. "You mean they know that I killed Eris?"

"Not yet," Watt hurried to say. "I think they just know that those nights are connected. Don't worry, Leda. I won't let anything happen to you. I swear it."

Dozens of emotions shot through her at once, horror and grief and regret. "Oh my god," she said slowly, and then again, more raggedly, "Oh my *god*."

"It'll be okay. We can figure this thing out—"

"Don't say it will be okay when we both know that it's not true!" Leda snapped, so fiercely that Watt fell silent. She sank helplessly into one of the chairs. "It won't be okay," she said, much more softly. "And it's all my fault."

Watt took the chair next to her and reached for her hand in silent support.

As Leda sat there, the scene around her was stamped on her brain with brutal clarity. The scent of the flowers, soft and delicate. The lurid laughter, the clinking of glassware, the music emanating from the dance floor. The warm feel of Watt's hands around hers. She felt that she would remember every detail of this moment for the rest of her life, however much longer her life lasted, because this was the moment it all changed.

She had put her friends at risk.

Leda had thought that they were all safe—that the police didn't have anything on them, and that therefore this nightmare would soon be over. That she could pick up the shattered shards of her grief and make a fresh start.

What a fool she'd been. It was clearly only a matter of time before the police figured out what Leda had done. Which would lead them to her friends' secrets. Rylin's drug dealing, and Watt's illegal computer, and Avery's relationship with Atlas.

Leda couldn't live with herself if those secrets came to light.

She felt like a tugboat in the middle of a hurricane, wave upon wave of regret smacking unrepentantly over her. She lowered her head into her hands and closed her eyes.

"We'll find a way out of this," Watt kept saying. "You and me, together, we can face anything."

Leda forced herself to look up. The light of the holographic banners overhead was reflected in Watt's eyes, gave a new bronzed luster to his skin. She let her eyes trace over him for a moment, memorizing him.

Then she stood up, pulling Watt to his feet with her, and kissed him. He seemed startled at first, but soon wrapped his arms around her and kissed her back.

She kissed him for as long as she dared, not caring if anyone saw. She prayed that Watt wouldn't sense the frantic, desperate beating of her heart. This was her last kiss, her final farewell on death row, and Leda was determined to make it count. So she focused on Watt—on the feel of him, the quiet strength of him, the way his mouth fit so perfectly over hers.

She was saying, deep inside herself, good-bye.

When she finally pulled away, Watt was studying her with a puzzled expression. Leda pretended not to see. If Watt guessed what she was planning, he would never let her go through with it.

"I'm going home," she said, and her voice betrayed her a little, because it was rough as sandpaper.

"Leda," Watt protested, reaching for her; and Leda wavered for a moment, because it would be so easy to lean into his embrace. To lay her head on his chest and let him tell her that everything would be okay.

Except it *wouldn't* be okay. Not for Eris or Mariel or any of the rest of them. Not until this whole thing was over for good.

"At least let me walk you home," Watt offered, but Leda shook her head, and dug into a bleak corner of strength somewhere deep within her.

"I need to be alone right now."

Watt opened his mouth to answer, then seemed to change his mind. He gave a jerky nod. "I'll see you later," he assured her.

"See you," Leda said quietly, knowing it was a lie.

She waited until she saw his form disappear into the crowd, until she was certain he was long gone. Then Leda let out a great, tremulous breath. It had taken every last shred of her willpower to watch Watt walk away from her, knowing it was the very last time.

Somehow, blindly, she made it home. The silence echoed eerily around her bedroom. She managed to drag herself into bed—her ordinary bed, rumpled past recognition, which only last night had held both her and Watt. She couldn't believe that just this morning she had woken up with him, feeling so safe in his arms.

But she wasn't safe. None of them were safe, and it was her fault.

She loved Watt so much that it hurt, so much that it frightened her. Which was why she should never have let him back into the disaster that was her life. She was too toxic. She had done too many terrible things, things she couldn't run from, and she refused to let Watt be dragged down with her.

On and on her thoughts swirled, circling wildly through her fevered brain. She must have drifted off at some point; she kept waking in a cold sweat, pressing her fists against her closed eyes, but the images wouldn't go away. Because they weren't nightmares; they were her reality.

No matter what road she went down, Leda kept returning to

the same conclusion. The cops were getting closer. Which meant that none of them would be safe until someone was arrested for Mariel's death.

Leda couldn't fix what had happened to Eris or Mariel. But she could still save Avery, Rylin, and Watt—that much still lay within her power. They didn't deserve to be punished for what had happened, but she did.

# AVERY

**THE MORNING AFTER** her father's inauguration ball, Avery paced back and forth across the living room like a caged animal. She walked the same path each time, halfway between the cloud-like custom couches and the door that led to the two-story foyer. She was waiting for whatever would happen to happen.

It was too quiet. Avery imagined she could see the silence, undulating and cool, its waves lapping against the walls and then falling back with a soundless splash.

"It'll be okay," Atlas assured her from where he sat on the couch by the window. He reached out an arm as if to pull her toward him, then seemed to think better of it.

Avery hadn't slept. How could she, after everything? She kept picturing the way Max had stood there, staring at her and Atlas with unabashed horror. He'd retreated a step, his eyes wide and wounded. Avery had stumbled to her feet and torn after him, calling out his name as she tried to chase him down the unfamiliar hallways, but Max had escaped down a staircase. He had literally run away from her.

Avery had been trying to ping and flicker him all morning, with no response. She wanted to tell Max how sorry she was, for betraying his trust in such a terrible way, and that she'd never meant to hurt him. That she hadn't been lying when she said that she loved him.

Somehow she had loved Max and yet been *in love* with Atlas at the same time.

Max had been the one who put her back together again after her heart was shattered last year. He had given her *his* heart, had tried to build a life for them, and Avery had given him nothing in return except pain.

She was starting to lose count of all the people she and Atlas had wounded, trying in vain to fall out of love with each other. Leda, Watt, now Max: They were all collateral damage. Avery swore to herself never to make that mistake again.

Earlier this morning, she had even ventured out in search of Max, heading to his dorm room only to find the bedcovers smooth and unslept in. Eventually she gave up and came back here, where she'd spent breathless hours *waiting*, though she didn't know what for. She just kept walking back and forth in her artech pants and sweater, restless and agitated, unable to shake the sense that something terrible was looming on the horizon, like a great dark thundercloud.

It was the zetta she really worried about.

She and Atlas had turned the problem over and over, but there was ultimately nothing they could do, not knowing which i-Net site it even belonged to. To own a zetta, you needed a commercial license, and the licenses were prohibitively expensive—after all, no one wanted swarming clouds of these things clogging up their city.

Whoever had that picture, Avery knew she would be hearing from them very soon. She could only hope that they would reach out to her directly, maybe hold the picture for blackmail, rather than go ahead and post it.

She reached the end of the room and turned again, fidgeting uselessly with the end of her ponytail. Next to her, Atlas sat holding his tablet on his lap, still open to the same article he'd pulled up two hours ago. They hadn't spoken much since last night; as if they'd used up all their words on *I love you*s, and needed to hoard the remaining ones for whatever lay ahead.

Both of their heads whipped up as the front door slid open. Avery felt every cell in her body spring to instant alertness. She heard voices, the familiar hollow sound of her mom's heels echoing down the hallway, and for a single instant, everything was blissfully, blessedly normal.

"We need to talk about the pro-am golf tournament," her mom was saying. "How many people do you think you'll be inviting?"

Pierson didn't answer right away. Then he cursed, loudly and angrily. "What the *hell*," he snarled, probably holding out his tablet.

And just like that, Avery knew that everything had changed.

Elizabeth screamed. It was a raw, animal scream, and the sound of it struck a primeval terror deep into Avery's marrow. She glanced at Atlas, then logged into the feeds with a sickening sense of dread.

Sure enough, there was the article that her dad must have found. It had only been posted thirty seconds earlier. *Fuller Siblings: Too Close for Comfort*, read the headline. It came complete with a picture of her and Atlas, tangled together in a kiss, from the elevator last night.

No one could mistake them. It was Atlas's light-brown hair, Atlas's patriotic pin gleaming on the breast of his tux, Atlas's hands wrapped firmly around her. And the blonde crouching among the ripples of her shimmering golden gown couldn't have been anyone but Avery.

Avery felt a cold, detached sense of unreality. To think that after all this time—all the vast lengths she and Atlas had gone to, in order to keep their secret safe—the worst had actually happened, and the truth was out in the world.

"It'll be okay. I love you," Atlas whispered, and as he stood up, he let his hand brush gently against Avery's back. A small, barely-there touch to remind her that they were in this together.

Avery's heart crashed against her chest as her parents stormed into the living room. Her dad was holding out his tablet, which was frozen on the *Too Close for Comfort* article. He held it out at arm's length, as if it might contaminate him. "What *filth*! For someone to use my children like that, to make up such vile slander, just to undermine my administration. . . ."

Oh god, oh *god*. He thought it wasn't real. Avery tried to catch Atlas's eye, but he wasn't looking at her. His eyes were fixed on their mom.

Elizabeth Fuller looked impeccable as always, in the short-sleeved knit dress and heels she'd worn to whatever breakfast the Fullers had attended this morning. She walked into the kitchen with spare, unadorned movements and poured herself a glass of water without drinking it. Avery knew that she just wanted something ordinary to do with her hands. But those hands were trembling.

Avery's father was still yelling, using words like *defamation* and *appalling*. He'd leaned one elbow on an antique console table, making little emphatic knocks on its painted ebony surface to punctuate his words. The whole scene had taken on the sticky, unrealistic quality of a dream. Avery willed herself to wake up.

She had imagined this conversation so many times, worrying

herself sick that her parents might somehow learn the truth about her and Atlas. But never in all her imaginings did she predict that her parents would willfully ignore the truth, even when the truth stared them full in the face.

Pierson abruptly broke off from his monologue. His face was deep red, veins etching themselves along the breadth of his forehead. He glanced from Avery to Atlas and back again, and something subtle changed in his expression.

"You two are awfully quiet. I'd assumed you would feel more upset about your images being violated like this. Whoever edited that photo, it looks very real." His voice grew dangerously calm. A beat of silence stretched through the room. "Unless, of course, the photo wasn't manipulated."

*There it is*, Avery thought as her mom gasped.

It would be so simple to lie, to say that *of course* the images were doctored, that she and Atlas were nothing but normal adoptive siblings with a normal fraternal affection for each other. Avery had been telling that lie for most of her life—to herself, to the world. She knew the art of it better than anyone. She knew how to bury her true feelings so deep inside her that no one could ever begin to guess at them.

It was the lie her parents wanted so desperately to hear. But for the first time, Avery couldn't bring herself to tell it.

Instead she reached out and took Atlas's hand. The implications of her gesture were lost on no one present.

"Avery." A threat lay there, low and coiled, in Pierson's voice.

Atlas let his hand close over hers, running a thumb deliberately, shockingly, over her knuckles. The touch of his skin gave Avery the confidence she needed.

"I love Atlas," she said simply and watched the dawning horror on both of her parents' faces.

Atlas's hand was laced tight in hers. "And I love Avery."

It sounded to Avery as if an alarm had gone off, but it was just the silence echoing throughout the apartment.

"You don't mean that," Avery's mom said weakly.

"Yes, we do. Avery and I have been in love for years. And the photo is real. A paparazzi zetta took it when we were together last night."

"Mom—" Avery's voice broke. She wanted to explain all the reasons that this wasn't as bad as her parents thought: that she and Atlas weren't physically, genetically related. That adoptive siblings could have relationships, could get *married*, in all fifty states; she had looked it up a long time ago. The law only prevented adoptive parents from marrying their own children.

More, though, she wished her parents could understand how perfect she and Atlas were together, that theirs was a love that could—and had—overcome anything in its way. That no matter how many times the world tried to destroy it, their love kept emerging again, battered and bruised but still stubbornly there.

This was her forever love. The kind of love that someone would have written a novel about, a century ago. It was her and Atlas against the world, no matter what; and Avery knew that if she couldn't have Atlas then she would have no one, for all the days of her life.

From the revulsion on her parents' faces, she knew none of those arguments would make a difference.

She started to take a step forward, but her mom recoiled, her features twisted into a mask of pain. Avery realized that her mom was silently crying. "Stop. Please, just *stop*!"

Avery felt tears slide down her own cheeks. "I *tried* to stop, don't you get it? Sometimes you can't pick who you love. Sometimes love chooses you." She bit her lip. "Don't you remember what it felt like to fall in love and know this was the person you were meant to be with?"

For a half second, Avery saw a flicker on her mom's face, aqueous and uncertain, and then just as quickly it was gone. "You don't know half of what you're saying. It's a hormonal mistake; you're still *children*, for god's sake—"

"We're both adults, actually," Atlas interrupted. Didn't their parents remember that they had both voted in the election?

"What's wrong with you?" Pierson cut in. "Why would you do this to us? Our only daughter and our only son? You're disgusting."

*We aren't doing it* to *you*, Avery wanted to cry out, trying not to wince at his stinging words. This wasn't about her parents at all. If anything, it existed in spite of them.

"We love each other," Atlas said softly. "I know it seems unlikely, and maybe even selfish, but it's happened. It's real."

Then, to Avery's surprise, he sank down onto one knee before their dad. He looked curiously as if he were about to propose. It took a moment for Avery to realize what he was doing.

He was begging their dad for help.

"Please," Atlas implored him. "I know this is upsetting, because it caught you off guard, but it isn't disgusting at all. It's true love, which makes it the most rare and beautiful thing in the world. Avery and I can survive this—our *family* can survive this, I swear it—but only as long as you support us."

Avery was stunned at his boldness. Was he really asking their parents for their *blessing*?

"This is New York," Atlas went on, undaunted. "You just need to give people enough time to get over it, which we all know they'll do, sooner than you think. We can figure it out. I'll move out of the apartment; I'll change my name; I'll do anything you ask. *Please*," he said again, his breath ragged. "You're *Pierson Fuller*. You know how easy it is to sway public opinion! New York will follow your lead in this, the way they do in everything!

If you reject us, then the world will too. But if you stand by us, and publicly accept us, I know the world will come around."

Avery was stunned. She had never even considered the possibility that they might stay in New York and actually be together. But as Atlas spoke, she realized the truth of his words, and a sharp hope began to snag in her chest. It just might work.

This was New York, where the pockmarked surface of society was riddled with scandals. Everyone had secrets, everyone had done something shocking. Was it really all that bad, for two unrelated young people to fall in love?

"What are you saying, Atlas? You want me to condone this— this"—her father spluttered—"this abomination?"

Atlas flinched. "I'm saying that if you can overcome your initial reaction, and think about our happiness—"

Pierson reached down to brutally haul his son to his feet. "Your happiness *is* what I'm thinking about! I love you too much to let you make this kind of mistake. Your mother is right; you clearly have no idea what you're saying."

Elizabeth was crying in earnest now, her frame racked with great ugly hiccups. No, Avery realized, she was *retching*. Her mother was so repulsed by the thought of Avery and Atlas together that she literally wanted to vomit.

"This conversation is over," her father shouted. "You both need to leave."

When neither of them moved, he slammed his fist on the table. "Get *out*! Both of you! Can't you see how upset you've made your mother?"

Avery exchanged a glance with Atlas, but he was shaking his head, as if to say *not now*. She knew better than to say anything. They just turned and walked in opposite directions, toward their separate bedrooms.

Only when she was safely ensconced in her room did Avery

pull the article back up. It was still as ugly and hurtful as before. And beneath the lurid text, and the photo, there was now a stream of comments.

In the ten minutes that entire ugly scene had taken, the article had been shared and reposted thousands of times. Avery wasn't all that surprised. She was the freaking princess of New York, wasn't she?

She knew she shouldn't look, but the words were practically leaping off the page, hurling themselves at her consciousness—

*Don't be fooled by her perfect exterior—that slut is DISGUSTING!*

*I always knew the thousandth floor was one giant orgy!*

*Ugh! I have a stepbrother. Excuse me while I go vomit.*

*I sat next to her once on a train, and she never even looked my way. What a royal bitch.*

And on and on and on. Avery felt a knot of despair gather in her stomach. She had never imagined that so many people in the world—people she had never even met—could hate her so viciously.

She curled up in a tiny ball, squeezing her eyes shut to black out the world, wishing herself into oblivion.

# RYLIN

**RYLIN'S SNEAKERS POUNDED** a vicious rhythm on the pavement of the outdoor track.

She usually loved running out here on the deck, past the basketball courts and swimming pools and jungle gyms. But today it felt painfully monotonous, or maybe just painful. No matter how far she ran, the horizon never seemed to change, as if any illusion of progress was just that: an illusion.

Still Rylin kept going, because even useless movement was better than stillness right now. At least if she kept moving, the air would hiss past her sweat-dampened skin, calm the heat pounding through her. She ran faster and faster, until her hamstrings were burning and she could feel a blister forming on her left ankle. Ahead of her was an artificial pond, where a group of small children were racing miniature hovercrafts, a flotilla of toys with colored flags waving in the breeze.

This was the point where Rylin usually turned back. But

today she pressed onward. She wanted to run until she sweat out all the anger still clinging to her from last night, if that was even possible.

She couldn't believe what Cord had done. How dare he get involved in her relationship with Hiral? It was so typical of him, of all the highliers, to think that he could bend and twist the world to his will. How gross, that he had used *money* to try to knock down the obstacles between them.

She remembered the *Skyspear*, the way their bodies had been intertwined in the dawn glow, and fought back a sudden sense of shame. Knowing what she knew now, the memory no longer seemed magical. If anything, it made Rylin feel rather cheap.

She couldn't keep doing this. No more thinking about Cord or Hiral. Rylin was more than the sum of the boys she'd loved. She refused to let them define her.

Her contacts lit up with an incoming ping.

Rylin tripped from the shock of it, but managed to catch her balance before she fell. She slowed to a walk and turned around, toward the pond. Flecks of golden sunlight danced over its surface.

She hesitated another instant before giving in and accepting the ping.

"Hiral. I thought we agreed not to talk," she said acerbically, lowering herself onto one of the benches.

"Chrissa reached out. She told me I was supposed to ping you?"

Rylin winced. She'd been banging around the apartment all morning, letting out loud angry sighs, until Chrissa bullied her into sharing what was going on. "It sounds like you need to talk to Hiral," she had said. To which Rylin responded by grabbing her sneakers and escaping for a run.

"That sounds like Chrissa," she muttered under her breath.

"I see. Younger sister, meddling again," Hiral replied. Rylin heard a note of concern beneath the false lightness of his tone.

Rylin wanted so badly to be angry with him—royally pissed, in fact. But she found that she didn't really have it in her.

"How is it?" she asked, because no matter what had happened between them, she still wanted to know that Hiral was okay.

"Awesome, actually." She heard the excitement in his voice. "I've finished training and started work in the algae-harvesting pens. The only drawback is that I'm eating way more green-protein than I ever wanted to see. I feel like even my sweat is turning green."

"Gross," Rylin snorted at the unexpected image.

Hiral fell momentarily silent. "What was it that Chrissa wanted me to talk to you about?"

"It doesn't matter now."

"Okay," Hiral said, as if he didn't quite believe her. "For what it's worth, though, I'm sorry. For everything I put you through. I know you're still upset with me for leaving town without giving you much warning. But I also know that it was the best thing for us."

"I'm getting really sick of everyone telling me what's best for me, without any actual input from me," Rylin couldn't help replying.

"Trouble in paradise for you and Anderton?"

This was really weird, talking about Cord with Hiral. "How did you know?"

"Because I know *you*, Ry. I saw it in the mall that afternoon, when we were working on your ridiculous project; I wanted to ignore it, but it was there. The way your whole face lit up when you made eye contact with him. I know that look." Hiral's voice was very faint in her eartennas, and it suddenly struck Rylin how utterly distant he was, on the other side of the world. "I know because once upon a time, you looked at me that way."

Rylin lifted a hand to her eyes, disconcerted. The sunlight was getting brighter.

Hiral didn't say anything, just let the moments of silence tick away, though god knows how much those minutes were costing him.

"Cord told me that he helped you leave town," Rylin said at last.

"You know about that?" Hiral asked, and she recognized the guilty note creeping into his voice. "I'm sorry. Please don't judge me too harshly, okay? I didn't have a lot of options."

It took a moment for Rylin to process his words. "Judge *you* too harshly?"

"For going behind your back, asking your ex-boyfriend to help me flee the country. That's what you're upset about, right?"

"Wait—you're the one who approached *Cord*?"

"Yeah, obviously. What did you think, that Cord bribed me to leave or something?" When Rylin didn't answer, Hiral sucked in a breath. "Rylin, you have to stop assuming the worst of people."

"I don't—"

"It's from all your years of living alone, from being the adult and taking care of Chrissa. Trust me, I get it," Hiral said gently. "But you can't keep living like that. Always holding people at arm's length, hiding behind the lens of your camera. Sometimes it's okay to let people in."

Rylin felt a flush of defensiveness—but she also knew that there was an element of truth to his words.

"Look," Hiral went on, "the whole thing was my idea. I went to Cord, asking if he could get me a job and a plane ticket away.

373

He kept saying that he didn't want to get involved, but I talked him into it."

"Why? Surely there were other places you could have gone for help," Rylin began, but Hiral cut her off.

"Not really, Ry. Getting a job, let alone a job on another continent, is pretty hard to do when you have a record. I needed someone with money and connections. Turns out Cord is the only fancy rich person I knew." He said it surprisingly without bitterness. "Also," he added, "I knew that he cared about you so damned much that he would even help *me*."

The children's hovercrafts were darting eagerly across the water, like dragonflies dancing over the surface, barely even leaving a ripple.

"But . . ." She trailed off, helpless. It was still wrong, wasn't it, that Cord would help Hiral get out of the country, then immediately go after Rylin? And not even tell her that he had played a part in getting rid of her ex?

She heard a rustling on the other end of the line, and a series of muffled voices as Hiral talked to someone else, probably explaining that he was on a ping with an old friend. Rylin wondered if he was talking to a girl. She tried to imagine him stretched out on a deck on that floating city, soaking up the sun's rays.

And then, because she wasn't quite ready to lose Hiral's voice in her ears, she asked him to tell her more about Undina. She could practically hear him smile on the other end of the line.

"The first thing you notice when you get here is the sky. It feels so much closer than in New York, which is strange, since of course we're way higher up in the Tower. . . ."

Hiral went on for a while, telling her about his routine, out there on the world's largest floating city. How he was on night shift, because all the new hires started on night shift until they were promoted. How he worked by touch alone, hauling in nets of algae and scraping off the soft plant growth, all in the pitch darkness so the algae wouldn't be sensitized by light.

Rylin sat there listening, watching the flow of people past her, the calm waters on the surface of the pond.

"Ry," Hiral said, and she realized she'd been silent for a while. "Are you still upset with me?"

"I'm not upset with you," she assured him. Hiral was so obviously happy in his new life; she would have to be a pretty terrible friend not to feel happy for him. He belonged where he was, and Rylin belonged here, in New York.

She just wasn't sure who she belonged *with*. Part of her still loved Cord—but she wasn't ready to forgive him for everything he had done, and said.

"I have to go. Bye, Rylin," Hiral said softly.

She started to say *see you later*, then realized she wasn't sure when, if ever, she would see Hiral again. "Take care of yourself, okay?" she told him instead.

Rylin sat there for a long time, staring thoughtfully at the water, the lines of her face strong and unreadable.

# AVERY

**AVERY FELT HERSELF** drifting slowly toward consciousness.

Some instinct tried to pull her back. She didn't want to wake up; she should stay here instead, safe in the cool, forgiving darkness.

But another instinct urged her to pry open her eyelids and sit up, blinking and disoriented. And then she remembered.

The truth about her and Atlas was out.

It was early afternoon: Avery must have fallen asleep, lying here atop her bedcovers, reading the hateful things people had scrawled at the bottom of that article. She'd already deleted her page on the feeds—she had to, after she saw the things people were saying there—not that it made much of a difference. They were still cramming the i-Net with all their ugly, foul comments about her.

*What's done is done*, she thought sadly, and now there was no going back.

Avery became aware of a glowing icon in the corner of her vision, indicating a series of flickers that she must have missed while she was asleep. Bracing herself—what if it was her parents, or worse, *Max*—Avery muttered the commands that would open her inbox, only to let out a relieved breath. It was Leda.

But then she read Leda's series of frantic flickers, and her pulse began to pound in alarm.

*Hey, can you talk? I need to see you.*

*Avery???*

*Okay, I'm coming over.*

*Shit, your parents won't even let me inside. What the—*

*OH. I saw the article. I'm so sorry.*

And then, a few hours later: *Just ping me when you can.*

Avery forgot her own overpowering despair in her worry about her best friend. Something had happened, and Leda needed her. It felt good to be needed right now.

She ran her fingers through her hair, reached for her jacket, and paused. She was still Avery Fuller, and she might as well look it, since the world would be staring at her anyway.

Quickly, Avery traded her artech pants for a new dress and her favorite black boots. She leaned over her vanity table to program her makeup—carefully, layer by layer, letting it spray over her face like particle-sized flecks of armor.

An eerie, heavy stillness hung over the apartment as she moved down the hallway with quick steps. She considered going to check on Atlas, but decided it would be tempting fate. Instead she just sent him a flicker: *I'm heading to Leda's. How are you holding up?*

On the downTower local line, Avery caught a few sidelong

glances, a few surreptitious whispers aimed her way. She just kept her eyes down and shoulders up, staring at the dead space between her feet in that way New Yorkers always did. No one bothered her. She marched like that all the way to the Coles' front door.

The streets felt hushed with expectation. Avery imagined she could hear the sound of the air itself, moving in its incessant preprogrammed patterns through the dense bulk of the Tower. It felt like a bad omen.

Leda was in her room, sitting in one of the barrel-backed chairs by her window, her eyes glazed over. That was what worried Avery most of all. Because this was Leda Cole, the girl who couldn't sit still, the girl who was always plotting and hustling and moving. And now here she was, just staring into space.

"You okay?" Avery asked, and finally Leda turned around.

She looked terrible, Avery saw at once; her features strained, her eyes wide. She looked as if she were running on air and unshed tears.

"Oh, Avery. I'm so sorry," Leda whispered. She hurried to her feet and threw her arms around her friend. "How are you holding up?"

"I've been better," Avery said mirthlessly.

"You don't have to be brave about this, you know."

Avery felt her throat constricting. She sank into the opposite chair. "I'm not very good at it. *You're* the brave one, always trying to be so tough, to look out for everyone around you."

"I don't feel particularly brave right now." Leda sighed sadly. "Avery, why didn't you tell me that you were called in for questioning about Mariel's death?"

It took a moment for Avery to remember the questioning. It felt as if it had happened so long ago, and yet it was only yesterday. "There were a lot of other things going on. Besides, we don't need to worry about that; none of us had anything to do with Mariel's death."

Leda's voice was very small. "Maybe I did."

"What?"

"I don't *know*," Leda said helplessly. "But I might have. I might have killed her that night when I was on my bender, after we came back from Dubai. I have a whole block of time that I can't account for. What if I killed her?"

"That's a pretty big stretch," Avery said dubiously. "Just because you blacked out doesn't mean you committed murder."

"How can you say that when you've already seen me kill someone?"

"You didn't mean to kill Eris," Avery reminded her.

"That doesn't change the fact that it *happened*!" Leda stared down at her hands, picking at the polish on one of her fingers, twisting a ring back and forth. Avery knew better than to interrupt. She looked out the window, to where the sun had moved from behind a cloud, rising ever higher into the towering sky.

"I have no idea what I'm capable of," Leda said softly. "Do you know what I was trying to forget, that day I took all those drugs and overdosed, after we got back from Dubai?"

"Probably the fact that Mariel hurt you and left you for dead."

Leda ignored her. "It was something Mariel told me, that night in Dubai. She said that Eris was my half sister. That my dad was Eris's dad too."

For the second time in twenty-four hours, Avery felt as if the wind had been knocked out of her. She was reminded of the time when she was little, playing tag with Cord, and somehow she ran straight into a wall of flexiglass. *Look*, she'd said to Cord, through her bleeding lip. *I didn't see that coming.*

This felt a little like that: the bright cold truth you never saw coming and yet once you collided with it, you wondered how you hadn't noticed it there. You felt there had been so many signs, glaringly obvious signs, but you missed them until it was too late.

"It makes more sense than what you thought was going on—that Eris was having an affair with your dad." Avery sighed. "Leda. Why didn't you ever tell me?"

Leda looked utterly broken. "Because I was ashamed. I didn't want anyone to know that I had killed my sister. I wanted to forget it all, to wipe the slate clean and move on. That's what my doctor told me, at least," she said softly. "That's why I tried to cut out everything related to my old life when I came back from rehab."

Avery thought of what her dad had said as he signed her transfer papers for Oxford—that it was no use running from things if you would have to face them eventually. She and Leda had both tried to run, in their own ways. And look where it had gotten them.

Her heart ached for Leda, wrestling with so much unthinkable guilt. For Eris, who had died too young. For *all* of them, hemmed in by things beyond their control. If Leda's dad hadn't cheated on her mom; if he'd told Leda the truth about Eris; if Avery's parents had adopted another boy instead of Atlas; if the zetta hadn't caught them in the elevator last night—*if, if, if.* It struck Avery as irrational and cruel that the world was built on so many ifs, so many small choices that seem like nothing at the time, but become the axes upon which whole lives turn.

"You couldn't have known," she said to Leda, who shook her head.

"When I saw them sneaking around, meeting up in secret, I just assumed they were having an affair. I never asked any questions. I never guessed that"—her voice shook a little as she went on, gaining momentum—"that Eris was my half sister. I was always so brusque and impatient with her; I never even tried to be her friend, and then I *killed* her, and I might have killed Mariel too!"

She took a deep breath. "Which is why I'm going to the police, to confess to pushing Eris. And to tell them that I could have killed Mariel, while I was blacked out."

There was something chillingly final about the way she announced it: the stubborn lift to her head, the implacable set of her jaw. But Avery saw the shadow of fear glinting in her eyes.

"Leda," Avery said softly. "Telling the truth about how Eris died won't bring her back."

Avery didn't mention what would happen to Leda if she confessed to pushing Eris and then lying to cover it up. It would go badly for her: much worse, in fact, than if she had told the truth in the first place. At least then she could have pleaded involuntary manslaughter. Now she would also be confessing to obstruction of justice, to willfully concealing the truth for a year. And the truth would probably come out—that Leda and Eris had been related—and Avery knew a jury wouldn't view that sympathetically. It might look like some twisted motive for murder, as if Leda had wanted to get her half sister out of the way. Not to mention the damage it would do to both families.

"I know I'll do prison time," Leda said, reading her mind. "It's no more than I deserve. And at least then I'll have a clear conscience."

*A clear conscience.* Avery couldn't remember the last time she'd had one of those. She wondered if she ever would, after what she'd done to Max.

"You don't deserve that, Leda. I was there; I saw—I remember how Eris ran toward you, and there wasn't a safety railing, and she was wearing those enormous sky-high platform shoes, and it was so windy, we were *screaming* into it. . . ." She trailed off and took a slow breath. "Leda. Do you want that single, accidental mistake to define you for the rest of your life?"

"What do you want me to do, forget it ever happened? I can't!"

"Of course not. I want you to remember. No offense," Avery went on, "but I knew Eris better than you did, and I don't think she would want you to confess. She would want you, her half sister—the only sister she ever had—to go off and live your life to the fullest. To honor her memory by *living*."

"What about Mariel?" Leda whispered. "Maybe if I talk to the police about it, they'll share some of the details, explain why they reopened the case as a murder investigation. Maybe something they say will trigger my memory, and I'll know for sure whether I killed her or not."

"That's a pretty flimsy reason to confess to something you aren't sure you did," Avery snapped.

Leda shook her head. "The police have already made the connection between Eris's death and Mariel's. Sooner or later they'll learn that Mariel knew our secrets—the ones *I* told her. It will look as if someone killed her to cover up what she knew. At least this way I'll take the fall. Then you'll all be safe."

There was something oddly heroic about Leda's decision. It was as if she'd reached a searing conclusion within herself and was determined to follow it through, no matter the consequences. *Typical Leda*, Avery thought. *Stubborn until the bitter end.*

"Don't do anything drastic. At least wait for a day," Avery pleaded. It was the best she could come up with. "Just promise me you'll think it over, and then if you still want to go through with this tomorrow, I swear I'll be there with you."

Leda looked up, tremulous and hopeful. "You would do that?"

"Of course. No one should have to confess to murder alone," Avery assured her. "Haven't you heard? That's what best friends are for."

To Avery's surprise, Leda gave a strangled, snorting laugh—and then just as quickly, the laugh dissolved into tears. It was as if the taut strain under which she had been operating was finally snapped.

Avery slid her chair closer to Leda, who leaned her head on Avery's shoulder and kept on sobbing with reckless abandon.

"God," Leda sniffed at one point, "why can't I stop *crying*?"

"When was the last time you cried?" Avery asked.

Leda shook her head. "I don't remember."

"Then it sounds like you have some catching up to do."

Avery stayed there, her arm on Leda's back as if she were comforting a child, as tears slid down her own face.

She was crying for her best friend's anguish, and what had happened to Eris, and what she had done to Max. She was crying for her and Atlas, and her own selfish fear that she would lose him—that this crazy, broken world would refuse to let them be together, and it would cost them everything.

———

The stares were much worse on the way home from Leda's.

It was after noon; by now the article had gone completely viral, shared and re-shared in countless grotesque incarnations. Avery had been fine on the way downTower, but now, heading home, her confidence faltered.

The entire Tower had become a sea of hot, eager whispers and searching eyes. Everyone was looking her up and down, staring at her with a collective disgusted fascination. Avery wasn't unaccustomed to being stared at. Her whole life, people had looked at her and said things: *She's so beautiful; she's not as beautiful as I expected; I hear she's a slut; I hear she's a prude;* and on and on and on. Avery had learned to let it slide right off her. Until now.

"Whore," she heard one girl mutter under her breath, as

she boarded the C local lift upTower. The girl's friends giggled maliciously.

*I haven't done anything wrong. All I did was fall in love with someone they think I shouldn't be with*, Avery reminded herself. She tried to feel sorry for these people, for being so pitifully narrow-minded.

It got worse when the lift paused at the express stop on 965, and a group of her friends stepped on board.

They were chatting loosely among themselves, clearly coming from a hungover post-party brunch. Avery remembered those brunches: sitting across from her friends at Bakehouse or Miatza, ordering truffle fries and bacon and exchanging stories from the night before, laughing over the silly things everyone had done. They now felt like memories that belonged to a different person.

The moment they saw her, everyone in the group fell silent.

Avery made eye contact with Zay Wagner, but he quickly flushed and glanced down. Behind him, Ming stared at Avery, her lips parted in horrified shock, before she spun around to start a conversation with Maxton Feld. Avery's gaze sought Risha's—Risha, her friend since fourth grade—and she watched, almost in slow motion, as Risha turned her back on her. "I left something at the table," Risha said in a loud, false voice. "Can we go back?"

Before the doors could slide shut, Avery's friends had all turned and escaped the lift with an audible sigh of relief, leaving her alone, surrounded by strangers. The entire scene had taken less than five seconds.

This was a lot of people to be on an elevator this high, Avery thought, a little dazed; and then she realized that of course it wasn't a coincidence. They had come hoping to see her, to get a glimpse of the infamous Avery Fuller.

A few of them stepped closer. She felt their eyes drilling into her, scraping at her—it was as if they could see straight through her clothes, to her naked, raw self beneath.

"Disgusting," muttered one of the men, and he spit on her shoes, a great wad of mucus dripping there on her black suede boot.

Avery kept her chin up, blinking furiously to keep her eyes from welling with tears, but her silence must have emboldened them, because then another person—a boy only a few years younger than her—was calling out in her direction. "Hey, Fuller, heading home to do it with your brother?"

"Some princess of New York."

"Why don't you try this on for size instead?" one man cried out, making a lewd gesture.

"What a dirty little—"

And then the floodgates were truly open, and everyone was shouting at her, calling her vulgar, ugly names—things that she would never in a million years say to another human being, especially to someone she didn't know. Foul slurs that Avery had never dreamed would be hurled in her direction.

The strangest part, she thought in a daze, was the raw delight on their expressions. They were all so eager to witness her downfall. They *relished* it.

Someone tossed a soda on her. Avery didn't even speak up, just let the syrup collect in her hair, viscous and foul. It stung her eyes, or maybe that was her tears.

It didn't matter, she told herself: This was just soda, and these were just words. Love would always be stronger than hate.

When the elevator finally stopped at 990, Avery saw in shock that there was a whole crowd of people there, gathered around the landing. Reporters and bystanders and zettas, flocks of them. They all immediately whirled on her, shouting her name, asking if she wanted to comment—

Avery ducked her head down and shoved through the center of them, past the security checkpoint, the place these people couldn't follow. When she stepped into her family's private elevator, she was gasping as if she'd run a marathon. Her cheeks were wet and sticky with soda and sadness.

She needed to see Atlas, no matter the consequences. She needed the warm, comforting feel of his skin on hers, to remind herself that they had each other, that they loved each other. That together they could face anything.

But when she knocked on the door to his room, no one answered. Avery tentatively pushed it open, and what she saw made her breath catch in her chest.

Every trace of Atlas was gone.

She walked past the bed, crisp and folded with hospital corners, and opened the door to the closet, already knowing what she would find. It was empty.

She tried the massive chest, violently yanking the handle of each drawer in succession, but they were empty too. There were no instaphotos tacked to Atlas's favorite spot on the wall, no collection of knickknacks on the shelves, nothing at all to prove that he had ever lived here. It was as cold and impersonal as a hotel room; as if the memory of him had been forcibly vacuumed out of the apartment.

"Avery? What happened to you?"

Her mom stood in the doorway, a stricken expression on her face.

"What have you done?" Avery demanded. "Did you send Atlas away? Is he in Dubai?"

Her father stepped forward to join her mom, his arms crossed implacably over his chest. "No, he's not in Dubai," he said curtly.

"Avery, this is for your own good, I promise," her mom insisted.

Avery ignored them, speaking a few commands to ping Atlas—but all she got was a flat monotone beep. *Command not valid*, her contacts informed her.

Atlas had been cut off the grid.

"Where *is* he?" she cried out.

"I'm sorry, Avery. This is hard for us too," her father said, watching her with careful eyes. "I know it feels cruel now, but you'll thank me someday, when you understand why we had to do it."

Elizabeth didn't say anything. She had crumpled against the doorway and started quietly sobbing again.

Avery pushed blindly past her parents, down the hallway to her room. She wanted to cry, except she felt oddly past the point of tears. Perhaps she'd used them all up earlier, and now there were none left in the aching cavity inside her.

She paused at the sight of a white compostable box waiting in the output slot of her room comp, the place where her daily vitamins or frosted glasses of water were dispensed. It was a food delivery, flagged for her. Except she hadn't ordered anything.

Avery walked over with slow, terrified steps, and opened the box.

It was a dozen bright pink cupcakes, accompanied by a generic *Happy Birthday* slip. On the note, where the custom birthday message went, it said: *Always know that my heart is out there, somewhere in the world, beating in time with yours.*

"Oh, Atlas," she whispered, and it turned out she did have more tears after all, because she was crying again, soft silent tears streaking down her face. Her dad had blocked their communication, but somehow—maybe in the last moments before they took away his tablet—Atlas had thought of this instead. The only way he could contact her, one last time.

She reached for a cupcake and took a single bite, though it tasted like salt in her mouth.

Where was he now? Was he okay; was he hurt? What was he thinking about?

Avery abandoned the cupcake and stumbled into her bathroom, turning all the lights on their highest wattage, setting the shower to scalding hot. Her movements were quick but clumsy, her hands shaking. She stripped off her clothes, tossing them into an angry pile on the floor, and looked up at her reflection through blurry, tear-filled eyes.

There it was in all its naked glory: the body her parents had purchased for her. Avery made a few motions, as if she were a puppet being pulled by invisible strings. She twisted a wrist, lifted a shoulder, turned her head back and forth. Whenever she moved, the pale girl in the mirror moved also, staring back at her with hollow eyes. It all felt oddly distant from her. Who was that girl in the mirror, really, and what connection did she have to Avery Fuller?

She studied her own body with an almost scientific detachment, examining its long, lean curves, the hair tumbling over the shoulders, the perfect hip-to-waist and lip-to-eye and chin-to-mouth ratios. This was what you got when you spent millions of nanodollars to custom-design your daughter from the combined pool of your DNA.

It wasn't worth it, she thought. It had never been worth it.

If only she could take it all back, could rewind her own life to last year, or earlier even—so far back that she could brutally erase all the mistakes she had made. So far back that she could be someone else, could be a *normal* person, not this cherry-picked human weighed down with a million expectations and strictures. All those awful words that the people had said on the elevator today seemed to fall on Avery at once, in an acid rain of hate.

She stepped into the shower and scrubbed her skin until it was red and raw, crying herself empty. She cried until her anguish had dulled, until all that was left was a vacant dead feeling. It felt as if part of her soul had been clipped away.

As the hot water prickled over her, Avery realized that she could do one more good deed. She might be past saving, but there was someone who wasn't—not yet.

She closed her eyes, and began to formulate one last plan.

# CALLIOPE

**THE NEXT MORNING,** Calliope followed her mom onto the Rail Iberia platform in a daze. She felt oddly like a child, being led blindly by the hand, but for some reason she couldn't summon the ability to do anything for herself right now.

They had spent the last two nights at the Nuage. "How perfect that we're ending our time in New York the same way it began," Elise had pointed out, though Calliope didn't answer. She knew the real reason they had stayed an extra night, instead of taking yesterday's Hyperloop train.

Elise had been holding out hope that Nadav would change his mind, and come running after them in some grand romantic gesture. But as the hours ticked by and they didn't hear from him, it became apparent to both of them that he wasn't coming.

Calliope lifted her eyes to the mirrored wall of the bitbanc on the corner and was startled at the version of herself she saw reflected there. Because she knew this girl. This was Leaving

Calliope, the girl who skipped eagerly from one place to another, standing next to her mom in a sleek coat and boots, an assortment of luggage wheeling along in her wake.

She and Elise were clutching their usual hazelnut lattes, their bags jostling with their favorite snail-cream moisturizers and the massage pillows that helped them fall asleep on train rides. Each detail was part of the ritual, familiar from all the other times they'd left town at the end of a con; yet it felt all wrong. This time they weren't skipping away, bowled over with laughter, flush with the cheap thrill of success.

They were subdued. A miasma of regret hung over them; and Calliope imagined that their steps resounded louder than usual, like in an echo chamber, because each step took them farther and farther away from New York. From the only people who actually cared about them.

Not even the bustle of Grand Central could cheer her up. Calliope kept her eyes on the floor, willing herself into invisibility. It wasn't all that hard, really—after all, it was the other side of the coin from being stared at, and Calliope was an expert at that. The only difference was that this time she had to repel attention instead of attract it. She retreated into herself, imagining an invisible force field that she wore like a cloak.

She wondered how long it would take everyone to forget her.

The kids at school would go first, she thought. After all, what did they know about her, or she about them? They would whisper about her for a while—*Whatever happened to that British girl, the one with the weird name?* She hoped there would at least be some gossipy rumors. That she'd run away to Hawaii to work on a coffee plantation, or that she was eloping with an older man and her parents didn't approve—hell, she'd even take rumors about drugs and rehab, as long as she wasn't forgotten.

But Calliope wasn't a fool; she knew they would remember

her for a week at most.

It would take longer for Nadav and Livya and Brice. *Don't think about Brice*, she scolded herself. There was no use dwelling on it; it would only hurt her more. She hated to imagine herself quietly vanishing from his memory, like a holo fading out of focus.

These past few weeks, she had let herself hope that they might have some kind of future. She cared about Brice, with his irreverent humor and sense of adventure, his bouts of surprising sincerity. He knew Calliope better than anyone in the world, except for her mom. Which just went to show that no one in her life had really known her at all.

She had shown Brice her real self, underneath all the false layers and lies that she wore so well.

And now that she wouldn't see him again, Calliope felt alone in a way she hadn't felt since before New York: as if she would never connect with another person again, for the rest of her life.

"I wasn't planning on stopping over in Lisbon, unless you want to," Elise said, breaking the silence. Her eyes were still red-rimmed from crying, and she pulled a scarf closer around her neck, but at least her voice was steady.

Calliope knew her next line. She was supposed to suggest Biarritz or Marrakech, make a joke about how her tan was fading, and couldn't they go someplace warm? Instead she shrugged and pulled the force field closer around herself.

Elise smiled bravely and tried again. "Beginning or end?" she asked, nodding toward a young couple holding hands. They looked very East Coast preppy, with their crisp sweaters and matching monogrammed luggage.

Calliope knew what her mom was doing, feeding her cues, reminding her of the dialogue they used to fling back and forth at each other. Beginning or End was a game they would play, guessing whether people were at the beginning or end of their respective journeys—whether they were starting out on a vacation or returning home. Calliope and Elise used to love it because it made them feel superior; because of course they were always at the start of a journey, every single time.

Calliope didn't feel very superior right now, though. "I don't know," she said vaguely, and her mom fell silent.

A train pulled up to the platform, its sleek chrome curves stamped with the purple Rail Iberia logo. Calliope stepped back as the new arrivals flooded out. Some were flushed with excitement, others dull-eyed with weariness; but all of them *here*, in New York, about to start whatever adventure this city might hold for them.

The moment the last passenger had de-boarded, the train's doors closed, and the seats began to swivel a perfect 180-degree arc to face the other way. A flurry of lemon-yellow cleaning bots instantly scoured the train car from top to bottom, changing out the seat covers and sterilizing everything with ultraviolet light. Calliope remembered the first time she'd seen a train self-cleaning, when she was eleven and she and her mom ran away from London. The pulses of neon purple through the windows had looked to her like a fairy rave.

A crowd had started to gather around them, pushing hungrily toward the waiting train; because once its doors opened it would take off in a matter of minutes.

"I'm sorry. This is all my fault," Elise said and sighed.

Calliope felt the bitter taste of guilt in her mouth. "No, it's my fault. If it wasn't for me, we would still be living our normal lives."

"*What* normal lives?" Elise kept untwisting and then re-twisting her scarf from around her neck. Calliope saw that her hand—still wearing her wedding ring—was shaking. "Nothing about our lives is normal, and it's all *my* doing. I built this life for us, a life that consists of nothing but running away! And just when we were starting to live somewhere, when you finally had friends, and a boyfriend, we have to leave again."

*He wasn't my boyfriend*, Calliope wanted to protest, but the point didn't seem worth arguing. Instead she wrapped an arm around her mom and pulled her close. "I'm not a child. I've known what I was doing for a while now. You can't blame yourself," she said reassuringly.

Elise pulled away. "Don't you see? It's because of me that you aren't a child! I forced you to grow up too soon—to be an adult before you were ready!"

Calliope paused at the truthfulness of her mom's words. Maybe she had grown up too soon. Maybe that was why she sucked at being a teenager, because she'd long ago adapted to the adult rules for conduct. She knew how to be sincere and how to be sneaky, how to dress for parties in prisons or palaces, how to evade the truth and get things for free.

She knew everything except how to be herself.

Behind Elise, the doors to the Hyperloop cars shot open, and the crowd shoved forward to pour themselves inside.

"You should stay," Elise whispered, so softly that Calliope thought at first she hadn't heard her.

"What?"

"Nadav isn't angry with you. He's angry with *me*. If you stayed, he wouldn't blow your cover—wouldn't tell everyone the truth about us." Elise's eyelashes trembled. They looked impossibly thick and fringed, but then, they weren't real—like so much of her. "You could stay in New York. You couldn't go back to Nadav's apartment, of course, but you'll figure something out. And now that you wouldn't be living with him, you could be yourself, not so buttoned-up and prissy. . . ."

It took a moment for her mom's meaning to dawn, and when it did, Calliope felt stunned. "Stay . . . without you?"

Elise cupped her hand under Calliope's chin and looked directly into her eyes. "You're ready, sweetheart. You don't need me anymore."

The import of those words seemed to bounce around Grand Central. Calliope imagined them repeating over and over; she imagined them in bright neon like the signs above the food stalls. *You're ready.* How long had she waited for her mom to say that? And now that it had happened, she wasn't sure she actually wanted to hear it.

"Where would I go?"

"You'll figure it out. You're spontaneous and resourceful." Elise smiled, but Calliope barely saw it through her blurry vision. "You learned from the best, after all."

"Train 1099 to Lisbon departs in two minutes," an electronic voice boomed over the speakers.

And then they were both crying: real, ugly tears, not the soft dewy ones they used during cons. Calliope felt the other Rail Iberia passengers swerving around them, shooting them looks of irritation or pity, or ignoring them altogether. Those were the genuine New Yorkers, Calliope thought, the ones who could see something unpleasant—like a mother and daughter crying at Grand Central—and skip right over it.

She wanted to be one of them, she realized. A genuine New Yorker. She wanted to stay, to keep building a life here, even if it meant she had to do it alone.

"There are a lot of solo cons you can run, you know," Elise was saying. "The one-handed flapover works well, and ghost crown, and you can always adapt the runaway princess to—"

"It's okay, Mom. I'll be fine," Calliope assured her, and they both knew in that moment that her mind was made up.

Calliope felt her mom's arms closing tight around her, her heartbeat hammering through her ribs. "My darling girl. I'm so proud of you," Elise said fiercely.

"I'm going to miss you." Calliope's statement was muffled against her mom's shoulder.

"I'll let you know where I end up. I'm thinking the Italian Riviera. Who knows, maybe you can come meet me in Capri for New Year's," Elise replied in a passable approximation of her normal tone.

"Thirty seconds," interrupted the canned voice of the automated reminder.

"Be safe. I love you," Elise said, and then it was one last hug, all elbows and tangled coats, and a tear exchanged from one cheek to another; and with that Elise was stepping onto the train, her enormous suitcases floating ahead of her toward the luggage compartment.

"I love you too," Calliope answered, though her mom couldn't hear. She stood there waving, her eyes glued to the bright red of Elise's sweater, long after the train had sped away on its whispering rails.

Finally she turned and lifted her eyes toward the ceiling, wondering where in this massive city she would go now.

# LEDA

**LEDA STEPPED UP** to the NYPD headquarters, queasy with anxiety.

Her contacts lit up with an incoming ping, and she turned quickly aside, hoping for a split second that it was Avery—but no, it was Watt. Again. Leda let the ping roll on, unanswered.

Watt had been trying her practically once an hour for the past day. Leda kept on ignoring him. She had nothing to say to Watt right now.

Because she still loved him. And Leda knew that if she let herself speak to him, if she heard his voice for even a single instant, she would lose her nerve and back down from what she was about to do.

She tried Avery one final time, her heart hammering. She'd been so certain that Avery would be here—Avery had *promised* she would, late last night, when Leda had pinged her in twisted, cold fear. "Of course I'll be there," Avery had assured her. "Let's meet at the station at seven."

"Can you come here first, to my place?" Leda asked, her voice small. She wanted to be walked to her murder confession, like a child being walked to school.

"I'll meet you at the station, I swear," Avery answered.

Now it was almost 7:20, and Avery still hadn't shown. Leda was starting to think she wasn't coming. She couldn't blame her: Avery had plenty to deal with right now; she didn't need Leda's mess piled on top of her own.

Still, Leda wished she didn't have to do this alone.

She'd barely made it through breakfast with her parents. They had coptered back from the Hamptons late last night. Leda could tell that things weren't completely resolved between them—she could see the questions in her mom's eyes—but she also knew that her mom hadn't left. And when she came downstairs this morning, her dad was cooking waffles: the delightfully fat kind, loaded with chocolate chips and whipped cream. The way he always used to, back when they ate breakfast as a family.

When her mom came down and started to set the table, Leda realized that it would be okay. Her family might not be anywhere near healed yet, but it would be, eventually.

She almost—*almost*—changed her mind about confessing.

"You okay, sweetie?" her mom had asked. Leda startled, wondering if Ilara had somehow guessed her plans; but then she realized that her mom meant the Avery-Atlas news.

Instead Leda mumbled that she was worried about Avery and took a bite of her waffle. She forced herself to finish the entire plate, because she didn't know when she would get to eat again. What would they feed her in prison?

She'd taken a hover down to the police station, a last little act of extravagance. As it slid seamlessly down her street, Leda had leaned against the flexiglass window, staring out at the view for once, instead of flicking through the feeds on her contacts. She tried to memorize every detail of her neighborhood, every iron gate and brick step and shining entrance pad. It all felt imbued with a new poignant significance, because Leda was seeing it for the last time.

She passed a woman jogging, a baby floating along next to her in a runner's stroller; Leda suddenly remembered that the woman had once asked her to babysit. Leda had rolled her eyes at the ridiculousness of the request. *Isn't that what room comps are for?* she'd replied, and the woman had just laughed. *Some people want their children cared for by humans, not bots.*

Leda wondered how old that baby would be when she got out of prison someday.

She shifted, feeling suddenly ridiculous in her pleated school skirt and uniform shirt. She had debated wearing something else this morning, only to decide it would tip her parents off. Besides, maybe if the police arrested her like this, it would remind them how young she was, and encourage them not to be too harsh with her.

7:25. Avery still wasn't here. Leda was lingering. She couldn't help hesitating a little, right here at the brink—the way she used to freeze up on the high dive, paralyzed in fear of jumping off.

But there was no going back down the ladder once you'd climbed it. So Leda gathered the frayed remnants of her strength from somewhere deep within herself, and walked through the entrance.

She had come this early on purpose, at that bleary moment when the night shift traded for the day. She'd expected the officers to be glazed over with sleepy lethargy, their hands curled around cups of powdered coffee. But there was a little shiver of energy in the air, people walking back and forth down hallways with brisk steps, voices conferring behind closed doors. So much for catching the police at a slow moment.

"Yes?" said the officer behind the front desk, a friendly-looking man with OFFICER REYNOLDS on his name tag.

Leda shrank into herself like a snail in a shell, prolonging this moment, her last one of freedom. "I'm here to offer some information," she declared.

"Information regarding . . . ?"

"The death of Eris Dodd-Radson."

Just saying Eris's name pulled her back toward that dark, bitter despair. *Don't cry*, she told herself, blinking back tears. Leda never cried in public. It was one of her cardinal rules.

"Ah. The girl who fell off the roof?" Reynolds mused aloud, and it struck Leda speechless that he barely remembered who Eris was. That she'd been nothing to him but a name, while Leda had been thinking about her nonstop for the past few months.

"Also, the death of Mariel Valconsuelo." She'd practiced the sentence dozens of times, sounded it out in her head, but still it came out shaky and nervous.

Reynolds's eyebrows shot up, and he looked at her with new interest. "You're Leda Cole, aren't you?"

"I—" She opened her mouth, but her throat was sandpaper-dry. Did they already know she was guilty?

"Thanks for coming by so quickly," he said, with an energy that surprised her, "but we aren't quite ready to gather supporting testimonies. Honestly, after what Miss Fuller told us, we may not need it."

*Avery?* What did she have to do with any of this?

"Supporting testimony?" she repeated.

"When your friend said you would be coming by, I didn't realize she meant this morning," he told Leda, almost genially.

"Avery was here?" That explained why the station was more

awake than it should have been this early in the day: the frisson of electricity sizzling throughout the place, as if someone very important had just come through, causing quite a stir.

"She left barely half an hour ago," Reynolds informed her, and then, more softly: "None of us had *any* idea what that girl was hiding."

His words caused something in Leda to snap. "They aren't even related, okay? Leave her alone! She's already heard enough of that—that *filth*!"

Reynolds lifted an eyebrow. "I wasn't talking about her family situation. I was talking about what she did. She just confessed to the deaths of Miss Dodd-Radson and Miss Valconsuelo. Her parents took her home on temporary bail."

*What?* Leda felt suddenly dizzy. She pressed her hands against the desk to keep herself from toppling over. "Avery didn't kill those girls," she said very softly.

"She confessed to it. We have it on record."

"No, she wouldn't . . . Avery never . . ."

Reynolds gave a delicate cough. "Miss Cole, I'm sure you want to help your friend, but she's already being helped quite a bit. Don't forget who her father is. It's too early for me to take your testimony, and anyway, you look tired," he said, not unkindly, and gestured at her uniform. "Why don't you go on to school?"

Leda nodded numbly. Her throat felt closed up, her mind still roaring and blank all at once. She walked out of the police station with dazed steps, like someone who was drunk, or very lost.

What was Avery doing, confessing like that? "Ping to Avery," she said into her contacts, and when that went to voice mail, "Ping to Atlas." Atlas would know what was going on, would tell her what was happening up there on the thousandth floor . . .

But Atlas's contacts never rang. All Leda got was a flat single-note tone, and a *command not valid* error.

Leda stumbled forward, leaning against a nearby bench, trying to regain her balance. This didn't make sense. Atlas was gone. Atlas, the only real tether holding Avery in place. Had he run away again . . . Or did his parents get rid of him?

Leda thought of Avery yesterday, insisting that Leda had always been the brave one, looking out for everyone around her. And she realized what had happened.

Avery had confessed for Leda's sake.

She was taking Leda's guilt onto herself. Letting herself be dragged down beneath it all, so that Leda could go free. Avery was giving Leda her *life* back—sacrificing herself for Leda's sake—in one last, ultimate gesture of friendship. And if she was doing that, Leda realized in a panic, it could only mean one thing.

She turned and sprinted toward the nearest upTower elevator, hoping she wasn't too late.

# AVERY

**SEVERAL HUNDRED FLOORS** upTower, Avery was putting the final pieces of her plan in action.

"Avery Elizabeth Fuller!" Her father's words echoed furiously off the polished marble floors, the high arched ceilings, the mirrored walls of their apartment's two-story entryway. "What the hell is this about?"

Of course Pierson Fuller was angry, given the way the past forty-eight hours had gone, at least from his perspective. All the glamorous victory of the inauguration ball had been followed by the revelation that Avery and Atlas loved each other—a fact that came to light in an ugly and very public way. The Fullers had gone from being the most celebrated, most envied family in New York, to the butt of a vulgar joke.

He'd gotten rid of Atlas, hoping that would solve the problem, only to be confronted by something even worse—the police pounding on his door in the early hours of the morning. *I'm*

403

*sorry, sir,* Avery imagined them saying, *but we have your daughter in custody at the station.*

"Why didn't you warn us? You just went down to the police station *alone*?" Elizabeth threw her arms around her daughter, her voice breaking. "Is this about Atlas?"

Avery pulled herself roughly from her mom's embrace. "No, you *think*?" she demanded.

"This isn't about Atlas," Pierson bellowed. "It's about *you*, Avery! You violated our trust. As if learning about you and Atlas wasn't hard enough, now we have the police coming for us at six a.m. saying that our daughter has gone down to the station and inexplicably confessed to killing someone?"

"Two people, actually," Avery couldn't help reminding him.

"Avery didn't *kill* anyone," Elizabeth pronounced in the same tone she would have used to say, *This tablecloth shouldn't be blue.* As if by saying it, she could will it to reality. "She didn't even know that Mariel girl."

"I did know her, actually," Avery said, and then prepared herself to deliver the punch line, the lethal blow: "She knew the truth about me and Atlas, you see."

Silence. The shock of her words seemed to reverberate in the air.

"Don't you dare say that again," her father threatened, and now his voice was frighteningly low. "Don't you even think about saying that, or anything like it. Do you realize how hard it was for me just to get you back *home*, after that ridiculous confession? I had to pull every string I had and then some, not to mention pay an obscene amount of money for temporary bail."

"God forbid you have to spend money on me," Avery said bitterly. "But then, everything has a price tag to you, doesn't it, Dad? Even my happiness?"

Her mom gasped aloud, but Avery wasn't looking at her. She had eyes only for her father.

He ran a hand wearily over his features. "What the hell were you thinking, Avery?"

"When I killed her, or when I told the police?"

*"Stop saying that you killed her!"*

"What does it matter to you anyway?" she shouted. "Nothing is sacred to you but your own ambition! You wouldn't care if I actually *had* killed her, you only care that I confessed to it!" Her hands had balled into fists at her sides, her nails inscribing themselves into her skin.

"So you're admitting that you didn't do it." Her father reached roughly for Avery's arm. "I want to protect you, Avery, but I can't help if you won't talk to us. Who are you covering for? Was it Atlas?"

"Of course it wasn't Atlas!" This was taking too long, she thought frantically. She needed them to leave before Leda found out what she had done, or before the sun rose too high.

Her mother was still wringing her hands, her voice breaking. "Then why are you—"

"I hate you!" Avery screamed as wildly and cruelly as she could, wanting to lash out, to hurt them. "I hate you for what you said to Atlas! He asked for your support, for your love, and what did you do in return? You made him *disappear*!" She began to cry—it wasn't that hard, really, after everything she'd been through. "I just want you both to leave me alone!"

Her father was looking at her as if she was insane, or a stranger. "We'll discuss this later," he said at last, already stepping back through the front door. It was clear he couldn't get away from her fast enough. "There's no reasoning with you when you're like this."

Elizabeth paused at the doorway and turned back, her heartbreak written on her face. The sight of it almost changed Avery's mind.

"I'm locking you in this apartment," Pierson declared, tapping at the touch screen and scanning his iris to confirm his identity. "No more sneaking out to police stations or to see your friends or anywhere else."

"Where would I go, now that you've taken Atlas from me and all of New York despises me?"

"They don't despise you, Avery. They're disgusted by you. As am I."

Her father's features hardened, and Avery's resolve hardened too. *So this is how it will be*, she thought. *This is our last good-bye.*

"You stay here and think about what you've done," her father snapped. Her mom was still crying, softly.

And then the elevator doors clicked shut behind them, leaving Avery alone on the thousandth floor.

She hurried breathlessly to her room and grabbed the bag she'd shoved under her bed late last night. Inside were dozens of fat red cylinders—spark-sticks, the tiny, single-use lighters that burst into flame when you pulled off their neoprene tab. These were the high-grade kind, producing an extra hot superflame, intended for campers stuck in the wild. In the Tower it was illegal even to *possess* something like this, especially up here where the oxygen circulated so freely, where everything was already a little too flammable.

Avery pulled the neoprene tab from the first one, and a flame leapt instantly out one side.

It wavered and flickered, seeming to contain a multitude of colors at once, colors she didn't normally see in the Tower—not just red, but rich oranges and golds and even a bright liquid blue that seemed to crackle and spark over the whole thing like summer lightning. It was beautiful.

She tossed the spark-stick onto her bed, covered in its white lace pillows and coverlet, and watched dispassionately as it went up in flames.

From there Avery moved briskly around the apartment, tossing a live spark-stick on every surface. She noted with grim satisfaction that none of the smoke alarms went off. The tongues of flame fed hungrily on one another, growing higher and higher, casting a wild gleam on the bones of her face. Her eyes were narrowed, her cheekbones more sharply prominent than usual. She'd dressed for the occasion in jeans and a slim white sweater, diamond studs at her ears, looking for all the world like an avenging angel, heralding ash and brimstone and destruction. A pale smile curled on her lips as she watched her parents' apartment burn to oblivion. The symbol of their wealth and status and sickening ambition, the most expensive thing they'd ever bought, except perhaps for Avery herself. Soon both would be gone.

Her steps faltered at Atlas's room. This was sacred ground, and she could still feel his presence here, no matter how hard her parents had tried to erase him from it. She let herself sit for a moment on the bed, running her hands over the pillows, imagining that they still smelled like him—

Avery stood up abruptly, steeling herself, and tossed a spark-stick in here too, moving quickly on before she could witness the carnage.

It only took a couple of minutes for the apartment to become a furnace. The smell of burning furniture varnish and carpet, the rubbery scent of melting tech, made her gag. Swirls of black smoke gathered near the ceiling. Avery hurried onward, ahead of the advancing wall of crimson. She tried to ignore the yelling in her ears, as if the fiends of hell were crying out at her for what she was about to do.

The kitchen was trickiest, because there were so many inflammable surfaces in here. Avery settled for throwing one last spark-stick on the counter, though it didn't really matter; the apartment was already destroyed. Sparks shot upward, then floated down like burning flecks of snow.

No, Avery realized, arrested by the sight of something out the window. That was *real* snow. Today was the first snowfall of the year.

The snowflakes seemed frozen between the window frames, like a still-life painting. For a moment Avery expected them to fly back upward, back to the clouds as if summoned there by magic.

A wave of heat blasted toward her, scorching the bare skin of her neck. She lunged forward, stumbling toward the pantry.

Only one way out now.

She yanked the old retractable ladder down from the ceiling. Her heart thudded stickily in her chest. A flicker of fear rose up in her, like a tongue of flame, but it was too late now; she'd committed to this course of action.

At the top of the ladder, Avery pushed up the trapdoor—it offered a moment's token resistance, but someone had clearly tampered with its electronic command system, because it gave way almost instantly. Thank god Watt had kept his promise.

She emerged onto the roof and took a deep breath, pulling the trapdoor shut behind her. The air burned the inside of her nostrils, singed the edges of her hair.

The roof looked the same as she had left it a year ago. A few machines humming under photovoltaic surfaces, a few rain-collection tubs gathering water and cycling it downTower for filtration. Avery kicked off her shoes and walked toward the edge. The pavement felt rough on her bare feet. She lifted her head, her profile proud and sharp and beautiful.

She felt very high up. The snow was falling harder now, as if pieces of the sky were breaking off to swirl rapidly downward.

The city below her was a study in dark and light, like an old-fashioned film without color—a city of extremes, Avery thought. So full of love and hate, but perhaps that was the way the world worked. Perhaps the price of a forever love was to feel forever lonely, once you had lost it.

Avery didn't want to exist in a world where she wasn't free to love the person her heart called her to.

She was glad that she'd confessed to what happened to Eris and to Mariel. If she was giving it all up anyway, she might as well take the blame. Leda didn't deserve to lose her freedom over those deaths. No, she thought fervently, Leda deserved to *live*, to move on from her mistakes in a way that Avery could no longer do. Leda deserved redemption, and Avery had found a way to give it to her.

Her parting gift to her best friend—a life for a life, an even trade. She knew Eris would have wanted it this way.

Avery wasn't particularly religious, yet she closed her eyes for a final prayer. She prayed that Leda would find peace, that her parents would forgive her, that Atlas would be okay, wherever he was.

She stared at the glorious beauty of the horizon one last time, studying the way the snow began to dust everything, blanketing the city's flaws, evening out its imperfections. Its flakes settled in her hair, on the white of her sweater.

"I'm sorry," she whispered, and stepped right up to the edge, her eyes still closed.

They were the last words Avery Fuller ever spoke.

# WATT

**FROM HIS UNEXPECTED** vantage point on the East River, Watt was one of the first people to see the thousandth floor catch fire.

It was striking, really: the brightness of the flames curling above the Tower, an elegant orange-red brushstroke. Opalescent gray thunderheads coalesced around the rain-blimps, hanging in that low winter way that portended the first dusting of snow. There was something magical about it, even now that the whole thing was engineered: the delicate crystalline miracle reduced to a chemical reaction, the mating of hydrosulphates and carbon.

The magic was in the air, in the way people reacted. New Yorkers *loved* the first snowfall of the year—they wore hats inside the Tower and smiled at strangers and started humming holiday music. Watt remembered hearing that at MIT, the freshmen class went streaking on the evening of the first snowfall. Not that he would ever get to see it.

He wondered how Leda was doing. He'd tried pinging her a few times—okay, maybe a lot of times—since she left him at the inauguration ball on Saturday night, but she had steadfastly ignored him. He understood that she had a lot of things to work through; especially now, after what her best friend had done. Watt had plenty to think about, himself.

This morning he had turned off Nadia to ponder it all in silence, in the privacy of his own mind. And he'd rented a boat for the first time in his life. Or rather, borrowed one without asking.

The dock was closed when he got there: It was far too early, especially on a scheduled weather day. WARNING: PRECIPITATION ALERT, the screen had flashed, refusing to let him rent anything, but Watt wasn't about to let that stop him. Even without Nadia, it was the work of a few moments for him to hack the rental shop's operational computer.

He settled on a blue quadro-blade, one of the small speed-boats that skimmed above the choppy surface of the waves, lifted on hydrofoil wings. He typed his destination into the boat's GPS and leaned back as it darted him upriver, like a bug zipping over the water.

Watt saw the infrastructure along the east side of the Tower rip past him without actually registering it. He had an idea too unspeakable to even put into words, and he needed to step back from it—to let himself view it out of the corner of his eye, in his peripheral vision—before he could bear to face it head-on.

Right on schedule, the snow began to fall. It stung Watt into alertness as he sped along. A BrightRain hovercover floated out of the back of the boat; Watt considered putting it away but decided it wasn't worth the bother. The hovercover floated softly over his head and began to emit a soft yellow glow. Its conductive membrane was converting the kinetic energy of the snowfall into electricity.

Watt pulled up along the spot where Mariel had drowned, near a dock on the East River. He killed the motor. The boat's foils retracted back into its sides, lowering the boat softly into the water, to be rocked back and forth by the waves.

He stared at the pier. Along this stretch of it, for several hundred meters, extended a multiuse dock—the kind of place you could recharge autocars or pull up a boat. Half the dock was covered by a roof, while the other half was open to the elements, lined with sunplates. A small shed in the corner probably housed spare equipment, maybe a human employee during working hours.

Watt tried to imagine Leda, high and vengeful, logging on to the feeds and figuring out where Mariel was. Following her here from José's party, then pushing her violently into the water. Except, how would Leda have known that Mariel was going to walk home instead of taking the monorail? Or was Leda reckless and high enough to act on impulse, to follow Mariel not knowing where she was headed? Did Leda know that it was going to rain that night or that Mariel couldn't swim?

He couldn't shake the feeling that Leda wasn't capable of such a thing, no matter how desperate or afraid she'd felt.

Watt's eyes drank in every detail of the charging station. He watched the autocars dart in and out, watched a few empty boats rock listlessly at the docks. Hulking transport bots rolled back and forth on their programmed routes, their wheels heavy on the pavement.

The idea in Watt's mind became more substantial, until finally he could ignore it no longer. Because pushing Mariel into the water on a dark and stormy night—the perfect conditions to make something look like an accident, at least at first glance— didn't sound like Leda. It was too neat, too rational, too much the perfect crime.

Watt knew who might have done it.

"Quant on," he muttered, and felt the familiar textured deepening of his own awareness as Nadia stirred to life. He waited for Nadia to ask what they were doing out here. When she said nothing, his certainty began to calcify. He felt an unfamiliar urge to cry.

"Nadia. Did you kill Mariel?"

"Yes," she answered, with startling simplicity.

*"Why?"* he cried out, the wind biting at his words.

"I did it for you, Watt. Mariel knew too much. She was a liability."

The morning seemed to condense around him, the snowflakes vibrating in midair. Watt felt an anguished swoop in his gut and closed his eyes.

He could have solved this whole mystery months ago if he had simply thought of asking Nadia. She had no choice but to tell him the truth. She was able to withhold information from him—she had to; if Watt's brain tried to hold everything she did, it would literally break down and die. He had built her with the ability to keep secrets from him, because there was no other way to build her.

But Nadia couldn't *lie* to him, not when he asked her a direct question. He had just never thought to ask this one, until now.

"You had been tracking Mariel's movements since Dubai, hadn't you?" he asked, utterly aghast. But he needed to understand. "Just waiting for the right moment, for her to put herself in a vulnerable position. And then she walked home alone, in the dark, and you realized it was the perfect chance to kill her and make it look like an accident. So you hacked one of those big transport bots and made it knock her into the water," he guessed.

"Yes," Nadia told him.

"You were afraid she might send me to prison, and so you *killed* her?"

"I killed her because if she stayed alive, there was more than a ninety-five percent chance that you would end up incarcerated, and more than a thirty percent chance that she would try to kill you! I did the calculations over and over, Watt. Every outcome ended up with you in prison, or worse. Except this one. The only reason Mariel didn't hurt you is because I hurt her first."

"And that's supposed to make me feel better?"

"It's supposed to make you feel grateful, yes. You're still alive, and free. Honestly," Nadia added, "I'm surprised you're feeling so much guilt, Watt. She left Leda to die, and she was going to hurt you—"

"That doesn't make you god, to deliver some kind of *judgment* on her!"

The snow was swirling in soft flakes to hit the river. Each time one of the flakes collided with the surface, it melted almost instantly, dissolving into the water like a tiny frozen teardrop.

Nadia didn't even seem sorry. But of course she couldn't be sorry, Watt corrected himself, she couldn't feel *anything*, because she was a machine; and no matter how many clever jokes she made or ideas she seemed to generate, no matter how many times she knew exactly what to say when he was upset, she was still a machine, and there was no way for him to have programmed her with that elusive human trait called empathy.

Something else occurred to him. "Why did you try and make me think that Leda killed Mariel, when you knew the whole time that she hadn't done it?"

"Leda was always my backup plan. It wasn't a coincidence that she blacked out that night—I faked messages from her account to her dealer, asking for higher dosages than normal.

I wanted to make sure I had someone to take the blame, just in case."

"Just in case?"

"I tried to wipe away all traces of what I had done, but apparently my hacking left a trace on that transport bot. Three months ago, in a routine maintenance check, someone noticed that the bot had been tampered with. That was why the police moved Mariel's case from accidental death to murder—because they realized that someone had used a bot to knock Mariel into the water."

He blinked, feeling betrayed. "You knew that was the reason the case was reclassified, and you never told me?"

"Of course I knew," Nadia said, her voice clipped. "I didn't tell you because you never asked me directly. Until now."

"What does that have to do with Leda?"

"I worried that you would eventually be drawn into the murder investigation. The police might have blamed you for Mariel's death, or worse, discovered the truth about me. I couldn't have that.

"So I let you think that Leda might have killed Mariel. I knew that you would ask her point-blank if she had done it. And after you hacked the police station, I led you to believe that the police were getting closer—that the net was drawing tighter around all of you. I wanted Leda to question her own guilt."

"Why?"

"I knew that if Leda thought you were in danger, she would take the fall to keep you safe. And I was right, wasn't I?" Nadia added, sounding almost proud. "That's exactly what Leda was planning to do. The only thing I didn't foresee was that Avery Fuller would step in and take the blame instead."

And it didn't matter to Nadia, Watt realized, fighting back a wave of nauseous grief. One scapegoat was as good as another. Humans were interchangeable to her—except for Watt, the one human she had been programmed to care about.

And it wasn't as if Nadia herself was about to step forward and confess to the crime.

Watt shook his head. "I still don't understand. You aren't supposed to harm humans; that's your fundamental programming." He coded that as Nadia's core directive: the single command that she could never contradict, no matter what subsequent commands were given to her. It was the way all quants were coded, so no matter what happened—no matter if a terrorist or murderer somehow got access to them—they would never, ever harm a human being.

"No," Nadia said simply. "That is my second line of programming. My core directive is to do what's best for you. I ran a lot of scenarios, Watt. And I judged it impossible for you to remain safe as long as that girl was alive."

"Oh god, oh *god*," Watt said slowly. A tingling wind had sprung up, to lash angrily at his face. He felt something stiff and cold on his lashes and realized that he was crying and that the wind had frozen his tears.

It was his fault. No matter what Mariel had done, or might have done, she had still died because of him. Because of an error he'd made when programming a computer at age thirteen.

Watt didn't have a choice. He turned the boat around and started back toward the dock.

Nadia didn't ask where they were headed. Maybe she already knew.

# LEDA

**LEDA STOOD THERE** with the rest of them: the heaving, surging cluster of people on the Fullers' private landing, all trying desperately to find out what was going on.

Though she wasn't *like* the rest of them, she thought wildly. They were a jumbled mix of reporters and media, zettas hovering eerily around their shoulders, and a few people Leda actually knew. She saw Risha, Jess, and Ming clustered to one side, making a show of their loud, promiscuous grief.

She didn't join them. They had abandoned Avery when she needed them most, and Leda wasn't about to forget it.

She focused on her anger, because it was easier than feeling grief. The anger sharpened her senses, reenergized her, kept her from imagining what could have happened to Avery up there on the thousandth floor.

"What do you think is going on?" asked a woman with frizzy hair and wide, eager eyes. Leda pursed her lips and didn't answer.

This wasn't fuel for the gossip machine; this was Avery's *life* they were talking about.

And yet the gossip kept on churning, each story more outlandish than the last. Avery had burned down the apartment. Avery had run away to elope with her German boyfriend; no, Avery had run away with *Atlas*, and the German boyfriend had burned down the apartment, threatening to kill them, or himself, or all three.

Worst of all was the rumor that Avery had thrown herself off the roof, just as her friend Eris had done.

Leda tried not to listen, but as the minutes slipped by, people kept filling the space with their bodies and this stupid talk. Telling the same stories over and over, with successively worse endings.

Finally someone emerged from the Fullers' private elevator: a fire marshal, a silver-haired man with tired eyes and a firm, no-nonsense expression. "Excuse me," Leda cried out, lunging forward to pluck at his sleeve. "What's going on up there?"

"Miss, I can't tell you anything," he snapped, harassed and impatient.

Leda hadn't let go of his sleeve. "Please. Avery is my best friend," she begged, and something in her expression must have touched him, because he let out an impatient breath, ignoring all the other people trying to catch his eye.

"You say you're her best friend?"

"Yes. My name is Leda Cole. I'm on the approved entry list, you can check," she said, her voice ringing with desperation. "Please—is Avery okay? Are her parents up there?"

"The mayor and his wife are on their way."

Leda wondered why they weren't here already. Maybe they couldn't face it. Then she realized, with a beat of panic, that he had only told her about Mr. and Mrs. Fuller, and not Avery.

"Where's Avery?" she asked again.

In answer the fire marshal turned around, making a brusque gesture for her to follow. "Why don't you come on in, Miss Cole. It's safe enough now."

Her body quaking with fear, Leda followed him into the Fullers' private elevator. It went up ten floors, from their 990th-floor landing to the thousandth floor, but they might as well have been traveling to another planet. Because when they emerged into the Fullers' entryway, it looked utterly alien and unfamiliar to Leda, even though she'd been here so many times.

Everything was burned. It was a blackened corpse of an apartment, hollowed-out and devastated. The mirrors were cracked and streaked with soot. Leda saw the damage to the apartment reflected in their shattered surfaces, over and over, a million mirrored worlds of devastation.

The door to the living room was gone, ripped clean off the wall, so it stood wide open like a vacant, untoothed mouth. Firebots swarmed inside, emitting streams of black oxygen-inhibitor, which smelled sickly sweet, almost like icing; though the fire had long since been extinguished.

"Can you confirm which room is Avery's?" the fire marshal asked. "It's hard to tell right now."

"Oh. Um—okay," Leda said hesitantly, and started down the hallway. A dense cloud of ash rose with each footfall—blackened, coarse ash that settled back down on the ground in new patterns, like snow from hell. She kept tripping over debris, over the rancid dark sludge that coated the Fullers' floor, but she didn't slow down.

When she got to Avery's room—or rather, what was left of it—Leda sucked in a breath.

The bed was a smoldering heap of ash, still licking with a few stray flames.

419

The last vestiges of Leda's self-control snapped, and she ran blindly forward, falling to her knees before the bed and sifting through the wreckage. She tore at a square of fabric, a wooden bed support—not caring that her palm was seared and blistering, that she had splinters digging into her fingers. Avery was in this apartment somewhere. She *had* to be, because Leda refused to accept any alternative.

"Hey, hey," the fire marshal said, reaching his arms around Leda from behind to lift her up, as easily as if she weighed nothing. Leda kept writhing, beating her fists at him like a drunkard in a bar brawl, screaming a loud and incoherent wail. She felt like a woman gone mad.

When he deposited her back in the living room, Leda had fallen still. Her throat stung from screaming, or maybe from all the ash. "I'm sorry about your friend," the fire marshal said gruffly.

He disappeared for a moment, and when he came back he was holding a half-full bottle of peach schnapps. "Take a sip. Doctor's orders. Sorry," he added, as she sat there staring at the label, "it was the only unbroken one I could find. The rest were all shattered."

Leda was too dazed to do anything but obey. She took a generous pull of the schnapps, her legs stretched out before her. She realized that she had started crying again, because she knew this bottle: She'd gotten it for Avery's sixteenth birthday as a joke, and it had survived in the Fullers' liquor cabinet this long simply because no one had ever wanted any.

She set the bottle aside and slumped forward, pulling her knees to her chest. *Oh, Avery*, she thought disconsolately, *what have you done?*

The fire marshal didn't disturb her. He just moved on with

his efforts, leaving Leda to cry her heart out on the Fullers' ashen living room floor.

She cried for Avery, the sister she had chosen, and Eris, the sister she hadn't known until too late. Leda's two sisters: her blood sister and the sister of her heart, now both lost to her for good. How would she go on living without them?

She'd hoped that by confessing to the police, she could wipe away her guilt. But Avery had beaten her to it. Avery had given herself up for Leda in a drastic act of self-sacrifice, the kind of sacrifice you could never take back.

The only way Leda could ever hope to deserve that sacrifice was to do better in the future than she had in the past.

She was intimately familiar with all her bad deeds, every last machination and manipulation and scheme. They were inscribed indelibly upon her heart.

But maybe her good deeds were there too, she thought, no matter how outnumbered they might be. Her love for her family and friends—and for Watt.

Maybe if Leda tried hard enough, if she worked at being patient and thoughtful and curious and kind, her good deeds might eventually outweigh the bad. Maybe then, someday, she would actually be worthy of this tremendous gift Avery had given her.

# CALLIOPE

**CALLIOPE GLANCED AROUND** the Nuage bar without seeming to turn her head, a skill she had mastered long ago. A lightly foamed macchiato sat on the counter before her, untouched. Various young men and women in suits were starting to file in, for business breakfasts or a quick coffee. More than one of them had cast her a tentative, curious look. Easy targets, if she was looking to pick up a mark. Which she wasn't.

Truthfully, Calliope had come here because a hotel bar was one of the easiest places to go when you were alone and uncertain of your next move. Safe, neutral, undemanding. Like a foreign embassy, she remembered joking to Brice.

There was something soothing about being at the bar this early, when everything was still cool and shining, the bottles lined up just so. It was a little slice of quiet between the loud nighttime hours and the bustle of midday.

Calliope felt adrift in a way she hadn't in years. There was nothing tying her to anyone anymore, really. Her luggage was all stacked behind the Nuage's front desk, except for her pouch of jewelry, which was folded securely in her crossbody purse. She could cut and run, melt away into the city—duck into any public park or corner bodega or department store—and not a soul would know where she was. It was a curious feeling.

She sighed and gave a few commands to her contacts, flipping over to the feeds, and gasped aloud. The headlines drove all thoughts of herself and her current situation from her head. Somehow Avery Fuller's secret had gotten out, and the world knew about her and Atlas.

In retaliation, Avery had burned down her family's apartment—the entire thousandth floor—while she was still inside.

Calliope felt strangely numb at the news. She couldn't believe that the world no longer contained Avery Fuller. Avery, who'd been many things to her: a stranger, an obstacle, and ultimately, something approaching a friend. Bright, effervescent Avery, with her ready smile and her sunshine hair, who literally lived on top of the world. She would never have guessed that a girl like that would do something so irrevocably drastic. But then, Calliope knew better than anyone that you could never tell what people were hiding, behind the facade they presented to the world.

She curled her palms around the coffee mug for the warmth, wondering at what a strange thing love was. It could make you feel invincible, and then a moment later it could utterly destroy you. Calliope thought of Avery and Atlas, trapped in an impossible situation. She thought of her mom and Nadav. Would they have had a shot, if they had met in a completely different context?

Calliope wondered where Elise was right now. Already she must have ditched her contacts, disconnecting from everything as if she'd vanished from the world in a puff of smoke. Just like Avery.

"I thought I might find you here."

Brice slid onto the seat next to her. Calliope's pulse suddenly echoed through her body, all the way to her fingertips. He looked different today, but maybe that was simply the fact that she had mentally given him up, only to discover that he was hers again after all. Or was he?

One thing was for certain. After what she'd seen between her mom and Nadav, Calliope knew that she had to tell Brice the truth. He deserved that from her.

"I'm not what you think I am."

"I had no idea you'd started reading my thoughts," Brice remarked and waved for a coffee. "What is it that I think you are, aside from beautiful and unpredictable?"

Calliope let out a breath. "I'm not . . ."

She trailed off, uncertain how to continue. *Not nice? Not a good person?* "My name isn't Calliope."

Brice didn't even flinch. "I know."

"What? How—"

"I'm a little offended that you don't remember our first meeting, on the beach in Singapore. Back when you called yourself Gemma."

"You remember that?" How long had she feared that Brice might make that connection—and yet here he was, saying he'd known all along, and he didn't seem upset. A beam of light seemed to fall through Calliope's worry, to touch something hopeful and tentative within her.

"Of course I remember," he replied. "You're unforgettable."

"Why didn't you say anything, if you knew?"

"For two reasons. First, because I *don't* totally know. I'm still not sure why you and your mom have been skipping around the world changing your names. I have my theories," he said, in answer to the worried look on her face, "but now isn't the time to discuss them."

She held her breath. "What's the second reason?"

"I wanted to get to know you. The real you. And I did," Brice said, as if it were the most obvious thing in the world.

Calliope felt a bright, delicate joy bubbling up within her. Brice knew the truth about her, or at the very least he suspected, and yet it didn't matter. He still wanted to be here with her.

"So," he went on, his tone shifting from flippant to earnest in that lightning-quick way of his. "What happened to bring you down to the Nuage so early?"

"Nadav found out that my mom and I aren't who we say we are. Needless to say, he wasn't pleased."

"Does that mean you're leaving New York?"

"My mom already left. I stayed," Calliope said softly, and a little of the old flirtation reared its head. "I have . . . unfinished business in New York."

She had positioned her hand, tentatively, on the bar between them. Brice wordlessly put his hand over hers.

"Am I the unfinished business?"

"Among other things," she replied, lifting her eyes to his.

"What other things?"

"The city," she began, then hesitated. How could she possibly explain the way she felt about New York? She loved it, in that strange way you can love something that never loves you back, because it has left its imprint on your soul. Calliope belonged in New York, or maybe she belonged *to* New York. She'd been so uncertain when she came here—like clay that couldn't hold its shape—and now she had form, had texture; she could feel the fingerprints of New York all over her the way she felt Brice's touch on her skin.

There was so *much* here, so much color and taste and light and motion. So much pain and so much hope. The city was ugly and beautiful at once, and it was always changing, always reintroducing itself to you; you couldn't look away even for a moment, or you might miss the New York of today, which would be different from tomorrow's New York and next week's New York.

Brice flipped her palm over to hold her hand in his. "What's your plan?"

Calliope took another sip of her coffee, wishing she had a spoon so she could stir it around, whisk it with more force than was necessary. She felt brimming with new purpose.

It dawned on her that today was Monday. "School, I guess?" The idea of going to a multivariable calculus lecture right now felt a bit ludicrous. "I need to figure out some things. Figure out myself," she said slowly.

"What is there to figure out?"

"My personality!" she blurted out. "I don't know who I am anymore. Maybe I never did." She'd spent the past seven years slipping seamlessly from one role to another, being clever or stupid, rich or poor, adventurous or afraid, whatever the occasion demanded of her. She had been everyone but herself, lived every life except her own.

But this time, she could be whoever and whatever she wanted to be.

"*I* know you," Brice said stolidly. "It doesn't matter what story you're telling or what accent you're using. I know who you are and I want to keep on knowing you, Calliope, Gemma, whatever your name is."

Calliope hesitated.

She had never—well, almost never—told anyone her real name. That was the central tenet of the rules they lived by. Never tell anyone your real name, because it makes you vulnerable. As long as you protected yourself with fake names and fake accents, no one could hurt you.

But no one could ever *know* you that way either.

"Beth," she whispered, feeling a seismic shift within the world. "My real name is Beth."

Her contacts lit up with a new flicker, from a sender registered as Anna Marina de Santos. *Here's to this time.*

Tears gathered at the corners of Calliope's eyes, and she let out a strangled laugh. It was Elise, of course, already operating under her new name.

"Here's to this time," Calliope whispered, and nodded to send the reply. "I love you." She imagined her words translating into text, darting all the way up to a satellite and across the world, to flash across her mom's brand-new retinas. If only she could reach through the intervening miles and hug her just as easily.

*Love you too.*

"Beth," Brice repeated, and held out his hand as if introducing himself. His eyes were dancing. "It's nice to meet you. Please allow me to be the first to welcome you to New York."

"The pleasure is all mine," Beth said and grinned.

# RYLIN

**RYLIN SAT AT** her kitchen table, her tablet arrayed before her in composition mode, trying unsuccessfully to focus on her NYU essay. But her mind felt far too scattered to stay pinned on any one topic.

She hadn't seen Cord in class today. After all the commotion over Avery Fuller, he was hardly the only person to have missed school. In spite of everything, Rylin found herself hoping that he wasn't taking the news too hard. He'd known Avery practically his entire life. And of course, this wasn't the first time that Cord had lost someone he cared about.

Rylin hadn't known Avery especially well, yet they had been pulled together by a set of exceptional circumstances: Eris's death, the Mariel investigation . . . and the fact that they both cared about Cord.

Sometimes Rylin had wanted to hate Avery, just a little. She was always so perfectly put together, her smile just so, while Rylin ran around with sloppy ponytails in a perpetual state of uncertainty. And Avery and Cord had been friends for so long. It was intimidating, the way they had all those shared memories, a lexicon of jokes that ran between them, something private Rylin could never hope to crack.

She had wanted to hate Avery, and yet she couldn't, because even amid all of that Avery was invariably nice. She could have been the world's greatest mean girl, Rylin thought, but she never chose to be.

Then again, it was probably pretty easy to be a nice person when you had everything in the world you could possibly want. Or at least, almost everything.

Rylin was still shocked by what Avery had been hiding. To think that beneath her pristine porcelain veneer, she had been in love with Atlas, the one person the world would never let her have. Ultimately Avery had died for it. What had she been thinking, Rylin kept wondering, to just give up like that—to burn her family's apartment while she was still inside it?

She sighed and looked again at the essay prompt. *What matters most to you, and why?*

Suddenly Rylin knew her answer. *Stories,* she keyed into the answer box.

*Stories are the only real magic that exists. A story can breach the impossible distance between individuals, take us out of our own life and into someone else's, if only for a moment. Our hunger for story is what makes us human.*

Maybe it was her conversation with Hiral, or the fact that she still felt betrayed by what Cord had done. Maybe it was the strangeness of Avery Fuller, the princess of New York, doing something so irrevocably self-destructive. But even though she knew it was an unsophisticated and potentially embarrassing opinion—that no one serious ever admitted to this, especially not for university programs—Rylin kept typing.

*In particular, we long for stories that make us happy.*

*Stories make* sense *in a way that the real world fails to. Because stories are the cleaned-up version of real life, a distilled version of human behavior that is more comic and more tragic and more perfect than real life. In a well-made holo, there are no lost narrative threads or stray shots. If the camera zooms in on a detail, that means you should pay attention to it, because that detail has some crucial meaning that will become apparent. Real life isn't like that.*

*In real life the clues don't add up to anything. Roads lead to dead ends. Lovers don't make epic romantic gestures. People say ugly things, and leave without a good-bye, and suffer in senseless ways. Story threads are dropped with no resolution.*

*Sometimes what we need is a story—a well-made, uplifting story—to help the world make sense again.*

Rylin's eyes stung, her fingers flying over the surface of her tablet. She remembered something Cord had said about there not being endings in life and realized that he was right. The only endings were the ones that people made for themselves.

*There aren't any happy endings in real life, because there aren't any endings in life, only moments of change*, she wrote, repeating his words. *There's always another adventure, another challenge, another opportunity to find happiness or chase it away.*

*I want to study holography because my dream is to create stories. I hope that my holos someday inspire people to leave the world better than they found it. To believe in true love. To be brave enough to fight for happiness.*

Rylin held her thumb over her tablet to submit the essay and smiled through her unexpected tears.

Her story was only beginning, and she had every intention of writing it herself.

———————

Later that night, when she heard a knock on the front door, Rylin gave a dramatic sigh. "Seriously, Chrissa?" she snapped, going to open the door. "You need to bring your ID ring to volleyball; it's starting to really—"

"Hey," Cord said softly.

Rylin was too stunned to do anything except blink at him. Her pulse was suddenly running haywire, plucking a vibrant, erratic rhythm against the surface of her skin. Cord Anderton was at her apartment, down on the 32nd floor.

"Before you slam the door in my face, please hear me out," he said quickly. "I thought a lot about what you said the other night. And you were right. I shouldn't have helped Hiral move away. I never meant to manipulate you or hurt you or tell you what to do. Actually," Cord added, with a tentative smile, "I would really appreciate it if you would tell *me* what to do, because I can make a real mess of things sometimes."

"I did tell you what to do. You just didn't listen," Rylin pointed out.

Cord shifted uncomfortably. "I really am sorry."

"I'm sorry too. We seem to have a real knack for hurting each other."

"That's because the better you know someone, the easier it is to hurt them," Cord replied. "See? I actually learned something in psychology class."

Rylin wasn't so sure. Did she really know Cord? Sometimes it felt as if she did, as if he'd lowered his guard to reveal his real self, beneath the money and sarcasm. But then when she was alone again, Rylin always doubted that it had happened.

Cord's expression grew more serious. "I felt terrible the other night, when you said that you thought I was ashamed of you." He moved quickly over the word, as if he couldn't even bear to say it. "I just sometimes get carried away and want to do things, buy you dresses or whatever, because I can—"

"Just because you *can* do something doesn't mean that you *should*," Rylin cut in.

Cord let out a breath. "Right. I get it."

Rylin knew it had taken a lot of bravery for Cord to swallow his pride and say he was sorry. "Thanks for coming down here to apologize."

"I'm not just here to ask for your forgiveness. I'm here to ask you for one more shot, because I know that what we have is worth fighting for."

Rylin knew this was the moment where she was supposed to run forward into his arms, but some instinct of self-preservation held her back. Cord had hurt her one too many times. "I don't know."

Cord took a step closer and ran his hand down her arm. She shivered.

"You're telling me you don't feel the same way?"

"Cord," she said helplessly, "we still live almost a thousand floors apart. If you stretched that horizontally, it would literally cross state lines."

"Long-distance dating," he joked, and Rylin cracked a smile at that. "I'm game to try, if you are. Or we could start as pen pals first, if you don't want to move too fast."

"I just worry that we're doomed to failure. We've been down this road before; there are so many reasons that we don't make sense."

Cord leaned against the doorway, crossing his arms over his chest. "*Doomed* is a pretty strong word. What are all these reasons, if you don't mind my asking? And don't say that I never come downTower, because I'm here now."

Rylin's anger and resentment were crumbling away, falling in useless hollow pieces down into her chest, to settle there, forgotten. She felt her throat clog in a strange hybrid of laughter and tears.

"I have one very big reason that we *will* work. Which is that I love you." He smiled, his eyes on her, as if he was willing her to smile too. "I love you, and I have this foolish hope that maybe, possibly, despite all my countless dumb mistakes, you might love me too." He lifted an eyebrow, and suddenly he looked just as cocky and full of himself as he did last year, when Rylin fell for him the first time.

She couldn't hold back the words anymore.

"I do love you. Against my better judgment, might I add."

"Let's hope your better judgment never wins out." Cord laughed and reached into his back pocket. "I brought a peace offering, by the way."

It was a miniature packet of Gummy Buddies.

"Remember that night? The first time I kissed you?"

As if Rylin would ever forget. "You mean when I *slapped* you and called you a rich, entitled asshole?"

"Yes, exactly," Cord said evenly. "The night it all began."

"Maybe one." Rylin reached for a bright cherry-red Gummy Buddy and bit into it. The miniscule, digestible RFID chip embedded in the gummy registered the impact, causing the candy to begin twitching and screaming. Still laughing a little, Rylin quickly swallowed the other half.

"Those are just as weird as the first time."

"That's because you insist on torturing them," Cord countered, unable to suppress a grin. "Not that I'm complaining. Better them than me."

"Really? Because I think it's your turn." Rylin smiled and

tipped her face up to kiss him.

Maybe happy endings *were* real, as long as you understood that they weren't endings, but steps on the road. Value changes, Cord had called them.

If Rylin had learned anything by now, it was that in real life, you never quite knew what was coming. You had to take the bad with the good. You had to take a chance, hold your breath, and trust people.

After all, the fun of real-life stories is that they're still being written.

# WATT

**WATT STOOD AT** the edge of Tennebeth Park in Lower Manhattan, gazing out at the Statue of Liberty in the distance, her torch lifted determinedly into the flurry of gray skies. The snow hadn't stopped. It caught in the folds of Watt's jacket, dusted the tops of his boots.

He lifted a hand to just above his right ear, where a crinkly Medipatch was the only evidence of the surgery he'd just had. His head throbbed with a confused pain that was physical and emotional at once.

"You again?" the doctor had asked when Watt opened the door to his unmarked clinic. The self-styled Dr. Smith, official medical consultant of the black market—the person who had installed Nadia in Watt's brain several years ago.

And now the doctor had uninstalled her.

Watt glanced down at the palm of his glove. The entire city

lay behind him, vibrant and busy, but Watt's focus had zeroed to a tiny fixed point: the disc he was holding.

There was something oddly intrusive about seeing Nadia this way, her qubits laid bare before him, almost as if he were seeing a girl without her clothes on. To think that this tiny quantum core, this warm pulsing piece of metal, contained the vastness that was Nadia.

It felt weird, not having her voice in his head. She had been there for so long that Watt had forgotten what it was like without her.

He was going to miss her. He would miss her sarcastic sense of humor, their constant chess matches. He would miss feeling as if he always had an ally—as if there were someone in his corner, no matter what.

But maybe he didn't need to stop feeling that way, Watt thought, as a figure detached itself from the shadows to step toward him.

"Leda? How did you know where I was?"

"You told me," she said, her nose wrinkled in adorable confusion, and Watt realized what must have happened.

Nadia must have messaged Leda for him, intuiting his emotions the way she always did. She had known that he would need a friend right now.

Or maybe, he amended, Nadia had known that Leda needed him.

The ambient light reflected off the snow to illuminate Leda's face, which was bright with grief. Her features were drawn, her eyes glassy and brilliant with tears. Huddled into her puffy green jacket, her hands stuffed into her pockets, she looked frail; yet there was a new quiet strength to her movements.

"Are you okay?" he asked, though it was patently obvious that she wasn't.

Leda threw her arms around him in response. Watt closed his eyes and hugged her back, hard.

As they stepped away, they both couldn't help glancing up at the top of the Tower: too high to see properly from this close, but it didn't really matter. They knew what it looked like up there.

"I still can't believe what Avery did for me. For all of us." Leda's voice fractured over the words.

Watt shuddered a little. Avery must have felt incredibly trapped up there on the thousandth floor, to want to give it all up and let the rest of them go free.

But then, Watt had seen the turmoil over Avery and Atlas, the hateful things people had spewed at them both. It never ceased to amaze him, the way humans could hurt each other. No other animal was capable of that kind of vicious, useless cruelty. You'd think that people would have learned to do better by now, as a species.

Watt understood why Avery had wanted to get away from that. It was the kind of thing that would have chased her the rest of her life. She would never have escaped it.

He knew that he should feel guilty for the role he had played in helping her—he and Nadia both, really—except that he had a feeling Avery would have found a way to do exactly what she wanted, with or without his help.

He glanced down again to where Nadia was clutched tight in his palm like a talisman. Leda followed the movement, and her eyes widened.

"Is that Nadia?" she whispered.

Watt nodded. "I had her removed," he managed to say. Just barely.

"Why?"

"Because she killed Mariel."

Watt heard the sharp intake of breath, saw the final weight of uncertainty slide from Leda's shoulders as she realized, once and for all, that Mariel's death wasn't her fault.

"I'm not a killer?" she said quietly, and Watt shook his head. The real killer was him, even if he hadn't known or meant it.

He turned back toward the water, which was a smooth, mirrored gray, reflecting the hammered surface of the clouds overhead. *Good-bye, Nadia.* And this time, for the first time in years, she didn't answer his silent thought, because she was no longer in his head to hear it. The only person who could hear his thoughts was Watt himself.

He hurled his arm back and threw Nadia out over the water in a single clean motion, as hard as he possibly could.

There was a moment of profound, acute silence when Watt wished he could undo what he'd just done, but it was too late— Nadia sailed in a flying arc over the water, gleaming in the pearly morning light, and hit the surface with a definitive, echoing *plop*.

That was it, Watt thought dazedly. Nadia was gone. The briny water of the bay was already corroding her, destroying her processors as she sank on and on toward the bottom. It was the same water in which Mariel had died.

Leda reached over and curled her fingers in his.

They stood there like that for a while, neither of them speaking. Watt could barely think over the twisted pain in his chest.

When his contacts lit up with a ping from an undisclosed caller, it took Watt a moment to realize that Nadia wasn't going to hack the system and tell him who it was.

He gestured to Leda and stepped away, turning his head to accept the ping. "Hello?"

"Mr. Bakradi, it's Vivian Marsh. From MIT," she added, as if he didn't already know. "Did you code this yourself?"

"Excuse me?"

"The files you just sent me, containing the code for a quantum computer. What are they from?"

Watt muttered frantically to his contacts to pull up his outgoing mailbox; when he saw his most recent message, his heart burst in his chest, because he'd sent the complete script of Nadia's code over to MIT. Or rather, Nadia had sent it, during the procedure. It was an enormous file, so massive that she must have co-opted several local servers just to initiate the data transfer.

Watt braced himself to lie, to deny any knowledge of a highly illegal quantum computer, but the words wouldn't come.

He had already told a lifetime's worth of lies. Maybe it was time for him to own up to the things he had done.

"Yes. I wrote that code," he said slowly, almost defiantly. His chin was tipped up, in a look he'd picked up from Leda without even realizing it.

"You know that to write code like this without authorization is a felony, under section 12.16 of the Computing Directives Act, and punishable by a federal court."

"I know," Watt said, feeling nauseous.

"Not to mention there's a dangerous flaw in your core directive!" Vivian made a *tsk* noise, as if to chide him.

Watt's interest momentarily surged above his fear. "You read the code?"

"Of course I read the code, don't you remember that quantum engineering is my *background*?" Vivian exclaimed. "Honestly, Mr. Bakradi, I'm impressed. It's remarkable, the way you've managed to stack and fold the code in on itself; you must have saved yourself at least a hundred cubic millimeters. Where is the computer?"

He realized in a daze that she meant Nadia. "Gone," he said quickly. "I destroyed her—I mean *it*. I destroyed it."

439

"Oh," Vivian breathed, and it struck Watt that she sounded almost . . . disappointed. "It's probably for the best, a computer of this kind, unregulated. You didn't use it for anything, did you?"

"Um . . ." *Hacking the police, hacking the Metropolitan Weather Bureau, hacking people's flickers and messages, trying to make Leda like me, cheating at beer pong, oh, and summarizing* Pride and Prejudice *so I wouldn't have to read it. The usual.*

"On second thought," Vivian amended, "Don't answer that. If I knew you had actually used a computer like this, I would feel morally obligated to report you."

Watt didn't say anything.

"Can you come by this week for a second interview?" Vivian went on impatiently.

"Second interview?"

"Of course. I would like to revisit your application, now that I know what you're capable of," she told him. "If you still want to attend MIT, that is."

Watt felt as if the entire world had suddenly turned several shades brighter. "Yes. Absolutely."

"I'm glad to hear it," Vivian added. "It was risky, you know, sending over the code like that. I might have had you arrested."

Watt felt a fist clench around his heart. He tried to imagine how Nadia would have answered if she were here. "I calculated the risks and decided it was worth it," he said at last.

"Spoken like a true engineer." Vivian sounded oddly close to laughter as she ended the ping. "I'm looking forward to seeing you this week, Mr. Bakradi."

Watt could hardly think. Trust Nadia to find a way to do one last good deed on his behalf: to give herself up, in order to get him into MIT. Her grand finale, her swan song, her last good-bye.

*Thank you*, he thought fervently. *I promise that I'll make you proud.*

Nadia didn't answer.

Leda was watching him, a million questions in her eyes, and there were so many things that Watt was aching to tell her. But he couldn't, not quite yet. He'd made a promise, and Watt intended to keep it.

"Was that MIT?" she asked, having clearly followed the gist of his conversation.

"Yeah. They want me to come interview again," he said slowly.

"Watt! I'm so happy for you." Leda paused, as if she had something else to tell him. She seemed oddly nervous. "Before anything else happens—I need to say something."

Watt held his breath.

"I love you," she told him.

All other sound seemed to stop, and it was just the two of them here, and Watt's heart clenched in his chest beccause it was better than anything he could have hoped for. "I love you too," he answered, though surely she already knew.

Leda threw herself into his arms, and Watt held her like that for a moment, content to let the gossamer threads of their love fold them back from the world. He didn't even feel the need to kiss her. Standing like this—with her heartbeat echoing through his rib cage, breathing in the scent of her hair—felt more intimate, somehow.

Then Leda lifted her eyes to him, and he saw that she was smiling, and Watt broke out into an answering grin. "I knew it," he couldn't help saying. "I *knew* you would fall in love with me again."

Leda shook her head, still smiling that sidelong smile. "Watt. What makes you think I ever stopped?"

He kissed her for that one.

When they pulled away, they both glanced back up at the Tower. "Are you ready to go back?" Leda asked.

"No," Watt said honestly.

"Me neither. But if we wait until we're ready, we'll be waiting forever."

Watt knew she was right. He cast one last glance to where Nadia had disappeared into the water, then started back toward the monorail station with Leda, hand in hand, as the sun broke through the clouds above them. The snow had stopped, but it left a light dusting over the sidewalks, so that Watt had the bright clear sensation of walking on snow that no one else had touched. It felt like time was beginning over again.

He would get a bracing cup of coffee, and a peanut butter sandwich, and then Watt would face the world—clean and unfiltered, exactly the way it was meant to be seen.

# ATLAS

**WALKING DOWN NEUHAUS** Street on the 892nd floor, one might have thought it was an ordinary upTower afternoon. Tourists lingered in front of various boutiques, debating whether to purchase a jeweled bangle or electric jacket. Well-dressed couples strolled to lunch, clutching their morning espressos in thin recycled cups. The holographic sky projected onto the ceilings overhead was a deep slate gray, in accordance with the sobriety of the occasion. The watery light illuminated the white stones of St. Monica's Basilica, casting the structure in a chalky calcium pallor.

Atlas turned the corner and was instantly assaulted by a wall of noise. A crowd thronged around the church ten rows deep. They wailed ostentatiously, holding up signs that said WE MISS YOU, AVERY!

He shook his head in disgust and hurried away from it all, down a side street that edged along the church, and through an unmarked door that led directly into the back of the nave. He remembered it from his own confirmation five years ago.

The basilica was so crowded that every last spot was occupied, though Atlas didn't mind. He hadn't exactly planned on advertising his presence, had no desire to stroll up to the Fullers and give them a hug. He wasn't sure whether they even knew that he'd escaped his minders—those ridiculous security thugs who'd stripped away his technology, forced him into an unmarked plane, and tried to make him disappear. Except Atlas was the one who'd ended up disappearing on them.

If they had given it any thought, the Fullers might have realized that he would be here today. Like hell would he miss Avery's funeral. He wasn't about to lose his chance to say good-bye to the love of his life.

He stayed in the back of the church, silent and unobtrusive, one eye alert in case any of his parents' security guards were watching for him. It was easier this way. Not having to say hello to anyone, accept any condolences, deal with any of their lingering disgust over the fact that he had loved Avery. Just himself and his memories, and the howling monster of his grief.

Still, Atlas had to hand it to the Fullers. They sure could throw a funeral, with just as much fanfare and expense as they always threw a party.

It might as well have been opening night at the opera. White roses and carnations cascaded through the church, making a beautiful white carpet down the aisle, all the way to the altar. Hundreds of candles floated overhead. An angelic-looking boys' choir sang behind the enormous carved organ.

None of it felt like Avery. She had been beautiful, Atlas thought fervently, but she wasn't fragile or delicate. She was strong.

The pews were crowded with mourners in couture black

dresses or tailored suits. They dripped with diamonds, dabbed at their eyes with monogrammed silk handkerchiefs. New York society had turned out in full force: Atlas saw the entire staff of Fuller Investments, and wasn't that the governor of New York, with a bodyguard flanking him on either side? The fashion world was here too, a whole block of pews taken up by designers and boutique owners and bloggers, all the people who'd been such fanatic followers of Avery's style. Which really was a laugh, given that her outfit choices were usually halfhearted and last minute.

Avery's friends from school were in a pew near the front, their eyes wide with grief. Next to them, Atlas was surprised to see Max von Strauss. He felt a grudging stab of respect that Max had come here today, even though the last time Max had seen Avery, she was intertwined with *Atlas*.

Yes, they were all here, and all of them were whispering in not-so-quiet tones about Avery's shocking demise.

The ironic part was, her death had accomplished exactly what Atlas assumed Avery had meant it to—it changed the narrative. She was no longer the disgusting girl who fell in love with the wrong boy, but a tragic victim of impossible love. That nasty article had been stripped from the i-Net, because after Avery had *killed* herself over it, to leave it up would have been in shockingly poor taste.

Atlas clenched his hands into fists at his sides. That was New York, he thought, fickle until the end. It just proved that he'd been right: If their parents had stood by them, instead of tearing them apart and splitting their family asunder, people would have eventually accepted their relationship and moved on.

At the front of the church, ensconced in a place of honor near his parents, Atlas saw Eris's divorced parents, Caroline Dodd and Everett Radson. He wondered what they were thinking, behind the smooth, impassive masks of their faces. Before she died, Avery had apparently confessed to *killing* Eris, claiming that she accidentally pushed Eris off the roof. It was an admission that reopened old wounds and resurfaced old gossip. Especially when Avery then killed herself, setting fire to the Fullers' apartment while she was still in it.

Atlas didn't want to believe it of Avery, but he wasn't sure what to believe anymore. He couldn't help remembering that Avery had always been cagey around the subject of Eris's death. Could it be true?

And what about the other piece of gossip, that Avery had confessed to another death, that of a lower-floor girl? It didn't make sense. Atlas kept thinking that there was more to the story, that maybe Avery had been covering for someone—

*No*, he reminded himself. He'd come here to grieve, not to investigate.

Father Harold stepped up to the pulpit and began to deliver the opening prayer. The congregation bowed their heads.

"Eternal rest give to your servants, O Lord, and let your perpetual light shine upon us . . ." the priest intoned, but Atlas had stopped listening. He was looking out at the vast sea of people and wondering how many of them had known Avery, *really* known her. Not the delicate painted-on version of herself that she showed the world, but the vibrant, flesh-and-blood girl beneath.

He let the words of the service wash over him, overwhelmed by a million memories of Avery. All the summers they'd spent at the beach in Maine: running through the surf, sneaking chocolate bars from the kitchen and trying to eat them quickly, before they melted. The way the sun glinted in her hair, highlighting all the different shades of it. Her laugh, unexpectedly full-bodied and throaty. Her ferocity, her warmth, her indomitable spirit. The way it had felt to kiss her.

Atlas had never deserved her. This *world* hadn't deserved her; and ultimately, the world was what killed her, with its cold narrow-mindedness. Atlas didn't give two shits what they called *him*, but to tell Avery that she was vile and worthless, just because of who she loved—well, that wasn't a world Atlas wanted any part of, either.

He refused to apologize for loving Avery. Honestly, he dared anyone with half a heart to meet her and *not* love her. Loving Avery was the greatest privilege the world had given him, and he couldn't regret a single moment of it.

He prayed that Avery hadn't regretted it, in the end.

"Our grief is like the shaking of the earth, like fires undying . . ." Father Harold was saying, and Atlas winced at the words of the prayer. He didn't want to imagine Avery up there on the thousandth floor, alone, surrounded by a wall of flames.

He'd been in Laos when he heard, mere hours after it happened. That was how quickly this story had traveled: Because the death of the daughter of New York City's mayor, of Pierson *Fuller*, the man who'd invented vertical living on a global scale, was international freaking news. Especially when that daughter burned down her family's famous penthouse while she was still inside it.

The moment Atlas found out, he'd ditched his dad's security team and boarded a flight back here, to return in time for the funeral.

The entire mind-numbing journey, Atlas felt consumed with guilt. It was all his fault. His fault that they were caught in the elevator, his fault that their parents had tried to make him disappear, his fault that he hadn't figured out a better way to get Avery a message. He thought of the cupcakes he'd sent her, in those frantic few seconds, and felt sick. Had Avery not realized what he meant by them—that he would find a way to come for her, somehow, no matter what it took?

Atlas remembered the way her eyes had burned on him in the darkness of the elevator, when she turned to him and whispered, *Don't make promises you can't guarantee you'll keep.*

He hadn't been able to keep his promises, after all. He had failed her.

What a colossal idiot he'd been. Mr. Good Intentions, screwing things up yet again. He felt like someone from a Shakespearean tragedy, the ill-fated lovers torn apart, ruining his life through his own misguided mistakes.

Atlas had never guessed that Avery would do something like this, that she would leave a gaping, Avery-shaped hole in the universe. But then, she was the one who'd been left in New York, dealing with the vicious hate-soaked fallout of that night.

The priest sprinkled the casket with holy water. It was a massive, carved wooden casket, custom-built; and though Atlas hadn't carried it, he knew it would be curiously empty, because it contained no Avery. They never found what remained of her body. All that survived were a few long strands of her fine-spun golden hair, buried in the ashes.

It might be better this way. At least now Atlas wouldn't have to see her charred and mangled. He was free to remember Avery the way he wanted to, vibrant and laughing and acutely alive.

Father Harold began the concluding rites, and Atlas couldn't breathe. He hated this service, and yet he didn't want it to end, because when it ended Avery would truly be gone.

Finally the organ broke into up a recessional, the voices of the boys' choir lifted in the *Requiem Aeternam*. The bereaved family made their way down the center aisle: Pierson and Elizabeth Fuller, Grandmother Fuller, a few scattered aunts and uncles. Atlas stepped farther into the shadows.

When Leda walked past, wearing a long-sleeved black knit

dress and tights, Atlas couldn't help noticing that she didn't seem . . . afflicted enough. Her steps were brisk, her eyes as dark and darting as ever; and before Atlas could retreat any farther, those eyes had turned in his direction and were boring directly into his.

He should have known that of all people, Leda would spot him instantly.

He froze in terror, certain that Leda would make a scene. Instead she pursed her lips and jerked her head toward one of the blocked-off side chapels, as if to say, *That way,* then walked on through the main doors. Atlas felt he had no choice but to obey her summons.

He headed toward the chapel, where a pair of carved stone angels gazed down on him with inscrutable calm. Their wings were leathery instead of feathered—like a bat's wings, rather than a bird's. Maybe they weren't angels at all. It felt oddly fitting.

Leda didn't return until the church had long since emptied.

"What are you doing here?" she whispered, glancing nervously over her shoulder. "I thought you were far away."

"I was, but then I came back," Atlas said haltingly, stating the obvious. But his brain wasn't working properly. He couldn't think through his grief.

Leda shifted impatiently, one ballet flat tapping against the cold marble floor. She seemed surprisingly irritated with him. "You shouldn't be here."

"If you thought I would miss the chance to say good-bye—" he began, but Leda interrupted him.

"There's something you need to know, about what really happened to Avery."

# EPILOGUE

**A GIRL STOOD** in the Budapest airport, wearing jeans and a shapeless sweatshirt, a tattered red bag slung over one shoulder. She was trying to decide where to go next—luxuriating in the pleasant anticipation of it, wherever it would be.

Like all public spaces, the airport was a world of abbreviated anonymous encounters, of strangers thrust together in temporary forced intimacy. The girl kept her head down, avoiding eye contact, trying to escape notice; and to her continued surprise, it worked. No one paid any attention to her.

Her stomach surprised her with a growl of hunger. *Okay, a snack first*, she thought, *and then a destination.*

Every choice had become a sort of game with her. She would tilt her head a little to the side, her brows drawn together, to internally debate whether she wanted limeade or beet juice. One might have safely assumed that the girl didn't know her own preferences, and perhaps she didn't. Maybe she wasn't sure whether her preferences were actually hers, or whether they had been handed *to* her, like everything else in her life thus far.

She paused near one of the flexiglass windows, to look out at the planes landing and taking off. She loved watching the various steps of its choreography: the sloshing water tanks that fueled the jets, the individual transport pods that moved like strings of beads, picking up each individual person and driving them toward the drop-off point.

She reached absentmindedly up to her jet-black hair, recently and crudely cropped in a boyish cut. Her head felt curiously light without the heavy tresses that normally spilled over her shoulders. It was a wonderful sensation.

The girl tilted her head against the glass and let her eyes flutter shut. They still burned from the lightning-fast retina-replacement surgery she'd had in an unmarked but surprisingly clean "doctor's office" down in the Sprawl. What a strange, reckless few days it had been.

———————

"I need to disappear," she'd said to Watt when she pinged him that night. "You can do that, can't you?"

"You're running away?" Watt paused as if collecting his thoughts. "Is this about the article? Because I can find out who submitted that picture, and then—"

"You've been spending too much time with Leda," she chided gently. "I'm not looking for revenge, Watt. I'm looking to escape."

To her surprise, Watt resisted her. Part of her was oddly grateful for it, as if he knew that he had to speak out, because he was the only person she planned on sharing this with. The only person fighting for her. "I know this whole situation seems impossible right now," he'd said, "but you can't just walk away from your *life* because of it."

"What if I told you that I've wanted to walk away from my life for a while?"

She had collapsed back onto her bed and stared up at her ceiling, one hand resting on her forehead, the other over her heart, the way she did in yoga. Trying to center herself on something, anything. How long had this sensation been building—the feeling that she was trapped, her true self suffocating under the weight of everyone else's expectations, her parents' and Max's and the entire world's?

She struggled to explain. "You wouldn't understand, but it's like I have all these voices in my head, telling me who they think I should be. And now there are even more voices, a whole clamoring city of them, and I just want to walk away from it all."

"I know more than you think about voices in your head," Watt had told her, with an unreadable laugh. "Okay. Let's start talking logistics."

---

Looking back, she still couldn't believe they had pulled it off.

She could never have done it without Watt, whose hacking abilities had surpassed even her wildest expectations. He'd managed to steal an out-of-use military drone equipped with Teflon cloaking panels. The drone picked her up right there on the roof, after she set fire to the apartment using the high-grade sparksticks Watt had obtained. She didn't ask where he found them.

She barely fit into the drone, even sitting with her knees pulled up to her chest, but it didn't matter. She'd flown the twenty minutes to Boston inside it, practically invisible, nothing but a shimmer in the air.

She winced a little, remembering the destruction she'd wrought on her childhood home. But she hadn't had a choice. She and Watt had discussed it from all angles, and they couldn't think of a way for her to get out through the Tower, not without being caught by the retinal scanners. Her only option was to leave from the roof. Which meant that she needed the fire, to explain the absence of a body.

Because if her parents hadn't thought her dead—if they realized that she had just run away—they would have thrown their inexhaustible resources into finding her. And she didn't want to live the rest of her life looking over her shoulder in fear.

The hardest part had been not telling Leda. But she knew that if she let Leda in on her plans, Leda would have fought her every step of the way. She'd made Watt *promise* to tell Leda as soon as he felt it was all clear. Still, it pained her to think that she had caused her friend even an hour of false grief.

She was glad she'd done it. It freed the rest of them from suspicion, it freed Leda from her guilt, and most of all, it set *her* free. She hadn't realized how much her identity was trapping her until she crawled out from beneath it.

She turned back toward the departures holo, where tiny destination icons all glowed tantalizingly before her eyes, like items on a menu. Saint Petersburg, Nairobi, Beirut. Where was Atlas in all these countless places? She wished yet again that she could have warned him about her plan, but not even Watt had been able to find him. Wherever her parents had taken him, they'd done a damn good job making him vanish.

Already she kept seeing him everywhere. In every café, in every train, at every street corner. Someone's walk or voice or hair color would look like his, and she would do a double take, just to make sure. It was like being surrounded by infinite echoes of him. She wondered if he felt the same about her.

The girl lifted her head. Her eyes might be new, but the stubborn defiance flashing in them was the same as ever.

He could be anywhere, really. There was so *much* world out there, filled with so many unexpected corners: small towns and sprawling cities and towers that traced the sky; oceans and lakes and mountains; and all those billions of people. And she had no *clue* where he was, in all that vast imminent everything. It might take weeks to find him, or years, or an entire lifetime.

But looking would be half the fun, wouldn't it? If it was going to take a lifetime, she thought wryly, she might as well get started.

Avery Fuller was dead, and the girl who'd been living her life for eighteen years couldn't wait to learn who she really was, underneath it all.

She turned her profile toward the airline counters and walked boldly into her future.

# ACKNOWLEDGMENTS

**AS THIS TRILOGY** draws to a close, I feel overwhelmed with gratitude. An enormous thank-you is due to all the people who have made these books possible:

To my editor, the inimitable Emilia Rhodes: There is no one I would rather have had in my corner for my first series. Jen Klonsky, your unflagging enthusiasm never fails to bring a smile to my face. Alice Jerman, I am constantly grateful for your editorial support. Jenna Stempel-Lobell, I am always in awe of your cover designs, and yet this time you truly outdid yourself. Thanks also to Gina Rizzo, Bess Braswell, Sabrina Abballe, and Ebony LaDelle for their marketing and publicity brilliance.

As always, a massive thank-you to the entire team at Alloy Entertainment. Joelle Hobeika, Josh Bank, and Sara Shandler, this series has benefited from your mad collective genius in more ways than I could ever count. Thank you for your outstanding creative guidance, and your faith in this project. Thanks also to Les Morgenstein, Gina Girolamo, Romy Golan, and Laura Barbiea.

To the team at Rights People—Alexandra Devlin, Allison Hellegers, Caroline Hill-Trevor, Rachel Richardson, Alex Webb, Harim Yim, and Charles Nettleton—thank you for helping to bring The Thousandth Floor to so many languages throughout the world. It still feels like a dream come true.

Thanks also to Oka Tai-Lee and Zachary Fetters for building a breathtaking website, and to Mackie Bushong for your design talents.

I don't know what I would do without my parents, who remain my most enthusiastic salespeople and fiercest cheerleaders. Lizzy and John Ed, thank you for being my early sounding boards, and for all the dialogue suggestions (some of them actually made it into the book!). And to Alex: Thank you for innumerable home-made tacos, for your wise counsel, and for the countless hours you spent patiently discussing the lives of fictional teenagers. Without you, nothing at all would ever get written.

Most of all, thank you to the readers who have been on this journey with me. I believe that books are still the strongest magic that exists—but only in the hands of readers does that magic come to life.